"And what brings t[...] Nora?"

Nora turned to find the sheriff at her elbow. "Just thinking about how weddings bring out the romantic in even the most unexpected of hearts."

She realized how that must have sounded and her cheeks warmed. She quickly changed the subject. "Is there something I can do for you?"

"Just the opposite," he said. "Thought I'd offer you a ride back to your place."

How thoughtful of him.

"I promised your brother-in-law I'd keep an eye on you in his absence," he added.

Well, so much for his romantic interest, Nora thought. "Thank you, I would be most pleased to accept your offer of a ride. Would you mind holding Grace while I fetch her things?"

He backed up a step. "Better yet, why don't I fetch her things for you?"

She'd never met a man so standoffish when it came to little kids.

She wanted to know *why*.

Winnie Griggs

A Baby Between Them
&
The Proper Wife

HARLEQUIN® LOVE INSPIRED®CLASSICS

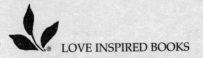

LOVE INSPIRED BOOKS

Recycling programs for this product may not exist in your area.

ISBN-13: 978-1-335-45462-1

A Baby Between Them & The Proper Wife

Copyright © 2019 by Harlequin Books S.A.

The publisher acknowledges the copyright holders of the individual works as follows:

A Baby Between Them
Copyright © 2012 by Harlequin Books S.A.

The Proper Wife
Copyright © 2011 by Winnie Griggs

Special thanks and acknowledgment are given to Winnie Griggs for her contribution to the Irish Brides miniseries.

www.Harlequin.com

Printed in U.S.A.

CONTENTS

Winnie Griggs is the multipublished, award-winning author of historical (and occasionally contemporary) romances that focus on small towns, big hearts and amazing grace. She is also a list maker and a lover of dragonflies, and holds an advanced degree in the art of procrastination. Winnie loves to hear from readers—you can connect with her on Facebook at Facebook.com/winniegriggs.author or email her at winnie@winniegriggs.com.

Books by Winnie Griggs

Love Inspired Historical

Texas Grooms

Handpicked Husband
The Bride Next Door
A Family for Christmas
Lone Star Heiress
Her Holiday Family
Second Chance Hero
The Holiday Courtship
Texas Cinderella
A Tailor-Made Husband
Once Upon a Texas Christmas

Visit the Author Profile page
at Harlequin.com for more titles.

A BABY
BETWEEN THEM

It is of the Lord's mercies that we are not consumed, because his compassions fail not. They are new every morning: great is thy faithfulness.
—*Lamentations* 3:22–23

To my fabulous agent, Michelle Grajkowski, who remains my biggest cheerleader. And to my fellow authors in this continuity series, Renee and Cheryl, who made this experience such a great one.

Chapter One

Faith Glen, Massachusetts, August 1850

Nora Murphy looked at her two younger sisters across the room and tamped down the pinprick of jealousy that tried to intrude on her joy at their good fortune.

After all, this was her sister Bridget's wedding day to Will Black, a good and honorable man who loved her dearly. Everyone in town was gathered to celebrate here at Will's home—Bridget's home now, too. It was a joyous occasion and it would be selfish to put her own feelings above her sister's.

So what if just a scant month ago Maeve, the youngest, had also married a wonderful man? No matter how it felt, Nora assured herself, it wasn't *truly* pitiable to be the oldest and the only one still single and with no marriage prospects. After all, at twenty-five she had a few years left to her before she'd have to don her spinster cap.

Strange how in just a little over two months—a seeming eyeblink of time—her whole world had changed. Back then they'd lived in Ireland amidst the terrible burdens of the potato famine and the sickness that had taken so many of their friends and neighbors, and finally their beloved da. Suddenly orphaned and facing eviction, they'd been left all but destitute and desperate. The startling discovery of a possible inheritance across the ocean in America from an old suitor of their mother's had been an answered prayer. She, Bridget and Maeve had left their homeland, headed for the land of promise with only their faith and the hope of finding a new home in the small town of Faith Glen, Massachusetts, to keep their spirits up.

They'd all taken jobs aboard the ship the *Annie McGee* to replenish their drained savings after purchasing their passage. Maeve, the youngest, had fallen in love with and married the ship's well-to-do doctor, Flynn Gallagher, before they'd even set foot in America.

And now Bridget, the middle sister, had married Will Black, a mill owner and Faith Glen's wealthiest citizen.

How wonderful that her sisters had found good, honorable men who loved them deeply and who could care for them extravagantly. It was surely a blessing from the Good Lord Himself. And she was certain the Good Lord had plans for her, as well. Whether or not those plans included marriage was another question altogether.

Father Almighty, I really do want to be obedient to You and to patiently await Your will for my life. But please be patient with me when I try to get ahead of You. I am prideful and too often try to control my circumstances.

"I brought you a glass of punch."

Pulled out of her musings, Nora found Sheriff Cameron Long, the man who employed her as housekeeper and cook, standing in front of her. He had a cup in each hand and was holding one out to her. His always-ready, lopsided smile was in evidence, giving him a boyish look despite his imposing size. Really, the sheriff could be so considerate.

When he wasn't being so maddeningly stubborn.

She looked up, meeting his gaze. Unlike her sisters, she had more of her father than her mother in her and had been the tallest of the three siblings. But Sheriff Long still towered over her, which was an uncommon but not entirely unpleasant experience.

"Thank you." She accepted the cup and took a quick sip. "'Twas kind of you to bring it to me."

He took a drink from his own cup. "If you don't mind my asking, what are you doing over here by yourself? As a sister of the bride I would think you'd want to be in the thick of things."

Nora waved toward the cradle that held her infant ward. "I'll rejoin them shortly. I just put Grace down for her nap."

She still found it hard to believe that no one had come forward to claim the newborn foundling who'd been abandoned during their voyage. Perhaps, for some reason, the child's family members couldn't reveal themselves. But whatever the case, Nora was guiltily glad they hadn't. The idea of giving Grace up now was too painful to consider.

As usual, the sheriff avoided more than a quick look Grace's way and merely nodded, then changed the subject. "I understand you made most of the cakes for this little gathering."

"It was my gift to Bridget and Will."

His smile broadened and his heather-blue eyes regarded her in that teasing way he had. Didn't he realize there should be a certain formality between an employer and his hired help?

"And a mighty tasty gift it was," he said, saluting her with his cup. "That was as fine a use of the Huntley-Black chocolate as I can remember. Most everyone is saying how good the desserts are and I saw several guests sneak back around for seconds."

Bridget's new husband owned and operated the Huntley-Black Chocolate Mill, a business that employed a large number of the town's citizens. It had given Nora a great deal of satisfaction to devise a recipe using Will's product for this reception. "I enjoy cooking and baking. I'm just pleased others take pleasure in the results of my efforts."

"And I'm pleased I get to enjoy them on a regular basis."

Her cheeks warmed at the more personal compliment. "Thank you. As I said, I enjoy cooking."

He finished his punch and she expected him to drift away, but instead he nodded toward the other side of the room. "They make a fine picture, don't they?"

Bridget had stooped down to say something to Will's three-year-old twins—her new stepchildren—and the youngsters were giggling. Will stood next to his bride, looking on with a besotted smile.

Nora nodded. "They do indeed. They are all blessed to have found each other."

"Do your Maeve and Flynn plan to stay here for a while?"

She followed his glance toward her other sister and brother-in-law. "No, I'm sorry to say. They'll be returning to Boston as soon as they see Bridget and Will off. Flynn has some patients to look in on tomorrow."

"Well, they can't get their new home built soon enough. The folks in these parts are really looking forward to having their own doctor right here in Faith Glen." Cam turned back to her. "And I'm sure you'll be glad to have your other sister close by."

"It *will* be good to have the three of us close together again." Maeve and Flynn were having a home built here in Faith Glen but it wasn't finished yet so they were currently living in Flynn's family home in Boston.

Nora cast a quick glance back over her shoulder to make certain Grace was all right. She smiled at the sweet picture the babe made as she slept.

"Speaking of your sisters," Sheriff Long said, "it looks as if they're headed this way."

Nora turned back around and sure enough, Bridget and Maeve were crossing the room toward her, arms linked and skirts swishing as they walked.

"Ladies." The sheriff gave a short bow as Nora's sisters halted in front of them. He smiled at Bridget. "I've already told Will more than once what a mighty lucky fellow he is."

Bridget smiled in return. "Thank you, but I feel like I'm the one who's been blessed."

Cam widened his gaze to include all three of them. "I must say, all of the Murphy sisters are looking especially fetching today."

Did his gaze linger on her just a heartbeat longer than her sisters? Nora pushed that ridiculous thought away. While she was honest enough to know she wasn't plain, she also knew she couldn't hold a candle to her sisters. Maeve was petite with beautiful curly red hair and the exquisite features of a porcelain doll. And Bridget was delicate, soft and dreamy-eyed with untamable hair that always gave her an ethereal look. Nora knew herself to be tall and rather thin, with hair that was plain brown and features that were pleasant enough but nothing out of the ordinary.

The sheriff held his hand out toward her and it took her a moment to realize he was offering to take her now-empty cup. Feeling her cheeks warm, she thrust the cup at him with a bit more force than necessary.

He raised a brow, but accepted the cup graciously enough. "I'll take care of putting this away for you and let you ladies talk."

"Must be nice having him pick up after you for a change."

Nora frowned at Maeve's words. "The sheriff is a good man and a fair employer."

Maeve raised her hand, palm out. "I didn't mean to imply otherwise. I just meant that after cleaning up after him all week I would imagine it would be a pleasant change to have him return the favor."

Nora merely nodded, then turned to her other sister. "Will you and your new husband be off soon then?"

Bridget's cheeks pinkened becomingly as she reached for her sisters' hands. "Yes. But before we leave for Boston, I wanted to thank both of you again for all you did to help make my wedding day so special."

Maeve, who'd supplied the beautiful gown Bridget wore, gave their sister a hug. "It was my pleasure. But, to be sure, your smile is the most beautiful thing you're wearing today."

Nora nodded her agreement before hugging her, as well. "And your joy is sweeter than my baking." She stepped back, taking both of Bridget's hands in hers.

"I only wish Mother and Da could've been here to see you today."

Romantically minded Bridget gave her a watery smile. "I do, too. Though I felt very close to them all through the ceremony."

Maeve patted her arm. "They would have been very proud of you."

Nora was certain of that, as well. She hoped their parents would also be proud of her. She'd done her best to hold their household together after their dear mother passed on ten years ago. But with Maeve and Bridget married now, the caretaker part of her life was over, at least as far as her sisters were concerned. She'd always thought she'd feel freer when this day came, not consumed by this sense of loneliness.

Of course she wasn't completely alone. While her sisters had new husbands and lives apart from hers now, the Good Lord had provided her with companionship of a different sort. Nora glanced back toward the cradle and smiled. Her sisters had husbands but she had this sweet, sweet babe.

"I see Grace is taking a nap."

At Maeve's comment, Nora refocused on her sisters. They had linked arms again and were facing her with identical determined looks on their faces. What were they up to? "Yes. Poor wee babe is worn out from being around so many people today. I should be getting her home soon."

Home. Such a small word for such a wonderful, wonderful thing. For the first time in her life, she finally had a place to call her own that no landlord could remove her from.

Bridget cleared her throat. "We have something to say

to you before Will and I leave for Boston. And we want you to hear us out before you say anything."

Nora's curiosity—as well as her concern—climbed. Something told her she wasn't going to be pleased with what they had to say.

"You've done a lot for us over the years," Bridget continued. "So now it's our turn to take care of you."

Take care of her? Did they think her incapable of handling things on her own? Nora felt a protest form, but before she could say anything, Maeve chimed in.

"That's right. I know you are working on making the cottage into a cozy home, but the new house Flynn and I are building here will have plenty of room. You and Grace could settle in with us easily enough. And Flynn would be as pleased as I to have you there."

"Or you can move in right here with me and Will," Bridget added quickly. "It would be nice to have you and Grace so close."

Something inside Nora tightened. She was grateful, of course, but at the same time she had to swallow a feeling of annoyance. "Thank you," she said, choosing her words carefully, "those are generous offers. But you're both newlyweds with new households. Bridget, in addition to your new husband, you have two precious children and a mother-in-law to care for now. And Maeve, you and Flynn are building a new home and starting up a new medical practice here. Neither of you need to be burdened with additional responsibilities right now." Besides, even if none of that were true, Nora would be uncomfortable living on what amounted to their charity.

Bridget drew herself up. "Nora Kayleigh Murphy, I'll have none of that talk. You're no burden, you're our sister."

As if the ground had shifted beneath her, Nora felt a

sudden change in her relationship with her sisters. Ever since their dear mother had passed on ten years ago, she'd done her best to look out for her sisters. And when their da had passed on just a few months ago, she'd felt the mantle of responsibility for their little family wrap even more tightly around her. But now the roles seem to have reversed. In their new elevated positions as married women, her sisters were now trying to take on responsibility for her.

"I meant no insult," she said, trying to smooth their ruffled feathers. "But that cottage was a gift to our mother. Remember how the mere idea of it gave us the courage to come to this country in the first place? The dream of having a home of our own gave us much-needed purpose through the long voyage." She looked from Bridget to Maeve and back again. "It just seems wrong somehow to abandon it now that we finally have it."

Bridget shook her head. "We wouldn't be abandoning the place altogether, Nora. The Coulters would still live there." James and Agnes Coulter were the elderly couple who'd been caretakers of the cottage for many years before the Murphy sisters even knew of its existence.

"Exactly." Nora pounced on Bridget's statement. "If it's sound enough for the Coulters to live in, then it's sound enough for me to live in, as well. Besides, the repairs are coming along nicely. Before you know it, it'll be a fine, snug little home."

"Perhaps it's fine now while it's still summer, but autumn will be upon us soon and with it colder, damper weather." Maeve's expression was unusually sober.

Keep your tone calm and reasonable, Nora told herself. "No more so than what we faced back in Ireland. In fact, I hear the weather is milder here."

"If you won't think of yourself, think of Grace," Bridget insisted. "Shouldn't she have the best accommodations possible?"

That set Nora back a moment. Was she being selfish and prideful? "I—" She rubbed a hand over the side of her face as she gathered her thoughts. "Of course Grace deserves the very best we can give her. But I'm not so sure what that is." She dropped her arm and drew her shoulders back. "This is not something to worry over today. Let us see how things fare when autumn gets here."

Bridget opened her mouth to speak, but Maeve placed a hand on her arm, shooting her a quick warning look. Turning back to Nora, she smiled. "Then we'll not say more until then." She wagged a finger Nora's way. "But don't think for a minute we've given up on this."

Nora was quite certain they hadn't.

Cameron Long set the two empty cups on the small side table that had been reserved for just that purpose. The three Murphy sisters stood together, pretty as butterflies in a spring meadow.

But to his way of thinking, Nora was the most compelling of the trio. He supposed it was the contradictions he sensed in her that intrigued him most. From the moment he'd first set eyes on her—tall and willowy with her hair pulled back in that tight little bun and her posture perfectly straight—she seemed to exude a no-nonsense air of practicality and discipline. But a moment later the infant she held had made some noise or movement that commanded her attention and her expression suddenly softened and she'd cooed some nonsense or other to calm the baby, and he'd glimpsed another side of her entirely.

From that day forward he'd made a point of trying to get to the truth of who the real Nora Murphy was beneath her prim facade. He'd found her by turns amusing, irritating and admirable.

Looking at her today, he saw something new. Her dress wasn't as frilly and fussy as the getups her sisters wore, but for once she'd worn something besides those serviceable homespun dresses she generally favored. The bright blue color and simple lines suited her perfectly. And while her sisters seemed somewhat softer and more relaxed than Nora, that touch of steel in her appealed to him.

Of course, she was a smidge on the bossy side, too, but he figured he could give as good as he got in that area. Truth to tell, it was a bit fun to watch her hackles rise and her finger start wagging and poking when she got riled.

All in all he was quite pleased that he'd ended up hiring Nora as his housekeeper instead of her sister. In fact, if he were the marrying kind, he'd probably set his sights on someone just like her. Not that that was either here or there. He'd decided long ago that he most certainly *wasn't* the marrying kind, and never would be. A man with a history like his had no business raising kids. It's why he never let himself get too close to any of the women he'd encountered over the years.

Shaking off those gloomy thoughts, Cam focused on the Murphy sisters again, then frowned. Something seemed to have upset his no-nonsense housekeeper. Not that she was making a big show of it, but he could tell by the appearance of that little wrinkle that furrowed above her nose whenever she was fretting over something. What could have put that crease there on what should be a happy day for her?

Before he could decide whether or not to saunter back over, the air seemed to clear and the sisters were hugging again. A tiny wail from the vicinity of the cradle diverted all three women's attention and Nora bustled over to tend to Grace. But he could sense the eldest Murphy sister still fretted over something.

Perhaps he'd find out just what was bothering her when he offered her a ride home after the reception.

Chapter Two

Nora swayed and rubbed Grace's back, trying to soothe the fussy infant as she watched Bridget and Will ride off in their carriage, followed closely by Maeve and Flynn in their own vehicle. The two couples would travel together on the road to Boston and separate once they reached the city—Maeve and Flynn to their home, Bridget and Will to the fancy hotel where they would spend their two-day honeymoon.

Grace finally settled down again, her head lolling against Nora's shoulder. The last of the guests were dispersing.

Well, all except Mrs. Fitzwilliam and the McCorkle boys. The Murphy sisters had met the starchy, well-to-do widow on the voyage over here from Ireland. She'd seemed quite patronizing and standoffish at first, but in time she and the sisters had become friends. Learning that the dowager was traveling to America on a quest to find her prodigal stepgranddaughter, her only living relation, had endeared her further to Nora and her sisters.

Though Mrs. Fitzwilliam had yet to find the runaway, she was no longer alone. She had, in fact, become guard-

ian to the three orphaned McCorkle brothers who had
also traveled aboard the *Annie McGee.* Mrs. Fitzwilliam
and the two younger boys had settled in Boston. The oldest boy, eighteen-year-old Gavin, had yearned for a bit
of adventure and had wheedled his way, in the most en-
gaging manner possible, into the role of Sheriff Long's
deputy-in-training.

Bridget had invited Mrs. Fitzwilliam and the two
youngest McCorkles to spend the night at their home so
Gavin would have an opportunity for a nice visit with
them.

Esther Black, Will's mother, stood near the gate, reassuring her twin grandchildren that yes, their father
and new stepmother would most definitely be returning in just a few days. Ben MacDuff, the sheriff's more
seasoned deputy and former mentor, was hovering near
Esther in a way that raised Nora's brow. Was something
brewing between the two, something deeper than friendship? Wouldn't that be lovely for them?

"And what brings that smile to your face?"

Nora turned to find the sheriff at her elbow. "Just
thinking about how weddings bring out the romantic in
even the most unexpected of hearts."

Seeing his quirked brow she realized how that must
have sounded and her cheeks warmed. Trying to cover
the moment, she quickly changed the subject. "Is there
something I can do for you?"

"Just the opposite. Thought I'd offer you a ride back
to your place."

How thoughtful of him. But Nora needed some time
alone to think over that conversation with her sisters and
the half-mile walk back to the cottage would be just the
thing. "Thank you but that's really not necessary."

"Sure it is. I promised Will I'd keep an eye on you in his absence."

Well, so much for his personal interest in her well-being. "Both my brothers-in-law worry overmuch."

His look chided her for her tone. "They don't just feel a responsibility for you, you know. They care about you, as well. Is that such a bad thing?"

He was right—she was being too touchy about her new status. She took a deep breath and smiled. "You're right. Thank you, I would be most pleased to accept your offer of a ride."

He nodded his approval. "You can say your goodbyes to Esther and the twins while I get the wagon."

A few minutes later, the sheriff had set the brake and hopped down to help her up. Since everyone else had either gone back inside or were on their way home, Nora stepped toward him. "Would you mind holding Grace while I fetch her things?"

He backed up a step. "Better yet, why don't I fetch her things for you? Just tell me where to find them."

She'd never met a man so standoffish when it came to babies. "Everything is in a canvas bag next to the cradle."

"Easy enough. I'll be right back."

True to his word, Cam was in and out of the house in just a few minutes. Swinging the bag with an easy rhythm, he deposited it in the back of his flatbed wagon then turned back to her. She noted the instant he realized he'd have to hold Grace in order for her to climb up into the wagon. His smile faltered and he darted a quick look around as if searching for someone to take his place.

But when she held Grace out to him, he swallowed hard, raked his hand through his hair and took the child, holding her as if she would bite him if he pulled her too close.

Nora climbed up quickly then reached down to take Grace from him. Looking as if he'd just survived a face-off with a bear, Cam quickly moved to the other side of the wagon and climbed up beside her. With a flick of the reins and a click of his tongue he set the horse in motion.

As the horse slowly plodded through town, Nora mulled over what the future might hold for her. How much time did she have to get things in order? "What are autumns like here in Faith Glen?"

He cut her a curious glance. "Well, now, the nights will start getting cooler come mid-September but the days will usually remain passably mild through October. You'll start to see more rain along about October or November, too."

The summer here in Massachusetts had been much warmer than what they'd experienced back in Ireland—it seemed that would work to her advantage when they moved into fall. She and Grace would be fine right where they were for another couple of months at least.

"If you're worried about how you'll fare at the cottage once the weather turns colder," he continued, "I promise I'll do my best to get the biggest of the cracks in the roof and walls fixed before the worst of it sets in."

He, Will and Flynn had already spent one entire day making repairs around the place when Bridget and Nora had first moved into the cottage a few weeks ago. Since then, all three had come by to advance the repairs as often as they could, but then Will had proposed to Bridget and wedding plans had superseded everything else. "That's kind of you. But actually, both Bridget and

Maeve have invited me to live with them." She tried to maintain a neutral tone. "All I have to do is choose between them."

From the too-even tone of her voice, Cam could tell Nora was not at all pleased with the idea. Is that what had upset her earlier? If so, was it the choosing between her sisters or the moving from the cottage that bothered her? "And what did you tell them?"

"That I'd think about it."

"And have you?"

She cut him a guarded look. "I haven't had much time. They only brought this up when they were preparing to leave earlier."

"But you're not overly pleased with the idea." Didn't her sisters know how their offer would strike their independent-minded sister?

She sighed. "I like having my own home." She frowned, as if just thinking of something. "Of course, Bridget and Maeve do each own a third of the cottage, as well."

The sisters had shown him the deed when they first arrived in town, so he was familiar with it. "That they do."

"But then there's Grace to consider." She seemed to be talking more to herself than to him. "A few windy drafts won't bother me, but if the repairs aren't all done in time…" She glanced his way. "No offense meant, but there's a lot of work to be done and you do have your sheriffing to do. I don't expect you to take on the role of my full-time handyman."

Cam could think of worse ways to spend his free time than in Nora's company. "Not full-time, but I *do* have two deputies, now." He let that sink in a moment since he'd hired Gavin McCorkle, a youth she'd met on her voyage over, at her insistence. "That gives me a lot more free time on my hands."

She worried at her lip. "But if you are going to spend more time working on the cottage, I'd want to pay you." She sat up straighter. "I suppose you could hold a portion out of my salary to cover it."

He knew good and well she needed every bit of that money to support her household, especially now that Bridget's wages wouldn't be helping supplement it. But he also knew better than to argue the point. "I'm certain we can work something out along those lines."

She fussed a moment with Grace's blanket and he could see the wheels turning in her mind. "Do you think I'm being selfish by denying Grace the opportunity to grow up in a fine home like the ones Bridget and Maeve could offer her?"

Nora Murphy was lots of things—obstinate, bossy, opinionated—but she was also the least selfish person he knew. "I think, as long as her needs are met and she feels truly loved, it doesn't much matter where she grows up."

He was rewarded with one of her rare approving smiles.

Looking considerably lighter of spirit, she lifted her head and changed the subject. "Any luck yet finding out who that girl was who nearly ran Gavin over?"

Cam flicked the reins, frustrated that he hadn't been able to resolve that particular matter to his satisfaction. The female thief had stolen his horse while he was helping with the repairs at the Murphy sisters' cottage a few weeks ago and had almost gotten away with it. Gavin's quick action had slowed her down and allowed Cam to recover his horse but she'd managed to elude capture.

That didn't sit well with him, not at all. It was his job to keep the peace in these parts and it was the one thing he was good at. Or at least he'd thought so until that wily slip of a girl had outfoxed him.

More worrisome than his injured pride, though, was the question of what she'd been doing near the cottage that day. The place was a half mile from town out near the shoreline and had nothing about it to tempt a thief.

Not only had he been there that day, but Will, Flynn and Maeve had been visiting, as well. Not to mention Mrs. Fitzwilliam and Gavin's two brothers who'd all come in from Boston to see the cottage the Murphy sisters had crossed an ocean to claim.

Had the little thief followed one of the guests there hoping to find an easy mark? Or had she been there for some other reason?

He didn't want to worry Nora with any of his as yet unfounded suspicions, though. "No, and no sign of where she's holed up yet either."

Nora's free hand fluttered then dropped back to rest against Grace. "I know she's a criminal, but I'm worried about her. She looked so young. The girl must be truly desperate to have turned to a life of crime." Nora shivered. "I hate to think of what might have happened to me and my sisters if we hadn't had this place to turn to."

Intrigued by the hint at what her past might have been like, he tried to learn more. "Were things so bad for you back in Ireland?"

She shot him an abashed look, as if sorry she'd said as much as she had. "There were some who had it worse. At least, thanks to the unexpected inheritance of the cottage, we were able to come here and find a home waiting for us."

She shifted Grace to her other shoulder. "Maybe Gavin's thief has left Faith Glen by now."

That was a very deliberate changing of the subject if he'd ever heard one. There was a lot she was leaving unsaid when it came to her former life. Was it so painful to talk about? Or did she just feel it was none of his business?

As for her question… "Maybe," he temporized. Because he doubted it, now more than ever. Just yesterday Ellen Kenny had mentioned that something had gotten into her root cellar and made off with some dried apples. Cam was inclined to believe it was a "someone" not a "something."

But again, there was no sense worrying Nora with that. He returned to the subject of her former life. "You never did say how you three came to possess the deed to Laird O'Malley's place. Was he a relative of yours?"

His question seemed to make her uncomfortable. She shifted in her seat and fussed with the baby for a moment. "Actually, he was a suitor of our mother's before she married our da. When she turned down his proposal, Mr. O'Malley left Ireland and came here. Apparently he never forgot her. He sent her the deed to the cottage and said it was for her and her heirs if she or they should ever need a place to call their own."

Cam remembered the deed had been dated twenty-six years past. "Pined for her all that time, did he?" If the late Mrs. Murphy was anything like her three daughters he could see where such a thing would be possible.

Nora nodded. "So it seems. But we didn't know anything about him or about the deed. We only found it by chance when we were packing up our things to leave."

Interesting. "So you were planning to leave your home *before* you knew about this place?"

She cut him another of those I've-said-too-much looks. But this time she didn't immediately change the subject. "The stone cottage where we'd lived all our lives did not actually belong to us, nor did the land. When our da passed, Mr. Bantry, the landlord, told us he'd decided to lease it to a relative of his instead. We had no choice but to leave."

Cam's brow lowered. "Are you telling me this Bantry fellow kicked you out of your home while you were still in mourning?"

"It was his right," she said with a shrug.

But he could tell the memory still stung. His hands tightened on the reins as he thought of what fate could have befallen them if they hadn't had Laird O'Malley's cottage to fall back on. It was a good thing an ocean separated him from this blackguard Bantry, otherwise he'd be sorely tempted to teach the man a lesson or two about looking out for those in his care. "So this bully Bantry kicks you three out of your home, you find a twenty-six-year-old deed to a cottage an ocean away, and decided, just like that, to come to America all on your own." He shook his head. "That took a lot of courage."

Her lips pinched into a prim line. "It wasn't as if we had many other choices."

She could downplay it all she wanted, he still thought it a brave thing to do.

Then Nora's expression softened into a smile. "Isn't it a wondrous thing how, twenty-six years ago, the Almighty was already laying the groundwork so that me and my sisters would be taken care of in our time of need?"

Her comment caught Cam off guard. A lesser person

would be grumbling to God for putting them through all that Nora and her sisters had obviously endured. Yet here she was, praising Him instead for the good that had come out the other side of that valley.

"How long have Will's mother and Ben known each other?"

She was obviously ready to turn the subject to a less personal topic. "Quite a while I'd guess. Certainly since before I wound up in Faith Glen, back when Ben was sheriff himself instead of stepping back to be deputy."

That expressive brow of hers rose. "Oh, I didn't realize you weren't raised here. Where are you from?"

Now it was his turn to shift uncomfortably. Trust his sharp-witted housekeeper to pick up on that. "I was born in Boston. I didn't move here until I was nearly sixteen." And that was all he was going to say on *that* subject. "So why the interest in Ben and Esther?"

"Oh, just something I noticed today that made me wonder if they were more than just casual friends."

"Ben and Esther?" He grinned at the thought. "Now wouldn't that beat all?"

She waved a hand. "Oh, I'm probably wrong. Weddings just tend to bring out the romantic in folks."

"Speaking of Ben," Cam added, "he and Gavin pounced on that last slice of the pie you left for me Friday. Thought I was going to have to wade in and referee when they started arguing over who got the biggest piece. They said to tell you it was the best they'd ever tasted."

He saw her cheeks pinken and her blue eyes light up at the praise. Delight looked good on her.

"That was nice of them to say. Maybe I should stick an extra pie in the oven come baking day. Wouldn't want

Faith Glen's fine, upstanding lawmen to be found squabbling over a bit of pastry."

Was no-nonsense Nora making a joke? "You won't get an argument on that score from me. Just add the ingredients to my tab at the general store when you do the marketing."

They rounded the last bend and the cottage came into view. Just as he had every time he'd been here since the incident with the horse thief, Cam carefully studied the area around the cottage for anything that might look suspicious or out of place. But, just as before, nothing seemed amiss.

Still, he'd make his rounds before he left, same as always.

He didn't intend to take any chances. As sheriff, it was his duty to protect Nora Murphy, whether she wanted that protection or not. The memory of another time, of another young mother he'd let down intruded, but he determinedly pushed it aside.

There was no way he'd ever allow such a thing to happen again on his watch. He didn't think he could survive such a tragedy a second time.

Chapter Three

Nora leaned back and inhaled a breath of in-this-moment contentment. The sight of the cottage as they rounded that final bend always filled her with such joy and pride. Already this felt like home to her. How could her sisters believe she would ever want to leave it?

She glanced down at Grace and made a silent pledge. *I promise you that, whatever else shall be, in this home you shall never want for love.*

"You know, I was thinking," her companion said slowly, "most of the urgent repairs are done on the place. Before you spend all your money on additional repairs, you might want to look into getting yourself a horse and wagon of your own."

Nora's cheeks heated in embarrassment. Had she overstepped on his kindness somehow? Since the day she'd moved into the cottage a few weeks ago, he'd insisted on bringing his wagon around to pick her up in the mornings and bring her back in the evenings. She'd protested at first, but as usual he'd ignored her. He'd said at the time that it was no trouble, but she wondered now if perhaps he'd changed his mind.

"Of course," she said quickly. "I didn't intend to take advantage of your kindness. You're a busy man and it's an easy walk into town from here—"

"Hold on," he said, interrupting her. "That's not what I meant. I don't mind one bit giving you a lift into town on workdays. In fact, it gives me an opportunity to start my rounds by checking things out on this side of town."

She wasn't entirely convinced that he was being completely honest. "Then was there some other reason you brought this up?"

"What I was thinking was that if there's ever any kind of emergency out here it would be handy for you to have your own transportation."

"Emergency?"

"You know, like if one of the Coulters or Grace got hurt or took ill."

"Oh, I see. I hadn't really thought of that." But she was thinking of it now. The Coulters *were* quite frail. And if something should happen to Grace...

"I can find you a good deal," the sheriff assured her. "I'll even loan you the money and you can pay me back a little at a time."

Seemed he was always doing that—loaning those in need the means to get by. Well, she wasn't one of his charity cases. "That's very kind of you but we've managed to make do this long, we can get by a bit longer until I can save up the funds."

"No offense, and I know you have your pride and all, but I really think we should go ahead and take care of this now."

Of all the high-handed— "Sheriff Long, I appreciate your concern, but this is really not your decision to make."

Her not-so-veiled reprimand failed to have the desired effect. "Now don't go getting all prickly on me." His tone contained the barest hint of amusement, setting her teeth on edge.

"Because," he continued, "as a matter of fact, this *does* concern me. I've worried about Agnes and James out here on their own for years now, but haven't been able to do much more than check on them regularly. If you had a vehicle—"

"Well, they're not on their own any longer," she interrupted. "I'm here to keep an eye on things."

"Yes you are, and that does relieve my mind a bit. But that doesn't change the fact that James and Agnes are getting on in years and you have an infant to take care of which limits your ability to just take off and go for help if help's needed. So, being the conscientious lawman that I am, I'd still feel obligated to come out here on a regular basis to check in on things. Now, if I knew you had a means to go for help if something…*unexpected* happened, then I wouldn't feel as if I had to come out here and check on things so often."

She clamped her lips shut and glared at him. He was trying to manipulate her but it wouldn't work. "I apologize," she said stiffly. "I had no idea you were inconveniencing yourself on our account."

She brushed at her skirt with her free hand. "Well, you can set your mind at ease. James and Agnes may be unable to get around very well, but I'm perfectly capable of running to town for help if an emergency should arise." She lifted her chin. "So there's no need for you to continue to check in on us any more than you do any other citizen of Faith Glen."

"But that's my job. You wouldn't want me to shirk my duties, would you?"

She held back her retort, settling for merely glaring at him. Not that he seemed at all appreciative of her restraint.

"Tell me," he asked equably, "how would you feel if James or Agnes got hurt or took ill while you were in town and they were alone out here with no way to go for help? I know I certainly wouldn't want something like that on my conscience. Especially if it was just a bit of pride that kept me from providing them with the means."

She felt her resolve fade, but glared at him resentfully. "You, sir, do not play fair."

The sheriff's little-boy grin reappeared, signaling that he knew he'd won.

But she wasn't going to let him have his way altogether. "I don't want anything fancy mind you. A serviceable cart and pony will do just fine."

He swept his hand out to indicate the rickety wagon they were currently riding in. "As you can see, my tastes don't usually run to fancy." He pulled the vehicle to a stop near the front of the cottage. "I should be able to find something for you to take a look at on Monday."

He hopped down and strode over to her side of the wagon. This time he didn't hesitate to take the baby from her, though he still held Grace with more trepidation than enthusiasm.

Once she was back on the ground and he'd returned Grace to her, the sheriff snatched the bag with Grace's things from the bed of the wagon and escorted Nora inside without waiting for an invitation.

They found the Coulters in the kitchen. Ben had driven them home earlier, and the older couple had already changed out of the clothes they'd worn to Bridget's wedding and were back in their everyday work clothes. Agnes sat at the table, darning a nearly thread-bare sock with knobby fingers that had lost much of their nimbleness. James sat nearby, reading silently from a well-worn Bible.

Both looked up when they entered. Cam set the bag on the table and turned to James. "Good news. Nora here has decided to get a cart and a pony to pull it."

Nora shook her head as she set Grace in the cradle that sat next to the table. Leave it to the stubborn lawman to make it sound like it had been all her idea.

James, however, seemed to approve. "Good thinking," he said, smiling in her direction. "Now, make sure you let Cam here help you pick it out. He knows a thing are two about livestock and wagons."

Nora nodded dutifully, refusing to look the sheriff's way.

"That's high praise coming from you, James," Cam said. Then he turned back to Nora. "James worked with horses and carriages for years before he moved here to Faith Glen."

Interesting. She was ashamed to say she hadn't given much thought to what Agnes and James's lives had been like before she met them. "It's reassuring to know I have such talent under my roof."

But James just waved off their praise. "That's all in the past now. But I should go out to the barn and make sure it and the barnyard are in good enough shape to house your horse and wagon when they get here."

The sheriff nodded. "You're right. Why don't the two of us go look things over and see if there's anything that might need immediate attention?"

James pushed himself up from the table. "It's been a while since anything other than the cow and a few cats sheltered in that old barn. And the fence around the barnyard couldn't hold in a spindly foal, much less a full-grown horse."

"Pony," Nora corrected.

James's brow went up and he glanced toward Cam.

The sheriff merely shrugged and smiled that infuriating humor-her smile of his.

Rubbing the back of his neck, James turned to face Nora. "Well, if that's what you think best, I won't speak against it." He nodded toward the counter. "There's fresh milk for Grace. I milked Daisy after we got in from the wedding."

"Thank you." Nora moved toward the milk pail. "I'm sure Grace will be fussing for her bottle any minute now."

James waved Cam forward. "Come along, boy. I'll show you what I think needs tending to first."

"Lead the way."

Much as the sheriff could irritate her with his high-handed ways, at times like this Nora couldn't help but admire Cameron Long for the way he deferred to the older man. He had a way of helping people without robbing them of their dignity in the process.

James, who walked with a limp he'd acquired before she ever met him, led the way, talking to Cam about spare timbers to brace up the barn's north wall.

"Cameron is a good man." Agnes made the pronouncement as if she thought Nora might argue with her.

Instead Nora merely nodded and proceeded to get Grace's bottle ready. When she finally spoke, she deliberately changed the subject. "It's a pity you and James couldn't stay for the reception," she said over her shoulder.

Grace started fussing and Agnes set down her darning and rocked the cradle with her foot. "When you get to be our age," the older woman answered, "you don't spend much time away from home. But the ceremony was lovely and Bridget was beautiful."

"That she was."

Agnes gave her a knowing look. "You're going to miss having her under the same roof with you, aren't you?"

Nora thought about that a moment. It would certainly be strange not having either of her sisters living in the same house with her. They'd never been all separated like this before. No more shared bedrooms and late-night whispers, no more working side by side at their chores, spinning stories for each other and dreaming together of their futures. She would miss that special closeness. But it wasn't as if she'd never see them again. Soon they would all be living in the same town and there would be opportunities aplenty to visit with each other.

She smiled at Agnes as she moved back to the table. "I suppose I will a wee bit. But it's the natural order of things for siblings to grow up and start separate families of their own." She lifted Grace from the cradle. "And I still have Grace, and you and James, here with me. That's plenty of family to keep a body from feeling lonely."

Agnes, her eyes a touch misty, reached over and patted Nora's hand. "You're a good girl, you are, Nora Murphy, to be adding James and me to your family. And we feel the same about you and that sweet little lamb you're holding, as well."

And right then, Nora knew with certainty that she

could not abandon this place, this life, no matter how much Bridget and Maeve tried to convince her otherwise.

Almighty Father, surely You didn't bring me to this place just to have me leave it. Help me to make the right choices to build a good life here for all of us. But always, according to Your will.

Agnes spoke up, reclaiming Nora's attention. "Do you mind if I ask you a question of a personal nature?"

Nora smiled. "You know you can ask me anything. What is it?"

"When you and Bridget first arrived here you mentioned that you discovered the deed to this cottage only a couple of months ago, and that none of you girls knew anything about Mr. O'Malley before then. I've been waiting ever since then for one of you to ask about him and I confess to being a bit puzzled that you haven't. Are you not the least bit curious?"

Nora shifted Grace in her arms, giving herself time to think about her response. Truth to tell, she'd been a bit afraid of what might come to light if she learned too much. Laird O'Malley had obviously loved her mother a great deal in his youth, and had continued to love her until he died. But had her mother returned that love? Had she secretly pined for this man who had traveled to America and never returned? And if so, what had she felt for their da?

No, Nora wasn't at all sure she wanted to know the answer to that question.

But Agnes was waiting for her response. "I already know that he was a generous man who loved my mother very much," she said carefully. "I'm not sure I need to know more."

Agnes studied her closely for a moment and Nora tried

not to squirm under that discerning gaze. Finally the woman resumed her darning. "I see. Do you mind if I tell you something of him? I think he deserves that much."

Nora knew it would be churlish to refuse, so she gave in graciously. "Of course."

"Mr. O'Malley was a good employer, fair and not overly demanding. He loved this place, especially the garden, which he tended to personally." She smiled reminiscently. "There was even a rumor that he had buried a treasure out there, but of course that's nonsense. Even so, after he died we would sometimes find an occasional youth sneaking out here and digging around, trying to find it."

Nora was relieved she hadn't gone down a more personal road. "So he was happy here."

"Ah, no, I wouldn't say happy." Agnes continued to focus on her stitches. "There was a sadness about him, a sort of lost emptiness that seemed to weigh him down. Many's a day he would spend walking along the beach and staring out over the ocean as if looking for a ship that never came."

Had he been yearning for her mother all that time? Better not to dwell on that. "Did he have many friends here?"

"He kept to himself for the most part. He wasn't shunned or outcast, mind you, he just never made much of an effort to get close to anyone, more's the pity."

Nora's curiosity got the better of her. "Did he ever speak of his life back in Ireland?"

"Not to me or James. But then, he was a very private person and never spoke about much of anything." Agnes sighed. "I always sensed the man had a good heart—he never uttered a harsh word in my hearing and he could be generous if he became aware of a need. It's such a sadness that he spent so much time dwelling on his past rather than enjoying his present."

She knotted and snipped her thread, then began putting away her sewing things. "Anyway, in his own way, Mr. O'Malley provided for all of us in this household and I just thought you ought to know the sort of man he was."

Grace had finished her bottle by this time, and Nora lifted her to her shoulder. "Thank you for sharing that with me. It sounds as if he was a very lonely man." How sad to have loved someone so deeply and not have had that love returned.

She remembered how dejected and hurt Bridget had been when it looked as if Will would be honor bound to marry another woman. Thankfully, it had worked out happily for them in the end, but what if it hadn't? Would her sister have recovered from that blow, especially after she'd already suffered being left at the altar once before?

Giving your heart so completely to someone else was a dangerous thing, especially if one had no assurance that the feelings were returned. She had made that mistake once. Back in Castleville, there'd been a young man, Braydan Rourke, who'd lived in the village near their cottage. Braydan was handsome and strong and had a winning smile and generous heart, much like Cam. He'd been kind to the Murphy family, helping them out when Nora's father had injured his foot and couldn't tend to his crops for a few weeks.

As she always had for their da, Nora had carried Braydan's noonday meal and flasks of water out to the fields, and during those breaks they had shared many a conversation. She'd been sixteen at the time and was enthralled when Braydan had confided his dreams of a better life to her. It embarrassed her now to remember how quickly and completely she'd fallen for him. At least she could take some small comfort in knowing that no one had suspected what a love-struck fool she'd been. Because when her da returned to the fields three weeks later, Braydan had not only left their farm but left Castleville itself without a backward glance and she'd never heard from him again.

It had been a painful lesson, but she'd learned it well. She would not so easily give her heart to a man again. Perhaps she was better off focusing her love on Grace.

James and Cam entered the kitchen just then, pulling Nora from her somber thoughts. The two men were sharing a laugh and Nora was caught again by how caring the sheriff was toward the Coulters, how boyish he looked when he was in a good humor and how his laugh could draw you in and make you want to smile along.

It would be so easy to develop stronger feelings for such a man. In fact, if she was honest with herself, she would admit that she already felt that little telling tug of attraction when he was around. His gaze snagged on hers and she could almost convince herself that his eyes took on a warmer glow. Almost without thought, she found herself responding in kind.

But then she dropped her gaze. That way lay heartache. She would not become another Laird O'Malley. Sheriff Long was her employer, nothing more. And if at times he seemed to treat her with special warmth, she needed to remind herself that that was just his way. Despite his nonchalant manner, she'd seen over and again how caring and protective he was of those around him. It was what made him such a good lawman. But she wasn't in need of his charity or his protection. Her life had been hard, but it had taught her how to take care of herself. And that was exactly what she would do.

As she fussed with Grace, Nora heard Agnes invite the sheriff to stay for dinner. She mentally held her breath while she waited on his response. When he refused, she wasn't certain if it was relief or disappointment that whooshed through her.

Later that evening as she lay in her bed, Nora found herself restless and unable to sleep. Not that this vague sense of discontent had anything to do with her earlier realizations about her relationship with the sheriff. No, it was most likely due to knowing Bridget was no longer part of the household—nothing more.

After all, it wasn't as if her heart was in any real danger since she'd come to her senses in time. And she was perfectly content to settle for Cam's friendship.

Turning over on her side, she steadfastly ignored the little voice in her head that wanted to argue the matter with her.

Chapter Four

On Monday morning, Nora patted Grace's back as she stared out the kitchen window at the gloomy weather. The rain had slacked off to a drizzle but it was still falling steadily. If it didn't let up soon it would make for an unpleasant ride into town this morning.

Not that she was one to let a bit of weather get in her way. There were four mouths to feed in this household, and, as her sisters had pointed out on Saturday, there was still lots of work to be done on the cottage itself before the cooler weather of autumn settled in. Work that required funds for supplies.

And there were more immediate needs cropping up every day. She'd awakened this morning to the sound of water dripping from the ceiling onto her bedchamber floor. Two hand spans over and those drips would have landed right on Grace. That had been a sobering sight.

But there was reason to be optimistic, as well. Just last night she'd had an idea for a way to bring in some extra money. She hadn't worked out all the details in her mind yet, but that was another reason she was eager to get to town today despite the weather—she'd really like to get Sheriff Long's opinion on this scheme of hers. After all, he had much more knowledge of Faith Glen and its people than she did.

Grace hiccupped and Nora patted her back. Then she frowned as she came back to this morning's weather. She didn't mind getting wet herself, but it wouldn't be right to take an infant out on such a day if it wasn't truly necessary.

But what other choice did she have?

"Surely you're not going to take that little lamb out in this rain." Agnes Coulter crossed the room, a soft smile on her face.

Nora shook her head. "I don't really want to." She glanced out the window once more. "Then again, perhaps if I wrap her really well…"

Agnes tsked. "You have another choice. You can leave Grace with me and James."

Nora immediately thought of a half-dozen reasons why she couldn't do that. The Coulters were elderly and frail. And they'd never had children of their own. Did they even know how to take care of an infant? And what about Grace's favorite lullaby—could either of them sing it to her when she got fussy?

She gave Agnes what she hoped was a convincing smile. "That's very kind, but I wouldn't want to impose on you that way. It's not raining very hard. Perhaps it will let up—"

"Don't be silly. I know you're as attached to that baby as a turtle is to its shell, but you can't keep her by your side all day, every day. You both need a break from each other occasionally."

Both women turned as the back door opened and

James limped in carrying a covered pail that no doubt contained fresh milk.

Agnes immediately started back across the room, her finger wagging like a gossipmonger's tongue. "James Barnabas Coulter, stop right there. Don't you dare go tromping water and mud across my clean floor." She made shooing motions with her hands. "Set that pail down and take yourself back out on the stoop and make use of the bootjack and dry off with that feed sack before you come back in."

"No need to yell at me, woman," James grumbled. "I was just trying to get the milk inside before Grace started wailing for her breakfast." But despite his aggrieved tone, James did as he was told.

Nora lay Grace down in the blanket-lined cradle and hurried over to retrieve the pail before Agnes tried to carry it herself. The older woman nodded her thanks and moved back toward the table, while Nora moved to the counter to strain the milk through a cheesecloth.

"This kind of weather is hard on his hip," Agnes said as the door closed behind her husband. "He doesn't like me to make a fuss over him, though."

Nora could hear the affection in the older woman's voice. The couple had been married for over fifty years she'd learned. Would she ever find that kind of love for herself?

An image of the sheriff, with his smoky blue eyes and straw-colored hair, floated through her mind at that thought. Realizing where her mind had drifted, Nora pulled herself up short, reminding herself of what she'd resolved just two days ago. There would be none of that. Better to remember that the man was not only her employer but more often than not she found herself at odds with him.

She watched Agnes's expression soften as Grace latched on to one of the woman's gnarled fingers, and Nora wrestled with the idea of leaving Grace in her and James's care. She'd barely been separated from Grace for more than a few hours since she'd first laid eyes on the squalling babe aboard the *Annie McGee*. The few time that they *had* been separated, Grace had been with one of her sisters. The Coulters, for all their kindness and good intentions, seemed hardly up to the job of caring for a baby. And she didn't want to put them to the test when she wasn't at least nearby to observe.

Nora set the bowl of milk aside and moved back toward the table. She resisted the urge to pick Grace up, instead letting Agnes continue to play with the child.

"See, Grace and I will get along just fine." Agnes smiled up at Nora, and then, as if she read something in Nora's face, her own expression changed to resignation. She reached over and patted Nora's hand. "It's okay, Nora girl. I understand."

Rather than making Nora feel better, Agnes's words shifted Nora's perception of the elderly couple. Yes, the Coulters still wore the frailness of their advanced years, but both Agnes and James had come a long way since she'd first met them. They moved with new purpose now, and the pinched, resigned looks they'd worn when she'd first met them were gone.

Besides, Grace was very little trouble and was still of an age where she stayed wherever she was placed. It wasn't as if they would have to chase after her.

As Agnes had said, she needed to accept that she couldn't have Grace with her every minute of every day, and this was an ideal time to see how both she and Grace would handle being apart.

Nora had a feeling that Grace would handle it much better than she would.

Taking a deep breath she smiled at her friend. "Actually, you're right, it would be irresponsible of me to take Grace out in this weather simply because I like the pleasure of her company. If you're certain you don't mind, I'd be most grateful to have you and James watch over Grace for me today."

Agnes's face split in a wide grin and she tapped Grace's chin. "Did you hear that, sweetling? You're going to spend the day right here with me and James."

Nora studied the woman's awkward movement and gnarled fingers and wondered if she'd made a mistake. But it would be too cruel to tell her she'd changed her mind now.

As Nora placed a clean apron and half-dozen fresh baked biscuits into a hamper to take with her, she thought that maybe she'd see if the sheriff would mind if she only worked a half day today. She mentally grimaced. One thing was for certain, he'd no doubt be glad she was leaving Grace with the Coulters for a change. She still hadn't figured out why Grace made him so uncomfortable, but there was no denying that she did. Would it be prying if she asked Ben if he had some insights into why?

Fifteen minutes later, Nora stood in the cottage doorway, tying the ribbon of her wool cape. She winced as she spotted droplets trickling down the wall near the parlor chimney. They were making progress on repairs but there was still so much to be done around here.

As she stared out at the lane, she wondered if perhaps she was assuming too much by expecting the sheriff to come out to fetch her in this weather. After all, he was under no obligation—

Right on time, she spied his wagon lumbering up the drive. Despite his sometimes lackadaisical demeanor, she had to admit the man was *always* punctual. He was wearing a long brown coat similar to what the fishermen back in Ireland wore, and what the sailors aboard the *Annie McGee* had worn. She thought wistfully about how nice it would be to have something to wear on a day like today that shed water so nicely. Perhaps she would add that to her growing list of necessary purchases.

As soon as the wagon drew near, she pulled the hood of her cape up over her bonnet and grabbed the hamper that rested at her feet.

No point standing on ceremony on a day like today.

And with that thought, she took a deep breath and prepared to dash out to meet him.

Chapter Five

By the time Cam had set the brake and hopped down from the wagon, Nora was already out the door. Fool woman, why couldn't she let a body help her every once in a while?

He waved her back to the house and she stopped short. Frowning at him, she turned and dashed back to shelter.

He reached under the wagon seat and grabbed the oil-skin coat he'd brought with him, then marched over to meet her. "Here, Ben sent this for you to use. It'll keep you drier than that bit of wool you're wearing."

Her eyes widened and her lips pinched into a straight line. No doubt she was unhappy with his tone. But there was a hint of appreciation in her eyes, as well. "That was very thoughtful of *Ben*." She didn't sound convinced that it had been his deputy's idea. Then she motioned him inside. "Come in off the stoop while I put this on."

He shook his head. "I don't want to track inside your house. Besides, I won't get much wetter than I already am."

She sighed, as if she were dealing with a stubborn child. But she didn't comment. Instead, she reached for the coat.

But Cam was having none of that. Instead he shook out the folds, stepped a little closer and held it up to assist her into it. After only the slightest of hesitations she allowed him to do so.

He was just being polite, he told himself. And if he happened to enjoy the fact that the action brought him close enough to brush a hand against her neck, to inhale the scent of cinnamon and flowers that seemed a part of her, well, that was just incidental.

Once the coat was wrapped around her, Nora turned to offer him a smile. "Thank you."

He cleared his throat. "Here." He handed her a fair-sized square of the oilcloth. "I didn't think you'd want to wear one of Ben's hats, but this will work almost as well. Just tie it over your headgear."

She took it without protest, quickly folded it into a triangle and covered her head, bonnet and all, tying it firmly under her chin.

That was one thing he liked about Nora, she didn't put on airs or complain. Good qualities to have in a housekeeper. And a friend.

He was relieved to note Grace wasn't anywhere in sight. It saved him the trouble of convincing her that the baby should stay inside on a day like today. "Glad to see you had enough sense not to take Grace out in this."

She nodded and he saw her worry at her lip a moment. "Agnes offered to take care of her and I couldn't turn her down."

He gave her an approving smile. "No reason why you should. It's about time you let Grace out of your sight for a bit."

She immediately stiffened and crossed her arms over her chest. "Of *course* I'm protective of her. That poor child was abandoned once already in her short life. I want to do all I can to make certain she feels loved and secure with me."

It seemed he'd gotten her back up yet again. He raised his hands, palms out. "I wasn't criticizing. It's obvious how much you love that little girl and I'm sure you're doing a fine job caring for her. It's just rare that I see you without Grace nearby."

Nora's feathers seemed a little less ruffled at that. "It's just for today." She glanced back over her shoulder. "You don't think watching Grace will be too much for them, do you?" She'd lowered her voice so that it didn't carry back to the kitchen.

He smiled. "They'll be fine." Then, wanting to reassure her further, he added, "And if it makes you feel better, Agnes worked as a nanny for some very prominent families in Boston for a number of years. I hear she was quite good at her job."

Some of the tenseness left her shoulders. "That's good to know." She gave a sheepish smile. "I suppose you think I'm being foolish."

"I'd never dare think such a thing," he said with mock seriousness. He was pleased when his teasing added a little spark to her expression.

Cam took the hamper from her and offered her his arm. "The ground is slippery," he said by way of explanation. "Ready?"

She nodded and took his arm. He could almost believe the no-nonsense Miss Murphy was suddenly shy. Almost.

They crossed to the wagon quickly, dodging puddles along the way. Cam made note of a number of maintenance issues that would need seeing to in the coming days.

He helped her climb onto the wagon and, once she was settled, handed up the hamper and then sprinted to the other side. As he took his own seat he saw her pull the coat more tightly around her. The sudden urge to draw her closer—to protect against the elements of course—surprised him.

He cleared his throat. "Sorry there's no cover on this wagon. I'm afraid even with the coat you'll be damp by the time we get to town."

She didn't seem concerned. "It appears to be letting up now. And a bit of soft weather won't hurt me."

"Soft weather?"

"Back in Ireland, when the weather turned all misty and damp, which was quite often, we'd say we were having a soft day."

There was a faraway look in her eyes, as if she were seeing her homeland in her mind. He flicked the reins, wordlessly directing the horse to turn the wagon back toward town. "Do you miss it much? Ireland I mean?" He kept his tone causal but he found himself tensing as he waited for her answer.

She seemed to consider his question a moment before speaking. "It's my birthplace and I have a lot of fond memories of growing up there." She grasped the seat on either side of her and leaned slightly forward. "Ireland will always be a part of who I am. But near the end of our time there, there was so much sorrow and pain, so much loss and uncertainty, that I'm grateful to be here and have this chance for a fresh start."

She flashed him a smile so full of hope and promise that it took his breath away. "Only yesterday I was thinking how nice it was that this place—both Faith Glen and the cottage itself—already feels like home to me."

Her words warmed him, made him sit up taller.

Not that he read anything special into them. He was merely glad to know his housekeeper was happy here.

Cam brushed that thought aside and changed the subject. "Oscar Platt over at the livery has a wagon and horse for sale that I think might be just right for you. He'll have it ready for you to look at after lunch if that's agreeable."

Her brows drew down. "I thought I'd said to find me a pony and a cart."

Was she going to be stubborn about this? "I think the horse and wagon will work out better for you in the long run," he said patiently.

But she wasn't appeased. "Sheriff Long, I understand that you think you always know what's best, but I'll have you know I have been making my own decisions for quite some time now."

He shook his head. No matter how many times he asked her to call him Cam, she insisted on using the more formal title of his office. But he did admire her spirit. "I'm sure you have, but that's not the point. Oscar owes me a favor and he's offering a good deal on the animal, which I am willing to pass on to you. You won't find a better value for your money anywhere." He raised a brow. "Unless you're so set on a pony and cart that you're willing to do without while you search for one? I suppose I can continue to worry about the Coulters for another few days."

She clamped her lips shut at that and they rode along in silence for a little while. When she finally spoke again, she surprised him by changing the subject. "I'd like to ask your opinion on a matter I've been mulling over the past few days."

So, she wanted his opinion on something, did she?

And from her tone it was something of import to her. Best not to read anything into that, though. No doubt she turned to him because he was her boss and the town sheriff—an authority figure of sorts. Still, she deserved his full attention.

He sat up a bit straighter. "Ask away."

"It's a matter related to finances."

Was she worried about owing him for the horse and wagon? Or the repairs that were still needed on the cottage? The woman did have more than her fair share of pride. "Go on."

"I mentioned to you on Saturday that my sisters would like me to move in with one of them. Well, I've decided, much as I love my sisters, that I would definitely prefer to stay right where I am."

That didn't surprise him at all. In fact it was the decision he would have predicted she'd make.

"The thing is," she said carefully, "in order to do so, I must prove to them, and to myself, that I can handle such a responsibility, both temperamentally and financially."

"Do you doubt that you can?"

"I believe I have the temperament and skill to do it, of course. But I spent some time after services yesterday figuring out what monies I'll need to provide for the basic needs of the four of us."

So, she considered the Coulters part of her responsibility, did she? Nora might have an excess of pride but she also had an excess of heart to match. "Perhaps you won't need quite as much as you think."

She gave him that prim spinster-aunt look. "Oh, no, I'm quite good at figures. After Mother passed on, Da left me to handle the household finances."

Another responsibility she'd shouldered. How old had she been when she'd taken that one on?

"Anyway, even being conservative," she continued, "the figures were daunting. And I know that there's not just food and everyday supplies to think about. I need to consider the repairs that still need to be done to the house and now to the barn." She raised a hand. "Whatever you were planning to say, please don't. I simply cannot let you continue to work at the cottage without pay."

She shifted in her seat. "There will be the added expense of the—" she paused a moment and eyed him primly "—the *wagon animal* to see to."

Still smarting over his insistence on a horse, was she?

"And while I am quite good at stretching provisions if I do say so myself," she sat up straighter, a proud lift to her shoulders, "I need to make certain there is sufficient food on the table each and every day for four people."

No doubt about it, in spite of her prickly exterior, Nora Murphy had a nurturing streak a mile wide. But where was she going with all of this? "If you don't think I'm paying you enough—"

She shook her head vehemently. "Oh, no, I've no complaints on that account. The wage you pay me is more than generous, and, the Good Lord willing, I truly think I can make it stretch to cover most of our expenses."

"So what is it that's worrying you?"

"There's something else I need to do to make the cottage truly a home for me and Grace as well as the Coulters."

"And that is?"

She clasped her hands in her lap, squeezing them tightly together. "As Colleen Murphy's daughters and heirs, the cottage belongs to all three of us. Since my sisters now have homes of their own, I would like to purchase their portions from them."

Now that *did* surprise him. Not the idea that she wanted to stake her claim to independence, that was absolutely in character. But that she thought her sisters would require, or even accept, payment from her. He didn't know Bridget and Maeve well, but he knew them well enough to know they'd be affronted at even the suggestion. "You really think they'd expect you to buy it from them?"

"Oh, I'm absolutely certain that they would simply give it to me if I asked them to, but that's not what *I* want. I won't feel like it is truly mine unless I do what's right and proper."

"And what's to say that them giving you their portions is not exactly what is right and proper?"

"My conscience. So, I need to find another way to earn money in addition to the work I do for you."

Stubborn woman. "I see. Then you want to cut down on the hours you spend working for me—is that it?"

"Not exactly. Actually, I think I have the perfect solution, but I wanted to get your thoughts on it."

He was both intrigued and a bit flattered by her request for his counsel. "I'm listening."

"I'd like to make pies and cakes to sell here in town." She announced her plan as if it was the answer to all her problems. Then she looked at him expectantly.

He tried to wrap his mind around what she'd just said. "Start a bakery business you mean?"

"Yes, but on a very small scale." She seemed less certain now. "You did say that folks seem to like my cakes and pies."

"Absolutely. I can't say as I ever tasted better."

His answer seemed to buoy her confidence once more. She smiled up at him with the raindrops glistening on her long dark lashes, vividly brightening her blue eyes, and he had to blink to clear his suddenly muddled thoughts.

"And Will has asked me to consult with his chocolatiers on how to improve his chocolates," she continued, "so perhaps I could somehow combine the two things."

Did she really understand the amount of work that would be involved in such an undertaking? "You'd have to make an awful lot of baked goods to make any sort of profit at it."

"I know. And I'm not afraid of hard work. But I would need your help."

She'd managed to surprise him yet again. "You want me to help you do your baking?" His only foray into baking was biscuits and he wouldn't exactly be bragging on his results.

But his question earned him a grin. "Nothing so challenging. I would, of course, do a lot of my baking at home. But I'd like to do some of it during the day, as well. Only, well, that would mean using your oven." She fluttered a hand in an uncharacteristically nervous gesture. "I promise not to do any less work for you than I already am." The words were rushed, as if she was trying to forestall an objection. "I can continue to clean and wash and cook your meals while my baked goods are in the oven."

He didn't for a minute doubt that she would be conscientious about her work. "Where do you plan to sell these delicacies?"

The look she shot him let him know she realized he hadn't answered her question. But she followed his lead. "I thought perhaps Mrs. James at the general store might be willing to sell some goods on commission for me and perhaps Rosie over at the boardinghouse would take some to serve to her boarders, as well." She stared at him expectantly. "What do you think?"

She really had given this some serious thought. "I think it's certainly worth a try. I might be able to drum up a few other customers for you, as well." That earned him a grateful look. "In fact," he added, "the workers over at the mill might be a good group to talk to."

"Oh, I hadn't thought about that. I'll speak to Will when he and Bridget get back into town." She eyed him uncertainly. "So you're agreeable to my baking while I work for you?"

"On one condition."

"And that is?"

"That you start small and don't work yourself to exhaustion."

She nodded. "I understand. I wouldn't be very useful as a housekeeper if I didn't have the energy to do my job."

Cam didn't comment. If she thought that was his reason then far be it from him to say otherwise.

Chapter Six

Nora shook her head over Cam's insistence that he drop her off at the door to his office, but she was grateful nevertheless. As he handed her down, she noticed that where the ends of his hair had gotten wet, the straw color had darkened to chocolate brown and had started to curl just the tiniest bit. She found her thoughts straying to what it might feel like to test the spring of that curl against her fingers.

Shaking off that totally inappropriate thought, she said a quick thank-you and bustled into the sheriff's office. She greeted Ben and Gavin, both of whom were sipping cups of the thick liquid that passed for coffee inside these walls when she wasn't around.

"Well, aren't you a pretty sight on a dreary morning." Ben's smile changed to a frown. "Where's Gracie? Nothing's happened to her I hope."

"No, no, Grace is just fine. But I didn't think it would be wise to take her out in this weather so I left her with the Coulters today."

He nodded. "I suppose that was the right thing to

do. I'm sure going to miss having that little girl around today, though."

Ben and Gavin had both warmed up to Grace quickly enough. They even helped watch her when Nora was particularly busy with some chore or other.

Nora turned back to Gavin. "Did you have a nice visit with your brothers and Mrs. Fitzwilliam after the wedding?"

Gavin nodded. "I sure did." Then he grimaced. "If only Mrs. F would quit trying to talk me into returning to Boston with them."

Nora raised a sympathetic brow. "She means well."

He shrugged. "I know. And I'm grateful that she's seeing that my brothers go to school. But that's not for me—this is where I want to be."

"Give her time. She'll come around." Nora untied her makeshift rain hat. "How goes her search for her granddaughter?"

Gavin shook his head. "No sign of her yet. I think Mrs. F is beginning to feel a bit discouraged."

Nora's heart ached for the older woman. "I will continue to pray for the two of them."

As she hung the hat on a peg, Ben rejoined the conversation. "You'll find a pair of freshly cleaned rabbits in there." He nodded toward the kitchen. "Andy Dubberly brought me those yesterday evening in exchange for a favor I did for him. Thought they might be good for lunch."

"How wonderful." Nora was genuinely delighted. This being a coastal town, fish was plentiful and inexpensive, so that was what she usually purchased when she did the sheriff's shopping. But red meat was a welcome change. "And I know just how to cook them." She was already going over the list of supplies she'd need to make her da's favorite rabbit stew. *Carrots, onions, turnips—*

"I have the stove already warmed up for you, Miss Nora."

Nora smiled at Gavin's not too subtle hint that he was ready for the morning meal. "Thank you. I'll have breakfast ready quick as can be."

She shook herself out of the borrowed raincoat. "And thank *you* for the use of your coat," she said to Ben. "It was most welcome on the ride in this morning." She hung it next to the hat. "It certainly kept me drier than I would have been without it."

Ben shook his head. "It's Cameron you should be thanking. The boy let himself into my place before dawn and grabbed my coat without so much as a knock or a may-I." Then the older man smiled. "But I'm very pleased to see he put it to such good use."

So it had been Cam's idea, not Ben's as he'd led her to believe. "Well, thank you anyway." She moved toward the kitchen. "Now, I believe this is a three-egg morning for the lot of you." She wagged a finger at the two deputies. "And no snatching the biscuits while my back is turned."

Nora found herself humming as she moved to the room she had nicknamed her "galley."

The sheriff and Ben had living quarters in a small two-story building behind the jailhouse. Ben lived on the lower floor and the sheriff on the upper. Both homes, if one could call them that, were quite small. They each had three very small rooms—a kitchen, a parlor and a bedroom.

Gavin, the newest member of the peacekeeping team, slept in one of the two cells at the jailhouse. He couldn't afford to stay at the boardinghouse and there was no-where else.

She'd decided almost from the outset to do the cook-ing in Ben's quarters instead of the sheriff's since it was on the ground floor and meant easier access for every-one. She also insisted on feeding them at the same time so neither had to eat their meals cold. But when Gavin came on the scene it really made Ben's tiny place seemed cramped and uncomfortable.

Especially since Cam wouldn't hear of her excusing herself to work elsewhere while they ate. Instead, he insisted she share their meals with them and would not even listen to her very reasonable arguments on why it was inappropriate for the hired help to sit down to dine with her employer.

I need to make sure you're keeping your strength up so you can handle these chores I hired you to take care of, he'd said. And, on another occasion he'd made the out-rageous statement that *I can't have a cook who won't eat her own cooking in front of me.* So she'd finally given in.

Which meant four people sat down to eat two meals a day in Ben's cramped quarters.

But when she'd returned to work the Monday after Gavin became a permanent resident, the men had had a surprise for her. She'd arrived at the sheriff's office to find that they'd cleared out the jailhouse storeroom and set up a makeshift kitchen in its place. The sheriff had *said* it was so he could eat in the office where there was more room, but she suspected it was as much for her benefit as anything else.

Whatever the reason, Nora had been delighted with the new arrangement. There was a brand-new stove al-ready stoked and ready for her to put to use. One wall was lined with shelves that now contained foodstuffs, cooking implements and rudimentary serving dishes. A small but sturdy table stood near the opposite wall. And the room even had a window that not only let in the sunlight but provided her with a view of Ben and Cam's living quarters.

Water had to be hauled in, of course, but there was a small water barrel in the corner and Gavin, bless him, usually took care of keeping it filled for her.

She'd nicknamed the storage room-turned-kitchen her "galley" because it reminded her of the kitchen aboard the *Annie McGee* where she'd spent a good deal of her time on their voyage from Ireland. She'd worked as a helper to the ship's cook.

So now she started her days in here, fixing up a hearty breakfast for everyone.

Nora continued humming as she cracked three eggs for each of the men and one for herself. The more she thought about her baking venture, the more excited she became. And now that she knew the sheriff wouldn't be opposed to her combining her job here with her new business, the way seemed clear for her to give it a try. It was certainly a generous concession from him, and she was determined to make certain he didn't regret it.

He was right about starting small, of course. Maybe two pies and a cake of some sort each day this week. Hopefully it would grow from there. And if things worked out well, perhaps one day she could have her own little bakery right here in Faith Glen.

By the time Cam came back in, Nora had the morning meal almost ready. "There's a fresh pot of coffee here on the stove," she called out to him. "You have just enough time to grab a cup before I serve breakfast."

Cam joined her in the galley, his large presence filling the small space. "Something sure does smell delicious. That's the kind of aroma a man likes to be greeted with on a day like today. I should have set up a kitchen in here ages ago."

Just as she turned to retrieve a platter, he reached around her to grab the coffeepot from the warmer. The minor collision that ensued caught Nora completely by surprise.

His arms reflexively closed around her to keep her from falling and she pressed her hands on his chest in an effort to maintain her balance. For a frozen moment of time they were locked in an embrace that took her breath away and pushed everything else aside. She couldn't move, couldn't think straight. All she could do was feel—feel his arms around her, feel his heartbeat beneath her palms, feel the warmth of his breath on her forehead.

Then everything came rushing back in, including her wits. Flustered, she took a hurried step back and he released her, dropping his hands to his sides. Unable to look at him directly, she cast a sideways glance his way, trying to figure out what he was thinking. But his expression was unreadable.

"I'm so sorry." She was appalled by the stammer in her voice and swallowed, trying to get herself back under control. Where was that resolve she'd counted on?

Before she could say more, he spoke up. "My fault entirely. I shouldn't crowd you here in what is indisputably your domain." If his tone was any gauge, he'd been entirely unaffected by the momentary contact.

She mentally cringed at the implication behind that betraying thought. Of course he'd been unaffected. It had been nothing more than a little everyday mishap. Her own reaction was no doubt due to the fact that she'd been caught off guard. She wouldn't allow it to be anything more.

His expression changed to one of concern. "I hope I didn't hurt you."

Mercy, did she look as rattled as all that? Nora attempted a reassuring smile. "No, no, I'm fine. Don't think anything of it." *Please* don't think of it.

"Well, then, I'll just leave you to your cooking. I can get that cup of coffee later."

"Nonsense." Glad of an excuse to turn away, Nora quickly poured him up a cup. She turned and handed it to him, careful to keep their hands from touching. Then she made shooing motions with her hands. "Now, if you'll leave me to finish up in here, I'll have breakfast ready to serve in just a moment."

Raising the cup in a friendly salute, he left the galley and joined Ben and Gavin.

Nora turned back to the stove but had to force herself to concentrate on the task at hand.

Because she could still feel the beat of his heart under her palms. And she didn't understand why that should make her feel so flustered.

Cam sipped his coffee without tasting it. Hang it all, what had just happened in there? It had been a simple accident, a reflexive response to a minor collision, nothing more. Yet it had affected him more than it should have, and from the expression on Nora's face just now, it had affected her, as well.

Only he wasn't sure in just what way. As far as that

went, he wasn't sure exactly what *he* was thinking or feeling about it either.

Truth to tell, he was having trouble getting his thoughts clear from the warm feel of her hands against his chest, the sight of her suddenly wide blue eyes and the sound of her quickly inhaled breath that inexplicably seemed to suck all the air from the room.

This was definitely *not* a good development. He liked Nora well enough. To be honest, maybe a sliver more than "well enough." But it wouldn't do for him to start having stronger feelings. And not just because she was his housekeeper.

"Hey, sheriff."

Gavin's hail brought a welcome break from Cam's muddled thoughts. "I'm listening."

"I almost forgot to tell you—Mr. Lafferty stopped by while you were out fetching Miss Nora. He said someone's been raiding his garden and he wants you to do something about it." Gavin shook his head. "He sure was mighty angry."

Ben snorted. "Amos Lafferty's not happy unless he's got something to complain about. Why, if someone walked up and handed him a fistful of coins he'd likely complain because it wasn't in a shiny leather pouch."

Cam grinned at Ben's very apt description of the town's most cantankerous citizen.

Ben leaned back in his chair. "It was likely just a deer or fox or some such deciding to take a midnight graze through his place."

Ben was probably right. Still… "All the same, I think I'll go have a look around after breakfast. If there *is* somebody raiding his garden I want to put a stop to it."

Ben shrugged. "Suit yourself. If you want to go tromping through a muddy garden in the rain on a wild goose chase, that's your business."

"I don't mind a bit of rain," Gavin piped up. "Can I go with you?"

Cam eyed his overeager deputy, then nodded. "Sure. You can ride Ben's horse since he plans to stay in out of the rain."

He moved to his desk and gathered the few papers that had accumulated since yesterday and stashed them in the top drawer. That effectively turned his desk into a dining table at mealtime, with each of the four of them taking a side.

Right on cue, Nora bustled across the room carrying a large tray. He knew better than to offer to help since prior experience had taught him that she'd only lecture him on how he should get out of the way and let her do her job. Still he watched her, looking for signs that she was at all rattled by their earlier encounter. But she seemed as efficient and unflappable as ever. She didn't once make eye contact with him, but that could be nothing more than her being distracted by planning for her new venture.

Five minutes later she had everything laid out before them and all four took their seats. After they said grace, Cam nodded to Nora. "Did you tell Ben and Gavin about your idea for a new business?"

Ben paused in the act of spreading jam on his biscuit. "A business venture? Are you going to be a woman of means soon?"

Nora laughed. It seemed there was no lingering nervousness on her part.

"Nothing so spectacular," she said. "I'm thinking about baking a few extra pies and cakes to sell around town."

"Well, now, I'm guessing you're going to have people lining up to buy them." Ben pointed his fork her way. "And if you need someone to do your tasting for you, I hereby volunteer."

"That's a mighty generous offer," she said dryly, "but I don't think I'll need to impose on you."

Cam noticed the way her eyes brightened when she was in a teasing mood. Not that he saw this side of her often. Which was really too bad.

Gavin, however, didn't seem to find the subject a teasing matter. "You mean you're going to be baking all kinds of desserts in here and we aren't going to be able to eat any of them?" The boy looked absolutely crestfallen.

Nora laughed. "Don't worry, Gavin, I'll still make sure you gentlemen have something fresh for dessert every day."

"Well, I for one think it's a dandy idea." Ben scooped up a forkful of egg. "And now that the folks in town have had a chance to sample your baking talents at your sister's wedding reception, I don't think you'll be wanting for customers."

Her cheeks pinkened. "Why, thank you, Ben. I certainly hope you're right."

Cam ate his breakfast in silence while Nora continued to banter with Ben and Gavin. Why was she so relaxed and easy with the other two, calling them by their first names and even lapsing into this teasing banter, yet at the same time she insisted on being formal with him? The whole thing got under his skin more than it should.

After all, they'd known each other a month and had gotten to know each other well. Was it too much to ask for her to treat him as more of a friend than a boss?

And being friends was all he wanted from her, all

he would *allow* himself to want from her. Because he'd decided long ago he couldn't have a family of his own, especially not one that included a child. There were too many inherent dangers for a man like him in a relationship like that.

Yes, sir, he'd accepted his own limitations in that area and moved on a long time ago. So why was he feeling so restless about the whole matter lately?

Nora absently pushed the broom across the floor of Ben's kitchen. Cleaning this place and the one upstairs was no hardship—they were so small and both men were fairly neat. It was no wonder, though, that the two men spent most of their time over at the sheriff's office. It must be lonely in their very separate, very small spaces. Not that either of them would ever admit to such a thing.

She'd made good progress this morning and was well ahead of schedule. Since Ben had provided rabbits for today's meal and the pantry was well stocked she hadn't had to go to the market. And without Grace to tend to, her work had gone much faster. And been much lonelier.

It was quiet in here today. Too quiet. Even the patter of the rain had faded away about thirty minutes ago. No doubt about it, she missed having Grace with her. Listening to the baby coo and gurgle and even fuss always provided welcome company during her workday.

Nora wasn't normally a talkative person, preferring to keep her own counsel. But her life had undergone so much change in the last few months that she'd found herself longing for someone to discuss things with, as much to sort it out in her own mind as to seek advice.

And it turned out that Grace was a very good listener. During those times when it was just her and Grace, she'd gotten into the habit of talking to her while she worked, holding entire conversations, as if Grace understood every word. She'd related some of her fears and dreams and plans, working through her own feelings about her new life in the process.

Somehow, talking to an empty room didn't seem quite the same.

And, oh my, but it certainly would have been good to have someone to talk to today of all days—someone who wouldn't comment or pass judgment but merely listen as she talked about the events of the day.

There was, of course, the advice she'd gotten from Cam about her baking venture. His opinion carried a lot of weight with her—he was intelligent, he knew the town and he knew her. Knowing she had his approval gave her the confidence she needed to carry through with her idea.

Yes, she should be planning her menus and shopping lists and identifying potential customers. Instead her traitorous thoughts kept circling back to that near-embrace that had resulted from her collision with the sheriff earlier. Yes it had taken her breath away and set her pulse to racing. But surely that was natural given how startled she'd been.

And it wasn't as if she had a lot of experience with that sort of thing. There'd been no time for courting back home in Ireland. After their mother's death she had become the lady of the house and had taken on many of the household duties that had formerly been her mother's.

If only her traitorous mind didn't keep returning to the sweet sensation of being held in his protective embrace....

So lost in her thoughts was she, that she nearly dropped her broom when someone knocked on the door.

"It's only me," Ben called from outside.

"Come in," she responded, glad for the moment to collect herself. Then, as soon as the door opened, "I've told you before there's no need for you to knock at your own door."

Ben shook his head as he wiped his boots on the rag rug she'd made to grace his threshold. "Wouldn't be right for me to barge in on a lady unannounced, even if that lady is sweeping my floor."

Nora had grown quite fond of Ben in the short time she'd been in Faith Glen. The impish quality he wore like a favorite suit made his age seem like a disguise. His dark eyes, hidden behind a pair of spectacles, seemed to look at the world with a youthful, mischievous air that made you both want to smile and to wonder what he had up his sleeve. Clouds of snow-white hair adorned the sides and back of his head, but only wisps clung to the top.

She leaned on the broom a moment. "If I'm in your way, I can work over at the jailhouse for a bit."

He waved her back as he crossed the room. "Nonsense. In fact, I came over here looking for a bit of company. Cameron and Gavin are out tromping through old Amos Lafferty's garden and it was getting lonely across the way by myself."

He pulled out a chair and sat at the small table, smiling up at her as he did so. "So, tell me more about your plan to start a business."

Glad to have a bit of company, Nora smiled and resumed her sweeping. "There's not a whole lot to tell, other than what you already know. The sheriff cautioned me to start slow, and I agree that's probably best—maybe two pies and one cake a day. Then, if it looks like folks really will buy my baked goods, I can do more."

"Oh, I have no doubt you'll do well." Ben tipped his chair back on two legs. "I just hope you don't get so much business you decide you don't need to work here anymore."

She smiled. "Don't worry, you three will always be my favorite customers. And let's not get ahead of ourselves. This may not work out."

He wagged a finger at her. "None of that false modesty. Folks are still talking about how good that cake you baked for the reception was."

Nora couldn't decide how to respond to that so she changed the subject. "Did you happen to check on the stew before you left the jailhouse?"

He nodded. "I gave it a good stir. The smells coming out of that pot are enough to tempt a stone. Those rabbits gave up their lives for a good cause."

Nora laughed. "Indeed. Rabbit stew was one of the first things my mother taught me how to cook, and it was my da's favorite dish."

Ben let the chair legs drop back to the floor. "Sounds like you had a fine family." Then he cocked his head to one side. "Speaking of which, I kind of miss having little Gracie around today. Of course, I know you made the right choice leaving her home in this weather."

"I miss her, too. But at least the sheriff is more comfortable not having her around." Nora wanted to take the words back as soon as they slipped past her lips. Yes, she was curious about his behavior, but she had no business fishing for information about her boss.

Ben gave her a searching look. "He's more fond of that little girl than you think, than even *he* thinks."

Nora tried not to let her skepticism show, but she

found that very hard to believe. So she settled for saying nothing.

Ben studied her for a long moment, his expression unusually serious. Finally he nodded, as if he'd reached a decision. "There's something you probably ought to know about Cameron."

Chapter Seven

Nora felt a momentary touch of panic. Much as she'd like to learn the sheriff's secrets, this was wrong. She put a bit more force into her efforts with the broom, keeping her head down. "I didn't mean to bring this up, Ben, and I certainly don't want to pry into his past." Well, that wasn't entirely true, but wanting didn't give her the right to actually do it. "The man has a right to his privacy. If there's something he thinks I should know, then he'll tell me himself."

Ben shook his head. "You're wrong. I love that boy as if he were my own son, but he's got hold of some foolish notions that are ruining his life. And I think it's time someone else shared the burden of knowing about the nightmares that drive him. Someone who cares about him and wants what's best for him." He gave Nora a challenging look. "I was hoping you might be that person."

The sheriff had nightmares driving him? Hard to believe. He seemed so strong, so confident. Yet she'd sensed there was something troubling him.

But did she have the right to hear his story before he

was ready to tell her himself? Still, if Ben thought her knowing could help…

Almighty Father, I truly do want to help Cameron. He's a good man and he's been nothing but kind to me since I arrived in town. I'd like to return the favor and help him if I can. Maybe this is one way to do that.

Hoping she'd made the right choice, Nora slowly moved to the table and sat down across from Ben. "Tell me."

He smiled approvingly. "Good girl." Then he sobered. "I warn you, though, this won't be easy to hear. Cam didn't have a pleasant childhood."

Nora clasped her hands together in front of her and mentally braced herself. Suddenly she was very afraid of what she might hear. "Go on."

Ben patted her hands, then raked his fingers through his sparse hair. "Cam loved his mother deeply. From what he's told me of her, she was a God-fearing woman, hardworking and a loving mother." His face hardened. "Unfortunately, he wasn't so blessed when it came to his father. Douglas Long was a terrible man, a monster. He was a thief and a drunk who'd spend every penny of his money on liquor and gambling, then lash out at his wife for not putting food on the table. And worse, he was a mean drunk who beat both Cam and his mother regularly."

Nora couldn't repress her gasp. "No!" She could hardly take in the idea of someone treating another person that way, much less his own wife and child. How had Cam borne such cruelty?

Ben's gaze softened and he patted her hand. "I'm sorry to distress you so, but I'm afraid it's true. Cameron lived like that for the first twelve years of his life. He and his mother tried to protect each other as best they could, but they weren't a match for his brute of a father."

Her heart bled for the little boy Cam had been and for the mother he'd loved. "You said the first twelve years of his life—is that when his father died?" Her eyes burned with the effort not to cry.

"No, more's the pity. That's when his mother died."

How awful to lose the loving parent in such a situation. Why couldn't God have taken the brute instead? "Did his father cause—"

"No, thank the Lord. Both she and Cam worked at a factory and apparently there was some sort of accident there. After that, with nothing to hold him at home, Cam ran away. He lived on his own in the city for a while—this happened in Boston. Eventually, when he was about sixteen or so, he ended up here in Faith Glen."

She wiped her eyes with the corner of her apron. "And you took him in."

Ben shrugged. "It wasn't a hardship. Cam needed a job and a place to stay and I needed a deputy."

Nora knew it was much more than that—like Cam's hiring of Gavin. But she let it pass while she swallowed the lump that had formed in her throat.

"Anyway," Ben continued, "it took me a long time to get the story out of him. He wasn't big on trusting folks as you might imagine. But the important thing for you to understand is this." He leaned forward as if to emphasize what he was about to say. "Cam is absolutely convinced that if he was ever to have children of his own, he'd turn out to be just as bad a father as his own was."

Nora straightened, outraged. "That's ridiculous."

Ben spread his hands. "I know. But on this one subject, Cam is just not objective. And because he feels that way, he won't let himself get close enough to a woman to contemplate marriage. And he definitely wants nothing to do with being solely responsible for a child."

Nora couldn't believe what she was hearing. "But he's *nothing* like his father, and could never be. Even I can see that after knowing him for only a month. He cares too much about people, all kinds of people."

This time Ben raised his hands palm out. "You don't need to convince me. I'm on your side." He captured and held her gaze. "You do realize you can't let him know I told you, don't you?"

"But—"

Nora jumped as the front door opened.

"Ben, I need to talk to—" Cam halted on the threshold, obviously surprised to see Ben wasn't alone. "Well, don't the two of you look mighty serious. What have you been conspiring about in here?"

Cameron stared from Ben to Nora as he wiped his damp boots on the rag rug that was almost identical to the one Nora had placed by his own front door. Now just what had put that guilty look on both their faces?

Instead of answering him, Nora popped to her feet, grabbed the nearby broom and started sweeping. Was she pushing it with a bit more vigor than absolutely necessary? Something had gotten her all agitated.

When he turned back to Ben, his friend gave him an unrepentant grin. "I was just wheedling Miss Murphy here into taking a break from her work to keep a tired old man company."

Was that it—was she worried he wouldn't approve of her taking a break from her work? Cam snorted. "Tired old man, my foot. You have more energy than that puppy

Gavin." He glanced Nora's way. "And Nora knows she can take a break anytime she wants."

Nora pushed the small pile of dirt she'd swept up toward the door. "I'll get out of your way so you two can talk business. I need to check on lunch anyway."

She turned to Ben and he felt some sort of understanding flash between them. "Thanks again for our chat. I appreciate your…encouragement for my baking business."

Ben nodded. "My pleasure. I have faith in you."

Cam watched Nora leave, frowning as something about her demeanor still seemed off.

But as soon as the door closed behind her, Ben spoke up. "That girl not only has a smart head on her shoulders but she has a good heart and isn't afraid of hard work. Some lucky man is going to snatch her up one day soon and we'll be stuck with each other's cooking again."

That prediction brought Cam up short. He didn't like that idea one bit. Only because it meant he'd lose a good housekeeper and cook, of course.

Ben hooked his elbow over the top of his chair. "Now what did you want to talk to me about?"

Cam shook off his momentary distraction and pulled up a seat. "About what I found out at Amos Lafferty's place."

"Are you telling me the garden intruder wasn't an animal?"

"I found some signs that it might be an animal of the two-legged variety."

"What kind of signs?"

"The rain washed most of the tracks away, but I found one footprint near his gate. And it was made by a foot much smaller than Lafferty's."

"You thinking the Grady boys might have been up to mischief again?"

"Maybe. Or maybe it was someone else."

Ben's gaze sharpened. "What are you thinking, Cameron?"

Time to let Ben in on his suspicions. "I'm just wondering if that little thief who tried to steal my horse is still here in Faith Glen."

"Now why would she be hanging around after almost getting caught? Makes more sense for her to move on to some place less...aware."

"I don't know." And that was what was worrying him. There was a part of this puzzle he hadn't figured out yet, and something told him it was a key piece.

"Did you mention this to Gavin?"

"Of course not. The fool boy is still half-besotted with her." He supposed a pretty face and an air of mystery and adventure would present a powerful attraction for a boy Gavin's age. But Gavin would have to learn to see below the surface if he was going to last as deputy.

"Besides," he said, focusing back on Ben, "I might be wrong, and you could be closer to the truth on the Grady boys. In fact, I think I'll have a word with them after lunch."

"Want company?"

"No need. Lem's a good man. If his sons are the guilty parties then I'll leave it to him to handle disciplining the pair. If they're not, then only one of us will have wasted a trip out there."

Ben didn't seem put out by Cam's answer. "Well, then, I think I'll wander on over to the Black house after lunch. Esther mentioned she might need some help with her garden while Will and Bridget are out of town."

Esther, was it? And when had Ben ever done any gardening? Had Nora been right after all about something developing between Ben and Will's mother? Come to think of it, Ben had become a regular at Sunday services lately and had inserted himself into the same pew as Cam, the Murphy sisters and the Black family. Cam had figured it was because he was in that pew, but the real draw might well have been something else altogether.

Cam was never one to beat around the bush, especially with Ben. "Nora seems to think you might be courting Miss Esther."

Ben smiled. "Now, didn't I tell you Nora had a smart head on her shoulders?" The older man got up and headed for the door, his step a bit jauntier than usual. "And speaking of Nora, you might want to keep an eye on her. If this bakery business does as well as I think it will, you might well be looking for a new housekeeper and cook soon even if she doesn't find herself a beau."

Cam refused to consider that possibility. "She seems to think she can handle both jobs."

Ben shrugged. "Let's hope she's right." He opened the door and his grin reappeared. "I'm off to Esther's. But tell Nora to save some of that lunch for me if I'm not back when she gets ready to serve it."

Cam followed more slowly, grinning at the idea of his old friend courting Will's mother. He supposed that proved it was never too late for a body to find love, or in Mrs. Black's case, find it again.

As for himself, well perhaps that didn't apply to everyone—

Tamping down the persistent image of Nora in his arms earlier and scampering away a few minutes ago,

Cam circled his thoughts back around to what he'd found out at Amos Lafferty's place.

And what it might mean.

Nora put away the last of the freshly washed lunch dishes and moved to wipe off the stovetop. What should she tackle next? She wasn't quite following her schedule today, which put her slightly out of sorts. Should she bake a loaf of bread to go with their evening meal? Should she work on the pile of mending the men had added to her basket? Or would it be all right if she just asked Cam for the rest of the afternoon off?

Nora chewed on her lip, fighting the urge to go with the latter choice. How were the Coulters faring with their nursemaid duties? Had they remembered to give Grace a bottle at midday? Were they keeping a close eye on her? Did they know to sing her a lullaby to help her sleep when nap time came around?

Did Grace miss having her near?

On the other hand, much as she missed Grace, Nora had to admit that she *had* moved through her chores much faster today. Without the precious distraction of tending to the baby's needs and pausing occasionally to just coo over her, she'd breezed through her tasks. Perhaps, instead of leaving now, if she continued to work for just another hour or so, she could complete all her normal chores and still get back to the cottage several hours earlier than normal. She'd make her sales pitch at the boardinghouse and general store tomorrow. And she could always take some of the lawmen's mending home with her to do there.

Pleased that she'd formed a plan that would allow her

to fulfill all of her obligations, Nora gave the stove one last swipe with her rag, then turned.

But when she looked up, Cam was moving purposefully toward her. Remembering what happened the last time he'd been in the cozy galley with her, Nora felt her whole being tense in a not unpleasant anticipation.

But he halted just inside the doorway and leaned casually against the jamb.

She raised a hand to tuck a nonexistent stray hair behind her ear. "Hello there," she said, doing her best to sound casual. "Was there something you needed?"

He looked at her as if puzzled. Had he heard something in her tone? Could he sense the nervous energy thrumming through her?

"I didn't mean to interrupt your work," he said diffidently.

She shook her head, giving him a bright smile. "You aren't interrupting." She reached for the nearby broom, glad to have something to occupy her hands. "I've finished with the dishes and was about to sweep up in here. But if you have something else for me to do—"

He waved her words aside. "Actually, I had a different idea. Since the weather's cleared up, I was thinking we could head over to the livery so you can have a look at that horse and wagon I told you about. Oscar should have it all ready for you to inspect by now."

His tone indicated he considered it just a formality, that *of course* she would agree with his judgment. Didn't he understand by now that she had a mind of her own? "Of course. Best to get this inspection over with so we can move on to a more sensible solution if we need to."

He raised a brow, as if she'd just issued a challenge. Which, she supposed, she had.

"You have to promise me you're going to give this a fair consideration," he said pointedly.

"Naturally."

"Good." He straightened and nodded toward the door. "Then put the broom aside and let's go have a look."

The walk to the livery stable was pleasant. The rain had long since stopped but the sidewalks were still damp, and the road muddy. Still, the sunshine felt good and the air smelled fresh and rain-washed. They exchanged greetings with several folks as they passed by. Nora found even those casual exchanges worth a smile. She was still something of an outsider here but it was amazing how quickly that was changing, how the townsfolk were already beginning to accept her as one of them.

"When are Will and your sister due to return to town?" Cam asked.

"This evening. They didn't want to stay away from the twins for too long."

Cam nodded. "It's obvious those youngsters are already attached to your sister."

"I assure you that feeling is returned. Bridget will make a wonderful mother." The subject reminded her of her earlier conversation with Ben. "I've often thought being a parent must be one of the most blessed and fulfilling callings of all. Don't you agree?"

"It's a tremendous responsibility," he said evenly. "And not one that everyone is suited for."

He hadn't really answered her question. "Oh, I agree. One must be willing to see to their children's needs—and not just their physical needs. A parent should put their child's welfare above their own." She cut him a sideways glance. "Sort of the way you do for the citizens of this town."

He grinned. "Are you saying I treat the citizens of Faith Glen like a bunch of children?"

The man could be so frustrating when he got like this. He knew good and well that wasn't what she'd meant—he was just trying to bait her.

But before she could say more, they had arrived at the livery and the moment was lost. Oscar Platt stood just inside the large open carriage door and strode forward when he saw them.

"Good afternoon, Sheriff, Miss Nora. I assume you're here to look at the horse and wagon. They're already hitched out back and ready for your inspection."

They followed him to the back where several wagons were stored. The vehicle he led them to was similar to the one the sheriff used, with a single seat in front and a flat bed in the back. The bed of this one was much shorter than the sheriff's, but it was more than big enough for her needs.

It was the horse, however, that drew her attention. The mare had a reddish-brown coat with a darker mane and tail. She held her head up at an alert angle and had bright, intelligent eyes.

Nora approached the animal slowly. "My, my, aren't you a beautiful lady."

"Her name's Amber," Oscar said, giving the animal's side an affectionate pat. "She's a fine animal, fine indeed. And you'll see she's nearly as good a saddle horse as she is a carriage horse."

This was not at all the kind of animal she'd expected. She was no expert but even she could see that this mare was first rate, the kind to demand a premium from a prospective buyer. She would never be able to afford such a horse. "Mr. Platt, I'm afraid there's been some mistake. I'm looking for an animal that's not quite so...so *fine*."

The livery owner looked confused and turned to Cam.

"Tell her how much you're asking for the horse and wagon together," Cam said.

Oscar named a figure that brought a frown to Nora's face. Not because it was too high, but for the exact opposite reason. "May I ask why you're selling her for such a low price, if she's as grand as you say she is?"

"Well, I, that is..." Oscar rubbed the back of his neck and again cast a help-me look Cam's way.

Cam cleared his throat. "I told you, Nora, Oscar owes me a favor so he's giving me his bottom-line price on this." He spread his hands. "And I'm passing that good fortune on to you."

Nora stroked the horse's muzzle as she thought about that. She suspected there was more to this than Cam was letting on. But the offer *was* tempting.

"What do you think?" Cam asked. "Perfect for your needs isn't she? And the wagon, too?"

"They're everything you say. I just—"

He didn't let her finish her thought. "Why don't we take a little ride to test it out?"

"Well, I suppose." She glanced toward the livery owner. "I mean if Mr. Platt doesn't mind."

The man waved them on. He actually seemed relieved that they were leaving. "Not at all. You two go on with you. I'm sure you won't find anything wrong with the rig or the horse."

Cam offered a hand to help her onto the wagon, then took the seat beside her. "This seat has a nice solid feel to it, don't you think?"

She ignored that and settled herself more comfortably. "Shall we drive around the square then?"

"I have a better idea. Why don't we give this horse and wagon a more thorough workout? A short ride on Farm Road maybe."

Nora's lips curved up at that. The sky had cleared and the day had turned pleasant. A companionable ride would be very nice. And she hadn't had the opportunity to explore in that direction yet. What the locals called Farm Road headed west away from the ocean and, as the name implied, led to a number of small farms and homesteads clustered around the town.

She gave him a bright smile. "If you're sure you have the time, a short ride would be lovely."

"Actually, I have a bit of business over at Lem Grady's place. I thought I'd combine our ride and my work. It shouldn't take more than a few minutes."

"Of course." So much for thinking he wanted to take a casual ride with her. Not that it mattered. Besides, it would be interesting to see him at work on official business.

The Grady place was just past the edge of town, and they arrived within ten minutes. Once there, rather than going to the house, Cam stopped the wagon near an open field where Mr. Grady and his two boys were digging up an old stump in the rain-soaked ground.

He set the brake then turned to her. "There's no need for you to trouble yourself getting down. It's still muddy out here, and I don't plan to be long."

Nora sat back and folded her hands in her lap but she watched curiously as Cam crossed the field to meet the three Gradys.

As she watched Cam, Nora mulled over the earlier

exchange in the livery, and a soft smile curved her lips. Yes, Cam had been very presumptuous in the matter of selecting a horse and wagon. But it was also obvious that he'd gone to some trouble to convince Mr. Platt to give her such a good deal. It was all the more endearing because he'd never take any credit for it.

Nora sat up straighter. Not that she should read anything into his actions. Cam was always looking out for folks, that's all this was. She shouldn't forget her resolve to not open herself up to that kind of hurt, and instead to focus her affections on Grace.

Chapter Eight

Nora couldn't hear anything that was being said, but from their expressions and movements she thought she could make out some of the conversation.

Cam had approached the Gradys in his normal casual fashion and Mr. Grady seemed pleased to see him. The boys, on the other hand, looked guarded, and toe-digging-in-the-ground apprehensive. Had they done something they shouldn't have?

A moment later, Mr. Grady turned a stern eye toward his sons. The boys reacted with vehement head shakes and gesticulations.

Cam questioned them a few more minutes, then finally shook hands with Mr. Grady and headed back to the wagon. As he climbed up and released the brake, she noted he had a thoughtful, somewhat troubled expression on his face.

"Did everything go as you hoped?"

"I just ruled out a couple of suspects in a bit of ongoing mischief."

Was that a good thing or not? She couldn't tell from his expression. "If it's not out of place for me to ask, did this have something to do with the produce missing from Mr. Lafferty's garden?"

He nodded. "But Lem says he can vouch that his boys were both home all night because he heard Arnie snoring off and on and Evan hurt his foot yesterday and is moving pretty slow right now. Lem's not one to try to lie to keep his boys out of trouble, so I believe him."

"Are you sure the culprit wasn't a deer or fox like Ben first thought?"

Cam shook his head, his frustration evident. "Not entirely, but all the signs point to a thief of the two-legged variety."

"I know it's wrong to steal," she said, "but perhaps whoever is guilty of this had no other food. Surely we can be forgiving of such a trespass."

"That'll be up to Amos Lafferty. Assuming we ever find the culprit."

"Well, I'm certain you'll find him eventually."

"Your confidence is appreciated," he said dryly. Then he cocked his head, studying her thoughtfully. "And speaking of food, have you ever tried your hand at baking a blueberry pie?"

"What's a blueberry?"

He raised a brow. "You've *never* had blueberries? Well, then, we need to remedy that immediately. It's one of my favorite fruits. And you're in luck. I know where there's a fine patch of wild berry bushes and they're hitting their peak right now."

"But, shouldn't we get back to town so I can finish up my work?"

"Whatever you have to do will still be there tomorrow." He looked like a child about to partake of a rare treat. "This will be an opportunity for you to stock up on an ingredient you don't have to pay for." His expression seemed to be issuing her a dare. "Unless you're worried about getting a bit of mud on your shoes?"

She wouldn't let the challenge go unanswered. "My boots are up to a bit of mud. As am I." Besides which, she was curious as to what this fruit tasted like.

Cam stopped the wagon at the Grady farmhouse and borrowed a pail from Mrs. Grady. Fifteen minutes later he pulled the wagon to a stop beside an overgrown field.

They picked their way over the damp ground and past scraggly brush until Cam declared they had arrived. "Here we are," he announced with a flourish. "Prepare to taste one of nature's most delectable gifts." He plucked a berry from the bush and handed it to her.

She studied the dark blue, smooth-skinned berry for a moment, then popped it into her mouth. As soon as she bit into it she tasted the sweet, slightly tangy flavor. Immediately she could imagine how well this tiny fruit would lend itself to a pie, either on its own or paired with apple or other berries.

"I can see why you like these so much."

He grinned. "I knew you'd enjoy them. So what do you say? Want to gather some up?"

"Absolutely."

"All right then. The best way to make sure you harvest only the best is to hold the pail under the clusters and brush your hand across them. Those that are ripe will let go of the branch easy enough. Make sure you don't pick any that still have red coloring on them, and you don't want any that aren't firm." He picked another berry and popped it in his mouth, as if unable to resist. "If we work at it for an hour or so we ought to be able to fill most of this pail for you."

"Oh, but surely you plan to take half of whatever we pick for yourself?"

"Don't worry, I'll be eating as we go. And I expect to see a blueberry pie on our table one day this week."

"That sounds fair. After all, since I've never cooked with these before, I'll need to experiment a bit."

He straightened with a mock indignant look. "So that's how it's going to be, is it? You plan to save your best for your paying customers, and leave the castoffs to us?"

She lifted her chin and matched his tone. "Of course. I'm a businesswoman now."

He chuckled and they worked in companionable silence for a while. The time passed quickly and before Nora knew it the pail was nearly full and it was time to go.

Cam carried the pail as they strolled back to the wagon, swinging it slightly with one hand while he took her elbow with the other. After only a few steps, though, she stumbled over a piece of uneven ground and he quickly tightened his hold to steady her.

"Are you okay?"

Feeling foolish at her own clumsiness, she quickly nodded. "Yes, thank you."

"Good." Rather than simply loosening his hold, Cam linked her arm through his and drew it close to his side. "The ground's a bit rocky here—we'll take it slower."

He was merely being gentlemanly, of course. Still, Nora remained acutely conscious of his hold for the rest of the trek back to the road and waiting vehicle.

When they reached the wagon, Cam set the berries under the seat, then handed her up. But he didn't immediately go around to the other side. Instead he leaned against the wagon frame and looked up at her thoughtfully. "I didn't think to ask this earlier, but how much do you know about driving a horse and wagon like this one?"

Nora straightened and tried to appear confident. "I've never actually driven one myself, but I've observed others do it many a time. It doesn't look very difficult."

Cam rolled his eyes. "Slide over. I'm going to teach you how it's done and then you're going to drive this wagon back to the livery."

Not having much choice, Nora did as she was told. The idea of learning how to drive excited her, made her feel as if she were taking another step to gain control of her life.

Once Cam had settled in beside her, he instructed her to take the reins. "Hold them in your left hand, so you can guide with your right. You want to thread them through your fingers so that the left rein is between your thumb and middle finger and the right is two fingers below that."

As she attempted to follow his instructions, Cam leaned forward. "Here, let me show you." He adjusted her hold, threading the reins through her suddenly tingly fingers.

She was glad his focus was on her hands and not her face, because she wasn't certain her expression was as neutral as she'd like it to be.

When he seemed satisfied that she had the reins held properly, he glanced back up at her. "The trick is to get the tension just right. Hold the reins so that there's no slack, but don't pull them tight or tug on them unnecessarily. You want the horse to know you're here, but not to be made nervous by it."

To Nora, that sounded completely contradictory. Or was it just that her mind was unaccountably addled?

When she hesitated, he leaned forward again. "Here, let me show you."

His hand closed firmly over hers and it was all she could do not to jump.

As soon as Cam grasped her hand he felt his pulse jump. The warmth and fragility of her smaller hand under his made him feel both powerful and fiercely protective.

He pushed those thoughts away as best he could and focused his attention on teaching her to hold the reins properly. "Can you feel that?" he asked without looking up. "The horse is there, solid and ready for your direction."

All *he* could feel at the moment was her hand beneath his, small, warm, fragile. Was that racing pulse under his palm his or hers?

Clearing his throat, he again tried to focus only on giving her instruction. "Amber here is a good horse, gentle for the most part, so she shouldn't give you any trouble. But gentle doesn't mean meek. She's got some spirit in her, as well, so make sure she knows you're in control."

"You seem to know this horse pretty well."

He ought to. He'd spent quite a bit of time looking for just the right horse for her. But she didn't need to know that. "You wouldn't expect me to let Oscar sell you a horse I hadn't checked out first, would you?"

He didn't wait for her answer. "Now, there are a few simple procedures you need to learn. When you're ready to start, release the brake by pulling that lever back. Then give the reins a little flick and say 'get up.' When you want to go left, tighten the left rein and when you want to go right, tighten the right. To stop, pull gently back on both and say 'whoa.'"

He leaned back. "Do you have any questions?"

"No slack, but don't pull too tight. She's gentle, but I should make sure she knows I'm in charge. Simple enough."

He smiled at her dry attempt at humor. "It'll probably take a little practice for you to get the feel of it, but you strike me as a fast learner."

"A lot depends on the teacher," she said with a half smile.

Was she doing that deliberately? "Well, then, start whenever you're ready."

She seemed nervous, but she gamely lifted her chin and reached down to release the brake. Sitting up ram-rod straight, she took a deep breath, flicked the reins and gave the command to go. She seemed almost star-tled when Amber obediently moved forward. A moment later her lips curved in a triumphant grin.

Cam's chest swelled with an almost paternal pride, feeling her victory was a shared one.

They made the trip back to the livery without inci-dent. Nora cautiously stopped the wagon well away from the building, but set the brake as if she'd been doing it for years.

Cam showed her how to tie off the reins then hopped down and helped her down.

Oscar was at the horse's head before she had her feet on the ground. "Well, what did you think?" His pleased-with-himself tone said he expected them to be won over. "The horse handles beautifully, doesn't she? And the wagon is sturdy and well sprung."

Cam decided to let Nora do most of the talking.

"It's just as you say." Nora crossed her arms. "And

I've decided that if we can come to an agreement on the terms, we have a bargain."

Uh-oh. He recognized that stubborn tilt to her chin. Nora was going to try to wrestle control and do this her way. But at least she had decided to forget about the pony and cart idea.

"The terms?" Oscar looked confused again.

Cam almost felt sorry for the man. He hadn't intended for things to get so complicated when he'd involved Oscar in this negotiation. He just figured Nora would accept the deal better if it came from someone other than him.

"Yes." She drew herself to her full height and faced Oscar without blinking. But Cam noticed a blush of pink staining her cheeks, as well. "Unfortunately, I don't have the funds to make this purchase outright," she continued. "But, as you are aware, I am earning a regular wage. I'm hoping you will agree to let me pay you in installments. I would pay you an amount from my wages every week, with the understanding that the full amount will be paid within six months."

"But I thought—" Oscar rubbed the back of his neck and shot a quick look Cam's way.

Predictably, Nora would not allow herself to be ignored.

"While Sheriff Long did kindly offer to loan me the money," she said firmly, "I would prefer to take care of this myself. If my terms are unacceptable to you, then I will have to, regretfully, decline your generous offer."

Again Oscar turned to Cam.

Keeping to his plan to stay out of the discussion as much as possible, Cam shrugged. "You heard the lady. It's her you need to deal with."

"Well, I—" Oscar rubbed his chin, and once more cast a pleading look Cam's way.

Relenting, Cam gave a quick nod to the hapless livery owner, then turned to Nora. "Perhaps Oscar here would look more kindly on your offer if you gave him an added incentive."

Her brow furrowed. "Incentive?"

He grinned. "Say, throwing in one of your pies along with his weekly payment?" With that, he casually moved back to the horse, leaving the two of them to carry on without him. He'd done all he could to bring this negotiation to a happy conclusion. They were on their own now.

Happily, Nora jumped on his suggestion with alacrity. "That sounds fair to me. One fresh-baked pie with each weekly payment. Your choice of filling."

Oscar rubbed his chin. "I've always been partial to apple."

Cam hid a smile at the livery owner's befuddled tone. "Does that mean we have a deal?"

"I suppose it does."

Cam turned in time to see Oscar wipe his hand on his pants and then offer it to Nora to shake, sealing their bargain.

Her expression was flush with victory as she walked toward him a moment later.

"It seems you now own a horse and wagon," he said dryly.

She gave him a diffident smile. "I hope you understand why I had to do it on my own."

Oh, he understood all right. The woman had too much pride for her own good. "Of course. You don't want to be beholden to me."

"Yes. No. I mean—" She took a deep breath. "I don't want to be beholden to *anyone*."

"You know, it's not shameful to accept help occasionally."

"But it's better to make your own way when you can." She brushed at her skirt. "Now, I'll go back to the jailhouse and finish up my work. It shouldn't take me more than another hour or so."

"How about you go home early today?"

He saw the flash of eagerness cross her face, followed immediately by a responsible frown. "But, I didn't finish—"

"As I said earlier, whatever it was you didn't finish will still be there waiting for you tomorrow. We should get this horse and buggy out to your place so James can get Amber settled in before dark. Besides, something tells me you're itching to see how Grace is faring with the Coulters."

Her expression turned sheepish. "Was it that obvious?"

He raised a brow. "In case it has escaped your notice, I'm a very perceptive person."

"Well, then, if you're sure you don't mind, I am a bit anxious to get back to her."

"I wouldn't have offered if I didn't want you to take me up on it."

She moved closer to the wagon. "I suppose you'll be relieved not to have to drive me home today."

Did she really think that was how this was going to happen? He hadn't worked this all out just to rob himself of the chance to drive her to and from her home. "Not so fast. You did well with that first lesson, but I don't think you're ready to go it alone just yet."

"But—"

"No arguing. As the sheriff, I'm responsible for making sure you don't put yourself or anyone else around here in danger. You can take the reins but I'm riding along with you."

"But how will you get back to town?"

"I've got two legs and your place is less than a mile away."

She tilted her head to one side, considering the matter. "I suppose I could have James drive you."

This was beginning to turn into a farce. "If it'll make you feel better, I'll saddle Fletch and tie him to the back of the wagon. Then I can ride him home."

She nodded. "Yes. That *will* make me feel better."

In a very short time his horse was saddled and tied to the back of her new wagon. He held his tongue but watched carefully as she took the reins once again. He was pleased to see she didn't falter. As he'd guessed, she had a natural aptitude for driving.

"One thing I didn't think about was the extra work this will mean for James," she said. "I hope it's not too big a burden for him."

"Don't worry about James. He used to be a groom, remember? He worked for the same prominent family in Boston as Agnes, that's how they met. Anyway, James managed an entire stable. He really likes working with horses. In fact I think he misses it quite a bit. So, in a way, you'll be doing him a favor by putting this horse and rig into his keeping."

The worry lines disappeared from her brow and she focused on her driving for the rest of the short trip to the cottage.

Cam relaxed, satisfied that Nora had finally accepted

the situation. He'd never had so much trouble helping someone as he did this strong-willed woman at his side.

And if truth be told, he'd never gained such satisfaction from it before, either. Part of it had to do with the challenge she presented—he did love a good challenge.

The other part...well, he wasn't ready to dwell on that just yet.

Chapter Nine

As soon as Nora pulled the wagon to a stop, James was out the door and headed their way. "Well, well, what have we here?"

She set the brake, proud that she hadn't needed reminders or instruction. "It's my new horse and wagon. What do you think?"

James barely glanced at her and Cam—his attention was all for the horse. He ran his hands expertly over the animal, making noises in his throat that Nora couldn't quite decipher. Finally he looked up. "It appears you have yourself a fine animal here." He folded his arms. "I guess you'll be wanting me to care for her along with the other livestock."

Nora was relieved to see the eager anticipation behind his gruff question. "I'm sorry if this is going to cause you extra work. I promise to help as much as I can."

He waved a hand dismissively. "Ach, you have enough on your plate already, what with your job in town and the babe to look out for. You just leave the care of this fine animal and rig to me."

"I'll admit that would be very helpful. But only if you're certain...."

His chest puffed out slightly. "Certain as can be. Now get along in the house with you. I know you're itching to see Grace after being separated all day."

Cam moved to the back of the wagon and untethered his horse. "Need any help unhitching the wagon?"

James glowered at him. "Cameron boy, I was hitching and unhitching wagons when your pa was still a lad. Even with this bum leg of mine I can handle a simple rig like this one. You go back to your sheriffing and leave this to me."

Nora noticed Cam's smile wobble just the tiniest bit. Was it the reference to his father?

Cam led his horse over to where Nora stood and together they watched James lead the horse toward the barnyard.

"He really does seem to like working with horses," Nora mused. "I haven't seen such a spring in his step since I moved in here."

"Everyone likes to feel useful."

"And speaking of that, I suppose we should save you the trouble of coming out here every morning and evening. I'll just let James transport me and Grace to and from town." Though she *would* miss their morning and evening drives, and the accompanying talks.

Cam frowned. "I thought we already discussed this."

She tamped down her urge to agree with him. This was a matter of doing what was sensible, not what was more enjoyable. "*You* discussed it. And in your usual high-handed fashion, I might add. Surely you can admit that it's much more efficient for James to handle this now that transport is readily available."

"Nonsense. As I've already informed you, I have to make my rounds every day so this isn't the least bit out of the way."

In the end, they compromised. James would provide transportation in the mornings and Cam would take her home in the evening.

A few minutes later, Nora watched Cam ride off, re-flecting on what a stubborn man he was. Still, she wasn't nearly as miffed that he hadn't given in to her as she ought to have been. Perhaps she was just tired.

The sound of a baby's cry caught her attention, and she bustled inside.

Tuesday morning dawned clear and warm. James had the carriage ready early and Nora smiled to see how proudly he sat there holding the reins. If for no other reason than that, she was pleased she'd agreed to this purchase. Conscious of the difficulty James had climb-ing, she insisted he not get down to help her up. In-stead, Agnes held Grace while Nora climbed aboard, then handed up both the baby and Nora's basket of baked goods.

Nora said a silent prayer of thanksgiving as they made the short trip to town. Her life was good. She had Grace. She had a job that put food on the table for all of her household. And she now had the added measure of in-dependence the horse and wagon afforded her.

Though part of her missed her morning chat with Cam, it felt quite satisfying to ride into town in her own wagon. She was one step closer to proving she could make it without having to depend on her sisters'—or anyone else's—charity.

Later, as she was finishing her after-breakfast cleanup chores, the door to the sheriff's office opened and Bridget breezed in.

"Good morning, gentlemen," she greeted the lawmen.

All three men scrambled to their feet.

"Good morning, Mrs. Black." Cam was the first to speak. "Welcome back."

Nora stepped into the galley doorway, smiling at the emphasis Cam placed on Bridget's new title. "I'll second that."

"Hello." Bridget gave her sister a quick smile, then moved toward the basket at Ben's feet. "Ah, and there you are." She dropped into a graceful stoop to pick up Grace. "Oh my, you seem to have grown so much in just the few days I've been away."

"I can see which one of us you missed more," Nora said dryly.

Bridget laughed, lifting Grace to her shoulder and then crossing the room to give Nora a one-armed hug. "And you, dear sister, have not changed at all since I left."

"Glad to have you and Will back in town," Cam said as he raised a brow. "I trust you're not here on official business."

Bridget waved a hand dismissively. "Oh, no, nothing so serious. I was just hoping to catch Nora before she went out to do the marketing so I could accompany her."

"You're just in time." Nora untied her apron and grabbed her basket. "I'm on my way out now." She eyed her employer and his two deputies. "Any requests for your meals today?"

Cam waved her on. "Whatever you decide will be fine."

"One of those peach cobblers for dessert would be nice," Gavin added hopefully.

Bridget gave Nora an eager smile. "I brought Grace something from Boston."

"Oh?"

"It's for both of you really." Her grin broadened. "I can't wait to show you. It's right outside."

Her curiosity piqued by Bridget's obvious excitement, Nora let her sister lead her out onto the sidewalk.

And there sat a small, sturdy-looking wicker cart. It had four wheels and a handle, and had a leather shade on the side opposite the handle. The bottom was lined with a thick, soft blanket.

"It's a baby buggy," Bridget explained. "Do you like it? I thought it would make it easier for you to handle both Grace and your parcels when you had shopping or other errands to run."

"It's lovely." Nora ran a hand along the wicker edge, admiring the graceful curve.

"See." Bridget placed Grace inside and covered her with a lightweight blanket that had been tucked to one side. "She can lay here all comfy and cozy and leave your hands free for other things."

Nora gave her sister a hug. "Thank you. I love it."

"I'm glad. When I saw one of these on the sidewalks of Boston, I knew I had to get one for Grace."

Nora squeezed Bridget's hand before stepping back. "Well, it was very thoughtful of you." She eyed her sister teasingly. "You're looking so happy. Married life certainly agrees with you."

"Oh, Nora, I *am* happy and so at peace. I never thought

I'd say this, but I'm actually grateful to Daniel McGarth for treating me as he did. If he hadn't left me at the altar last year I would never have come to this wonderful country and would never have met Will."

"The Almighty certainly has a way of working things out for us."

Bridget grasped the hands of the baby buggy and they headed toward the general store. "And I'm going to see even more of this wonderful country. Will has a business meeting in New York City next week. So we've decided to go as a family. And we're traveling by ship. Caleb has shown such an interest in sailing vessels that we thought this would be a treat for him and for Olivia, too."

"That sounds lovely. And I'm certain the children will see it as a grand adventure." She gave her sister a teasing smile. "And so will their stepmother if I'm not mistaken."

Bridget didn't deny it. "We're leaving on Friday and plan to return on Wednesday. Esther is staying behind— she says sailing doesn't agree with her. Oh, and Maeve and Flynn plan to come down on Monday to check on the progress their builders are making, so they will be available if you should need anything."

Nora tried not to take offense. "Really, Bridget, I don't need checking up on. I'll be perfectly fine. And if I do need help with anything, I've made a number of good friends in Faith Glen that I can turn to."

"I know. Still, I worry about you out there in that isolated cottage."

Nora straightened, happy to have a surprise of her own to share. "Not so isolated any longer," she said proudly. "I am now the happy owner of a fine horse and wagon which are already sitting in our barn."

Bridget paused midstep. "You are?" She started forward again. "That's marvelous, of course. But when… how?"

"I purchased them yesterday. Did you know that James was once a groom for a well-to-do family in Boston? You should see how much pride he takes in caring for them. He's been quite pleased with life in general since we brought the animal home."

"We?"

Now why would Bridget pick that word to pounce on? "Sheriff Long helped me with the selection and purchase. He also taught me how to drive the thing."

"You mean you actually drove the wagon?"

Nora laughed. "I drove it home from the livery myself. It's really not so difficult a thing. And I have a feeling James will be doing most of the driving in the future."

"But, and I don't mean to be indelicate, but how could you afford such a purchase?"

Nora brushed a bit of lint from her skirt. "I made an arrangement with Mr. Platt. I will pay him something out of my wages every week until the debt is cleared." She gave her sister a sideways look. "That and a pie a week as interest."

But Bridget didn't smile. "Nora, if you needed money, you should have come to us. Will would have been glad to—"

Nora didn't let her finish. "You weren't here when I struck the deal. And it's better this way. When the final payment is made I will truly feel as if I earned this purchase."

Bridget shook her head. "You have always been so stubbornly independent. But at least Cam helped you make the selection." She paused a moment. "Wait a minute. Does this mean he won't be driving you to and from town every day?"

Nora couldn't quite interpret the look Bridget was giving her and so decided to ignore it. "Yes and no. James will drive me and Grace into town in the mornings, and the sheriff will drive us back home in the evenings. He insisted."

"I see."

There was that look again. "It's only because I don't always finish at the same time every day. It saves James the trouble of waiting on me or me on him."

"Quite practical." Bridget gave her a knowing grin, then turned serious. "But, Nora, won't you let me help you with this? Remember, I know precisely how tight your budget is."

Nora gave her sister a teasing nudge. "It is less so now that we have one less mouth to feed." Then she sobered. "Actually, I've come up with a plan to help me supplement my wages and perhaps even build a little nest egg. I'm starting my own business."

"Oh my goodness, you're just full of surprises this morning. What kind of business?"

"A baking business."

"A baking business? Nora, you can't be serious."

Bridget's reaction stung just a tiny bit. "Don't you think my pies and cakes are good enough for folks to want to buy them?"

Bridget waved a hand, dismissing her question. "Don't be a goose. Of course they are. But baking is long, hot work. Where will you find the time or energy to do this?"

Bridget's words eased the sting somewhat. "The sheriff has agreed to let me do some baking during the day while I'm working, and I have Saturdays, as well."

"Of course he did. But still, that leaves you *no* free time to rest."

"I'll rest on Sundays." She didn't want to argue with her sister, especially not today. "Oh, Bridget, be happy for me. If this goes well, I'll have enough money to supplement what the purchase of the horse and wagon takes from my weekly wages and perhaps some extra to put toward the rest of the repairs at the cottage."

"How many pies and cakes do you plan to bake?"

"I'm not sure yet." At least Bridget had stopped trying to talk her out of this. "As many as I get orders for."

"So you haven't started yet?"

"Actually, I'm just about to." She lifted the cloth from her basket. "I have an apple pie to give to Rose Kenny over at the boardinghouse and a chocolate almond custard pie to give to Mrs. James at the general store."

"*Chocolate* almond custard?"

Nora smiled. She'd known that would divert Bridget's attention. "That husband of yours asked me to experiment with chocolate powder in my recipes and this is one of my better outcomes."

"It sounds delicious." Then her sister frowned. "Did you say *give?*"

Nora nodded, proud of her plan. "I thought I would show good faith by giving them their first pie for free. Then, if they are satisfied with how their customers react, they can place an order for more."

"Clever." Bridget's expression turned somber. "Are you doing this because you don't want to accept help from me or Maeve? Because there's no shame in accepting a helping hand from family."

"No, that's not it. At least not entirely," she added honestly. "For the first time in my life I have a chance to determine how my life should be lived. I truly *want* to do this."

"Well, in that case, you can put me down for five pies every week. And I want one of those chocolate almond custard pies in my first order."

Nora gave her sister's arm a squeeze. "Don't be silly. If you want pies I'll give them to you."

"Oh, no. If you won't take charity from me then you can't expect me to take it from you."

"But it's not charity, you're family."

Bridget's raised brow and pointed look were quite eloquent. Nora laughed sheepishly. "Oh, very well. I'll have your first pie ready tomorrow." She gave her sister's arm a light squeeze. "That makes you my first customer."

By this time they'd reached the general store. Bridget lifted her chin. "Now, let's go inside and see if we can line up another for you."

Mrs. James seemed more interested in the baby buggy than in Nora's baked goods. In the end, however, she agreed to accept the pie Nora offered her, but was skeptical as to whether she would want to purchase any additional ones. But she promised to see if she could find a customer for it.

Rose, on the other hand, not only accepted the pie enthusiastically but immediately put in an order for two pies a day to serve her boarders, confessing that baking was her least favorite chore.

As they stepped out of the boardinghouse, Nora caught sight of a young girl scurrying quickly away. There was something vaguely familiar about her, but she couldn't quite place her.

"What is it?"

Bridget's words pulled her back to the present. "Nothing," she said, giving her head a mental shake.

"You looked miles away just now."

Nora waved a dismissive hand. "I just thought I saw someone I recognized, but she was gone before I could be sure."

"Should we try to catch up to her?"

"Oh, no, it wasn't important. Just one of those things that will nag at me until I remember."

Bridget tugged on her gloves. "Well, I should be getting back home. The twins will be ready for some outdoor play by now." She released the handle of the buggy and bent down to kiss Grace's cheek. "Tell James and Agnes hello for me and that I'll be out to the cottage for a visit soon."

Once her sister walked away, Nora headed back to the sheriff's office, pushing the buggy with a spring in her step. "Did you see what just happened, Grace? I already have orders for nearly twenty pies a week. I know that part of that order came from my sister, and is likely as much duty as desire, but I'm a businesswoman now and I must treat it as such."

Grace gurgled in response and Nora laughed. "You're right. I'm hardly a businesswoman yet. But, God willing, I will make this work."

Wednesday afternoon, Cam returned to the office from his midday rounds to find both of his deputies were out. He could hear Nora humming softly in the kitchen and could smell the enticing aroma of cinnamon and baked apples.

Almost without thinking, he crossed the room and leaned in the kitchen doorway, watching Nora at work.

She was bent over the oven, removing a pie with a perfectly browned crust, so she didn't notice him right away. As soon as she set the pie on the counter, she slid a cake pan into its place. Then she stood and wiped the sweat from her brow with the back of her hand. He frowned as he realized how hot the small room was. Perhaps he should add another window in that north wall.

"A body could practically live on the smells coming from in here."

She jumped, then whirled around to face him.

"Sorry, didn't mean to startle you."

She relaxed. "Oh, that's okay. I didn't hear you come in is all."

Feeling the need to keep the conversation going, he asked the first thing that came to mind. "Do you know where my two deputies disappeared to?"

"Ben said he had to help Miss Esther with something—I'm afraid I don't remember just what. And Gavin went to help Andrew Dobbs get his cow out of a bog."

Cam grinned, glad he hadn't been in when the call came in for help with that particular problem. It would be a good learning experience for the boy.

He nodded toward the pie cooling on her worktable. "So, how many orders do you have so far?"

Her expression changed to one of pleasure. "Bridget wants one pie every weekday, Rose wants two, Mrs. James wants a pie and a cake every day and a few of the ladies around town who've heard about my undertaking have placed onetime orders."

He was pleased for her but Ben's warning that she might leave them niggled at the back of his mind. "I told you you wouldn't have trouble getting orders."

"And I'm very pleased that you were right." She started rolling out some pie dough on a floured surface.

He watched her for a moment, admiring her deft movements and air of confidence. "I've been wondering," he finally said, "is your baking skill something you come by naturally or did you have to work to learn it?"

"A little of both." She lifted the thin sheet of dough with practiced ease and set it into a waiting pie tin. "I learned from my mother, of course," she said as she began fluting the edges of the dough. "She was the best cook in our village."

Nora was such an intriguing mix of pride and modesty. "Yet your sisters aren't quite as talented as you are."

"Maeve and Bridget were younger than I when Mother passed on. Besides, they have other skills, other interests." She started spooning a mix of blueberries and sliced apples into the crust. "And cooking is something I've always enjoyed so I spent a lot of time in the kitchen with my mother."

He heard the wistful note in her voice. "How old were you when you lost her?"

"Fifteen."

He felt a pinch of sympathy. She'd almost been of an age to spread her wings, only to have them clipped by that loss.

Then she turned the table on him. "What about you? How old were you when you lost your mother?"

He shifted uncomfortably. His past was not something he was interested in talking about. But he'd started this conversation. "Twelve."

Her expression softened in sympathy. "That must have been a difficult time. Do you have any siblings?"

"No." He knew his voice was terse but she didn't seem to notice.

"Then it must have been doubly hard for you."

Given what his childhood had been like, it was probably a blessing that he *hadn't* had siblings to share his fate. "It taught me independence."

It looked as if Nora wanted to say more, but Grace started to fuss, effectively distracting her.

Relieved to have an end to that particular conversation, Cam turned to leave. But Nora wasn't quite done with him.

"Oh, dear, there are times when I wish there were two of me." She cut Cam a hopeful look. "Would you mind entertaining Grace for just a minute? I need to check on the cake I have in the oven."

Entertain Grace? How did one entertain an infant?

Chapter Ten

Cam glanced back over his shoulder, hoping against hope that Ben or Gavin had slipped in unnoticed. But no such luck.

Nora seemed oblivious to his discomfort. "Just talk to her and wiggle your fingers in front of her face. I'll only be a minute."

Okay, that didn't sound too difficult. And it wasn't as if she were leaving him alone with Grace. Cam moved toward the basket where Grace lay, her little face scrunched up as if she would be expressing her displeasure very soon and with great gusto. What did one say to an infant? He glanced toward Nora but she had her back to him.

"Okay, ladybug, if it's attention you're looking for, you've got it. I'm all yours."

She hushed and stared up at him as if she'd understood his words. He smiled at the fanciful notion. "That's better. Now, Nora says you need to be entertained but I think you just want to make certain we haven't forgotten you. As if we ever would. Nora thinks you are exceedingly special, and I must say, you do have a way of lighting up a room."

"I think she likes you."

Cam looked up to see Nora smiling at him with a softly approving expression on her face.

Cam straighten and cleared his throat, feeling as if he'd been caught doing something foolish. "Yes, well, I need to get back to work."

As he moved to his desk, Cam couldn't shake the image of the way she'd looked at him, as if he'd done something heroic rather than just distract an infant for a few seconds.

A man would do a lot to earn a look like that.

Nora's Friday morning routine got a welcome interruption when Bridget stopped by to tell her goodbye before leaving on the trip to New York. The two sisters had a nice long chat while Nora prepared the lunch ingredients to throw into the stewpot.

Bridget was understandably excited about her upcoming travel and chatted on about all of the family's preparations and plans, making Nora laugh out loud at some of her stories. Finally she halted in the middle of a story about Caleb's idea of what he should pack, and gave a self-conscious grin. "Listen to me. I haven't let you get a word in since I walked in here."

Nora smiled indulgently. "I enjoy listening to your stories."

Bridget snagged a blueberry from the bowl on Nora's worktable. "You always were a good listener. Now, your turn. Tell me what's going on with you. The bakery business seems to be going well. I'm hearing good things from your customers."

Nora felt a glow of pleasure that her baking was being so well received. "I feel truly blessed that the people here have been so willing to support my efforts. The whole thing has grown much faster than I expected. I had to do a bit of quick rearranging with my routine this week to fit everything in." Then she grinned. "And for the price of one pie a week of his very own, Gavin has agreed to do my deliveries."

Bridget laughed. "Was that his idea or yours?"

"I suggested it, based on a bargain I made with Mr. Platt, but Gavin jumped on it. He had been lamenting the fact that so few of my baked goods made it to their lunch table and the idea of having a pie all to himself perked him right up."

Bridget laughed again. "He's a growing boy." Then she sobered. "So is it all going as well as it appears?"

Nora grimaced. "Except for one thing. It seems I've reached my limit as far as what I can produce. I actually had to turn away a customer yesterday."

"But, surely that's a good thing?" Bridget placed her elbows on the worktable. "I mean, it's better than not having enough customers to buy your wares, isn't it?"

"Yes, of course. But it also means I'll never be able to earn more than I am today." Was she being greedy to want more?

"Oh." Bridget plucked another blueberry and chewed thoughtfully for a moment. "Is there some way you could find other items to bake, items that cook more quickly and can be parceled to more customers, things like cookies or tea cakes?"

Nora stopped what she was doing and looked at her sister with new appreciation. She'd never cooked those types of items before but she felt certain she could master them. "Bridget, that's a wonderful idea." Her mind started turning over possibilities. "I would have to do a little experimenting, of course, but I think I could get quite a few additional items baked each day if I worked it just right."

Bridget laughed. "Glad I could help." She wagged a finger Nora's way. "Just make sure you don't wear yourself out with all this extra work. There are people who count on you to be at your best." She reached down and adjusted Grace's blanket. "Like this precious babe given into your care."

"Don't worry, I won't take on more than I can manage." Nora went back to stirring the stew that was simmering on the stove. She appreciated her sister's concern but she was much sturdier than those close to her seemed to realize. In fact, to provide for her household and achieve her goals, she could be quite resourceful.

The outer door opened and Nora felt a little stab of disappointment to see it was Gavin rather than Cam. Silly of her, of course.

The young deputy sauntered across the room and sniffed the air. "It sure does smell good in here."

Bridget laughed. "The aromas from Nora's cooking are more alluring than any fancy perfume." Then she nodded toward the paper in Gavin's hand. "What do you have there?"

"It's a letter that just arrived from Mrs. Fitzwilliam. She said to tell you both hello."

"Everyone is doing well I trust," Nora said.

Gavin nodded. "Yes, but she's feeling frustrated that her investigator hasn't located her granddaughter yet."

Nora wiped her forehead with the back of her hand. "I've been praying for a happy reunion between them."

Bridget nodded. "As have I. I hope the girl is all right." Then she stood. "Well, I enjoyed the visit but I should be going now. I want to stop by and visit a moment with Agnes and James before we leave."

Nora nodded. "They'll be pleased to see you."

Bridget crossed the small room and Nora opened her arms for a hug.

"Take care of yourself," Bridget said.

"Of course." Nora squeezed her sister's shoulder then stepped back. "Enjoy your trip and make certain you pay special attention to all the wonderful sights. I want to hear all about them when you get back."

Bridget exchanged a few words with Gavin then gave a final wave as she headed out the door.

As Nora went back to her cooking, she reflected on the unexpected and interesting turn her sisters' lives had taken since they'd left Ireland. Still, she didn't envy them their big houses and ability to travel to exciting places.

But if she was honest with herself, she did envy, just the tiniest bit, the happiness and loving families they'd found. She offered a silent prayer asking for forgiveness for that envy, and then added another prayer for guidance.

She hadn't forgotten what Ben had revealed to her about Cam's childhood. In fact it had been on her mind quite a bit lately. She was certain the Almighty wanted to use her and Grace to help him somehow—she just hoped she recognized the opportunity when it came.

Which didn't mean she had changed her resolve to guard her heart. She wasn't sixteen any longer, she was a grown woman and she wouldn't repeat the mistake she'd made with Braydan Rourke. No, she was concerned for a friend, that was all.

Nora entered the cottage that evening with a smile on her face. She had dozens of ideas spinning in her head for how to implement Bridget's idea of smaller bakery items and, since tomorrow was Saturday, she planned to spend most of the day trying them out.

And Cam's announcement that he intended to come by tomorrow to "do a little work around the place" had only added to her happy mood. It would be good to see progress being made on the repairs to the cottage.

Why his upcoming visit would cheer her up beyond that she refused to consider.

She found Agnes in the kitchen, darning a sock.

"I understand your baking business is doing quite well," the woman said by way of greeting. "In fact I hear you've had to turn away a few customers."

So, apparently Bridget had discussed her concerns during her visit out here this morning. Nora felt a momentary twinge of annoyance which she pushed away as best she could. She placed Grace in the kitchen cradle and gave Agnes a smile. "A body can only do so much. And I'm working on a few ideas to help me produce more."

Agnes gave her a pointed look. "Wearing yourself out is not the answer. But what if you had some help?"

Nora paused. Surely Agnes knew she couldn't afford to hire anyone. "What do you mean?"

Agnes set her sewing in her lap and met Nora's gaze. "I mean *I* can help you with your baking."

Nora was deeply touched by the generosity of the older woman, but she had no intention of taking advantage of her that way. "Oh, that's very kind of you to offer but I couldn't—"

Agnes raised a hand to halt her protest. "Nonsense. I figure James and I are benefiting from this new endeavor of yours so we might as well do what we can to help.

James is already taking care of your horse and driving you to town in the mornings. Helping with your baking will give me a chance to contribute, as well."

"But you already help me watch over Grace and do the housework. There's no need—"

Agnes sighed deeply. "Of course, if you don't think my cooking will be good enough, I'll understand."

Nora was horrified. She hadn't meant to hurt Agnes's feelings. "Oh, no, that's not it at all. I just don't want to impose—"

The grandmotherly woman beamed at her. "It's settled then. I know I'm not as good a cook as you are. But there are many things to be done that don't require a lot of skill. Like peeling and slicing apples, hulling nuts, measuring out ingredients, keeping an eye on the oven and such."

As Agnes picked up the sock and began plying her needle once more, Nora had the distinct impression that she had been rather expertly manipulated into accepting her friend's help.

Agnes was a lot more wily than her sweet appearance indicated.

The next morning, Nora rose before dawn and, as soon as she had Grace fed and freshened up, stoked the stove and went to work on her baking. Mrs. Ferguson, the wife of the foreman out at Will's chocolate mill, had placed a large order for a family gathering she was hosting Sunday afternoon. Happily, she had left the flavors up to Nora. Which gave Nora the perfect opportunity to do a bit of experimenting. She planned to try to mix Will's chocolate with both blueberries and maple syrup for what she hoped would be two very deliciously distinctive pies.

Nora sang softly as she worked, as much to entertain Grace as to keep herself company.

Before she could get the first pie in the oven, Agnes and James joined her in the kitchen.

Nora gave them a guilty grimace. "I hope my rattling around in here didn't wake you."

"Not at all." Agnes crossed to the cupboard to fetch two cups while James moved to the stove to get the coffeepot.

"No sense frittering the day away in bed," Agnes continued as she placed the cups on the table. "Getting an early start on your baking, are you?"

Nora nodded. "I promised Mrs. Ferguson I'd deliver her order this afternoon." She turned to James, who was filling the coffee cups. "I'm hoping you'll drive me to her place once I have everything ready."

"Of course." James lifted his cup and inhaled the steaming brew as if it were ambrosia. "I suppose you'll need something to pack your pies in so they're protected from the jostling. I think there are some bits and pieces of lumber out in the barn that I can use to fashion a few shallow crates from."

Nora started to protest that she didn't want to cause him extra work, then, remembering what Cam had said about folks needing to feel useful, thought better of it. "Oh, that would be wonderful, if you're sure it's not too much trouble."

"You just leave it to me." James's chest expanded noticeably. "I'll take care of it as soon as I tend to the animals."

When James headed outdoors a few minutes later, Agnes carried their cups to the counter. Then she turned back to Nora. "Have you had your breakfast yet?"

"The biscuits are almost ready to come out of the oven. I'll have one with a bit of jam in just a minute."

"Nonsense. That's not a proper breakfast. As soon as James brings in the fresh eggs I'll get a proper breakfast whipped up." She looked around. "In the meantime, what can I do to help?"

"If you would keep an eye on Grace for me while I roll out this pie crust that would be lovely."

"Of course." Agnes smiled fondly at the cradle. "But that's hardly work."

Nora smiled and waved toward a bowl on the counter. "Well, you did mention something about peeling and slicing apples."

Agnes nodded and moved toward the drawer where the knives were stored. Nora watched her, and offered up a quick prayer of thanksgiving. It was as if in her adult years she had been gifted with the grandparents she'd never known as a child.

Strange how it was that none of the three other people living in this house were related to her by blood, but she felt as close to them as if they were her true kin.

Thirty minutes later, as Nora and the Coulters were pushing back from the breakfast table, there was a quick knock at the back door and Cam stepped inside. "Mmm-mmm, it sure does smell good in here."

Nora waved him in. "If that's a hint that you're hungry, there are a couple of biscuits left from breakfast that you can have with some of Agnes's strawberry jam."

"Now there's an offer too good to refuse." He nodded toward the pie cooling on the counter. "Been hard at work already I see."

Agnes pulled a clean plate and coffee cup from the

cupboard. "Isn't it wonderful how well Nora is doing with this new business of hers?"

"That it is." Cam took a seat at the table. "The smells wafting from my office have made it a very popular place for folks to visit lately."

Cam reached for one of the biscuits from the platter, then paused. "Oh, I almost forgot." He dug into his pocket and pulled out a letter which he held out to Nora. "This came for you just before I headed here this morning."

Nora wiped her hands on her apron and accepted it. "It's from Maeve." Why would her sister send a letter when she was supposed to come for a visit in two days? Worried, Nora quickly ripped open the missive and scanned the enclosed page.

"I hope it's not bad news," Agnes asked, and Nora heard the anxious note in her voice.

A moment later her hand went to her throat. "Oh my goodness."

"What is it?" Cam pushed back from the table and stood. "Are your sister and Dr. Gallagher all right?"

Nora looked up quickly to find three pairs of eyes studying her in concern. "Maeve and Flynn are fine," she reassured them. "But there's been a terrible fire at a local hotel there in Boston." She closed her eyes momentarily before continuing. "Two people were killed and over thirty were injured, some of them quite severely. Flynn and Maeve are postponing their visit so they can provide medical assistance."

Agnes wrung her hands. "Oh, those poor people."

Nora sent up a silent prayer that the injured parties

would find strength and healing. She would miss seeing Maeve and Flynn, but she knew they were doing what they needed to do.

She turned to Cam, who had returned to his chair. "Thank you for bringing this out to me."

"It was no problem. I just wish it could have been happier news."

James, who still sat at the table, leaned back in his chair. "You planning to do some work out here today?"

Cam nodded as he slathered a generous dollop of jam on his biscuit. "I thought I'd work on the roof."

"By yourself?" James asked.

"I know Will and Flynn have helped out before, but they're both busy men. I figure if I wait until they're able to lend a hand it might never get done."

"Anything I can do to help?" James asked.

Nora held her breath waiting for Cam's response, ready to intervene if he accepted James's offer. Allowing James his dignity was one thing, but there was no way she'd let the elderly man try to climb a ladder up onto the roof.

But she should have known Cam would handle it well.

"Thanks," Cam said easily, "but I can't let you do that. It wouldn't be right, being as Nora here is paying me for my labors."

Nora jumped in quickly. "That's right. Besides, James, you've already promised to fashion those crates for me."

Cam raised a brow. "Crates?"

That spurred a lengthy back and forth discussion between the two men on what James was trying to do and the best way to go about it.

Agnes and Nora exchanged knowing smiles and went back to their kitchen work.

* * *

By midmorning Nora was ready to escape the hot kitchen for a spell. Thinking that her handyman-for-the-day might be feeling something of the same, she grabbed a few items from the larder, placed them in a basket, then carried it and Grace outside. She set the basket down and shaded her eyes, looking up to find Cam pounding away at the roof with a hammer.

When he spotted her he paused and leaned back on his heels. "Well, hello there. Dare I hope you have something in that basket for me?"

She grinned. "If you're ready for a break, there's a jar of apple cider, some berries and a couple of slices of cheese I might be willing to share."

He stood, apparently quite at ease on the pitched roof. "Now, that sounds really good. Just give me a minute to climb down."

She watched him, admiring the animal-like grace with which he moved, and the play of muscles in his back and arms as he descended the ladder. Was it wrong of her to admire such agility and strength? After all, God had formed him this way.

Nora shifted her gaze to Grace. Not wrong perhaps, but dangerous to her peace of mind.

A moment later he had made it to the ground and she was able to give him a friendly smile. "I've been baking all morning which means the kitchen is nearly as hot as the inside of my oven. So I thought we might find a shady spot out here to have our snack."

He returned her smile, pulling a large handkerchief from his pocket to wipe his hands. "Good idea. How about under that tree over by the garden?" At her nod he scooped up the basket. "You *are* going to join me aren't you?"

She planted a kiss on the top of Grace's head. "We certainly are."

He gave a satisfied nod, then led the way, whistling. Within minutes he had set the basket beneath the tree and spread the picnic cloth.

Nora carefully placed Grace on the blanket between herself and Cam, then pulled the simple fare from the basket.

"Colleen's Garden."

She looked up quickly to see Cam studying the weathered sign nailed to the nearby tree.

"Colleen was your mother's name, wasn't it? I remember it from the deed."

"Yes." Nora leaned back on her heels. "Apparently Laird O'Malley planted all of this for her." She looked around at the garden. She had done lots of weeding these past few weeks but it still needed a great deal of work to bring it back to life. "It must have been quite lovely at one time."

Knowing Cam was bound to be thirsty, she shook off the wistful musings and poured him up a large glass of the cider.

He drained it quickly then held his glass out for more. As she poured, he glanced toward an old rickety bench that sat a little ways from the tree. "Looks like that was part of the original setup, as well. It doesn't appear to be very safe, though. Probably best no one tries to sit on it until I can get it fixed."

"Don't worry. None of us here plan to risk our necks that way. Though it would be lovely to have a comfortable place to sit out here." She sat back again as he retrieved the glass from her, then she watched as he absently swatted at a fly that flew a little too close to Grace's face. How could this man ever believe he would harm a child placed in his care?

Please, Heavenly Father, give me the words and the opportunity to help Cam see how wrong his thinking is on that score.

He set his glass down, bringing her focus back to the present. She smiled at him. "Now, if you'd say grace for us please…"

Cam did as she'd asked and then they both helped themselves to the simple fare.

As she munched on a handful of berries, she studied the roof. "You're making good progress, but I don't want to take advantage of you. Please don't feel obligated to get it all done today."

He reached for a piece of cheese. "It's my day off and I don't have anything else to take up my time at the moment. Besides, another few hours and I should have this roof all squared away."

That was good news. She wouldn't have to worry quite so much about the next rainstorm to come through. "I certainly appreciate all of your efforts. I know how hot it must be up there."

He gave her a dry smile. "Don't forget you're paying me. It's not like I'm doing this just to be nice."

He wasn't fooling her. To be nice was exactly why he was doing this.

Before she could comment, though, he nodded toward the house. "I think the next project we should tackle is to work on the windows. I noticed the pane in one of them is broken and that several of them have cracks around the sills."

She agreed. "Let me know what materials are needed and I'll talk to Hattie over at the general store about ordering them."

"I can take care of that for you."

She eyed him suspiciously. "Just make certain it goes on my tab."

"You're the boss." Then he grinned. "Out here at least."

If only she was certain he believed that.

"I take it the baking you're doing this morning is for one of your customers. How many items are in the order?"

"Mrs. Ferguson ordered four pies and two cakes for a special dinner party she plans to hold tomorrow. I tried a couple of new flavors for her, and incorporated some of the chocolate from the mill. I hope she likes them." Then she felt her cheeks warm as she realized that he wouldn't be interested in her experiments.

But he didn't seem particularly annoyed. "I'll be glad to deliver those baked goods for you when I head back to town this afternoon," he offered.

"That's very kind of you. But I wouldn't want to cheat James of the opportunity." She smiled in response to his raised brow, then expanded on her statement. "I do believe James is looking forward to having an excuse to hitch up the wagon today since he didn't need to take me to town this morning."

Cam nodded. "I see. In that case, I shall withdraw my offer."

She leaned back, supported by her palms. "He and Amber have become best of friends, you know. In fact, I'm almost certain I'm missing an apple from my baking supplies this morning and there was a suspicious bulge in his shirt pocket when he went out to milk Daisy. I wouldn't be at all surprised to learn that apple somehow made its way into Amber's feed bag this morning."

She saw him brush away another fly that had gotten too close to Grace's face and decided to try a little experiment of a different sort.

Chapter Eleven

Nora popped up, and brushed the dust from her skirt. "I just remembered, I meant to bring some of my new cookies out here for you to try." She gave him a bright smile. "If you'll keep an eye on Grace for a minute I'll be right back."

She saw the sharp flicker of emotion in his eye. But he didn't refuse outright. "That's not necessary. There's more than enough here to—"

"Nonsense. It's a new recipe and I'd like to see what you think." She moved toward the house, not giving him time for further protest. "I'll be quick as a sneeze."

She kept moving forward, resisting the urge to look back. He might not be comfortable watching over Grace, but she wanted him to see that she didn't have even the tiniest concern that Grace would come to any harm under his care.

Cam's even-tempered disposition, however, was another matter altogether.

Cam rubbed the back of his neck, watching Nora abandon him with little Grace. Then he looked helplessly at the baby. "Well, ladybug, it looks like you're stuck with me for the moment. How about we make a bargain to make the best of it?"

Grace looked up at him with wide eyes, her arms and legs pumping jerkily in a movement that nevertheless communicated pleasure.

"Good girl. I'll take that as a yes." He lowered a finger to tap her chin and before he knew what she was about she'd latched on to it. He froze and then felt a strange pressure in his chest.

He stared at her hand, wondering at how tiny and fragile it was, yet how perfectly formed. The child was so utterly helpless, yet blissfully unaware of her fragility, blindly trusting that all her needs would be met. And deep inside him, an aching desire to protect her took hold of him. This child deserved a father, someone to cherish her and keep her safe.

It caused an almost physical hurt to know that someone could never be him. She deserved better. "Yes indeed," he whispered softly, "I do believe you're going to be a heartbreaker when you grow up."

"She's easy to talk to, isn't she?"

Cam started, surprised he hadn't heard Nora's approach. He slid his finger out of Grace's grasp, surprised to find himself doing it reluctantly.

"Probably because she isn't much of a talker herself." He stood and brushed off his pants. "Thanks for the refreshments and the company, but I really should get back to work now."

She smiled softly, as if seeing through his words to what he was feeling inside. Which was a ridiculous thought since there *was no* deeper meaning to his words.

"Aren't you going to taste these cookies?" she asked.

"Of course." He took one from the dish she held out and bit into it. And smiled. "*Very* good. If you're planning to add these to your wares I predict they'll sell well."

He reached for another and lifted it in salute. "I think I'll take this one with me."

He headed toward the ladder, hoping that putting some distance between himself and the two females behind him would clear his head. Those thoughts he'd been having about Grace were an impossible dream, and a dangerous one at that. He'd forgotten for a moment that he was the last person alive who should be responsible for a child's welfare.

He couldn't let himself forget that again.

Nora watched Cam climb the ladder back onto the roof, then she slowly bent down to collect the items from their picnic. What had just happened? She was certain Cam had been enjoying his time with Grace, had noted the soft smile he gave the babe and the easy way he spoke to her.

So what had sent him scurrying away just now without a backward glance?

She worried at her bottom lip. At some point she would have to tell him she knew about how his father had treated him. Would he feel betrayed?

She stroked Grace's cheek with a knuckle. "If anyone can convince him that he can be trusted around children, I do believe it has to be you, young lady. After all, you're his ladybug." She smiled again, pleased that Cam had a nickname for Grace. It gave her hope that he wasn't completely opposed to interacting with little ones.

Perhaps this *had* been progress of a sort.

And perhaps it was another test of her patience.

* * *

By midafternoon, Nora had finished her baking. She carefully packed her baked goods in the shallow crates James had devised—praising him for their clever construction—and helped him load them into the bed of the wagon. In addition to the goods for Mrs. Ferguson, Nora also packed up two dozen of her cookies to be split between Rose and Mrs. James as an enticement for them to order some in the future.

As James headed the wagon toward town, Nora noticed Cam was no longer working on the roof. She glanced around and found him working on that rickety old bench in the garden and her heart did a strange little flip-flop.

It was one thing for Cam to see to the soundness of her home—one could almost argue that he did it out of a sense of responsibility since he'd been looking after the Coulters for the past few years. But to fix something like the bench, something almost frivolous—its only function was to give her enjoyment—that could only come from the goodness of his spirit, and it touched her deeply.

How could he *not* know his own worth, his innate goodness? Humming, she went back inside and poured a glass of apple cider, then carried it out to him. "Hello there. You look like you could use a bit of refreshment."

Cam glanced up and wiped his forehead with the back of his hand, the one that still held his hammer. "Thanks. I could at that." He looked around. "Where's lady—Grace?"

"In the house. Agnes is keeping an eye on her." She nodded toward the bench. "It was so kind of you to work on this after all your hard work on the roof."

"It turns out it only needed a little shoring up." He patted one of the arms. "I just finished up. What do you think?"

"It's lovely." The broken boards on the back of the bench had been replaced with sturdy new ones and the arms were now attached securely. The seat was freshly braced and no longer seemed in imminent danger of collapsing. And all of the wood looked smooth and clean—freshly sanded perhaps? "May I try it out?" she asked.

He stood and waved an arm with an exaggerated flourish. "Of course."

Nora sat on the restored bench and spread her skirts primly as if seated on a throne. "Very nice. And very comfortable."

"So you approve?"

"Absolutely." She smiled up at him. "In fact, I can easily see Grace and me spending many an hour out here, enjoying the beauty of the garden."

He gave a satisfied nod. "Then I guess I'm finished for today." He bent down to pick up a small saw and handful of nails from the ground. "I'll see you at church service tomorrow."

She felt a stab of disappointment that he was leaving. "You could stay for dinner if you like."

He smiled. "Thanks. But dinner is still a couple of hours away and I have a few things to take care of before dark."

Cam saw Nora's cheeks pinken and realized she probably felt rebuffed by his refusal of her invitation. That hadn't been his intention, he really did have something to take care of. He planned to do a little more scouting around to see if he could find where the horse thief he was convinced was still in the area might be hiding.

But he didn't want to go into all that right now, so instead he gave her a reassuring smile. "By the way, I think with three to four more Saturdays like this one, we'll have the whole place weathertight and ready for the winter."

He saw her expression change to one of relieved delight. "Do you really think so? Oh, that would be wonderful. I can't thank you enough." Then the practical side of Nora stepped back to the fore. "But don't forget to figure out what I owe you for today's work."

He nodded. "I won't forget. I plan to keep track of everything you owe me and then we'll settle it all up when the job's done."

She gave him one of those suspicious looks that let him know he hadn't entirely fooled her, so he decided to take his leave before she had a chance to say anything else.

Saluting her with his hammer, he turned and made his way to his horse, and his thoughts turned back to his mission.

Why was the horse thief of a few weeks ago performing minor acts of mischief around town? And what was keeping her here? Did she have ties to the community? Or had she found herself somehow stranded here? Or was he completely wrong and were the horse thief and the mischief maker two completely different people?

Whatever the case, he aimed to get some answers, and get them soon. Because the idea of leaving Nora and Grace vulnerable to whatever plans a possible criminal might have in mind was totally unthinkable.

* * *

Nora added a little more salt to the pot of squash on the stove and tasted it again. Perfect!

James was out in the barn taking care of the evening milking and Agnes was in the parlor doing some mending, so she moved the pot away from the hottest part of the stove. She set it down on a spot where it would stay warm and at the ready until they were gathered for dinner.

Glancing out the window, she smiled at the sight of the garden bench. All in all it had been a lovely day and Nora felt a sense of deep satisfaction and renewed optimism that she really could make everything work out as she'd hoped.

She moved toward the cradle, checking on Grace. She exhaled a sigh of relief to see the little girl was now blissfully sleeping. Grace had been more than normally fussy this afternoon and, much as Nora loved her, it was nice to finally have a moment of peace and quiet. As if she'd heard Nora's thoughts, Grace stirred restlessly. Nora hummed softly for a few minutes until the baby quieted again.

Nora eased the muscles in her neck. It was stuffy here in the kitchen—maybe she should carry Grace to the parlor. Then again—Nora chewed on her lip, considering her options. She really didn't want to risk waking Grace up again after it had taken so long to get her settled. Perhaps she'd just open the outer door for a bit.

Putting thought to action, Nora crossed the room and propped open the back door. A slight breeze had stirred up and she stood on the threshold for a moment, savoring the cooler air and the peaceful evening. The sun hadn't gone down yet, though it was already reaching for the horizon.

Today's baking had exhausted her supplies—and her. But with the money she'd earned this week she should be able to replace everything and have enough left over to pay Mr. Platt what she owed him this week.

Thank You, Father Almighty, for all the many blessings You showered on me today, and every day. Help me to remember that, even in the dark times, You are there watching over me.

She moved back into the room and checked on Grace again. The child stirred in her sleep and Nora lightly brushed her cheek with a knuckle. What a joy and a blessing to have this precious child in her life.

Unbidden, she thought of Cam. He deserved to know this kind of joy, as well. And if she had it within her to help him, she would. Even if it was a joy he'd share with someone else.

She sighed and restlessly pushed her thoughts in a different direction. Perhaps now would be a good time to make her shopping list. She checked once more that Grace was sleeping well, then moved to the roomy larder, leaving the door open so she would hear if Grace started crying.

She studied the shelves. Another sack of flour was definitely needed. There was still enough sugar on hand, but she was short on salt. She was running low on chocolate but should have enough to last her until Will and Bridget returned.

Nora paused as she heard Grace fuss. But the baby quieted almost immediately and Nora relaxed. Taking a nap this late probably meant the baby wouldn't sleep through the night, but Nora didn't really mind. Tomorrow was Sunday, a day of rest. They could both nap in the afternoon if they needed to catch up on missed sleep.

A minute or two later she stepped out of the larder, satisfied she had a complete list. Perhaps she would also look at the seeds when she went to the general store. It wouldn't hurt to expand on their small kitchen garden. It had probably been all Agnes could manage on her own, but Nora was here to help her now. The more fresh herbs and vegetables they had, the better. And before spring arrived, Grace would be ready for some soft foods. Best to put up a good supply now.

Speaking of Grace, she was sleeping well. Nora moved toward the cradle, wanting to take another peek at her.

Then she froze and felt the blood drain from her face.

The cradle was empty.

Chapter Twelve

Where was Grace? Nora felt a momentary touch of panic jangle through her, then the only reasonable explanation occurred to her. Agnes must have picked her up when she started fussing earlier. Nora headed to the parlor, exasperated that the older woman would take the baby without telling her, but relieved that it was nothing worse.

But when she reached the parlor, Agnes was bent over her sewing, with no infant in sight. A cold finger clawed its way down Nora's spine. "Agnes, where is Grace?"

Agnes looked up, a puzzled frown on her face. "Isn't she in her cradle?"

Nora didn't answer. Instead she spun on her heel and raced back to the kitchen. Perhaps James had taken her outside. *Please God...*

She shot out the back door, wildly scanning the area behind the cottage for James, trying to reassure herself that there was no need to worry. A heartbeat later she spotted a figure running toward the tree line. And from the description she'd heard, she recognized that long yellow braid.

It was her—the horse thief who'd nearly run right over Gavin a few weeks ago. And the bundle in her arms was wrapped in Grace's blanket.

No! Dear Jesus, don't let her get away with my baby!

Nora took off at a run, yelling at the fleeing girl to stop. She had to catch up with her, had to make her give Grace back. What could she possibly want with Grace? *Don't let her hurt my baby, please...*

But the kidnapper disappeared into the woods while Nora was still several yards away. A moment later Nora plunged into the thicket behind her, ignoring the thorns and whip-like branches while calling frantically for Grace. She tried to pray, but all that came out was *God please, please, please* over and over.

The third time she stumbled, she stayed down, struggling to catch her breath. Panic threatened to suffocate her when she realized she had no idea which direction she should go in. She needed to be still, to just listen. Surely she would hear the girl running, Grace crying—something to tell her where they were. But the only sounds that she heard were the wind, the birds and insects.

A noise like the crack of a branch came from somewhere to her right, and Nora was up and running again.

Sometime later—minutes or hours, she wasn't really sure—a pair of arms grabbed her from behind. Nora screeched and began struggling for all she was worth. Did the little thief have an accomplice? Well, they would have a harder time taking her than they had with Grace...

"Nora, hold still, it's me."

She finally quieted and focused on her captor. "Cam." She said his name dully. Then she started struggling again. "We have to stop her. She's got Grace. That horrid horse thief has my baby."

He pulled her close against his chest. "I know. James rode into town and told me what happened."

The fight drained out of her. "Why did she do this? Oh, Cam, what if she's hurt?"

Cam had never seen his proud, no-nonsense housekeeper so distraught. There was a brittleness about her, as if she would shatter at the slightest touch. Her normally tidy hair had escaped its pins and was framing her face in wild disarray. There were scratches on her arms and face that she didn't seem to know were there. Her dress had two rips that he could see, and likely more. And worst of all, she was trembling.

Cam smothered an oath, directed against the kidnapper and against his own inability to fix this right this moment. The thought of any little one, much less Grace, at the mercy of a conscienceless criminal was tearing him up inside. He had to get his ladybug back safe.

"I know, Nora honey. And we'll find her. But you need to let me take you back to the cottage in case the person who took her decides to bring her back."

He saw a desperate kind of hope flare in her eyes. "Do you think that's possible?"

He tried to balance between reassurance and not promising the impossible. "Anything is possible. Now come on. Gavin is right over here. He'll see that you get home okay and stay with you."

"But—"

He had to get her home before she hurt herself or made herself ill. "Agnes and James are very worried. You need to be strong for them."

She stiffened stubbornly. "I want to keep looking."

He brushed the hair from her face, wishing there was

something he could do to comfort her. "It'll be dark soon. And time spent standing here arguing with me is time I could be out looking for Grace."

He saw the struggle play out on her face. Finally her shoulders drooped in acceptance and she nodded. Then she placed a hand against his chest. "Please, find her."

"I will." He desperately hoped he could keep that promise. *God, I know I haven't been much for praying, not in a long time, but please help me find Grace. Not for me, but for Nora and Grace herself—they need each other.*

An hour later the sun had gone down, blanketing the countryside in darkness, and Cam was forced to call a halt for the night. Even with lanterns it was too dangerous for the searchers to be stumbling around out in the woods. Still, he himself kept looking in the more open areas for another hour until he finally accepted that it was useless. In the dark he could walk within a few feet of the kidnapper and never know it.

He trudged up to the cottage, dreading having to tell Nora that Grace had not yet been found.

Before he got very close, the door flew open and Nora raced outside. The light from the half moon revealed in aching clarity just how much of a toll the wait and worry had taken on her. From the corner of his eye he saw Agnes and James standing in the doorway, holding each other. Gavin stood in the shadows behind them.

But his focus was all on Nora.

She halted a few paces from him and he saw the hope drain from her expression, quickly followed by anger.

All he could say was "I'm sorry."

She launched herself at him, beating against his chest

with balled fists. "How could you come back without her? You promised. You never liked her, did you? If you won't keep looking then I will."

Her words stung more than her blows, but he pulled her close, trapping her fists between them. "Neither one of us is going back out there tonight. We won't do Grace any good by tripping all over ourselves in the dark. The kidnapper has obviously gone to ground somewhere— we could pass right by her any number of times and not find her."

Her eyes blazed up at him, angry and defiant. "That's not true. You should at least be able to hear her. You promised to bring her back to me. Grace wouldn't be totally quiet while so much was going on, especially if she hasn't had her dinner. Not unless—"

He put a hand to her lips. "Shh. Don't think that way. Grace is fine. Why would the girl take her if she didn't want her for herself?"

Her angry determination finally gave way to resignation. "Oh, Cam, why did she take Grace? It makes no sense."

He almost preferred her anger to this air of numb defeat. "As soon as we find her, we'll ask her," he said as bracingly as he could. "And we *will* find her." He gently squeezed her arms then released her. "Now, let's go inside where we can sit."

She nodded and allowed him to lead the way back to the cottage.

Agnes straightened as they approached. "You must be tired and hungry," she said to Cam. "There's still some food left from dinner."

He cut a quick glance Nora's way. Would she want

him at her table or was she still angry? "I wouldn't turn down a bite to eat."

With a nod, Agnes moved down the hall, tugging James along with her.

Gavin remained just inside the doorway. "Any sign of her at all?"

"Nothing concrete." Cam turned back to Nora. "Why don't you go on with Agnes and I'll follow in a minute."

She eyed him suspiciously. "Is there something you're not telling me?"

He tapped her chin then traced an X over his chest. "Cross my heart, there's nothing new to report. I just need a word with my deputy."

She didn't appear convinced, but finally nodded and then trudged down the hall toward the kitchen.

He turned back to Gavin. "I think the kidnapper has a home base of some sort where she's been hiding these past few weeks. We'll need to thoroughly search all of the inlets and woodlands. For now, go on back to town and get some sleep. Pass the word that we're starting again at first light and that the sheriff's office will be the gathering point. And we need everyone to report on any abandoned outbuildings, thickets and caves they can think of where someone wanting to hide might take refuge."

Gavin nodded, his expression sober. "Do you really think we'll find her?"

"We have to." He couldn't let himself believe otherwise. If for no other reason than Nora needed him to be strong. "You can take my horse. No point in you doing any more walking than you have to."

"But what about you? No offense, but you must be worn out. It wouldn't be right for me to ride and you to walk. Unless you're planning to take Miss Nora's horse."

"I'm not planning to take Miss Nora's horse and I don't intend to do any more walking tonight." At Gavin's confused expression, he elaborated. "I'm staying right here."

Gavin's brow rose to near his hairline. "You mean all night?"

"That's exactly what I mean." Though he had a feeling he'd have to argue the point with Nora. "Someone should be here in case the kidnapper tries to come back. Just make certain you have Fletch back here at first light."

For a minute it looked as if Gavin would say more, but apparently the boy thought better of it. With a nod he stuffed his hands in his pockets and moved toward the paddock.

James met him in the hallway as soon as he stepped inside the house. "Don't mind what Nora said," the older man told him. "We all know you're doing your best."

Not Nora. "Apparently my best isn't good enough."

"Don't say that." James patted his shoulder. "You're going to find our Grace and bring her back. Just have faith."

Cam desperately hoped James was right. When he entered the kitchen Agnes was just setting a glass of what looked like apple cider on the table. Nora stood next to the counter with her arms wrapped around herself as if she were afraid she would fly apart otherwise. A heaping plate of food sat on the table, ready for him.

Agnes tsked when she saw him. "Your arm is bleeding. You should have said something."

Cam, who'd barely felt any of the scrapes and scratches he'd received, looked down to see a particularly deep scratch above his wrist, covered with dried blood and dirt. He grimaced as he studied it. "Sorry, but I don't think I tracked any blood into your house."

Agnes waved that comment away. "As if that was what I was worried about. Nora, see if it needs bandaging while I finish getting his meal served."

Nora nodded and motioned him over, but didn't speak and didn't meet his gaze.

Cam washed his hands and face, then let her take a look at his cut.

"It's started bleeding again," she said dully, "but it looks clean and not too deep." Her gaze remained fixed on his arm. "I don't think it'll need much doctoring beyond wrapping it."

She put words to action, winding a long strip of gauzy cloth around his wrist.

Though she seemed to have her emotions under control, she still wouldn't look up to meet his gaze. Was it deliberate? Was she still angry that he'd failed to find Grace?

He couldn't blame her—he was angry at himself, as well. This was partly his fault. If he'd tried harder to find the girl after she took his horse or if he'd warned Nora to take extra precautions because the criminal might still be skulking around here, then maybe Grace would never have been taken in the first place.

As Cam took his place at the table, Agnes stood. "If you will excuse us, James and I are going to retire for the night." She eyed Nora. "Don't you worry about cleaning the kitchen tonight—I'll take care of that in the morning."

Nora nodded, but didn't respond otherwise.

Cam ate in silence, watching her peripherally as he

did so. She stood as if carved from stone, stiff, silent and cold.

Finally he couldn't take the silence any longer. "Do you want me to send word to your sisters?"

"No, thank you." Her tone was flat, unemotional. "I'm not certain we could get word to Bridget before she's due to head back. And Maeve and Flynn have those burn patients to tend to."

She had obviously already given this some thought.

Nora took a deep, ragged breath. "Besides, we'll have Grace back before either of them can get here." Her fierce expression dared him to disagree.

Cam made a noncommittal sound, not trusting himself to say the right thing at this point.

She rubbed both her arms. "I saw you send Gavin off on Fletch. I want you to take Amber when you go, and please don't argue with me. You need to be at your best tomorrow when you start the search again."

So she wasn't totally oblivious to what was going on around her. "There's no need. I'm not going anywhere."

He was surprised when she didn't immediately protest.

"That sofa in your parlor is bed enough for me for the time being." He braced himself for her to argue with him now that she'd had a moment. It said something about her state of mind that she merely nodded.

The dark smudges under her eyes worried him, as did the fragility of her appearance. If only he had the right to hold her and offer her a bit of comfort. "I know you probably think sleeping is an impossibility right now," he said as he stood, "but it's best if you at least try to rest." He carried his plate to the counter and she drew herself in as he passed, as if wanting to avoid the least bit of contact.

He wasn't certain how much more of this he could take. "Tomorrow is going to be a long day," he said gruffly. "So upstairs with you."

For a moment he thought she'd argue. The Nora of this morning certainly would have. But this Nora didn't say a word.

After a moment she pushed away from the counter. "I'll lay a sheet on the sofa for you. Good night." The words were uttered in a hoarse whisper, then she crossed the room and headed for the stairs. Cam had to force himself not to go after her.

But even if he did, what then?

He sat back down at the table, folded his hands and bent his head. *God, I know I messed things up in a big way again, but please don't let that sweet little girl suffer for my mistakes. Do what You will to me, but bring Grace back home to Nora.*

And to me.

Chapter Thirteen

Cam was a young boy again and a woman was crying, hunched over so he couldn't see her face. But he knew the sound of that sobbing and knew it was his mother. He wanted to help her but his feet remained rooted to the floor. Then the figure shimmered and changed and now it was Vera McCauley holding the broken body of her three-year-old son. She looked up at him and her tearstained face twisted into a mask of hatred. Still, he couldn't move and couldn't look away.

Cam struggled to wake up, aware that he was having that old nightmare, but unable to escape from it. Then the image changed again. Now it was Nora, sobbing over a too-still Grace.

No! This wasn't real.

Finally he woke, flailing at the tangled sheet, damp from his sweat, breathless from the effort to push through. He ran a shaky hand through his hair. It had been years since he'd had that nightmare. He'd thought—hoped—it was gone for good. Now it was back, with an additional ugly twist.

He sat there for a moment, waiting for his racing pulse to slow, for his ragged breathing to return to normal.

Then his head came up. What was that noise? Cam forced himself to go very still, straining to hear. A moment later he heard the sound of muffled movements coming from the kitchen. Had the kidnapper returned? Between one heartbeat and the next he was on his feet and moving stealthily into the hallway. The sounds were more evident now and there was soft lamplight spilling out from the kitchen doorway. Whoever was in there was being mighty bold. Or mighty careless.

He reached the end of the hall, his senses on full alert, his body ready to pounce on whoever had dared break into Nora's home.

The rattle of dishes brought his brow up. Had the intruder decided to steal a meal? "Stop right there," he ordered as he stepped into the room.

With a tiny squeak of fright, the shadowy figure spun around to face him, a hand to her chest.

It was Nora. He was disappointed not to be facing the kidnapper, but it wouldn't do to let her see that. "Sorry, I didn't mean to startle you."

She took a deep breath. "That's okay. I hope all my fumbling around in here didn't wake you."

"No, I woke on my own." No need to mention his nightmare.

"I couldn't sleep either. I thought I'd come down and fix a cup of cocoa. Would you like some?"

"That sounds good." What sounded even better was that there was no hardness, no hint of accusation in her tone.

She added some extra milk to the pan on the stove, then stirred in some cocoa powder and sugar.

A few minutes later she had poured them each a cup and carried them to the table. But she didn't take a seat right away. She took a deep breath and then met his gaze. "I want to apologize for the way I acted earlier."

The tightness in his chest loosened the tiniest bit. "There's no need for that."

"Yes there is. I know with complete certainty that you did absolutely everything you could. And I know that you'll keep looking. You've been nothing but kind to me ever since I arrived here and there's no excuse for me to say such awful things to you."

Cam wished he deserved such accolades. "I know this is hard on you. If beating on my chest and yelling at me helps you feel better, then you just go right ahead."

She gave him a watery version of her normally dry smile. "You may live to regret you said that."

"It's all part of being the sheriff," he said, trying to match her tone. Then he sobered. "We're going to start back up at first light. Nearly every able-bodied man in town will be out looking."

She nodded and swallowed. Her eyes cut toward the baby bottle that still sat on the counter, waiting. Her clasped hands tightened, whitening with the effort.

He moved closer, touching her arm, trying to comfort her with his presence. "Grace will be all right." *Please God, let that be true.*

"That awful girl should have taken the bottle, too. How will she feed her? *What* will she feed her? Does she even have access to fresh milk?" Nora met his gaze, her eyes filled with unshed tears. "Oh, Cam, my baby is out there, probably frightened and hungry."

"Ah, Nora honey." He opened his arms and she stepped into them. He hugged her in a protective embrace, aching to do more, knowing it wouldn't be fair to her, and wouldn't be enough for him. Her tall, slender form felt so soft, so fragile. She was trembling and he longed to protect her from all hurts, all ugliness, to slay any dragon that would dare approach her. But he knew with aching certainty that there was nothing he could do that would ease this particular pain. She probably wasn't even fully aware that his arms were around her.

So instead he just stood there, silently holding her, trying to wrap her in whatever comfort he could provide by his presence. He swayed, almost as if they were dancing, until finally her trembling stopped.

"She'll be all right," he whispered. "We *will* get Grace back safely." *Dear God, please don't let me fail another child, another mother.*

Don't let me fail Nora.

He couldn't resist planting one soft kiss to the top of her head. Nora turned her face up at that and suddenly his lips were on hers. She didn't push him away; in fact, her arms went around his neck. She tasted sweet and innocent and totally wonderful. He wanted to communicate all he was feeling into that kiss—all of his protective urges, his desire to comfort her and absorb her hurts, his love—

That thought drew him up short and he used every bit of willpower he had to pull away.

Nora looked up at him, her eyes wide, her expression confused. She tucked a strand of hair behind her ear with hands that visibly shook. "I'm sorry. I—"

"Don't you dare apologize." Didn't she realize it was him who'd taken advantage of her? He took a deep breath. "We're both tired and worried, that's all."

Something in her expression flickered, there and gone

before he could identify it. She nodded and swallowed hard, then gave him a shaky smile. "I'm afraid our cocoa has gotten cold."

Relieved that she'd let it drop, he returned her smile. "It's summer. It'll probably be better cold."

Her eyes were overly bright orbs in a too-white face. "I don't want to be alone right now," she whispered.

"Then you won't be." He led her to a chair and seated her. His hand itched to stroke her hair but he picked up his cup of cocoa instead. "Why don't you tell me what life was like for you in Ireland."

He watched her as she talked and tried very hard not to think about that kiss.

And that one very unsettling thought.

Thirty minutes later, Nora yawned widely, then gave Cam a sheepish grin.

His answering smile had a teasing quality to it that warmed her to her toes. "Looks like someone might finally be ready for a bit of sleep."

"I've been sitting here talking your ear off and keeping you up half the night." She pushed her chair back from the table.

He stood, as well. "You didn't make me do anything I didn't want to." Then he gave her a probing look. "Are you going to be okay?"

She nodded and made an effort to smile. "I might actually be able to get a little sleep before the sun comes up." Though she doubted it. But it wasn't fair of her to keep him awake longer than she already had. She lightly touched his shoulder. "I appreciate you keeping me company."

As she moved toward the stairs, Nora realized how inadequate that thank-you had been, but she had been too much of a coward to say more. The way he'd held her tonight, keeping her together when she'd felt that she would shatter into a million pieces, had touched her on a level she didn't even fully understand right now. As for that kiss, that had touched her in an entirely different way. For one blissful moment she had felt cherished and loved and had been filled with certainty that this man holding her would slay all her dragons for her. Then he'd apparently come to his senses and disengaged.

She knew he'd merely been trying to comfort her. But somehow, it had felt like more. Or maybe, she thought as she trudged up the stairs, that was just wishful thinking.

Perhaps she'd turned into what she feared most. Someone doomed to experience an unrequited love.

Nora was downstairs before dawn the next morning. She'd gotten very little sleep, and when she awakened from her third doze she'd decided it was useless to keep trying. When her mind wasn't dwelling on the way that sweet kiss had made her feel, it was going over all the terrifying possibilities of what might be happening to Grace. Even if the kidnapper meant Grace no harm, would she know how to feed a baby or even have access to milk? Did she have clean nappies? Would she be gentle and sing her lullabies?

As early as she had risen, Cam was up before her. She found him pulling on his boots as she entered the kitchen.

He gave her a probing look. "Good morning." ·

She nodded, willing the heat to stay out of her cheeks. "James must still be in bed—the stove is cold. As soon as I get the fire going I'll fix you some coffee."

"No need. I'm headed out right away."

She wanted to protest—no doubt he needed some nourishment. But her desire to have him find Grace stopped her. "At least take some of this bread left over from supper."

He stood and accepted the bread, eyeing her as if trying to read her mood. Good luck to him on that—she wasn't sure of it herself.

"I feel so useless," she said as she paced the room. "I should be out looking for her myself."

Cam shook his head. "Like I said before, you need to be here in case the kidnapper brings Grace back. And there *is* something you can do to help."

"What?" Anything to keep her hands busy, to feel she was doing her part.

"We'll use this as a check-in point for the search teams. If you can keep a full pot of coffee and something to eat for when they report in, that'll be a big help. It doesn't have to be anything fancy—just filling."

She'd hoped it would be something more directly related to the search, but she nodded. "Of course." Cooking was something she could do, something to keep her occupied.

Cam placed a hand on each shoulder, stopping her from pacing. "You have to keep strong, not give up. We *will* find her."

Unable to say anything, Nora merely nodded.

"You have to keep strong," he said again, "for all of us." Then he gave her shoulders a light squeeze. "For me," he whispered.

The way he was looking at her stirred something inside Nora, caught the breath in her throat, pushed the rest of the world away. For one long moment she thought he might kiss her again.

Then the sound of activity outside broke the spell and turned both their heads. Without a word, Nora all but ran to the front door, only vaguely aware that Cam followed. Could it be—

In the shadowy morning light, she spotted Gavin riding in on Fletch. Trying not to let her disappointment show, she waved to the young deputy. "Come on back to the kitchen when you get the horse tethered. I'll have some breakfast ready in just a bit."

"Thanks. That sounds real good." Gavin dismounted and wrapped the reins around a fencepost, then moved toward the cottage. "That is, if there's time before we set out."

"You won't be part of the search party," Cam said firmly. "I need you to stay here with Nora and the Coulters."

Gavin stopped in front of Cam, a mutinous expression on his face. "But, I want to help look for Grace."

"I know you do, and I appreciate that, but you're needed here."

"Needed for what?" There was something suspiciously like a pout coloring Gavin's tone and expression.

"There's always the chance that the kidnapper will return, either to bring Grace back or do further mischief. We need someone here who can keep watch for anything that looks suspicious."

Cam's jaw tightened. "I need to know that you are here so I can fully concentrate on the search."

Nora felt her heart flutter slightly at that. Did Cam really believe what he'd said or was he just trying to placate Gavin?

Whatever the case, Gavin seemed somewhat mollified. "I suppose I can do that."

"Good, because I'll be counting on you."

Nora had all but forgotten it was Sunday. Wanting
to stay close to home in case something turned up, she,
Gavin and the Coulters decided to hold a small prayer
service of their own, led by James. He selected Romans
8 to read from, a chapter that brought her great comfort,
and then he spoke with simple but surprising eloquence
on what the passage meant to him.

Afterward they sang several hymns and Nora was surprised by the purity of Gavin's voice. One of the hymns,
"The Solid Rock," spoke to her in a way it never had
before.

Dear Jesus, she prayed silently, *I know I tend to try
to control everything myself rather than leaning on You
for help. Please help me to remember, especially when I
go through trials, that You indeed are my hope and my
rock. That whatever shall come to pass, You are always
in control and that You will never put me through any
trials that I cannot bear.*

Later, as Nora was preparing lunch, Gavin pulled up
a chair at the table to keep her company. He plucked an
apple from a bowl on the table and polished it against
his sleeve. "I can't believe I ever wanted to get to know
that girl better," he said. "I wish now she'd never come
to Faith Glen."

Nora had no trouble agreeing with that sentiment. But
that kind of thinking wouldn't help anything. "Well, she
did and there's nothing we can do to change that."

"Even so, I sure hope when we catch her that the sheriff throws her in jail and never lets her out."

At least he said "when" and not "if." But she couldn't let his comment go unchallenged. "That's not a very charitable thing to say."

"Surely you can't tell me you're feeling kindly toward that sneaky little thief after what she did."

"Kindly" wasn't what she was feeling at all. But Nora chose her words carefully. "I will admit that I would find it hard to give her a hug. But I've been keeping her in my prayers. Not because I'm particularly charitable. But because she has Grace and I cling to the hope that she is a good person at heart and that she is being kind and loving toward my baby." *Please, God, let that be the case.*

Gavin didn't say anything for a few minutes and she saw him think things over as he bit into the apple. Finally he nodded. "I suppose that makes sense. Maybe I ought to say a few prayers for her myself."

She gave him an approving smile. "That would be very nice."

The rest of the day seemed to drag on forever. Ben and a few other men came by at noon to report on their progress and to grab a quick bite to eat before heading back out. Gavin tried, with little success, to pretend he didn't mind being left behind again.

Throughout the afternoon, ladies from the town came by with offerings of food and kind words. Esther Black was among the first to arrive and she stayed until just before dusk. She'd brought her knitting with her and calmly sat in the kitchen keeping Nora and Agnes company, chatting over inconsequential matters, and letting the conversation ebb and flow comfortably.

Nora was both grateful and surprised by the woman's

gentle strength. And when Ben came by to take her home, Nora had no doubt Esther and Ben would do quite well together.

And through it all, she kept an eye out, hoping to see Cam return with her baby in his arms at any minute.

Cam's shoulders sagged with defeat as he trudged up to Nora's front door. He tried to steel himself for the disappointment he would see in her eyes as he returned empty-handed yet again, but still, when he saw it, it hit him like a physical blow. He would actually prefer to have her pound angrily against his chest as she had yesterday.

She gave him a tremulous smile, then waved toward the back of the house. "Come into the kitchen and I'll fix you something to eat." She led the way. "Esther brought a ham and Mrs. Donnelly brought by some shepherd's pie. You can have your pick. Or both if you like."

Cam heard the strain in her voice. She was very close to breaking down. "I think perhaps we should go ahead and send word to your sisters in the morning."

She turned and her gaze flew to his.

He recognized the question and the fear she was trying to hold at bay and he touched her arm reassuringly. "No, I'm not giving up, not by a long shot." He'd keep searching for that little girl until she was found, no matter how long it took. "But I think you need to have your sisters here with you. And I think they deserve to know what's going on."

"But—"

He didn't let her finish her protest. "Nora, honey, I know you're a strong, proud, independent woman. But if this was happening to one of your sisters, if it was one of their children who was taken, wouldn't you want to know about it, to be there for them?"

"Yes, of course I would."

"Then don't you think they deserve the same consideration from you?"

"I… Yes, I suppose you're right."

He gave her shoulder a squeeze. "Good. I'll have Gavin send someone to Boston with a message at first light. Who knows, Flynn may even have a way to get word to Will and Bridget."

She nodded, looking at him with such trust and heartache that it was all he could do to not take her in his arms right then and there.

To comfort her of course. But he'd already strayed too far across that line.

He took a deep breath. "Now, I'll join you in the kitchen in a minute. I just need to have a word with Gavin before he heads back to town."

A few minutes later Gavin was dispatched with instructions to get word to her sisters and Cam took a seat at the kitchen table.

Nora set a plate in front of him then stepped back and clasped her hands together. "I want to apologize again for the way I attacked you last night."

"I told you, there's no need for that." Especially since he was still burdened by his own guilt.

"Yes there is." She took a deep breath. "Knowing what I do about your upbringing, I realize it must have brought back painful memories for you."

His gaze sharpened and he went very still.

Chapter Fourteen

Cam couldn't believe that now, in the middle of this nightmare, his past was rearing its ugly head. "My upbringing?" he said softly.

"Ben told me about your father."

Cam swallowed an oath. "Ben should mind his own business."

"Please don't be angry with him." She took a chair across from him. "He cares about you."

He could do with a little less of that kind of caring.

She leaned forward, putting her still-clasped hands on top of the table. "I won't even try to say I understand what you went through."

The last thing he wanted from her was pity for the poor mistreated boy he'd been. He wasn't that boy anymore, hadn't been for quite some time.

"What I do understand, and thank the Almighty for, is that you are a much more honorable man than your father was."

He jabbed his fork into his shepherd's pie with a bit more force than necessary, wishing she would drop this whole line of talk. "You don't know me nearly as well as you think you do."

"I know with every fiber of my being that you would *never, ever* strike a child or a woman. Or anyone else for that matter, unless it was in defense of someone."

Her championing of him would be flattering if it wasn't so misguided. "There are other ways of hurting folks besides hitting them."

Her brow furrowed. "What do you mean?"

He had to shut this off—now. Time to be blunt. "Let's just talk about something else."

She leaned back, her posture stiffening and her lips pinching together. "Very well," she said primly. "What would you like to talk about?"

This was ridiculous. His tired mind couldn't think of anything but the kidnapping. Then he figured if Ben could discuss his personal life, then he could talk about Ben's. "How about your suspicion that something might be brewing between Ben and Esther?"

That brought a gleam back to her eyes. "Oh? Has Ben said something?"

"Not specifically. But ever since you mentioned the possibility, I've noticed my deputy has been spending a lot of time in her company. And he's been keeping an eye on things over at the Blacks' house while Will and the rest of the family are out of town."

"Oh, it would be such a wonderful match. They're both such good people. They deserve to have a bit of romance at this point in their lives." She sighed. "Everyone does."

She started then, as if embarrassed by what she'd said.

Pushing her chair away from the table, she stood. "Let me get you some dessert. I made buttermilk pie today."

Cam watched her cross the room, wondering if she included him in that "everyone."

And why did that matter to him so much?

Nora lay on her bed trying to wait for the darkness to fade into the gray of near-dawn. The cradle lay next to her bed, haunting her with its emptiness. She missed Grace so much it was like a physical ache. She could almost hear the echo of Grace's cries. Would she ever hear that sound for real again?

Father, You are the Great Comforter, the Almighty One. You have Your eye on even the tiniest sparrow, and it's not possible for anyone to hide from You. So I know You're watching over Grace, wherever she is. You know how much I want to have her back with me, but if that's not in Your will, please, please keep her safe and happy.

Nora uttered her amen aloud, then glanced at the window again. Had the sky lightened just the slightest bit? She had no doubt Maeve would come as soon as she got word, and it *would* be good to have one of her sisters here with her. They'd always looked out for each other and drew strength from each other.

Cam was putting on a strong front when he was with her, but she could tell he was taking this every bit as hard as she was. Whether he would admit it or not, he cared a great deal for her little girl.

That faint mewling sound wafted in through the window again, and this time she sat bolt upright in her bed. That hadn't been her imagination—it had been a real cry. It might just be a stray cat but she had to be sure.

Trying not to get her hopes up too high, Nora climbed

out of bed and slipped on a robe as she headed down the stairs. The house itself was eerily quiet, as if holding its breath. The parlor and Coulters' bedroom were both at the front of the house and the sound had come from the back, so perhaps no one else had heard it.

She didn't attempt to light a lamp—her eyes were accustomed to the dark. And she knew she had to be very quiet so as not to frighten away whatever, or whoever, it was.

God, if You'll give my baby back to me I won't even try to catch the kidnapper. I won't look for vengeance, just joy. I'll leave it to You to deal with her in Your own way, Your own time.

When Nora reached the foot of the stairs, she started toward the kitchen.

But the nape of her neck prickled as she sensed a presence behind her. Whirling around, her heart in her throat, she put a hand to her lips to stifle a scream a heartbeat before she recognized the shadowy figure as Cam. A question formed on his lips and she quickly transferred her fingers to his mouth, indicating he should be quiet.

He nodded, then, when she moved her fingers, "Why are you up?" His words were a mere whisper of sound.

"I heard something outside. I wanted to investigate."

She could sense his whole being come to full alert. He nodded, then quickly stepped in front of her, indicating she should wait.

Nora didn't argue, but there was no way she planned to obey that command.

He moved with surprising speed and stealth to the back door.

There was another fussing sound and this time she could tell Cam heard it, too.

He was out the door in a flash, and Nora was right behind him. Luckily the sky was clear and the first fingers of dawn were lightening the horizon so she could make out shapes. The girl, bent over a basket lying at the edge of the garden, was taken by surprise at their sudden appearance. She spun around and took off at a run.

Cam, still barefoot, gave chase but Nora ignored both of them. Heart pounding like fists against her chest, breath catching in her throat, she raced toward the basket. *Please, God, please, God, please—*

And there, her face scrunched up in a peevish grimace, lay Grace.

Nora dropped to her knees and started laughing and crying at the same time. Her whole body was trembling so hard she barely trusted herself to pick Grace up, but she couldn't hold back for long. With a cry, she lifted the squirming infant, hugging her against her chest, rocking back and forth. "Oh, my sweet, sweet girl, I was so worried, so scared I'd never see you again." Then she held her away, anxiously studying her. "Are you truly okay, my sweet little one?"

To her relief there were no signs of injuries. "Thank you, Heavenly Father. Oh, Grace, I promise I'm going to take such good care of you. You won't—"

Gavin appeared around the corner of the house just then, carrying a package wrapped in butcher paper. "Miss Nora, what are you—" Then he spotted Grace and his steps quickened. "Well, glory be! You found her. Is she okay?"

Nora was still studying every inch of Grace in the increasing morning light. "She sounds hungry, but otherwise I think she's fine." Her nose twitched as Gavin neared and her mind registered that his package undoubt-

edly contained fish. Apparently the townsfolk were still
sending food as tokens of support.

Before she could inquire, though, angry squeals coming from the distance snagged her attention. In her joy at
finding Grace she'd almost forgotten that Cam had given
chase to the kidnapper. She turned to see him holding
on to the arms of a twisting, kicking blonde whirlwind.

"I'm coming!" As if suddenly realizing what was happening, Gavin dropped his package and sprinted toward
the pair.

Nora pulled Grace back against her chest. No one
would take her little girl away from her again.

"Praise God Almighty, is that really Grace?"

Nora turned back toward the house to see James and
Agnes standing on the back stoop. She stood, and started
back toward the house. "Yes it is."

"But how…"

"I'm not certain, but I think the kidnapper brought her
back." Nora tilted her head toward the three who were
slowly moving toward them. "The sheriff and Gavin have
her in custody."

"Oh my goodness."

Then Grace started crying in earnest. "I think she
must be hungry."

"Well, of course she is." James stepped down from
the stoop and touched Grace's cheek briefly with one
work-roughened finger. "I'll go right now and get a pail
of fresh milk so you can feed her proper."

Nora saw the moisture in his eyes and smiled her
thanks.

"Let's get her inside," Agnes said. "I'll get the stove
warmed up and we'll fix coffee for the menfolk."

Nora carried Grace into the kitchen, rocking her in

her arms and crooning a lullaby. It was so good to feel that sweet weight in her arms again, to have that tiny heart beating against her own. She felt as if she would never let her go again.

A moment later, Cam and Gavin escorted the disheveled and cowed-looking kidnapper as far as the kitchen stoop.

"Do you mind if we come inside for a minute?" Cam asked through the open door.

Why would he feel the need to ask? "Of course not. Come on inside."

"All three of us?"

Oh, that was it. He was worried about her reaction to the girl. "Yes, of course. Agnes is working on getting breakfast ready."

Cam all but dragged the reluctant girl inside, while Gavin carefully guarded the rear, as if he expected the girl to somehow break away and make a run for it.

But from the way she stood there, it appeared to Nora that there was no fight left in the girl.

"Have a seat." Cam led the girl to the table and pulled a chair out with his free hand. "I'm going to let go of you, but if you so much as make a move to get up, I'm going to get a rope and tie you down. Understand?"

The girl nodded, her eyes downcast.

"Now, let's start with your name."

"Mollie Kerrigan."

Nora started at the sound of her voice. The girl was Irish—a recent immigrant from the sounds of her.

"Well, Mollie," Cam continued, "you've been causing quite a bit of trouble here the past few weeks. I've got a lot of questions for you. But we're going to start with why you kidnapped Grace."

The girl didn't say anything.

Nora, feeling slightly more charitable now that Grace had been returned and had apparently suffered no ill effects, tried a softer tone. "Please, tell me why you took my baby."

The girl looked up finally and stared at Nora defiantly. "She's *not* your baby."

Nora recoiled, clutching Grace tighter. "Of course she is. Or as close as makes no never mind."

"No, she's not." The girl's chin lifted. "I know, because I'm her *real* mother."

Chapter Fifteen

Nora felt the blood drain from her face and had to sit down before her legs buckled. Mollie was lying. What she said was impossible.

Cam moved to stand behind her and she looked up, searching for his gaze. She wanted to protest, to restate her own claim on the baby, but her mouth refused to form any words.

He gave her shoulder a light squeeze, then turned back to the girl. But his hand stayed where it was, lightly resting on her shoulder.

"You have any proof of that?" he asked.

"Only my word." Mollie must have realized how empty that sounded to the rest of them, because she tried again. "I had the baby aboard the *Annie McGee* just one day out from port. I wrapped her in a scrap of gray wool and left her between sacks of oatmeal in the kitchen's storage room because it was warm and dry there, and because I knew there was a woman who'd come by soon to find her. I didn't want a man to find her."

Nora finally found her voice. "Anyone who was on

board the ship could know all that. It doesn't prove you're the mother."

Mollie faced Nora defiantly. "She has a small birthmark on her back just below her left shoulder. Other than that, she's absolutely perfect."

Cam turned to meet her gaze, a question in his eyes. Nora nodded, reluctantly acknowledging the truth of what Mollie had said. Then she turned back to the girl, still not ready to believe her claim. "You've had her for the past few days, so of course you know about the birthmark."

The girl's lips pinched together. "When I placed her in the storeroom, I made her a pallet out of an empty flour sack and an old apron that I found hanging on a peg by the door. The apron was folded in quarters."

Nora's doubts were starting to fade and she was grateful for the warmth of Cam's hand on her shoulder. "If you're truly her mother, why did you abandon her?"

The air of defiance sloughed away, replaced by drooping shoulders and downcast eyes. "Because I was alone, and scared, and didn't know what else to do."

Cam cleared his throat. "Where is Grace's father?"

Mollie's face turned scarlet and she didn't say anything for a long moment. "We were planning to run away to America together as soon as we could earn enough money for our passage." Her voice wavered. "But when Elden—that's his name—found out I was going to have a baby, he ran off without me."

Nora felt her heart stir in spite of herself. To be abandoned like that, just when Mollie would need her husband the most, must have been a terrible blow.

"So you got on that ship to follow your husband to America?" Cam asked.

If anything, her face grew redder. "Elden's not exactly my husband. He never married me like he promised he would when we ran away together."

Nora heard a gasp but wasn't quite certain who it came from.

"I loved him," Mollie said defiantly. "My parents are dead and my grandmother hates me. But Elden was really nice to me, kind and caring. At least at first. And he promised if I came with him we would have wonderful adventures together." She rubbed her arms. "I thought he loved me."

She looked so forlorn, so lost, Nora had to hold herself back from offering a hug.

"And yes, I stowed away on the *Annie McGee* because I wanted to follow him here." Mollie seemed unable to stop talking now that she'd started. "And I gave my little girl away because I thought if the baby wasn't around, maybe Elden would want me again. Besides, I knew I couldn't take care of her myself and she'd have a better life with someone who could."

Mollie cast a longing glance Grace's way before lowering her gaze again.

"But I couldn't seem to put her out of my mind like I thought I could. It wasn't long before I realized what a fool I'd been to give up my precious baby for a faithless man."

Nora tried not to let the girl's story touch her. "You could have come forward and claimed her at any time before we docked."

The girl's shoulders drooped further. "I had nothing to offer her. I was stealing whatever scraps of food I could find just to survive, which meant I went to bed hungry most nights. And I was a stowaway. If I'd come forward there's no telling what the captain would have done to me."

Nora had a feeling Captain Conley would have been more understanding than Mollie feared but there was no point saying that now.

"I truly planned to leave her in your care. I could tell that you and your sisters were fond of her and you had more to offer her than I did."

Nora was still trying to find some hole in the girl's story. "So why did you follow us to Faith Glen?"

"I just wanted to make certain my little girl would truly be okay. That was all I planned to do, honest, and then I intended to go away and never bother you again."

She met Nora's gaze with eyes that begged her to understand. "But I couldn't make myself leave. The more I saw of my baby, the more I wanted to be with her. And besides, I didn't really have anywhere else to go."

Nora wanted to yell that Grace was *not* her baby, but the tense, uneasy feeling in the pit of her stomach mocked that assertion. Instead she pushed harder on the other points. "So rather than coming to me, you just snuck in and took her out of my home, leaving me to worry about Grace until I was nearly sick with it."

"I didn't mean to. I knew the sheriff was looking for me and that it was only a matter of time until he found me. So I planned to leave."

Cam had been looking for her? Nora swung her gaze around to his and saw the truth of that in his face. Why hadn't he said something?

From the corner of her eye she saw James slip inside with a pail of milk and basket of eggs. She started to get up, then saw Agnes reach for the bottle. Grateful, she settled back in her chair and returned her focus to the conversation around the table.

"I couldn't leave, though," Mollie was saying, "without getting one last look at her. Then I saw you," she nodded toward Nora, "leave the baby all alone in the kitchen and I realized I could get a closer look, maybe even touch her cheek, kiss her forehead, say goodbye proper-like."

Cam must have realized the guilt she felt at Mollie's words because he gave her shoulder another gentle squeeze.

"But you didn't just look." Nora couldn't control the accusatory tone that colored her words.

"I didn't plan to take her, truly. She started fussing and I picked her up just to quiet her. It was the first time I'd held her since the day she was born. She was so small and perfect, and when I held her she stopped crying and smiled at me. Just like that, something came over me, all of a sudden like. The next thing I knew I was running out of the house with my baby in my arms."

Nora tried again to tamp down any softer feelings toward this girl who had claim to her baby. "Her name is Grace."

"That's a very nice name." Mollie looked up again. "I know it was an awful thing to do, especially since you've been so good to her and all. I know you must have been worried something awful, and I'm really, truly sorry for that. But she's my baby and I wanted her with me."

You can't have her. "But you brought her back."

"After I stopped running, I realized I'd made a terrible mistake. Much as I wanted her with me, I knew I couldn't take care of her. I tried, but truth is I can hardly fend for myself. I want better for her than that. I want her to have the kind of life someone like you can give her."

The girl turned to Cam. "What do you plan to do to me?"

Cam dropped his hand from Nora's shoulder and she wanted to protest. Instead she hugged Grace closer.

"By your own admission, you're a stowaway, a thief and a kidnapper." Cam's voice held an authoritative, no-nonsense edge. "I'll have to arrest you."

Mollie nodded, seeming resigned to her fate. "I thought so."

Cam turned to Gavin. "Head back to town and let the other searchers know we've found Grace and there's no need to keep looking. Let Ben know exactly what's happened and to get the cell ready for a prisoner." He glanced Nora's way. "I'll borrow your wagon, if that's okay, to transport her into town."

Gavin nodded and headed for the door.

Agnes, who'd been working at the stove while the discussion with Mollie was going on, handed Nora the baby bottle and turned to Cam. "Before you leave I insist you eat breakfast. No point in all this food I've cooked going to waste."

While the others ate the eggs and ham Agnes had prepared, Nora gave Grace her bottle. The little girl sucked at it greedily, obviously more than ready for her feeding. Had Mollie fed her much at all?

Mollie dug into her plate of food with nearly as much enthusiasm. It was likely the first decent meal she'd had in quite some time. Nora also noticed her slipping glances Grace's way throughout the meal.

"Just out of curiosity," Cam asked, "where did you hide out?"

Mollie stopped eating long enough to answer his question. "There's an abandoned shack out in the woods about a half mile south of town. It's not much but it had a roof and four walls to keep the weather and the wildlife out."

Cam nodded. "I know the place—Lem Grady and his boys were supposed to check it out first thing yesterday morning."

"They did. I hid and watched them go over every corner of it. Then as soon as they left, I figured it would be safe to hide out there for a while."

Mollie seemed proud of her cleverness and Nora had to admit she seemed to have a good head on her shoulders, in a cunning, not-quite-trustworthy sort of way.

Once the meal was over, James volunteered to hitch the wagon. Agnes offered to hold Grace while Nora ate, but Nora turned her down. As foolish as she knew it was, she couldn't bring herself to physically let go of Grace until Mollie was out of the house.

Once breakfast was over, she followed Cam and Mollie as they headed outside. The three of them walked in silence until they reached the wagon and then Cam turned to her. She hadn't had a chance to say anything to him since he'd captured Mollie, and suddenly words failed her. A simple thank-you seemed inadequate for all he'd done, yet right now they were the only words she could muster. "Thank you. For everything."

"Just doing my job." But his eyes told her a different story. Then he touched her arm. "You've been through a lot these past few days. I don't expect you to come in for work anytime soon. Take as much time as you need."

"I appreciate the offer, but I'll be there tomorrow." She jiggled Grace. "We both will."

He appeared ready to say more, but then seemed to think better of it. Instead he nodded and turned to hand Mollie up onto the wagon seat. When he turned back to Nora he smiled. "Thanks again for the use of your wagon. I'll bring it back later today after I get our prisoner settled in."

Nora nodded, trying to sort through the emotions swirling inside her. She'd sort through her feelings for Cam later.

As for Mollie...

Part of her wanted to dislike this girl who had caused her so much anguish, and who had the potential to cause so much more. But the other part of her felt a stirring of unwanted sympathy for everything she had endured.

A moment later she watched Cam head the wagon toward town, and let out a deep, shuddering breath, releasing her ambivalent emotions with it. For now, at least, she would ignore everything but her joy at the miracle of having Grace back, safe and sound.

The rest could be sorted out later.

Chapter Sixteen

Nora spent most of the morning fussing over Grace. She bathed her and put a fresh gown on her. She cooed over her, crooned to her and examined her multiple times for any signs of injury she might have missed. Even when Grace took her nap, Nora hovered over her cradle, watching her sleep.

Near noon, Cam returned with the wagon. He helped James unhitch the horse, then joined Nora and Agnes in the house.

"Lunch will be ready in another thirty minutes or so," Nora said by way of greeting. "Would you care to join us?" She felt unaccountably shy, as if something in their relationship had shifted these past few days. Would it return to normal soon? Did she want it to?

He grinned, apparently feeling none of her ambivalence. "My timing was in no way accidental. I was hoping for an invitation." He glanced toward the cradle. "How's Grace?"

Nora beamed. "She's fine. In fact she doesn't seem to have suffered any ill effects at all." Then she asked a question of her own. "Is your prisoner settled in?"

"As much as can be expected."

He didn't sound particularly pleased. "Is something wrong?"

He waved a hand. "I've been dealing with gawkers most of the morning. Ever since I brought Mollie in, no fewer than two dozen townsfolk have made excuses to stop by. It seems everyone wants to get a look at the female kidnapper who caused all the fuss the past few days."

"That's natural I suppose," Nora said. "The search did disrupt a lot of lives for a short time." Though it hadn't seemed such a short time while it was happening.

Before Cam could respond, the sound of a carriage intruded.

"Now who—" Then realization hit her. "Oh my goodness, I forgot we told Gavin to send word to Boston."

Nora popped up and ran to the door. Sure enough the carriage had stopped and Maeve was already halfway out of it. Nora wasted no time running to meet her.

"Nora, oh, Nora, I'm so sorry. We came as soon as we heard."

The sisters nearly collided in their desire to embrace.

"It's all right now," Nora reassured her sister. "We have her back." She squeezed her harder. "We have her back," she repeated. Oh, how she'd missed having her sisters nearby. She hadn't realized how much until just this moment.

When they finally separated Nora noticed that Flynn had stepped out of the carriage behind Maeve and was talking to Cam in low tones. He had his doctor's bag with him at the ready. Apparently he'd come prepared for the worst.

"We would have been here sooner," Maeve said, "but

the young man who carried your message got lost trying to find us." She looked around. "Where is Grace? I have to see her for myself."

"She's inside with Agnes and James." Nora linked her arm through Maeve's as they moved toward the open door. "I'm so sorry I didn't send word when we recovered her. My mind has been a bit scattered."

Maeve gave her arm a squeeze. "Of course it has. I'm just glad it all turned out so well." She searched Nora's face, as if looking for reassurance. "Grace *is* okay, isn't she?"

"She seems none the worse for the experience. Of course if you and Flynn would examine her just to be sure I'd be most grateful."

Flynn spoke up from behind them. "I don't mind at all. In fact, I insist."

As soon as they entered the kitchen, Maeve gave James and Agnes a quick greeting and then reached for Grace. "Oh, dear, sweet Grace, let me have a good look at you. How you've grown since I saw you last."

Flynn performed a thorough examination and pronounced Grace healthy, then they all gathered around the table.

"So, tell me what happened." Maeve looked from Nora to Cam. "All I know is that Grace was taken. How long ago did this happen? Who did this terrible thing and how did you get our baby back?"

Nora spoke first. "It happened on Saturday." Was that really just two days ago? "Do you remember the day Bridget, Grace and I moved into this cottage? How this strange girl came out of nowhere and stole Cam's horse? Well, she's the same person who kidnapped Grace."

Maeve leaned forward. "But who is she and why would she do such a thing?"

"Her name is Mollie Kerrigan." Nora paused a moment, then took a deep breath. "And she claims to be Grace's mother."

"Grace's… But how… I don't…" Maeve looked as shocked as Nora had felt when she got the news.

Nora gave her a sympathetic smile. "I know, it's difficult to believe. But Mollie stowed away on the *Annie McGee* and didn't have anyone or any resources to take care of her baby, so she left her where she'd be easily found. Then she followed us here because she wanted to be close to Grace. Of course, I didn't learn any of this until she brought Grace back this morning."

"She *brought Grace back?*"

Nora stood and moved to the stove. "Yes. Because she realized she couldn't be the mother Grace needs, and she believed that I could." She stirred the contents of the pot, then moved it to a cooler area of the stove. "Now, the fish soup is ready and the bread is already cooling on the sill. There's more than enough for everyone so let me get the dishes on the table and we can continue this discussion over lunch."

Maeve rose and went to the cupboard. "It smells wonderful. Flynn's cook is really good at what she does, but I've missed your cooking."

They talked throughout the meal, Maeve and Flynn asking additional questions about what had happened the past few days, and Cam and Nora providing what answers they could. Then Nora asked them to share a little of what they had experienced working with victims of the fire in Boston. Once again Nora admired the dedication of the newlywed pair for the healing work they did.

When they were done with the meal, Agnes shooed them from the kitchen, insisting that she and James would take care of the dishes while the "young folk" had a nice visit. Cam and Flynn drifted out to the barn where Nora suspected they would have a more frank discussion about the kidnapping.

Nora and Maeve carried Grace out to the garden to enjoy the bit of afternoon breeze.

Maeve smiled in delight when she spotted the bench. "Oh, you've had it repaired! It looks nice."

Nora nodded. "Cam took care of that. He's been making repairs around the place for me."

Maeve gave her an arch look. "Has he now?"

Nora felt her cheeks warm. "I intend to pay him for his labors, of course," she added quickly.

"Of course."

Maeve's dry tone warmed Nora's cheeks further. She hadn't had much time to reflect on how her and Cam's relationship had changed over the past couple of days. All that she knew right now was that it *had* changed in some subtle, mysterious way.

As they settled themselves on the bench, Maeve reclaimed her attention. "That reminds me. Bridget stopped for a quick visit before they headed to New York and she mentioned you were starting a bakery business."

Nora nodded. "I'm just beginning but I think it's going well."

"Everyone always said you were the best pie maker in all of County Galway. Some even said you were better than Mother herself."

Nora waved off the compliment and gave her sister's hand a squeeze. Then she changed the subject. "I'm sorry if I pulled you and Flynn away from those poor hurting people who need medical help. But I'm selfish enough to be glad to have you here for a bit."

Maeve returned her smile. "There are other doctors to see to the patients, but I only have two sisters." Then her lower lip trembled. "Oh, Nora, when I think of all you must have gone through! That must have been such an awful, wrenching experience. Are you truly sure you're okay?"

Nora took a deep breath. "I won't deny it was a nightmare while it was happening. But it's over now and it turned out fine."

Maeve's expression took on a slightly accusing cast. "You should have sent word sooner. We would have come right away to support you through it."

"I knew you had other responsibilities taking care of your patients. And I kept praying they would find her any minute."

Maeve gave her hand another squeeze. "But you're my sister. Besides, I love Grace, too, you know."

Nora laid a hand on hers. "Oh, Maeve, I didn't mean to imply you didn't. To be honest, I don't think I was quite rational at the time it was happening. Forgive me?"

Maeve's face cleared and she leaned over and gave her a hug. "Of course I do." When she settled back she grimaced. "Is that wicked girl truly Grace's mother?"

Nora felt her thinking shift and certainty settled into her heart. "She is." Saying that out loud cut worse than she'd thought it would.

Maeve didn't appear convinced. "But, just because she claims she is doesn't make it so. She's done so many awful things—how can you be so sure she's not lying about this?"

"She knows too many details about Grace. And there's

a similarity in their features that can't be denied. She's Grace's mother all right."

"Where is she?"

"Cam has her locked up over at the jailhouse."

"Grace's mother, a criminal. So hard to believe."

Nora winced at that stark description. Her ambivalent feelings of this morning began to surface again, stronger than ever.

"What's she like?" Maeve asked.

Nora thought it best to let Maeve form her own opinion. "You should meet her and see for yourself."

Maeve shook her head. "Not right now. I don't think I could be very nice to her at the moment."

Nora couldn't imagine her little sister being deliberately mean to anyone. "There'll be time enough later I suppose. She's not going anywhere." She touched Maeve's arm. "But please, meet her before you return to Boston."

Maeve was silent for a long moment, then reluctantly nodded. "If I remember correctly," she said, "Gavin seemed smitten with the girl during his last encounter. How is he reacting to her now?"

"His infatuation with her ended as soon as she took Grace," Nora said dryly. "I think he's been harder on Mollie than anyone else. Except maybe Cam."

"I must admit, I have trouble feeling very charitably toward her myself."

"I don't think she would ever have deliberately hurt Grace. Even when she abandoned her on the *Annie McGee,* I think she was only trying, in her own way, to do what was best for her daughter."

"What's going to happen to her now?"

"I suppose she'll end up going to prison for a time." That idea didn't sit so well with her.

Maeve apparently sensed some of her ambivalence. "And how do you feel about that?"

Nora tried to gather her scattered thoughts. She wanted to say that justice was being done, that Mollie was getting what she deserved. But it wasn't that simple.

When she looked at Mollie she saw the girl-woman who had lied and cheated and stolen to get herself where she was today. The person who'd taken Grace from her and put her through two days and nights of gut-wrenching, heartbreaking worry. The person who could still lay claim—

No! She wouldn't even think of that possibility right now.

Yet this was also a girl who was hurting and needed a friend. A girl who'd felt alone, abandoned and scared. A frightened girl who had given birth alone while hiding in the dank bowels of a ship. A girl who'd eventually decided to do the right thing for her baby and risked capture to do so. A girl who, for all her faults, was still a child of God.

Finally she met Maeve's gaze. "I want to help her."

Chapter Seventeen

Cam and Flynn stood out by the barn, leaning against the newly patched fence. Cam had already filled Flynn in on the grittier details Nora had left out of her recounting, and reassured him about Nora's and Grace's ongoing safety. He'd even admitted, with some trepidation, his spending the past two nights in the house and was relieved when Flynn merely thanked him for the protection he'd offered his sister-in-law.

Now they stood in companionable silence, staring at Amber prancing about the enclosed barnyard.

When they heard steps approaching, Cam knew before turning around that it was Nora. Strange how attuned he was to her presence.

"That's a fine horse you've acquired," Flynn said.

"Thank you, but Cam here had more to do with the selection than I did."

Cam smiled. Nice to hear both her easy use of his name, and her acknowledgment of the part he'd played.

"Still," Flynn continued, "I know it'll be a relief to your sisters to know you have a means of transportation now." He straightened. "And speaking of your sisters, I did send word to Will and Bridget about this matter before we left Boston. I imagine they'll be here tomorrow at the latest."

Cam sensed something different about Nora, something unsettled. "Is something the matter?"

She met his gaze and straightened. "Actually, I've made a decision, and I'd like to have a family meeting to discuss it."

Family meeting. Surprising how deeply that exclusion cut. "I suppose I should be getting back to town anyway. Ben is probably ready for—"

Her look stopped him. "Actually," she said with a diffident smile, "if you have time, I'd like for you to join us, too. This is going to affect you as much as anyone. And I'd really like your thoughts on the matter."

That last comment made the invitation feel much less like an afterthought. He nodded. "Of course."

Cam and Flynn followed her back to the kitchen and the whole group took seats around the table, including Agnes and James. Grace lay sleeping in a cradle situated between Nora and Maeve. Cam was seated on Nora's other side. He wasn't sure if that had happened naturally or not, but he was glad to be there.

For a while no one said anything as Nora seemed to take a moment to gather her thoughts. The sober, determined look about her made her appear isolated. Cam wanted to give her hand a squeeze but held himself in check.

Finally she looked around the table. "I've been doing a lot of thinking this morning about what's happened, and about Mollie herself. I know she's done some terrible things, but she's suffered through a lot of hardship and pain, as well. Is it really necessary to have her spend time in jail? I mean, does it serve any useful purpose?"

Had she let the girl's story soften her heart? "She broke the law, Nora," he said, refusing to apologize for locking up a confessed kidnapper. "I had no choice but to arrest her."

Nora gave him a reassuring smile. "I know you were doing your job, Cam, but if Grace is truly her baby, can we really call it kidnapping?"

He refused to be swayed by such slippery logic.

But Flynn spoke up before he could. "That's not the only law she broke."

Nora shifted her gaze back to the others at the table. "I know. She also tried to steal Cam's horse, but she didn't keep it long."

"She didn't *try,* Nora," Cam protested. "She actually succeeded in stealing Fletch. How long she kept him is beside the point."

"But if you don't press charges on the horse stealing…"

"Why wouldn't I? Nora, she's a *criminal.* She's done lots of very bad, unlawful things."

"She abandoned her baby," Maeve said. "Twice."

Cam could see Nora trying to hold her frustration in check.

"But look at how young she is," she argued. "And her life hasn't been easy. It appears she hasn't had much in the way of family or friends to help her along the way."

"We had a difficult time too," Maeve insisted. "But we didn't resort to stealing."

"But we had each other," Nora reminded her. "And then you found Flynn."

Maeve glanced quickly at her husband and squeezed his hand, then turned back to Nora, a softer look on her face.

Cam frowned. Nora might be winning her sister over, but not him. "I'll admit, if what she told us is true she's had lots of trials and troubles to deal with. But how do we know she's telling the truth?" He raised a hand to stop whatever counterargument she was about to make. "And even if she is, that's no excuse for breaking the law. As your sister pointed out, other folk have had it as bad or worse and they got by without turning to crime."

Her expression immediately softened and the sympathy in her expression told him she was thinking of his past. He quickly spoke up again. "No matter what her situation, she could have just asked for help, rather than stealing and lying."

"Yes, she could have. But, for whatever reason, she didn't and we can't go back and change that. I want to help her now."

Nora's willingness to forgive was admirable, especially after all that had happened, but he didn't understand this misguided determination from a woman who was usually so practical and levelheaded. "Why? Why would you want to help someone who wronged you so deeply?"

"Because she's Grace's mother."

That simple statement silenced them all for a moment.

Finally Flynn spoke up. "What do you suggest we do? Surely you don't think she shouldn't have to suffer *some* sort of consequences for what she's done?"

"Of course not. Just because someone is sorry doesn't mean they don't have to make reparations for what they've done. But putting her in prison doesn't do her or any of the people she wronged any good. Especially since I don't think she's a danger to anyone or likely to repeat her crimes."

Cam wasn't so sure about the last part but decided to hold his peace on that score—for now. "So, as Flynn asked, what do you think we ought to do?" He knew she'd have a plan—she always did. And he also knew he wasn't going to like it.

"Wouldn't it be better," she replied, "not just for Mollie but for everyone involved, if she did what she could to make it up to the people she wronged? We could make a record of everything she's stolen and everywhere she's trespassed, and determine the lost value. Then we give her a way to earn money so she can pay it all back."

She'd obviously already put a lot of thought into this scheme of hers. "You do realize that letting her out of jail might not be doing her a favor, don't you? She might not be interested in working off her debts."

"If she doesn't want to work in exchange for her freedom, then I'll drop this whole plan without another word. But I really don't think that'll be the case. I sense that, deep down, there is something good in Mollie. We just have to help her find and nurture it."

"Everyone in town knows her story by now." Cam was still trying to get her to see reason. "Who do you think will be willing to take a chance and hire her?"

"You will." She lifted her chin. "Mollie can help me do the cleaning at the jailhouse and at your and Ben's places. That way you can keep an eye on her, the townsfolk can see you trust her, and she can pay you for the use of your horse and earn a little toward paying the shipping company for her passage."

He raised a brow. "But that's taking away money you need."

"Actually, I can use the time I save to spend more hours on my bakery business. It will let me fill those orders I've had to turn away."

Cam found his own frustration level growing. "And suppose she tries to run away again the first chance she gets?"

"Then you'll find her and bring her back, and this time she'll have much harsher consequences to deal with. But fear that she might not accept our help is no excuse not to offer it."

She looked around the table, and he saw the way she braced herself. "And there's another thing. Mollie will need a place to stay. Renting a room would take most everything she earns so that's not a good solution."

Cam sat up straighter. He had a good idea what was coming next and if he was correct he didn't like it one bit.

She took a deep breath. "So I plan to invite her to stay right here at the cottage."

He'd been right. Of all the fool, pigheaded, poorly thought-out notions. Apparently Maeve and Flynn felt the same way. Their protests were swift and overlapping.

"Oh, Nora, you can't let that girl near Grace—"

"Absolutely not. You're my wife's sister and I have a responsibility to—"

Cam was in complete agreement. Just because Nora was feeling softhearted didn't mean he would allow that girl to live under the same roof as her and Grace. Not to mention the Coulters.

When she turned to him, he gave her his answer in one terse sentence. "Not on my watch."

He refused to be moved by her obvious disappointment.

"It's the right thing to do," she insisted. "Mollie needs

good people around her to teach her to trust again." She stared Cam down. "The way Ben did with you."

That approach wasn't going to work with him. "Ben didn't have to arrest me to get my attention."

She brushed aside his comment. "Besides, if she lives with me, she'll be able to spend some time with Grace under my and the Coulters' watchful eyes. I can also teach her how to care for a baby and observe to see if she really can take on such a responsibility."

He saw her hand slide down to touch the edge of the cradle.

"You can't seriously be thinking about handing Grace over to her?" Maeve asked.

"No, of course not. But as Grace's mother, Mollie has a right to be part of her life."

Cam tried again to make her see reason. "I know she seems sympathetic enough now that she's been caught, but she has yet to prove herself trustworthy. She could even be dangerous."

"I don't think so. Remember, she *did* bring Grace back of her own accord."

Was she so determined to look for the good that she could ignore the bad? "Nora, she didn't once offer to make amends for any of her wrongdoings. She left Grace out in the yard, *hoping* you would find her quickly, and then up and ran off again. She's here now *only* because we caught her. If we hadn't, she'd still be out there doing goodness knows what."

"You need to listen to what he's saying," Flynn added. "I can't agree to leave that criminal here with you unless I'm absolutely convinced she's harmless. And maybe not even then."

"But—"

"No buts." Flynn could sound very authoritative when he tried. "If Cam wants to allow Mollie to work off her debts rather than go to prison, that's his business. But allowing her to stay here with the four of you is completely out of the question."

Nora leaned forward earnestly. "But I truly believe, for Grace's sake as well as her own, that Mollie needs to spend time with Grace. And the only way for that to happen is for her to stay here with us. Please, trust me to know what I'm doing."

"I have to ask this." Cam locked gazes with her. "Do you really think you can trust that girl not to try to abduct Grace again?"

He saw a vein in her throat jump, but she nodded. "Yes, I do."

Cam let out a frustrated breath. "That's very trusting and even charitable of you, Nora, but you need to let common sense prevail over your softer instincts."

Nora grimaced. "I'm no paragon." She expanded her gaze to include them all. "I still have trouble forgetting that Mollie abandoned her newborn baby. And that just a few days ago she stole that beautiful little girl away from me without so much as an explanation, leaving me to worry my heart and soul raw over Grace's fate." She took a deep breath then let it out slowly. "But in her own way, I think Mollie really does love Grace, so I have to believe she has good in her. And when it comes down to it, I have no right to judge her." She glanced around the table again. "None of us do."

She looked to the Coulters. "But I'm not the only one this affects. Agnes, James, can you be comfortable having her in the house with us?"

Agnes looked at her husband and took his hand in

hers. There seemed to be a moment of silent communion between them, then she turned back to Nora. "Everyone deserves to have someone who believes in them, to have a chance to make things right with their life if they're willing to take it. We're willing to stand behind your decision to help the girl."

Nora gave them an approving smile. "Bless you for your generous spirit."

"Well, my spirit is not so generous." Flynn's tone was firm. "I cannot allow you to endanger yourself this way. And I know Will will feel the same way when he hears of it."

"It is kind of you to be concerned about my welfare, Flynn, but I'm capable of deciding this for myself. I'm only discussing this with you all because I want you to understand why it means so much to me."

Cam hid a smile at this appearance of her stubborn, independent streak. There was a lot to admire in her spirit if not in the plan itself.

"Nora, be reasonable," Maeve pleaded. "Your heart is in the right place, but if you won't think of yourself, think of Grace and Agnes and James."

"Mollie wouldn't hurt us," Nora insisted. "She's not violent. And if she steals from us or runs away, then we will survive just fine."

Flynn softened his tone. "You want to believe everyone is as well-intentioned as you and your sisters are, but the truth is that there are bad people in this world. And until I'm convinced that she is as harmless as you believe, I can't allow you to put yourself or Grace in danger." He gave Maeve's hand a squeeze, as if to reassure himself that she was safe, as well.

Cam's jaw tightened. Flynn had a brother's right to

look out for Nora, and while he didn't out and out mention his partial ownership of the cottage, Cam knew Nora was aware of her brother-in-law's ability to enforce his will in this matter.

He couldn't bear the hurt, defeated look in her expression, especially not after all she'd gone through the past few days. "What if she had protection here?" he asked impulsively.

Flynn frowned. "Are you talking about giving Nora a weapon? I don't think—"

"No, not a weapon." How could Flynn think he would do something so reckless? "A person."

Flynn studied him suspiciously. Cam couldn't blame him. "What did you have in mind?" the doctor asked.

"As lawmen, Ben, Gavin and I all have a responsibility to provide protection to the citizens of Faith Glen, including this group here. In that role, we could take turns staying here at night, acting as prison guards." Not that he intended to let Gavin and Ben take very many "turns." "Sleeping in the parlor, of course," he added quickly.

Flynn frowned thoughtfully. "That seems to be a possible compromise. But I'm still not certain this is the right thing to do."

Nora crossed her arms. "I am."

Maeve placed a hand on Flynn's arm and a look passed between them. Finally Flynn turned back to Nora. "Let us agree to this much at least. We'll make no decision until Will and Bridget return and we can get their input."

Nora jumped on the suggestion, obviously relieved that the door hadn't been shut completely. "Agreed."

"Bridget offered us rooms in her home." Maeve was obviously ready for a change of topic. "We plan to stay there at least until they return. Longer if you need us to."

Cam still had one more issue he wanted to nail down. "In the meantime, supposing you got your way in this, where exactly would you have Mollie sleep?"

"She could take Bridget's old room," Nora answered, "the one upstairs across from mine."

Cam stood and turned to Flynn. "I think the two of us should have a look and see what would be required to make it secure."

"All right. At the minimum we'll want to be able to lock it from the outside."

Cam noticed Nora open her mouth to protest, but then she clamped it shut again. At least she was learning to pick her battles.

Nora watched Cam and Flynn leave the room together and felt some of the tension ease from her body. Cam's last-minute change of heart toward her plan had been both welcome and unexpected. Did he finally believe in what she was trying to do? In her?

She knew Flynn was only looking out for her, but she hated that he had such control over what she did. The sooner she could buy her sisters' shares of the cottage, the happier she would be.

"Don't blame Flynn." Maeve placed a hand over hers on the table. "He only wants what's best for you and Grace. We both do."

"I know. But you understand why I want to do this, don't you?"

"I understand that you have a good heart and that you always try to take care of those who have no one else."

Nora smiled at her sister's exaggerated praise, and her

avoidance of a direct answer. "I keep thinking about what might have happened to us if we hadn't had this place to come to. Mollie didn't have that chance."

"I know. And I agree that she had a rough time of it." Maeve's expression grew solemn. "But you need to see the other side of this, as well. She wasn't in our situation, not really. It sounds like she had a good home and a grandmother to watch over her at one time. Even if the woman didn't treat her well she provided for her. And Mollie threw that away to run off with a not-so-nice boy who made shiny promises she couldn't resist."

Nora was surprised by Maeve's rather straightforward assessment. When had her baby sister developed such a mature outlook? "I'm not blind to her weaknesses," she explained. "Mollie looks for the easy way out of her troubles, she doesn't take responsibility for her choices and she doesn't realize what havoc her actions cause. But she wants what's best for Grace and she has now seen how difficult life can be. I think she's ready to learn a better way and she deserves a chance to do so. So yes, I know she's not without her faults, but neither is she a villain."

Maeve gave her a hug. "Then that's good enough for me. I'll support you in any way I can." She released Nora. "Now, let's talk about how we're going to convince the others."

Chapter Eighteen

The next morning, Nora walked into the sheriff's office, pushing the baby buggy before her.

Cam frowned. "I told you not to worry about coming in today."

She glanced toward the cell, nodding a greeting Mollie's way, then turned back to Cam. "I know. But I'm ready to get back into my regular routine."

He studied her closely. "Are you sure?"

She nodded. "I wouldn't be here if I wasn't."

He smiled. "To the point as always. In that case, welcome back. We'll all be glad to have something besides our own cooking to eat."

Cam walked over to the stroller and had a look at Grace. "How's ladybug doing this morning?"

Nora smiled. "She's doing fine. And if you'll keep an eye on her for me I'll get breakfast started."

He grinned down at the infant. "I think you and I have the better part of that deal," he told Grace.

Nora's heart swelled with happiness as she went into the jailhouse kitchen. Cam had come a long way from not wanting anything to do with Grace. Was he finally beginning to understand that he was not his father?

Humming, she grabbed a bowl from the shelf and pulled eggs from her basket. Behind her she heard Gavin come in.

"Miss Nora's here!"

She smiled at the obvious pleasure in his voice. "Good morning, Gavin," she called over her shoulder. "Is this a two- or three-egg morning?"

"Three please." He stepped into the doorway. "It sure is good to have you and Grace back."

"Thank you. I'm happy to be back." And she most definitely was.

"Did you bring any of those big fluffy biscuits with you?"

She laughed. The hopeful question made it quite clear just what Gavin was most happy about. "I certainly did. And I brought along some plum jelly to go with them."

The sound of Ben entering and talking to Grace completed her feeling of things returning to the way they should be. These three very different men were part of her family now.

A few minutes later, Cam took Gavin's place in the doorway. "Smells good."

She smiled over her shoulder. "I'll be ready to serve in just a minute." Did he feel that same little tug of anticipation when they were together, that extra little tingle of awareness?

"Anything I can do to help?" he asked.

She shook her head. "Thanks, but there's no need. I'm almost finished."

He didn't move away but rather crossed his arms and stared at her with his smoky blue eyes. "I saw Flynn over at his building site when I made my rounds yesterday evening. The house looks like it'll be finished soon."

"It'll be good to have him and Maeve here permanently." Why did the room always feel so much smaller, more intimate, when Cam was in here with her? She wouldn't let herself wonder if he felt the same way. No, he'd made his lack of interest in her beyond friendship perfectly clear.

She lowered her voice. "Did you say anything to Mollie about my plan to help her?"

"Not yet. I thought we'd wait until Will and Bridget returned home and a definite decision was made."

Nora nodded. "That's probably best." She arranged five plates of food on a large wooden tray, then selected five cups from a nearby shelf. "Do you know if she prefers tea or coffee?"

"Tea."

Pleased that he'd taken the time to find that out, Nora prepared enough tea for two cups while she poured up three cups of coffee for the men.

She met his gaze, trying not to be distracted by the way he was looking at her. "I think it would be safe to let Mollie eat with us, don't you agree? I mean, it's not like she can escape with all three of you here keeping an eye on her."

Cam rolled his eyes, then nodded. "But only while she's eating. Then it's back inside the cell she goes."

"Of course. You're in charge."

And she wouldn't have it any other way.

Cam wandered out of the kitchen and moved to his desk. He had found himself on edge around Nora ever since Grace had been taken. At first he'd put it down to the tension that had permeated that whole situation. It was only natural, after all, that the heartbreak she'd been going through would touch him—it would have touched any man with half a heart. And the fact that she'd turned to him for comfort had only made it that much more intense.

But he was no longer sure that was the whole story.

Because he was ready to concede that she'd gotten under his skin way before that terrible incident, he just hadn't wanted to admit it before now.

The thing was, what did he plan to do about it?

She knew the whole ugly business about his father and it hadn't seemed to change her opinion of him. That was a testament to her own goodness. After all, if she was willing to forgive Mollie who'd wronged her so terribly, why wouldn't she have sympathy for someone who'd gone through what he had?

What she didn't know about, though, was his darkest secret. The one that triggered his nightmares. The one that kept him from ever pursuing the future he longed for. The one that no one, not even Ben, could ever know about.

So he had his answer. What did he intend to do about it?

Not a single thing.

Nora got word midafternoon that Bridget and her family were back home. It was Cam who gave her the news and he insisted Nora immediately take Grace and go reassure her sister that everything was okay.

And Nora, in turn, insisted that he accompany her.

By the time they arrived at Bridget and Will's home,

Nora could tell that Maeve and Flynn had updated them on most of what had happened.

Bridget ran to greet Nora, hugging both her and Grace as if afraid they would suddenly disappear if she let go.

When they all finally took their seats in Bridget's parlor, Nora looked around and suddenly felt as if she was on trial.

"Maeve and Flynn told us what you're wanting to do," Bridget said. "And we've all been discussing it at great length."

Nora couldn't discern from Bridget's expression how she felt about it.

"We think your motives are admirable," her sister continued, "especially given what you've been through."

Nora sensed a "but" coming.

"But we're concerned that your trust may be misplaced," Maeve said, right on cue. "However, we also know how much this means to you and how determined you can be to follow through on your plans to help someone."

Did this mean she would have their blessing?

"Cam's offer to volunteer his and his deputies' protection for your household seems like a good compromise," Flynn conceded. "But we have a few stipulations."

Stipulations? Nora braced herself. "And those are?"

"I had an idea yesterday while I was inspecting the construction on our home," Flynn explained. "We could add a structure to your cottage, a simple, single room on the back that was connected to the cottage but that had a separate entrance. It would allow Cam or one of his deputies to stay there as a guard in relative comfort and close proximity, without giving anyone cause for censure."

Nora wrinkled her nose. "Add a room? But doesn't that seem a bit extreme?"

"Not at all." Flynn tugged on one of his cuffs. "In fact, the men I have working on our home can take care of something simple like that in one, maybe two days."

Will leaned forward. "And since Flynn plans to take care of having the room built, I will see that it's furnished properly."

Nora tried to sound grateful. "That's very generous of you gentlemen, but it's really not necessary. I'm sure after just a few days' time, you will all see that Mollie is no danger to anyone and it will no longer be necessary for anyone to stay at the house to act as her jailer."

"We're going to build an extra room onto the cottage," Maeve said firmly. "And Will and Flynn are going to take care of the costs and the details."

Wasn't Maeve supposed to be on her side? "But—"

"And while we're at it we're going to make certain that the existing structure is weathertight," Bridget added.

Nora tried to protest again.

"It won't do you any good to argue," Maeve said firmly. "As you well know, Bridget and I each own a share of the cottage, and we want to do this, so you're outvoted."

When had her sisters gotten so bossy? They had never ganged up on her so forcefully before. She swallowed her pride and nodded. "I see I don't have much choice in the matter. And if this is what it takes for you all to feel comfortable going forward with my plans, then so be it."

"Good." Flynn looked genuinely pleased. "You can expect the work crew first thing in the morning."

Nora stood and reached for Grace. "I'll take my leave

of you now. I still have work to finish up at the jailhouse before I head home this evening."

Cam stood. "There's no need—"

She shot him a determined look. "I plan to put in a full day's work for a full day's pay." She hefted Grace to her shoulder. "Besides, we may have settled this matter amongst ourselves, but I have yet to speak to Mollie about it."

As they made their way to the door, Bridget moved beside her. "Don't be angry, Nora. We are only trying to do what's best for everyone."

She gave her sister a tired smile. "I'm not angry. I just wish it could have been handled differently."

Later, as Cam drove her back to his office, she let out some of her frustration. "One day I will own that cottage outright. But now, with the addition of this room, it will cost me more to do so."

"Why is it so hard for you to accept help?" he asked mildly.

"It's not that. It's just—" She stopped. What *was* it? "It's just that I don't want to be a burden on my sisters," she finished lamely.

"You're not a burden. Both Will and Flynn can afford to help you without any hardship whatsoever."

"But they shouldn't have to," she insisted.

Cam shook his head, his disagreement with her attitude obvious, and they made the rest of the short trip in silence.

When they arrived back at the sheriff's office, Cam was still trying to decide what he thought of the way this plan had been worked out among Nora and her family. But right now he needed to give Nora a bit of privacy to speak to Mollie. First he sent Gavin out to return his horse and wagon to the livery. Then a quick, meaningful look Ben's way was enough to have Ben remember an errand he needed to run.

Once they were alone, Cam unlocked Mollie's cell door and Nora went inside and sat next to Mollie on the cot.

He moved his desk chair to just outside the cell. He intended to keep a close eye on this little interaction. He figured he'd learn quite a bit about Mollie's character in the next few minutes.

"I want to talk to you about something," Nora began.

Mollie cast a quick glance his way, then focused all of her attention on Nora. "Yes ma'am. What about?"

"What do you think will happen to you now?"

Mollie picked at some threads on her raggedy skirt. "I suppose there'll be a trial and I'll go to prison for a long time." Her voice trembled slightly.

"What if I said there was another way for this to turn out?"

Hope flared in the girl's eyes. "What kind of other way?"

"Well, Sheriff Long and I, along with my family, have been talking things over, and we don't think you'll be helping any of those folks you wronged by spending your time in prison. In fact, we're wondering if you might better serve them and yourself by paying them all back instead."

The hope in her eyes died immediately. "That sounds good, but I don't have any money."

"You could earn it."

Mollie perked up. "How would I do that?"

"You could help out different people around town.

And you could start by working here at the sheriff's office."

Mollie gave her a confused look. "But, don't *you* work here?"

"That's right. And I would still do the cooking and mending. But I'm trying to start a new business which is going to require more and more of my time. I thought perhaps you could take over the cleaning and we would split the wages."

Cam mentally shook his head. She had managed to make this sound as if Mollie would be doing her a favor.

"Then if you do a good job here," Nora continued, "and prove yourself to be trustworthy, we could find other work in other places for you to do."

"I'd work very hard for a chance like that." Mollie lifted her head. "When Elden and I first ran off, I scrubbed floors at an inn to earn money and the innkeeper said I was a good worker."

Nora folded her hands in her lap. "Of course you'd have to turn over most of your wages to the sheriff to pay off your debts."

Cam raised a brow at that. So he was going to play banker in this little scheme of hers, was he?

Mollie glanced his way again and nodded emphatically. "I understand that, Miss Murphy. And I won't use any more of that money for myself than I need to. Why, I'll pitch a tent beside the road to live in if I have to. It'll just be good not to have to always be running and hiding anymore."

This time it was Nora who cast a quick glance his way. He gave a small nod of encouragement, more to show support for her than for her plan.

With a small smile, she turned back to Mollie. "That's

the other thing I wanted to talk to you about. I would like for you to come stay at my home."

Mollie was obviously surprised. "Why would you do that?"

At least the girl recognized how extraordinary the offer was.

"Well, for one thing," Nora said, "I'm one of the people you need to pay back. If you lived at my place you could do some odd chores in the evenings to take care of your debt."

Interesting. No mention of Mollie needing to spend time with Grace.

"I'm afraid there'd be lots of rules for you to follow," Nora continued, "and some restrictions on your freedoms, especially at first."

"I understand. I just appreciate that you'd trust me enough to give me this chance."

Nora sat back. "Then I guess the question is, are you willing to follow the rules and work hard to repay your debts? And to live under my roof?"

"I am." Mollie glanced toward the buggy where Grace slept. "In fact, I'd like that a lot." Then she turned back to Nora. "Mind if I ask you something?"

Nora sat up straighter. "Of course not."

"Why are you being so nice to me?"

Nora tucked a stray hair behind her ear. "I think everyone deserves a second chance." She stood. "Please don't prove me wrong."

Cam stood and opened the cell door for Nora to exit.

Then he leaned against the open doorway and stared down at Mollie. "There are a few things I need to say before we go through with this plan Nora just described to you."

"Sir?"

"First, you're going to be watched closely. Me or one of my deputies are going to be nearby at all times. If any of us gets even a hint that you're thinking about running off or breaking the law in any fashion again, then the deal is off and it's back to jail you go."

"Yes, sir. And I promise you won't have any trouble like that out of me."

"Next, we're going to sit down and you're going to tell me every single thing you stole or person you wronged from the time you slipped aboard that ship headed for America. And I do mean everything. I warn you, I know some of it already so I'll more than likely know if you leave anything off."

"Yes, sir, every single thing."

"We're going to make a list and then, where possible, we're going to let the victims set a value on how much you need to pay back for them to feel compensated, including your passage to America. And until you've paid it all back you won't be completely free to do as you please."

"Yes, sir."

"Promptly at eight o'clock each night you're going to go into the bedchamber Nora here assigns you at her home and someone is going to lock you in for the night. You are not to attempt to leave that room until it is unlocked the next morning."

Nora made a disapproving sound behind him. "I don't think—"

He didn't turn around. "I'll have no arguments, from either of you, on that point."

"It's okay, Miss Nora," Mollie said, "I understand. I

haven't given any of you much reason to trust me yet. But that's going to change, I promise you."

Cam nodded. She was saying all the right things, but did she mean them? "All right then. Me and Nora's family have some work to do out at her place to get things ready for your stay. Once that's done, we'll give this plan of hers a try and see how it all works out."

For Nora's sake, he hoped the girl was as eager to make amends as she seemed. He couldn't bear to see Nora disappointed again.

He waved Mollie out of the cell and over to a chair by his desk. He lifted his own chair and followed her. "In the meantime, let's get started on that list."

Just as Flynn had promised, bright and early the next morning, four workmen showed up at the cottage, accompanied by three large wagonloads of lumber and other equipment. Right behind them were Flynn and Maeve, Will and Bridget, and Cam.

Did her sisters' husbands and the sheriff plan to roll up their sleeves and get to work, as well? Within minutes it was obvious they did, as they helped unload the wagons. Once that was done, everyone went to work. James took care of the horses and wagons while the rest of the men started on the construction. Maeve and Bridget joined Nora and Agnes in the kitchen, each carrying a large basket.

"What's this?" Nora asked suspiciously.

Maeve started unpacking her basket on the kitchen table. "A pair of already plucked chickens and some fresh vegetables. Bridget has two jars of lemonade and some blueberries. We figure there's going to be quite a few mouths to feed for lunch today."

It wasn't enough that they were building her an addition to her home—they thought they had to put food on her table, as well. "I had planned to take care of that," she said stiffly.

"Don't worry," Bridget said with an unrepentant grin. "We intend to let you do all the cooking while we visit with Agnes and Grace."

Nora felt some of her annoyance ease and she returned her sister's grin. "I'm going to hold you to that."

Throughout the morning the hammering continued. It made Grace fussy so the sisters carried her out into the garden and then took walks along the beach with her. Nora joined them when she could get away from the stove and enjoyed the time spent with them. They did a lot of catching up with each other's news and slipped into the easy camaraderie she was afraid might have been lost to them when they went their separate ways.

When the men stopped to take a break, the ladies stepped outside to admire their work.

Nora tried to imagine what it would look like when it was completed. "It's so much bigger than I expected. You could almost fit both upstairs bedchambers in there."

Cam shrugged. "It's nearly as easy to build a large room as a small one."

Will nodded. "And we figured that when this is all over, you might want to move into it yourself."

The room was situated on the back side of the house and opened into the small room next to the kitchen that Laird had apparently used as an office when he lived here. It also had an outer door that faced the kitchen stoop. Then Nora looked again at the roofline that was taking shape. It extended well beyond the walls of the new room. "Are you planning to build a porch back here?"

"That we are," Flynn answered.

"But that wasn't part of the deal." Though if she was honest with herself, she was quite taken with the idea.

"We're not doing it for you," Cam said with a completely straight face. "It's for James. We're building it so he has a place to take off his boots before tracking into your kitchen when he comes in from the barn every morning."

"That's right," James answered. "I can't stand to have Agnes go on about my dirty boots every morning. That wife of mine is quite determined to drive me to distraction on the subject."

Nora couldn't resist a smile as she gave in. "Well, I wouldn't want to have that happen. And I'm sure we'll all enjoy having a back porch and will make good use of it."

By noon the four walls were up and the workers were constructing the roof and the floor of the porch. Because of their numbers, they ate in shifts and Nora found herself grateful that her sisters had brought along the extra foodstuffs. Those carpenters had worked up quite an appetite.

Cam was among the last of them to sit down at the table and she joined him. For a few minutes they had the kitchen to themselves. "So, do you think you'll manage to survive having to accept this generous gift from your sisters and their husbands?" he asked.

He knew her so well. "It will be difficult, but yes, I think I will survive."

He reached over and squeezed her hand. "That's my girl."

His words and tone as much as his touch set her pulse racing unexpectedly. He felt it, too—she could tell by the way his eyes darkened and then focused more sharply on her, as if she were the only thing he could see, the only thing he wanted to see.

For a moment neither of them moved, barely breathed. The tightness in her chest had become almost unbearable.

"Nora—"

Whatever he was planning to say was lost when Maeve bustled into the room. They simultaneously yanked their hands back and focused on eating their lunch.

"Bridget thinks Grace is ready for another bottle," Maeve said with a laugh. "I declare, that child is growing so fast, she—" Nora's sister paused, looking from Nora to Cam as if sensing something was wrong. "Sorry, did I interrupt something?"

"Not at all," Nora answered quickly. "We're just getting a bite to eat."

"I see." A secretive smile curved Maeve's lips. "Well, don't let me stop you. I'll just fix this bottle and be on my way again." Maeve reached for the pail of milk, humming cheerfully as she did so.

Nora and Cam continued to silently focus on their plates, even after Maeve had departed. Finally, Cam stood. "Thank you. That was delicious, as usual."

Was he going to leave it at that? "Cam, what—"

"I think we should be able to finish things up today." Cam didn't turn around as he placed his dish in the sink. "That means we can begin your project with Mollie tomorrow if you think you'll be ready."

Okay, so he didn't want to talk about it. "Of course."

He rubbed the back of his neck. "Which reminds me, I need to make certain that bedchamber door can lock securely from the outside. I'll grab the materials I need and take care of that right now." And with that he headed out the back door.

Nora slowly moved to the sink with her dishes, feeling totally dissatisfied.

What was going on with Cam?

Just as Cam had predicted, the workmen finished the construction, right down to the installation of two glass-paned windows, well before dark. Then they tackled the other critical repairs to the house, tightening loose boards, repairing or replacing sills, patching over chinks in the walls. When they were done, Nora was certain she no longer had to worry about drafts and leaks. They'd be able to face the coming winter with a snug, dry home.

Finally, Flynn walked up and gave her a short bow. "We're ready for your inspection."

Surprised by their desire to have her review their work, Nora nodded. Accompanied by her sisters, she walked through the large new room, inhaling the scent of sawdust and paint, admiring the craftsmanship of the well-sealed windows and square corners, enjoying the solid feel of the floors and the warmth of the sunlight streaming in through the windows. She pictured the curtains she would hang there, something light and cheery but not too feminine. And maybe some colorful rag rugs to warm up the floor.

Smiling, she opened the side door and stepped out onto her new back porch. The workmen were all standing there, including the sheriff and her brothers-in-law, waiting for her reaction. Agnes and James stood there, as well.

"I love it," she said with absolute sincerity. "It's perfect."

The men all smiled back at her.

"I have a chocolate blueberry pie and a buttermilk pie fresh from the oven waiting in the kitchen. I insist you all have a large slice and a cup of coffee before you go."

Before anyone could move, the sound of horses and wagons intruded.

Bridget clapped her hands. "That must be the furniture Will and I are giving you."

Sure enough, several wagons paraded into her front yard. In addition to the bed, which she had expected, she saw a chest, a padded chair, a small table, two rocking chairs and something she couldn't quite make out.

"Oh, Bridget, this is too much. I can't take all of this."

Bridget didn't even turn around. "Of course you can," she said brightly. "All you have to do is stand back and let the workmen do their jobs." Then she went back to directing the men unloading the wagons.

Within short order, the bed, complete with bed linens, along with the padded chair, chest and small table had been installed in the new room. The remaining items, the two rockers and what turned out to be a porch swing, were installed on the back porch.

She looked around at the circle of her family and friends who had done this for her and realized once again just how blessed she was. She might not want to lean on them so heavily as they seemed to wish, but they loved her and that was what mattered.

"Thank you all for this," she said, her voice catching for a minute. "And not just for the construction and the furnishings, but for caring so very much."

Her sisters squeezed her in a hug. "Goose!" Bridget said. "Of course we care. We love you."

"You're our big sister," Maeve added. "We need you at your best to look out for us."

How could she have doubted her sisters' motives, their undiminished love for her? Just because they were starting new lives didn't mean they were going off and leaving her behind.

It was she who, out of her fear and loneliness, had erected unnecessary barriers.

But no more. The Murphy sisters were family, come what may. Whatever they did for each other, they did out of love. She knew that now.

She saw Cam out of the corner of her eye. Somehow she had to reach him, help him understand how, like her, his thinking was painfully flawed in one small but important area of his life.

But how could she get through to him?

Chapter Nineteen

The next morning when Nora arrived at the sheriff's office, Cam opened the cell door and set Mollie free.

"You don't ever have to go back inside there," he told her, "if you stay on the straight and narrow. But if you do anything to hurt Nora or Grace, or slip back into any of your old ways, then our deal is off and it's back in here to face the music. Understand?"

"Yes, sir."

Nora immediately put the girl to work scrubbing floors while she herself started in on cooking their breakfast. She kept a close eye on Mollie, though she tried not to be obvious about it. Gavin, however, had no such compunction. He was still angry at the girl for the kidnapping and no amount of reasoning could change his mind.

After breakfast, Nora led Mollie across the way to Cam's and Ben's living quarters, with Gavin trailing closely behind. As they climbed the stairs to Cam's place, Mollie looked back over her shoulder at Gavin.

"You're the one I nearly ran over with the horse that day at Miss Murphy's place, aren't you?"

Gavin's scowl deepened. "I am." His tone was curt.

Nora opened the door and led the way inside. She didn't comment, deciding to let the two work this out on their own.

"Well, I'm very sorry for that and I'm glad you weren't badly hurt. I know that probably doesn't mean much, but I truly am. When those children saw me I got scared the sheriff would catch me. I knew if he found out I'd come here as a stowaway he'd throw me in jail."

"As he should." Gavin wasn't showing any signs of softening.

She nodded. "You're right. And if I'd known he was such a good man I wouldn't have feared it quite as much." She gave a sketchy grin. "But even so, being put in jail is never a pleasant thing to consider."

"Then you shouldn't do anything illegal."

Nora figured that was enough discussion on that topic. "Okay, Mollie, let me show you where the mop, broom and cleaning rags are, and go over what needs to be done. Ben's rooms are downstairs and you'll do the same down there as up here."

Once Nora was certain Mollie understood what needed to be done, and had observed her work for a few minutes, she left the girl under Gavin's watchful and very suspicious eye. Crossing back to the jailhouse, she placed Grace back in her buggy and headed for the general store.

Mrs. James greeted her with a smile. "Good morning, Nora. Glad to see everything is well with you and little Grace."

"Thank you. I'm starting back into my baking today. Would you like to place an order?"

"Two of your cinnamon pound cakes and an apple pie if you can manage that."

"Of course. I'll have them ready for you this afternoon."

Nora made quick work of her shopping, then eyed the dry goods section, intending to get the seeds for the kitchen garden. But then she spied the bolts of fabric. She'd noticed this morning how soiled and tattered Mollie's dress was. The girl very likely only had the one.

Making up her mind, Nora pushed the stroller toward the fabrics, then studied the bolts, selecting a simple green color that she knew would complement Mollie's complexion and eyes.

Mrs. James cut it to the proper length for her, then folded and handed it over. "That will make a lovely dress for you," she said. "Are you making it for a special occasion?"

Nora smiled. "No, nothing special." Not feeling the need to volunteer anything else, she quickly paid for her purchases and returned to the sheriff's office.

She got lunch started and placed a pie in the oven, then relaxed and gave Grace her bottle. Once the infant was sated she lapsed into a morning nap.

Nora returned to the kitchen, ready to do more baking. She hummed as she worked. There was her standing order to complete, of course. But she also did a little experimenting, trying a new combination of flavors in one pie and playing with size and thickness in a batch of cookies. It was fun to try new things, new ways of making her desserts.

"Sounds like someone is having a good time."

Nora glanced over her shoulder, surprised she hadn't heard Cam return. "I'm playing with flavors in here and they're turning out well, if I do say so myself."

"Dare I hope me and my deputies will get the benefit of some of your experiments?"

She smiled piously. "One should always have hope."

He shook his head at her rejoinder, then looked around. "So where is Mollie?"

Nora put the pie she'd been assembling into the oven, then turned back to him. "She's cleaning across the way. Gavin is keeping an eye on her."

"How is she doing so far?"

Nora didn't hesitate but chose her words carefully. "She doesn't do things exactly the way I would, but then everyone has their own ways, and she's getting the job done. I truly have no complaints about what I've seen of her work or her attitude so far."

She moved forward, stepping past him. "In fact, while I've got a few minutes, I probably should go check on how she's doing."

She bent over the buggy and saw Grace was sleeping. "Oh, she's napping. Would you mind keeping an eye on her for a few minutes? I won't be long and I hate to wake her."

She saw that familiar distressed look in his eyes.

"I don't think that's such a good idea. I mean, I might be called away on official business."

"You can always just step out the back door and call if you need me to come tend to her."

"Still, I think it best—"

Ben walked in just then, interrupting Cam's protest. As if he'd just been rescued from a burning building, Cam greeted his deputy with a broad smile. "Ah, Ben's here. He'll be glad to help you, I'm sure."

"Of course I will," Ben said agreeably. "I'm at your disposal, Nora girl. What do you need?"

Recognizing defeat when she saw it, Nora smiled Ben's way. "Just keep an eye on Grace for a few minutes while I step out back. She's napping and I don't want to wake her." She shot Cam a frustrated look. "Seems the sheriff here is afraid his official business might get in the way."

Cam cleared his throat. "That's right. You never know when an emergency situation might arise."

Ben made a shooing motion with his hands. "You just go on about your business now, we'll watch over little Gracie for you."

As Nora crossed the narrow alley to the lawmen's quarters she shook her head in disappointment. She'd thought Cam was beginning to get over his apprehensions about being around children, but apparently she'd been wrong.

This misguided fear of his was robbing him of the potential for so much happiness. She had to find a way to help him see the kind of man he truly was.

The kind of father he could be.

That thought set a fluttering in her stomach.

Father Almighty, I want to help Cam see the truth of this matter, but I'm not sure how anymore. Please help me to find a way. Present me with the right opportunity, the ability to recognize it and the courage to act on it.

Later that afternoon, when Cam drove them home, Nora found herself seated between Mollie and Cam. The addition of an extra adult forced her right up next to Cam. During that short ride, which felt unusually long today, she was all too aware of his presence beside her. Every bump and sway of the wagon caused them to brush against each other, and each brush sent tingles through her. Did he feel even the tiniest bit of that unsettling reaction? Or was he truly as unaffected as he seemed?

"This will be your room."

Mollie looked around at what had briefly been Bridget's room. "It's nice. In fact, it's been a very long time since I've slept in a place so clean and comfortable looking. Thank you for letting me use it."

Nora studied Mollie thoughtfully. "Don't you have any possessions to store here at all?"

"No. I had a few things I hadn't already sold off when I boarded the ship—some extra clothes, a hairbrush and mirror, a couple of hair ribbons—but I lost it all when my carpetbag was stolen on the docks in Boston."

Nora led her from the room and back down the stairs. "Well, then, you'll have to borrow one of my dresses and a nightdress until we can get you some additional clothing of your own. Do you sew?"

"I've done a bit of embroidery work and some mending, but I've never actually made an article of clothing before."

Nora nodded to herself. She thought she'd detected undertones of a genteel upbringing in the girl's voice. This reference to embroidery work and lack of practical sewing skills confirmed it. What had driven Mollie to leave that life behind for this one? "No need to worry," she said. "Agnes and I will teach you. You never know, that's a skill you might be able to use at some point to help you earn some money."

"I'm willing to try to learn anything you want to teach me."

The girl was certainly making an effort to have this arrangement work out. Nora moved toward the kitchen.

"Now, I think a nice long bath may be in order before we do anything else."

Mollie stopped in her tracks. "Do you mean it, Miss Murphy? It's been so long since I've had more than a dip in a pond or a quick wipe with a wet rag."

"Yes, a *real* bath. Now, the washtub is in the back room, right through there." She pointed to what had formerly been Laird's office. "I'll put the large kettle on the stove to heat up some water. There's a bucket over by the back door you can use to start hauling water to fill the tub."

Once Mollie was happily settled in the tub, Nora went to her room and looked over her dresses. It didn't take much time. Besides the one she had on, she had three others, and one of those was the special blue dress she'd worn to Bridget's wedding.

She picked up the brown one—serviceable but not too worn—grabbed her sewing bag and went downstairs. She paused long enough to scoop up the basket that held Grace and went out on the back porch.

She set Grace's basket on the floor of the porch near the swing, then sat down and threaded her needle. It was so nice to sit out here and enjoy the evening breeze. And the swing was quite comfortable.

She smiled as Grace gurgled, swinging her arms with such abandon. Apparently Grace liked it out here, as well.

When she looked up again she saw Cam headed back from the barn. He stepped on the porch and sat in one of the rockers. "Getting some mending done?" he asked.

"I'm shortening this so it will fit Mollie."

"Giving her the clothes off your back now?"

"Just until we can get her some of her own."

"And where *is* Mollie?"

"She hasn't run off if that's what you're worried about. She's taking a bath." Nora grimaced. "And I told her to wash the dress she was wearing while she was at it, so I need to get this finished quickly." She looked up momentarily from her sewing. "By the way, I meant to ask, how did the list of her transgressions turn out?"

"She was surprisingly forthcoming. Perhaps it was because she wasn't certain how much I already knew. But the list is long. Mostly small stuff, though. Like the produce from Amos Lafferty's garden."

"Have you talked to any of the people affected yet?" she asked. "Do you think they'll be satisfied with having her pay them back rather than serve time in prison?"

"Oh, I think getting reparation is going to be accepted by the victims quite well. It's the rest of the townsfolk you'll have worry about."

Nora's hands stilled for a moment. "What do you mean?"

"They're not getting anything out of this and to their way of thinking I'm letting a thief, and maybe worse, walk free among them." He raised a brow. "Don't forget, it was just a few short days ago that they were scouring this area because she'd kidnapped an infant."

How foolish of her not to have realized that. "Do you think that'll mean problems for Mollie?"

Cam shrugged. "If she works hard, does as she ought and doesn't get into any more trouble, I think folks will eventually accept her." He paused but she could tell he wasn't finished. "*Your* attitude will go a long ways toward smoothing the way for her," he finally added. "If folks see that you've forgiven her they are more likely to look for the good in her themselves."

Nora nodded and resumed her sewing. What Cam

had said made sense, but the responsibility that added to her shoulders seemed daunting. She offered up a silent prayer for help not to stumble in her efforts.

Cam watched Nora ply her needle, the quick efficient movements counterbalanced by the soft frivolity of her humming. It was so reflective of the contradictions that made her so uniquely Nora that it made him smile. He watched the light breeze tease a wayward tendril into escaping her bun and he itched to twine it around his finger to see if it felt as soft and playful as it looked.

This is how God meant for family life to be, he thought. Not the dark, ugly thing he'd grown up with that was filled with fear and hate and guilt. But this—this sense of warmth and peace and fulfillment, along with just a touch of mystery and the push-pull of attraction.

A gusty breeze scurried across the porch just then and Nora lifted her face into it, eyes closed and lips slightly parted, as if welcoming a lover's kiss.

It was a spontaneous, artless gesture, but the sweet arch and smoothness of her neck, the innocent pleasure in her expression, took his breath away. What would she do if he closed the distance between them, took her in his arms and gave her the kind of kiss he longed to, the kind of kiss a suitor gave to his lady to communicate the depth of his feelings?

Cam stood abruptly, caught off guard by the turn his thoughts had taken. When had he started feeling this way?

It didn't matter. He wasn't her suitor. And he wouldn't ever be.

And he'd better find somewhere else to be before he forgot that.

Chapter Twenty

After dinner that evening, Mollie helped clear the table and clean the dishes. Once that was done, it was time to feed Grace. Nora quickly filled the bottle with milk fresh from the evening milking, then picked Grace up.

Glancing across the room, she caught Mollie watching them. The girl looked away and busied herself with wiping the counter, but not before Nora had seen the sad longing in her eyes.

"I'm feeling the need for a bit of fresh air," she said impulsively. "Mollie, would you like to give Grace her bottle tonight?"

She could feel Cam staring at her but refused to look his way.

"Me?" Mollie's expression was both hopeful and fearful at the same time. "I don't…I mean, I might not do it right."

"Of course you can. Grace does most of the work anyway. Come, sit here at the table and I'll show you."

Mollie slowly walked to the table. "I don't think she likes me. I mean she mostly cried when I had her last."

When you took her from me you mean. Nora quickly

pushed that ugly thought aside. For this arrangement to work, she had to let go of all those feelings.

"One of the things you need to understand," she explained to Mollie, "is that Grace can sense your mood. If you're nervous, or irritable or frightened, she'll feel it and it will make her fussy, as well. So when you're holding her, focus on *her,* not on your own feelings. Think about how beautiful and precious she is, and how blessed you are to have her with you. Because if what she feels is your love, she'll feel safe and secure, and it will soothe her like nothing else can."

"She *is* precious."

Nora wanted to hold on to Grace, to make it clear that Grace belonged with her and no one else. Instead she nodded. "That she is. Now, hold out your arms."

Mollie did as she was told and Nora gently eased the infant into her waiting embrace. "Very good. Just make sure you support her head properly. Like that, yes."

Mollie stared down at her sweet burden.

"Here," Nora urged, "take the bottle and touch it to her lips. She'll latch on quickly enough." Grace started sucking at the nipple, right on cue. "There now, looks like you have the hang of it already."

Mollie couldn't seem to tear her gaze away from Grace. "She's so beautiful. She has my mother's eyes."

"Just about the most beautiful baby there ever was."

"Does she have a middle name?"

Mollie's question caught Nora unawares. "No. I mean, when we found her we had to give her a name so we could call her something other than 'baby,' so we decided to call her Grace. We never moved beyond that."

Mollie continued to stare down at the feeding infant. "I always thought that if I had a little girl I would name her after my mother, Abigail. Do you think we might give her that as a middle name?"

"I think Grace Abigail is a very lovely name."

Mollie smiled softly and stroked Grace's cheek. "Hello, little Grace Abigail."

Nora felt a lump form in her throat and tamped it down as best she could. "Well, now, time for that fresh air."

Mollie looked up, her eyes wide and staring as if her lifeline was being taken away.

Nora managed to smile. "Don't worry. Agnes is here to help you if you have questions. She actually has much more experience with babies than I do." Then with a wave, Nora headed quickly out the door.

She'd barely stepped off the porch before she heard someone step out of the house behind her. It was Cam, of course—she didn't even have to turn around to be certain of that. She didn't stop but in a moment he was beside her, matching his steps to hers.

"You're not worried Mollie will run away?" she asked. Better to keep the conversation on neutral ground.

"Agnes and James will keep an eye on her for me."

She stumbled over a bit of uneven ground, and he grabbed her elbow to steady her. Then, instead of letting go, he tucked her hand on his arm. She thought about pulling away but decided it felt good there.

"That was a very kind thing to do," he said quietly.

She shrugged. "It's just a feeding."

"We both know it was more than that."

Sometimes she wished he didn't know her quite so well. "It's why I brought her here." But she hadn't planned to start so soon.

"I know."

Neither said anything else for a while, and soon they were strolling along the beach. Nora tried to lose herself in the muted slap-lapping sound of the waves and the crunching sand beneath their feet, in the brisk scent of salt water and sea spray, in the awe-inspiring sight of an ocean that seemed to go on forever.

Finally the panic within her subsided.

She slowed her pace and found a grassy dune above the beach to sit on. She wrapped her arms around her knees and stared out at the water. "I'm not giving Grace up, you know. Not yet."

"I know."

"Mollie has to prove herself worthy and able first."

"I know."

"And maybe not even then. I mean, Mollie and I could both raise her, together." She laid her head on her knees and turned her neck to finally look at him. "Couldn't we?"

His smile was achingly gentle. "You could. Absolutely."

It wasn't until he touched a finger to her cheek and pulled it away damp that she realized she was crying.

Cam pulled Nora to him and placed her head on his chest. He'd give his right arm to be able to take the hurt from her, but he was helpless to do so.

"This is silly," she said with a slight catch in her voice. "It's only one feeding."

Cam made a noncommittal sound, not wanting to lie. Because he could see the writing on the wall. It was happening just as he feared it would. Nora was too honorable a woman to separate a mother from her child, even if she had to shred her own heart in the process. How she would be able to bear this he couldn't fathom. Because she loved that little girl as deeply and sacrificially as if she were her own flesh.

Nora finally lifted her head away from him, but remained in the circle of his left arm. His chest mourned the loss of her warmth, but his arm rejoiced in the sweet weight it supported.

He looked down and saw that her tears had stopped. But he knew the hurt hadn't.

She met his gaze and smiled softly. "You love Grace, too, don't you?"

"She is lovable," he answered lightly.

Her nose wrinkled in irritation. "Be serious, Cam. I saw the way her kidnapping ate at you and I see the way you look at her sometimes, like you can't help yourself. You love that little girl. Admit it."

Why was this so important to her? "All right, yes, I care a lot about her."

"Yet you won't let yourself get any closer to her."

"I have my reasons. Personal, *private* reasons."

"But this is so wrong, in so many ways. You'd make such a wonderful father, Cam. Don't you *want* children of your own someday?"

He pulled his arm back, grabbed a rock from the ground beside him and flung it as far as he could. "Yes! Is that what you want to hear? Yes I want to have children of my own, to have a family of my own. There are times when I see other fathers with their families and know I would give just about anything to be them for just a day." He stopped just short of saying *I want to have a family with you.* "But I know better than to pine after something I can't have."

She touched his arm, sending shock waves clear through to his gut.

"If this is about your father," she said, "then you have to see how blind you're being. You are not like him. You will never be like him. You are an honorable man."

She was pushing again, making him think about things he'd rather forget. "It's not about my father. At least not entirely."

"Then what is it?"

Cam stood and brushed off his pants. "Let this be, Nora. You can't fix everyone and everything. Some wrongs can never be righted."

He held out his hand to help her up and she took it. But to his surprise, when they were face to face, her eyes were filled with sorrow. "I'm disappointed in you, Cam. I thought you were a man who was fair and honest."

"I am."

"No, you aren't. You encouraged me to share my stories with you, how my mother and my da died, how we were run out of the only home we knew with no place else to go—or so we thought—and of the difficult decisions we faced. And in talking to you, I learned to see God's hand in everything that came to pass. You winnowed out of me my dreams of independence and you are helping me find a way to realize them. And you helped me see that it's naught but sinful pride to refuse help when it comes from a loving, generous spirit."

He rubbed the back of his neck, a little embarrassed by her recitation of the many things he'd done for her. "I was just trying to—"

Her eyes blazed back at him. "I *know* what you were trying to do. You were trying to help me without making me feel beholden to you. Because you're a good man, a good friend."

Did she think of him as *only* a friend?

"But if you are truly such a good man," she continued, "then you need to learn to take help and godly counsel as well as give it. If you don't trust me enough to share your worries, then talk to Ben or the preacher or Will." She spun on her heels and headed back toward the cottage.

As he followed in the gathering dusk, Cam let her words roll around in his mind, testing them for soundness. Could she be right?

Then the image of Vera McCauley's grief-twisted face screaming up at him blotted out everything else and Cam shuddered. Never again. The only way to prevent a repeat of the tragedy was to go on as he had before.

He stared at Nora walking away from him and ached for what might have been.

Then his lips twisted in a self-mocking smile. Whatever else had happened out here this evening, he'd succeeded in making her forget her own pain, if just for the moment.

Chapter Twenty-One

For Nora, the next three weeks passed both quickly and slowly at the same time. It felt almost as if her whole world were changing yet again and there wasn't anything she could do to stop it. She wasn't even sure if she *should* stop it.

The closeness that had developed between herself and Cameron was gone, replaced by the kind of casual friendship one had for a likable acquaintance. They talked every day, ate most of their meals together and he continued to drive her home every evening. And as for those evenings, there was no "taking turns" to stand guard over Mollie. Cam seemed to be a permanent resident of the new room at the cottage.

But there was no casual chatting in the doorway of the kitchen, no accidental brushing of hands and no repeat of that walk on the beach together. And the more time that passed, the less likely it seemed that they would be able to go back to what they'd had before.

Nora felt bereft, as if she'd lost something very special. Had this been her fault? Should she not have pushed him so hard? How could she help him if he wouldn't let her get close anymore?

But romance was definitely in the air for one of the lawmen. Ben finally proposed to Esther and the two declared their intention to get married in a few short weeks. Ben turned in his resignation at the same time, announcing that he and Esther planned to do some traveling after they got married.

Nora was tickled pink for them. She could see the joy in both of their faces and was happy that two such giving, generous people had found each other in this autumn of their lives. God's timing was truly perfect.

Gavin, too, was pleased by the announcement, but Nora knew it was for entirely different reasons. He was pleased, of course, that his friend had found happiness. But with Ben's retirement, Gavin was no longer just a deputy in training but was now Cam's right-hand man. And it also meant he would be able to move into Ben's place once Ben and Esther tied the knot. He seemed understandably thrilled that he'd soon be able to give up sleeping in a jail cell.

On the other hand, Nora's bakery business continued to grow beyond anything she had imagined. Now that Mollie was handling most of the cleaning Cam had hired her for, Nora had more time for baking, and the townsfolk were buying everything she could produce. She had learned to make miniature pies, and those, as well as her cookies, were big hits with the workers over at the chocolate mill. Her current goal was to save enough money to buy a second stove.

Things with Mollie were going very well, also. The girl was proving herself to be as good as her word. She tackled every job assigned to her and did it conscientiously. She took instruction from Nora and Agnes on how to sew and glowed with pride when she completed the work on her first dress. She even used the leftover scraps to make a little bonnet for Grace, utilizing her embroidery skills to add pretty touches to the finished project. On Sundays Mollie accompanied Nora and the Coulters to church services and was appropriately demure and teachable. She was beginning to win over many of the townsfolk.

Even Gavin, who remained intractable when she was under his watch, looked on her with something approaching approval when he thought no one was watching.

But the biggest change in Mollie, from Nora's perspective at any rate, was how comfortable she was becoming with Grace. Nora continued to care for Grace during the day, but in the evening, when they were back at the cottage, she turned over more and more of the responsibility for Grace's care to Mollie.

Nora tried to stay optimistic. She had grown fond of Mollie. Perhaps, if the girl wanted to settle down permanently here in Faith Glen after her debts were paid, and live at the cottage with Nora, then they really could both have a hand in raising the little girl.

When Maeve and Flynn's house was finally completed, the extended family members were all invited to take the grand tour of the place. The couple was planning a larger gathering the next day, an open house for the whole town to get to know their new doctor, but first Maeve had declared she wanted a "family only" gathering.

Nora looked around when she arrived, surprised at what a crowd her "extended family" now included.

Bridget and Will were there of course, along with their two children and Esther. And now that Esther was an engaged woman, it also included Ben. Nora herself had brought Grace, of course. Agnes and James had come, as well, as had Mollie, who was now like a niece to her. And because Mollie came, Gavin felt the need to be there, as well, to "keep an eye on her."

The last person to show up, to her surprise, was Cam. Why was he here? Did he consider himself part of the family?

But Maeve stepped forward and welcomed him literally with open arms. "Sheriff, I'm so glad you accepted my invitation. The party wouldn't be complete without you."

So perhaps she had misunderstood what Maeve meant by "family only."

"Now that everyone is here," Maeve announced, "I'd like to show you through our new home."

The home was indeed beautiful. Spacious and elegantly furnished, there were six bedchambers, a large dining room, a study, a library, a visitors parlor, a private parlor and a music room. There was even a bathing room furnished with the latest and most luxurious of fixtures.

When the inside tour was complete, Flynn and Maeve led them through wide glass doors out of the music room and onto an elegant stone terrace. They all took positions along the low stone wall that edged it, admiring the view that encompassed a gracefully sloping lawn, well-manicured gardens and a large pond.

"You picked your home site well," Will remarked.

"Thank you." Flynn gave Maeve's hand a squeeze. "My wife wanted lots of green to look at. I don't think she cared much for Boston."

"You know I'm content wherever I am as long as you're there," Maeve answered. Then she gave an impish grin. "But I do admit to liking this home better than the one we left behind in Boston."

Then Flynn spread his arms wide. "We hope you will enjoy yourselves. Our home is completely open to you. Walk around the place, inside or out, to your heart's content. There's a croquet set on the lawn for any of you who might be interested in playing and a chess set in the study. The cook is preparing a nice meal of baked fish and roast leg of lamb. We'll eat here on the terrace in about an hour."

The group drifted apart in very short order. Will challenged Flynn to a game of chess. Maeve and Bridget, along with Gavin and Mollie, headed for the croquet set. Caleb and Olivia followed behind with cries of "can I play, too?" Esther moved inside and sat at the piano. Ben stood beside her, ready to turn the pages of her music, and James and Agnes sat nearby, ready to be entertained. Within minutes, the lovely strains of a waltz floated through the open doorway.

Nora was content to sit on one of the terrace benches and hold Grace as she watched her sisters. She smiled when she saw Maeve and Bridget each take one of the twins and let them "help" hit the croquet ball with the mallets.

"Your sister has a beautiful home."

Startled at the sound of Cam's voice so close, Nora looked up just as he took a seat on the other end of her bench. "Yes, it is," she agreed.

"It gives your other sister's home some competition for the largest house in town."

Nora smiled. "I'm quite sure Maeve and Bridget don't

feel any sort of competition on the matter." Now their husbands might be a different matter, but there was no need to voice *that* thought.

"And you?" he asked. "Do you wish you had a big fine house like your sisters have?"

"I'm quite content with my cottage." Nora meant that with all her heart. "I have no use for six bedrooms, I can't play any instruments so a music room would be useless and I have no books so I have no need for a library."

"Isn't there anything you would change?"

I'd like a large family to fill it. But she couldn't say that aloud. Instead she gave an answer that she knew he would appreciate. "A larger kitchen with two ovens would be nice."

He smiled. "I hear your baking business is doing really well."

Nora nodded, wondering why he'd sat down beside her. It was the first time he'd deliberately sought her out since that evening on the beach. Was he trying to make amends? Or was he merely at loose ends?

They sat in a not uncomfortable silence for a while, until Maeve and Bridget climbed the steps to the terrace, arms linked, smiles on their faces. Nora felt a momentary twinge of jealousy as she recognized they had a common bond that she lacked. But she was able to release it without a qualm a second later.

"Game through already?" she asked when they drew close.

Bridget laughed. "Caleb and Olivia got tired of it. Caleb decided he'd prefer to see if there were any turtles around the pond, and Olivia refused to be left behind. Mollie offered to keep an eye on them."

Maeve laughed. "And Gavin is keeping an eye on Mollie." Then she held out her hands toward Grace. "May I?"

Nora reluctantly handed the baby off. She watched her youngest sister's face as she cooed down at the infant and saw a banked longing there. She guessed it wouldn't be long before Maeve and Flynn announced they were starting a family of their own.

Feeling suddenly restless, Nora stood and moved across the terrace to lean against the stone wall. She could feel the heat from the sun-warmed stones through her dress, but it was more soothing than uncomfortable.

Less than three months ago she had been desperate, destitute and uncertain of her future. Today she had a comfortable, snug home that no one could ever evict her from, lots of new friends who would drop everything to help her and a baby who'd touched her heart deeply. Also she was well on her way to having a thriving business of her own.

So why couldn't she be content?

Father above, I know I'm being impatient and prideful, but I'm trying to do better. I know I should be content with whatever lot in life is mine, but I also know that You want us to come to You with our longings. So I'm coming to You with mine. Please—

Cam joined her at the wall and rested his elbows next to hers. But before he could say anything, a child's scream rent the air. In a flash Cam was gone from her side and sprinting across the lawn. Nora lifted her skirts and was right behind him. What had happened?

Oh, dear Jesus, I'm sorry for my selfish prayer of a moment ago. Just let the children be okay.

She arrived at the pond a few heartbeats behind Cam. To her relief, both of the children were safely on the bank, though Caleb was soaking wet, and both he and Olivia were crying.

But Gavin and Mollie were in the pond, and Mollie seemed to be supporting an unconscious Gavin. Before she'd fully registered that fact, Cam had waded into the pond with them and lifted Gavin in his arms to carry him out. Concerned for Gavin, Nora tried to put aside her worries while she comforted Olivia and Caleb, and made certain they stayed safely away from the water.

Bridget came up behind her, breathless from running, and obviously concerned for her stepchildren.

"They're okay," Nora quickly assured her. "I think they just got a scare." She left Bridget to attend to the children and stepped forward to help Mollie out of the water, while Cam placed Gavin on the grass, well away from the edge of the pond.

"Is he going to be okay?" Nora asked, concerned by the fact that the boy hadn't yet opened his eyes.

Cam met her gaze without answering, his expression reflecting his own worry.

By this time, Maeve, Flynn and Will had also joined them, and Flynn had his medical bag at the ready. Flynn knelt down beside the much-too-still deputy and asked the others to give him some room. "Someone tell me what happened," he commanded in his strongest no-nonsense physician's voice.

It was Mollie who answered. "He slipped and fell backward into the water," she said, worry coloring her voice. "I think he must have hit his head on something because he sort of groaned and then went still." She wrung her hands, oblivious to the state of her own clothing. "I waded in and held his head up out of the water until Sheriff Long came, but I didn't know how else to help him."

"You did just as you should," Flynn reassured her. He gingerly felt along Gavin's scalp and suddenly the boy groaned and finally stirred. His eyes fluttered open and he looked around at them as if not quite certain what was going on. "What happened?"

"You took a fall and went in the water," Flynn said. "Now hold still while I examine you." His hands were busy, exploring Gavin's head and neck with practiced, efficient movements. "Tell me how you feel. Where does it hurt?"

Gavin grimaced. "My head feels like it's been hit with one of those croquet mallets, I'm soaking wet and I have water in my boots, but other than that I'm okay."

Flynn slid his hand under Gavin's back. "Can you sit up?"

"I think so." Gavin put word to action and in moments was sitting up and answering Flynn's questions in an intelligible manner. From his responses, it was obvious his confidence and sense of humor had survived intact.

Now that the concern for Gavin had abated, Mollie turned to face Bridget. "I'm so sorry, Mrs. Black. This is all my fault. I know I was supposed to be watching your little boy and girl, but I only took my eyes off Caleb for a minute."

"Tell us what happened." There was a hardness in Will's voice that commanded attention. He had stooped down to check on his children but this in no way diminished his presence.

Nora wondered if Mollie was about to face the considerable force of a father's anger. Instinctively she moved closer to the girl to lend her moral support.

But Mollie, obviously distraught over what had happened, kept her attention focused on Will and Bridget. "The ribbons on Olivia's shoe came undone and I stooped down to tie them up again because I didn't want her to trip on them. I told Caleb to stay close, but he saw a lizard and went chasing after it before I could stop him. He tripped and fell into the pond." She glanced toward the deputy. "Gavin was lightning quick, though—he went right in and plucked Caleb out. But then *he* slipped on the wet bank and fell backward." Mollie pushed her hair off her forehead. "I made sure both children stayed sitting down away from the pond while I was helping Gavin." She took a deep breath. "Like I said, this was all my fault, I should have been watching more closely. I can only say again how deeply sorry I am."

Nora's heart warmed with pride for Mollie. Yes, a near disaster had happened under her watch, but children had a way of slipping past even the most watchful of caretakers. The important thing was, Mollie had taken responsibility for her actions, had kept her wits about her when it counted and hadn't tried to run away. The girl had definitely come a long way in the past few weeks.

"It wasn't her fault." Gavin stared past Flynn to Will and Bridget. "She *was* watching the twins real close like she said. And Caleb wasn't in any real danger. The pond only comes up to his waist on this end."

Caleb threw his arms around his father. "I'm sorry I didn't mind Miss Mollie, Papa. Please don't be angry."

Will's face softened as he stroked his little boy's head. "I'm not angry, Caleb." He glanced Mollie's way. "Not at anyone."

Then he looked back at Caleb, tilting the boy's head up to meet his gaze. "But now you see what can happen when you don't mind what you're told. You must promise me you will do better in the future."

The little boy nodded contritely. "Oh, I will, Papa." Then he qualified his promise. "At least I will *try.*"

Nora hid a smile at the toddler's innocent honesty.

Flynn closed his bag, reclaiming everyone's attention. "I don't think Gavin has a concussion but he's going to have a whale of a headache for the rest of the day. Just to be safe, someone should keep a close eye on him for the next twenty-four hours." He turned to Gavin. "You shouldn't make any sudden, jarring movements or do any heavy lifting for the next few days. And if you have any dizzy spells you come back to see me right away. Understand?"

Gavin started to nod then winced and thought better of it. "Yes, sir."

Flynn stood and turned to Mollie. "It's a good thing you acted so promptly, young lady. You most likely saved Gavin from drowning."

Gavin looked at Mollie, a new appreciation gleaming in his eyes. "Seems I owe you my life."

Mollie blushed.

Nora wondered, was she embarrassed by being the center of everyone's attention? Or was it just Gavin's approving smile that put the pink in her cheeks?

Will rose and moved to help Flynn stand Gavin up, thanking the boy for rescuing Caleb from his dunking. As everyone began to make their way back toward the house, Nora looked around for Cam. She finally spotted him, standing with his back to the trunk of a nearby oak tree.

When had he moved away from them? More importantly, *why* had he moved away from them? She saw the strained look on his face, the clenched fists at his sides and headed his way without further hesitation.

She stopped in front of him and it seemed to take a moment for him to register her presence. Even then he didn't meet her gaze directly.

She said the first thing that popped into her head. "You should change into some dry clothes."

His lips barely curved as he smiled. "I will in a minute."

"Is something the matter?"

"I know how she feels." His voice was hoarse, ragged.

Something was definitely the matter. "What do you mean?"

"I know how Mollie feels. The awful feeling of things going out of control caused by one moment of inattention, the helplessness to turn back time and fix it."

There was an underlying meaning to his words that she wanted desperately to understand. "But everything turned out okay."

His gaze locked on hers and he seemed to really see her for the first time since he'd started talking. "Yes. This time it did."

"Cam, does this have something to do with your own troubles?" She held her breath, wondering if he would push her away again.

He held his peace for a long moment and she braced herself for the forthcoming rebuff. But then he let out a long breath and nodded. "You're right. You deserve the whole story. And then you'll finally understand." He muttered something under his breath that sounded suspiciously like "then it'll be over."

"I'm listening." Nora's heart pounded in her chest,

sending her pulse scurrying through her veins. She sensed that everything between them would change after this. And she wasn't certain she would like where it went.

Cam indicated they should walk and Nora fell into step beside him, following the edge of the pond. "After my mother died," he began, "and I left my father's house, I was on my own for a while. I worked in one of the factories in Boston, earning just enough to keep myself fed. One of the ways I survived was by finding a second job. When I wasn't working in the factory, I helped a lady I'd met there by watching her little boy in the evenings when she went out to work *her* second job. She didn't have very much, so she couldn't pay me, but she let me sleep in her apartment so I had a roof over my head."

Nora's gut clenched in sympathy for the harsh childhood he'd had. It was a wonder he'd grown into such a good, even-tempered man.

"The apartment she had was just a tiny garret room in a four-story tenement, but it was better than sleeping on the street. Her little boy, Tommy, was three years old— just about Caleb's age. I didn't mind watching him—he was a sweet kid, full of curiosity and energy. After a while, it was almost like having a little brother."

She smiled, picturing what a great big brother he would have made to such a child.

Cam raked a shaky hand through his hair and she knew he was getting close to the difficult part of his story. "But then one hot July evening a moth flew in the open window and Tommy tried to catch it. I didn't realize what was happening until it was too late. Tommy followed that moth right out of that fourth-story window."

Nora couldn't stop the gasp that sprang from her lips and her hand flew to her throat. "Oh, Cam, how awful."

He didn't seem to hear her, his gaze was focused on something in the far distance. "I raced down the stairs, hoping, praying that somehow there'd been something there to cushion his fall, that he'd be okay."

She knew instinctively that that had not been the case.

"His mother found him before I did. She was kneeling on that grimy sidewalk, holding the broken, bloody body of her only child." He swallowed hard. "When she saw me she started screaming, telling me it was all my fault, that I had killed her baby."

Nora grabbed his hand and squeezed it, the need to touch him, to console him, overwhelming her. "Oh, Cam, she had to have been out of her mind with grief. But no matter what she said, it *wasn't* your fault."

"Tommy died while under my care, because I didn't watch him closely enough." His face hardened. "Don't you understand? My dad was a mean drunk and a miserable human being, but as far as I know, he was never responsible for anyone's death." He grimaced. "I can't say the same about me."

What a terrible burden he'd carried all these years. "You were just a boy—"

His eyes blazed at her, but she knew his anger was all directed inward. "Don't try to sugarcoat this, Nora. I was twelve years old. Old enough to be on my own, old enough to hold down a man's job and old enough to know exactly what my responsibilities to Tommy and his mother were."

He pulled his hand out of her grasp. "Now, if you'll excuse me, I think it's time I changed out of these wet clothes. Give my regrets to your sister and Dr. Gallagher. I'll see you at your place this evening."

And with that he marched off toward the town square without so much as a backward glance.

Chapter Twenty-Two

Nora took her time returning to the house. She ached for Cam, for the lonely, guilt-ridden boy he'd been, for the torments that still haunted him as a man. So much about him was clearer now. And so much had become clearer about her own feelings for him.

Quite simply, she loved him. She loved his courage and his honesty, his generous spirit and his ability to feel the pain of others. She loved his stubborn determination, even when it was misdirected, and his maddening tendency to hold himself to a higher standard than those around him. And she loved the quiet, unobtrusive way he had of helping others while allowing them to maintain their dignity.

For good or ill, she was totally, achingly, deeply in love with Sheriff Cameron Long. She wasn't nearly as certain how he felt about her.

But one thing was certain, no matter how long it took, and no matter how much he rebuffed her efforts, she would make it her mission to help him see his own character.

She climbed the shallow stairs to the terrace to find

everyone gathered there, including Gavin, who now seemed to be wearing some of Flynn's clothes. A quick glance Mollie's way showed her to be wearing one of Maeve's dresses. It seemed the Gallaghers went the extra mile when it came to the comfort of their guests.

Nora let everyone know about Cam's departure, giving his need to change clothes as an excuse. If anyone thought it odd for him to leave without saying goodbye to his hosts, they didn't say anything.

Later, as they sat around the outdoor table enjoying their meal, Maeve turned to Gavin. "I have a surprise for you. Your brothers will be at the open house tomorrow."

Gavin's face split in a wide grin. "Sean and Emmett? That's terrific. It seems like forever since I saw them."

"You have brothers?" Mollie asked from her seat between Gavin and Nora.

"Yep. In fact they were the two boys who spotted you that day you nearly ran me over with the sheriff's horse out at Miss Nora's place."

"Well, glory be." Mollie smiled wistfully. "I always wished I'd had siblings. Where have they been staying?"

"In Boston. A woman we met on the ship coming over here took us all under her wing and she's been taking care of my brothers since we got here."

"That's right," Maeve interjected. "Mrs. Fitzwilliam and the boys plan to stay overnight with us so you'll be able to have a nice long visit."

"Mrs. Fitzwilliam!" Mollie popped up from her seat and Nora saw her face drain of color. "Mrs. *Elizabeth* Fitzwilliam?"

"Why yes, dear." Maeve stared at Mollie in concern. "Do you know her?"

Mollie nodded and sank back into her seat as if afraid her legs would buckle. "She's my grandmother."

"Your grandmother!" The three sisters stared at each other, starting to put the pieces of the puzzle together.

Nora felt excitement bubble up inside her at the realization of what this meant. God's ways really were mysterious—and magnificent.

Gavin, however, still didn't seem convinced. "But her granddaughter's name is Mary."

Mollie's nose wrinkled. "Mary is my real name, but I go by Mollie—it's what my parents always called me. But grandmother never would. She said Mollie was too common." She seemed truly distraught now. "That's how it always was between us. Please, she can't know I'm here."

Gavin stared at her earnestly. "But, Mollie, she's been looking for you. That's why she came to this country. She thought you were already here and wanted to find you and make certain you're okay."

"But, I thought—surely she was happy to see the last of me? We didn't get along at all and she was constantly berating me and telling me what a hoyden I was."

Gavin's brow came down. "I know she can be gruff and unbending at times, but in the short time me and my brothers have been with her I've seen below that to a very lonely and well-intentioned woman. She's been very good to all three of us, boys who were strangers to her before we boarded the *Annie McGee* and who were far from genteel. And she's mentioned you often, how she wishes the two of you had been able to get along better and how she hopes you haven't run into difficult situations."

Mollie didn't appear at all convinced. "She may have been nice to you, but she wasn't like that with me. If she's been looking for me, it's only because she wants to tell me again what a disappointment I am to her. I just couldn't bear to go through that again."

Nora touched Mollie's arm, claiming her attention. "Don't you think *everyone* deserves a second chance?" she asked gently.

Mollie stared at her for a long moment, then slowly nodded. "Of course." She swallowed hard. "I'll meet with her tomorrow."

"Good." It was Nora's turn to put on a brave face. "And you can introduce her to her new great-grand-daughter."

That evening, dusk was settling in before Cam showed up. He seemed to have recovered from his earlier dark mood and conversed easily with everyone around the supper table. He listened to the news about Mollie's relationship with Mrs. Fitzwilliam with suitable interest and even added his own reassurances to the still-nervous girl.

But Nora wasn't fooled. Without being able to put her finger on exactly what had changed, she sensed that he'd somehow distanced himself from the rest of them.

Or was it just from her?

Later, before Nora could pull him aside for a few words in private, he excused himself, declaring his intention to turn in early.

Nora watched him exit through the kitchen door, feeling her heart grow heavy. Was he so afraid to spend time alone with her? Or rather did he now resent her for having forced his story out of him?

Mollie was apparently unaware of any undercurrents. She was full of nervous, bubbly chatter that she seemed determined to share with Nora. She talked about the beautiful home the Gallaghers had built, declaring it to be finer than even her grandmother's. She talked about the incident at the pond, about how quick and gallant Gavin had been in his rescue of Caleb. And about how scared she'd been for both Caleb and Gavin. But mostly she talked about her nervousness around facing her grandmother the next day.

Nora, whose mind was still on Cam, only half followed the girl's conversation until she mentioned Grace's name. She immediately gave the girl her full attention. "I'm sorry, what was that?"

"I said, I know the transgression my grandmother will have the most trouble with is the fact that I had a baby out of wedlock. I just don't want her to look down her nose at Grace the way she did with me. Grace is the one good, innocent thing that came from all my wickedness."

Nora smiled reassuringly. "I don't think you need to worry about that." At least she hoped this was true. "She's been very fond of Grace, ever since she spent time with all of us on the *Annie McGee*. And look at how your grandmother has behaved toward the McCorkle brothers. It's obvious Gavin cares for her. Doesn't that speak of a softer side of her?"

Mollie shook her head. "That sure doesn't sound like the grandmother I left behind in Ireland. I half expect to see a stranger who happens to have the same name as my grandmother show up at the Gallaghers' tomorrow."

Nora gave Mollie a pointed half smile. "People change."

Mollie grimaced. "All the same, I'd prefer to see how she reacts to the rest of my story before I tell her about Grace."

"That's up to you, of course," Nora said diffidently, "but I think you'll be pleasantly surprised."

With a skeptical nod, Mollie excused herself and then bustled off to make certain her dress for tomorrow was immaculately clean and perfectly pressed.

Nora turned and stared at the door Cam had disappeared through earlier. Could he change, as well? Or at least his understanding of who he was?

Please, God, he's helped me in so many ways. Let me be the one to help him now.

The next morning Nora and Bridget waited with a very nervous Mollie in Maeve's parlor. It had been decided that Maeve, Flynn and Gavin would greet Mrs. Fitzwilliam and the two younger McCorkle brothers when they arrived. Then Flynn would take charge of Sean and Emmett, enticing them outdoors with the promise of fishing in the pond, while Gavin and Maeve accompanied Mrs. Fitzwilliam here to view a "little surprise."

The carriage had arrived a few minutes ago, so the moment of truth was upon them.

"I don't know if I can go through with this," Mollie said for what must be the twentieth time.

And just as she had the other nineteen times, Nora reassured her. "Of course you can. Just remain calm, trust in the Lord to guide you and let your grandmother see your heart." She patted Grace's back, glad the waiting would be over soon.

"You've both changed a great deal since you last saw each other," Bridget added. "She'll probably be every bit as nervous as you when she sees you."

Mollie looked skeptical, then her expression turned to panic as the door swung open.

Mrs. Fitzwilliam was the first to enter the room and her smile turned to shock as she recognized the girl standing before her. "Mary?" She took hold of Gavin's arm, as if she needed the added support. "Praise God, is that really you?"

"Yes, Grandmother, it's me."

"But how did you come to be here?" The matron allowed Gavin to lead her across the room. "I've been scouring all of Boston for you."

Mollie gave a tremulous smile. "It's a long story." She took her grandmother's hand and gave her a peck on the cheek. "But first, I must know why you've been looking for me."

"Why?" Mrs. Fitzwilliam appeared affronted by the question. "Because you're my granddaughter, of course. I was concerned for your well-being. And," she cleared her throat in an almost-apologetic manner, "I was afraid that there were some misunderstandings between us that we needed to clear up."

"Misunderstandings?" Mollie's lips pinched defensively, then she shot a look Nora's way and took a deep breath. "Please sit down so we can talk more comfortably."

Mollie had elicited promises from the Murphy sisters and Gavin that they not leave her alone with her grandmother, so it had been decided that Nora, along with Grace, would remain for as long as Mollie needed the support. Mrs. Fitzwilliam took a seat in a throne-like wingback chair while Nora and Mollie sat on a love seat across from her. Maeve, Bridget and Gavin quietly excused themselves.

Now that the initial surprise was over, Mrs. Fitzwilliam's

demeanor took on a hint of imperiousness. "So, tell me this long story that ends with you being here in Maeve's parlor."

Mollie reached for Nora's hand, and Nora gave it a comforting squeeze, adding a silent prayer that this would go well.

Then, taking a deep breath, Mollie launched into her story, telling her grandmother all of the unpleasant, unsavory details without excuses, leaving out only the parts that involved Grace.

Mrs. Fitzwilliam let her speak without interruption, but her expression grew sterner with each confession.

When Mollie finished, she sat back and there was a long moment of complete silence.

Nora could sense Mollie holding her breath, waiting for her grandmother's response. She gave the girl's hand another squeeze, not surprised to feel a slight trembling.

Finally Mrs. Fitzwilliam straightened. "It seems you were lucky that your foolish acts were discovered by such charitable people as Nora and Sheriff Long." The woman's tone was stern, disapproving.

Mollie nodded. "It is something I have thanked God for every day since the moment I was arrested." She took a long, steadying breath and lifted her chin. "I know that I was willful and disobedient, Grandmother, and that I've done terrible things. I'm truly sorry for all of that, and am trying to make reparations. But I will understand if you can't find it in your heart to forgive me."

Still Mrs. Fitzwilliam's frown did not soften.

Nora tried to keep her expression even, but she felt a surge of disappointment. *Please, God, don't let her pride get in the way of a second chance for her and her granddaughter. Show me a way to help them reconcile.*

Grace started fussing and Nora suddenly smiled.

"Mollie, I believe there is one more very important thing you have to say to your grandmother." She cut her eyes toward Grace purposefully.

Mollie's gaze shot to Nora and she gave a slight shake of her head. But Nora wouldn't allow her to drop her gaze and finally the girl nodded.

Taking a deep breath Mollie turned to Mrs. Fitzwilliam. "Grandmother," she said with obvious trepidation, "I would like you to meet your great-granddaughter, Grace Abigail Kerrigan Murphy."

Nora was both surprised and touched that Mollie had given the Murphy surname the place of honor in Grace's name.

Mrs. Fitzwilliam, for once, seemed struck speechless. Then she turned to Nora. "Is this true?"

Nora nodded. "Mollie was aboard the *Annie McGee* and had the baby there. Grace is her daughter all right." That admission was still difficult for her to make.

The woman's expression had softened at last, glowing with a dawning sense of wonder. She held out her arms. "May I hold her?"

"Of course." Nora stood and placed the baby in her arms.

"What a sweet little bairn you are." Mrs. Fitzwilliam's smile and tone were doting. There was no doubt Grace, at least, had won a place in her heart.

Then Mollie stood and took Grace from her, handing the baby back to Nora. "We still need to settle matters between us," Mollie said to her grandmother. "And until we do, I'd prefer we not expose Grace to our bickering."

Mrs. Fitzwilliam nodded. "I see you have a mother's love for her child." She folded her hands in her lap. "If I seemed harsh to you it is because I felt you were not being totally honest with me. Now that I understand what you were holding back, and why, I want to apologize."

There was a great deal more discussion between the two women—explanations, admissions and tears as well as assertions of changed outlooks, forbearance and deeper tolerance. But in the end, grandmother and granddaughter hugged with genuine affection and promises to start fresh.

"Now, my dear," Mrs. Fitzwilliam said happily. "You must pack up your and Grace's things so that you may return with me to Boston tomorrow."

The words hit Nora like a punch in the stomach and her hands tightened reflexively around Grace.

But Mollie was already shaking her head. "I can't do that. I belong here."

"Nonsense!" Mrs. Fitzwilliam sat up ramrod straight, some of her imperiousness returning. "You belong with your family."

"Grandmother, I still owe money to a lot of people here, debts I'm working to pay off." Mollie cast a shy glance Nora's way. "And I have friends here." She raised her head determinedly. "I'm sorry if that makes you unhappy, but this is where my life is now."

Mrs. Fitzwilliam lifted her chin. "I can take care of those debts for you. As for your friends—" she smiled magnanimously "—you can come back to visit in Faith Glen as often as you like. Just as Emmett and Sean come to visit Gavin."

"Those are *my* debts, not yours," Mollie insisted. "And I promised Sheriff Long and Nora that if they gave me the chance to make things right, I would work until I paid off every last one of them. It wouldn't be right for me to just let you snap your fingers and make them go away."

Nora wanted to cheer. Mollie was turning into a fine young woman, one with backbone and character.

Mrs. Fitzwilliam eyed the stubborn tilt of Mollie's chin. "You can't be so selfish as to think only of yourself. What about Grace?"

Some of Mollie's confidence seemed to crumble and she glanced quickly at Grace. "What do you mean?"

"If you stay here what will your daughter's future be like? A poor washerwoman's daughter with no prospects? On the other hand, think of the advantages I can provide for her. She can have the best care, pretty clothes and a proper education. She can mingle with the cream of society."

Mollie shook her head. "I'm sorry, but while being able to provide fine things would be wonderful, I don't think it is the most important thing in a child's upbringing." Then she squeezed Nora's hand. "Besides, it's not for me to say whether Grace stays or goes. She belongs with Nora."

"What foolishness is this?" Mrs. Fitzwilliam turned to Nora, her smile taking an almost cajoling aspect. "Nora, you know I've grown quite fond of you and your sisters. And of course it was generous beyond measure for you to take both Grace and Mary in and care for them as you have." She spread her hands. "But you must agree that a child's place is with her mother."

Nora started to say something, she wasn't quite sure what, when she felt Mollie's hand press firmly on hers.

"Grandmother," Mollie said with great deliberation, "this is between Nora and me and we will do whatever is best for Grace. It's not something I will allow you to interfere in."

260 A Baby Between Them

Mrs. Fitzwilliam sat back, obviously disconcerted by her granddaughter's forceful words.

Then Mollie softened. "Please, let's not allow this difference to put a wedge between us again. Can't we still be friends at least, even if I stay in Faith Glen?" Her hands trembled slightly. "Just like you and Gavin."

Mrs. Fitzwilliam rose from her chair and marched toward her granddaughter. Mollie stood, as well, and the two women faced each other, neither saying a word. Then the older woman reached over and gave Mollie a hug. "We can be more than friends, my dear. We are family."

Once her surprise receded, Mollie returned the hug with a fierce abandon. "Thank you, Grandmother."

Nora felt tears well in her eyes. She was so happy for the two of them that she felt ready to burst with it.

Thank You, Father Almighty, for letting me witness this beautiful reconciliation.

Mrs. Fitzwilliam stepped back and briskly brushed the wrinkles from her skirt. "I suppose I will need to follow Dr. Gallagher's example," she said severely, "and build a residence here in Faith Glen. What a great bother that will be."

Nora hid a smile. The woman was trying to sound disgruntled but it was obvious she was quite taken with the idea.

"Do you mean it?" Mollie asked.

The woman huffed. "I wouldn't say it if I didn't. It's the sensible thing to do. After all, there's nothing to keep me in Boston save the theater, and I can travel back when the fancy takes me. Sean and Emmett will, of course, be happy to be closer to their brother, and moving here is apparently the only way I'll be able to spend much time with my granddaughter and great-granddaughter."

She lifted her chin and turned toward the door. "Now, I must go at once and speak to Mr. Black and Dr. Gallagher to learn the best way to go about procuring land and constructing a home."

Once the reinvigorated woman had left the room, Nora turned to Mollie. "What you said about Grace—"

Mollie stopped her with an upraised palm. "I meant what I said. Both Grace and I owe our lives to you. That's a debt we can't easily repay." She smiled. "Now, shall we go see how your sisters' husbands are reacting to my grandmother's barrage of questions?"

Mollie took Grace from her as she made to rise, and Nora didn't try to take her back once she was standing. Instead she led the way from the room.

I'm not losing Grace, she told herself. *Mollie can continue to live with me and together we can raise Grace.*

She would just have to do her best to ignore the little niggling doubts that were creeping into her heart.

Chapter Twenty-Three

Nora leaned on her spade, wiping her forehead with the back of her hand. She glanced at her two sisters, working beside her in the cottage garden, Colleen's Garden, and smiled. Maeve had been living in Faith Glen for two weeks now and while the three sisters didn't get together every day, they made time to see each other two to three times a week.

Today they had decided to do some work in the garden.

The sound of children's laughter caught her attention and she glanced toward the nearby lawn where Caleb and Olivia were playing. Mollie was watching Grace this morning and Gavin was watching Mollie.

As for Cam, that distance she'd first noticed after he'd told her his terrible secret remained firmly in place. And the realization that she had no idea how to break through it was killing her.

"Nora."

At Bridget's hail, Nora brought her focus back to the present. "Yes?"

"You looked like you were miles away." Bridget's

voice had a teasing edge to it. "I was asking where we should plant this last rosebush."

"It's your garden," Maeve added, "so we need you to select the spot."

Her garden. That sounded good. She pointed to an area between the bench and the tree and walked toward it. "How about over there?"

Both sisters nodded approval and they strolled forward, tools in hand.

"It's really quite beautiful and peaceful out here," Bridget mused.

Nora agreed. The garden was now almost fully restored to its former glory. The weeds were gone, the beds were neatly planted and bordered, and the fall flowers were beginning to bloom. There was even a new stone birdbath in the center, a gift from Mrs. Fitzgerald.

As she speared the ground with her spade, Nora's thoughts turned back to Cam. To be honest, he was never far from her thoughts these days. She missed the easy camaraderie they'd shared, the way she'd been able to seek his counsel when she needed it, even his high-handed way of making decisions when he wanted to help her out in some way. If only—

Her spade struck something hard, sending a jarring wrench up her arm.

"Sounds like you hit another rock," Maeve said. "I hope it's not a big one this time."

Nora tapped it again. "I don't think it's a rock." The three sisters stared at each other for a minute, then eagerly went to work on the hole. Finally they unearthed a metal box about the size of a loaf of bread.

"Pull it out," Maeve urged.

Bridget peered into the hole. "Whatever can it be? Do you think Laird put it there?"

Remembering Agnes's story about the supposed treasure Laird O'Malley had buried out here, Nora didn't waste time on words. She got down on her knees and tugged the box out of the hole, her curiosity growing by the minute.

The sisters moved to the nearby bench and Nora placed the dirt-covered box on its seat. "There's no lock," she said after a quick check.

"Should we open it?" Maeve asked.

Bridget obviously had no reservations. "Of course we should open it, goose."

Maeve nudged Bridget away from the box. "You do it, Nora. You're the oldest and you found it."

With a nod, Nora reached down and tugged on the lid. It resisted at first, and then, with a low groaning of rusty hinges, it flipped open.

Inside was a bundle of letters, tied with a yellow ribbon, and addressed to Laird O'Malley. "That's Mother's handwriting," Nora whispered.

"Laird kept her letters." Romantically minded Bridget sighed. "But why would he bury them out here where he couldn't read them?"

"Perhaps he did it when he knew he was dying," Maeve offered. "So no one else would have them."

"Then perhaps we shouldn't read them." Nora closed the box. She wasn't entirely sure she wanted to know what her mother had said to this man who had loved her so deeply.

Bridget placed a hand on the lid. "But if he truly didn't want anyone to find these letters, wouldn't he have burned them? Perhaps he left them here, hoping his Colleen would come, or her descendents, and would see how much he still cared at the end."

She lifted the lid and handed them each a letter. "We *have* to read them, or his efforts would have been for nothing."

Nora slowly opened the one Bridget had handed her. It was short but eloquent, full of hope and promise. She glanced at the date penned in her mother's hand and breathed a sigh of relief. "This one was written before she married Da."

"Mine, as well," Maeve replied.

"This one, too," Bridget added.

Both of her sisters sounded as relieved as she felt. Nora thumbed through the remaining half-dozen letters. "All of them are." Then she paused over the last one. "Listen to this. It's dated just before Mother married Da." She began reading aloud to her sisters.

My dear sweet Laird,
I wanted to tell you this in person but your mother tells me you will be gone for some time. I have decided to marry Jack. I know that is not the answer you wanted, but I must follow my heart. He is a good man who loves me deeply and I know that we will be happy together.

While I will always have a special place in my heart for you, as we have discussed time and again, I cannot marry a man who does not share my love for Jesus. I wish you well, my darling, and pray you will find much happiness. I hope in time you will find your way to accepting the abundant joy

of what our Heavenly Father offers so that I will
see you again someday in heaven.
With much affection,
Colleen

Nora put the letter down and looked at her sisters, seeing the same tears glistening in their eyes that she felt in hers.

"So that was why she never married him," Bridget whispered.

"That poor man." Maeve swallowed. "I hope, in the end, he came to know Jesus."

"I think perhaps he did," Nora said slowly. "I saw his headstone in the churchyard. It had John 14:6 engraved on it."

Maeve nodded, quoting the familiar scripture. "Jesus saith unto him, I am the way, the truth, and the life: no man cometh unto the Father, but by me."

"Oh, I wish Mother could have known." Bridget's eyes were gleaming with unshed tears again. "That would have made her so happy."

"She knows now," Nora said softly. She set the letter back in the box and closed the lid. "I think we should put this right back where we found it. I can plant that bush a few feet to the left."

Bridget and Maeve both nodded agreement.

As they placed the box back in the hole and Nora began scooping dirt back on top, Bridget leaned against the handle of her hoe and looked around.

"This is so beautiful," she said. "Not just in the way it looks but in the sweet spirit that resides here. Mother would have loved it."

Nora nodded. "It's more than just that," she said. "*I*

love it here, and not only because it is the refuge we ran to when we were turned out back in Castleville. I love this garden. I love the new family I've found—both the ones you two married into and the Coulters. I love this town and its generous people who welcomed us so wonderfully."

And, whether he's willing to accept it or not, I love Cameron Long. But she didn't say that out loud.

The trio made quick work of planting the last rosebush then decided it was time to have a bit of light refreshment. As they headed back to the house, Maeve and Bridget paused to talk to the twins and admire the miniature structures they'd constructed of twigs and vines. Nora proceeded on to the house, mentally planning what she would serve her guests. When she stepped onto the back porch, however, she stopped short. Gavin and Mollie sat on the porch swing, and both were radiating happiness and cooing over Grace who lay gurgling happily in Mollie's lap.

It was the perfect picture of a happy family. And it broke a small piece of her heart.

Gavin spied her first and scrambled to his feet, his face flushing guiltily. "Miss Nora. Hello. I, uh, I was just…"

Mollie rose more gracefully and stood beside him, intertwining her hand with his. "Gavin just proposed to me," she said, her joy obvious. "And I accepted."

Chapter Twenty-Four

That afternoon, Nora sat on the same grassy dune she and Cam had once shared, but today she shared it with Grace. The little girl lay on a blanket beside her, gurgling happily and whisking at the air with her hands and feet.

She smiled down at the child's vigorous play. Grace was getting so big. Soon she would be rolling over on her own and then later learning to crawl. There'd be no stopping her then.

Nora leaned back on her hands, listening to the seabirds and staring out over the ocean. So vast, so majestic, so timeless—a metaphor for God himself.

After a time, she smiled back down at Grace. "Thank you, little one, for coming into my life when you did, for adding sunshine and unconditional love and purpose to my world when I was struggling to find all three. You've given me a sweet taste of motherhood and a fathomless joy. I will always, *always* love you, no matter what."

The distant sound of footsteps intruded but she didn't look up. She didn't have to.

"I figured I'd find you out here." Cam plopped down beside her, sandwiching her between himself and Grace.

"I like the sound of the ocean waves."

"I heard Gavin proposed to Mollie."

Nora nodded. "Mollie is over the moon. And I'm very happy for them."

"You don't think it's too soon? It wasn't very long ago that he wanted me to lock her up."

Nora shrugged. "Who's to say how long it takes someone to fall in love?" She tried not to think of her own experience with romantic love. "It looks like there'll be two weddings this month." She hoped her tone was as light as she intended. "I assume Ben's wedding will come first so Gavin can have a place to move his bride into."

"That's the plan. Which means Mollie will be moving out of your house soon."

"Yes." She kept her eyes focused on the ocean, not trusting herself to meet his gaze just yet. "Which I guess also means there's no need for you to spend your nights out here anymore either." They both knew there'd been no need for quite some time.

She reached over and tickled Grace's toes, smiling when the baby laughed. "And Grace will be going with Mollie of course." Her traitorous lip betrayed her, trembling on the last word.

"Ah, Nora honey." He pulled her close against him and stroked her hair. She couldn't bring herself to pull away. "You know you don't have to do this."

"Yes, I do. Cam, it's okay, really." She rested a palm against his shirt, right over the spot that protected his heart. Her own pulse responded to the strong, warm beat beneath her hand.

He placed his own hand over hers, his gesture comforting, protective. And something else she didn't dare dwell on.

"I've made my peace with it," she assured him. "Mollie has turned into a fine young woman and Gavin will make a terrific father. You only have to see how he is with his brothers to know that." She forced a smile. "And they'll be right here in Faith Glen where I can watch Grace grow up and maybe be a part of her life."

Cam brushed the hair off Nora's face, wishing he could brush away her pain as easily. She was hurting inside, but, being Nora, she wouldn't let it defeat her. "She'll be lucky to have you in her life." As would anyone. "It's okay to cry if you want to," he told her. Though her tears would be like daggers to him. "I won't tell anyone."

"I'm going to miss her, of course, more than I can say. And Mollie, too, truth be told. But I think I understand now, something of what God has been doing with my life."

She always seemed to look for lessons in her circumstances. "What do you mean?"

"For a long time I was angry with Him for all the people He's taken from me. I wouldn't admit it at the time, but the anger was there just the same. But what I've learned these past few weeks, since Mollie came along, is that I should instead be grateful for the time He allowed me to have with those special people."

Cam ached for the hurt she'd felt, and admired her ability to find joy in it.

She pulled slightly away from him and met his gaze with eyes that shone with her passion for this lesson she'd learned. "Imagine, for three months, I had the privilege of getting to be a mother to the most beautiful baby in the world, got to keep her safe while He worked in her mother's life to bring her back to His side. That privilege could have been given to anyone else on that ship, but God put Grace in *my* hands." She paused, staring out over the ocean again. "Who am I to be angry that He didn't leave her with me longer?"

Cam looked into her face and saw how deeply she believed every word of what she was saying. Her faith was amazing and beautifully submissive—it both astounded and humbled him.

Then she surprised him yet again by moving out of his embrace and sitting up with her hands clasped together on her knees. "Now, enough on that subject. The matter of Grace is settled and while it may feel bittersweet now, we will both resolve to be happy at the outcome."

He nodded. "Yes, ma'am. So what shall we discuss? The weather? Mrs. Fitzwilliam's building plans?"

She cut him a prim look of disapproval for his levity. "Actually, I do have some things I want to say to you, and you *will* sit there and listen to me."

Uh-oh. That statement didn't bode well for him.

"But first I want to ask you a question and I want you to be totally honest, no matter what you think I *want* to hear, because this is important. Promise?"

Seeing her earnestness, he nodded. "Of course—I promise."

"Do you think it's a mistake to hand Grace over to Mollie? Do you think that Mollie will be a bad mother, that she might not take proper care of Grace once she's on her own with her?"

She'd seemed so sure of her decision a moment ago. Was she having second thoughts now? Or was she just trying to get a different perspective? Well, she'd asked him to be honest. "No, of course I don't think she'll be a bad mother. Mollie loves Grace, it's as obvious as the sun in the sky. She'll put Grace's well-being above her own and no one could take better care of her." He tapped her nose. "Except you."

Nora gave him an approving smile. "So, just because her momentary inattention allowed that accident down by the pond, she shouldn't cut herself off from ever taking care of children again?"

He stiffened. Too late he realized where she was going. "What happened at the Gallaghers' is not the same as what happened all those years ago when I was supposed to be watching Tommy."

Her gaze never left his. "It's not?"

"No." Maybe if he was blunt enough she would drop the subject. "For one thing, nobody died."

To his surprise, she didn't back down. "But that's no thanks to Mollie. Her lapse of attention could quite easily have resulted in a much more tragic outcome. Maybe next time it will."

He clamped his lips shut, wanting to put an end to this discussion. He'd come out here to comfort her, not dredge his past up again.

But apparently Nora wasn't finished with him. "And what about me?" she asked. "My lapse had much more serious consequences. Maybe *I* shouldn't be left alone with a child again."

Now she was being just plain ridiculous. "Nora, you've been the most careful mother I have ever come across."

She shook her head and he saw the sadness creep into her eyes. "Have you already forgotten that it was my fault Grace was kidnapped?" She reached down to let Grace grab hold of her finger. "I left this sweet, helpless babe, who depended on me to keep her safe, all alone in the kitchen, knowing the outside door was wide open. Thanks to my negligence, a stranger walked right into my house and stole my baby. We got her back eventually, but only because the kidnapper returned her. If Mollie had decided to leave town with her, we might have never seen Grace again, might never have known what became of her."

She shuddered and Cam felt as if he'd been punched in the gut.

Had she really blamed herself for what happened? He should have realized what she was going through and reassured her. "Nora, honey, you couldn't have anticipated such a thing. And you were just in the next room. You can't be with her every second. No one blames you for what happened."

She raised a brow and he suddenly remembered the point she was trying to make.

"Exactly." She poked him in the chest. "So, if things had turned out differently, if we'd never seen Grace again, should I have vowed never to take on responsibility for a child ever again, have cut myself off from the possibility of having a family of my own someday?"

Everything inside him protested that vision. Nora was made to be a mother. She had so much love to give, so much warmth to share. To let that one lapse ruin her future was unthinkable. Especially since he knew that what she saw as a lapse would make her even more diligent in the future.

His own situation was entirely different.

Wasn't it?

Nora apparently tired of waiting for him to answer her. "You told me the dark secret from your past and put it forth as the reason why you will never let yourself be responsible for a child again. Now I'm going to explain to you why you are absolutely, positively, completely wrong in your thinking."

She stared earnestly into his eyes. "What happened was a tragic accident, but an accident nonetheless. I know you like to think you are somehow more capable of looking out for others than most people and so should be held to a higher standard than anyone else, but that kind of thinking is not only misguided, it's just plain prideful. And pride is a sin." Her lips curved slightly. "I should know."

He couldn't share her smile.

"You care about people," she continued. "You care deeply. It's why you became a sheriff, and why you're so good at it. It's why you keep a close eye on trouble-makers and an even closer eye on folks like the Coulters who have no one else to care for them."

He tried to say something but she wasn't finished.

"When Grace was taken—" she shivered "—you were the first one out looking for her each day and the last one to come back in every evening. There was no doubt that you cared very deeply about Grace and would have been as devastated as I if we hadn't found her." She narrowed her eyes as if in accusation. "That's not a man who should think twice about the kind of father he would make."

She reached down and lifted Grace, blanket and all, then stood over him with her precious burden.

"God will forgive you for what happened if you ask Him to. You just need to learn to forgive yourself."

He saw some strong emotion flicker in her expression that he was afraid to identify.

"Do something for me," she said. "Sit here awhile, stare out at God's marvelous creation and really think about what I've said." Then she turned and walked along the beach, back toward the cottage.

Cam, his heart weighted down by the sadness in her eyes, turned and stared out over the ocean as she'd requested.

He plucked a handful of rocks from the ground beside him and began flinging them, one at a time, toward the water.

Nora was a sweet, tender, generous person. She was facing the end of her role as mother to Grace and she was doing it with dignity and grace despite her heartache.

Yet in the midst of this turmoil, she had taken time to try to heal his hurts, as well. And it hadn't been a half-hearted attempt. His lips curved in a tender smile as he thought about her passionate defense of him.

He only wished things could be as simple as she tried to make them sound.

He flung one last rock and then leaned back, letting the peace of his surroundings flow over him. Despite his resolve to the contrary, her words kept coming back to him, over and over.

She'd said his problem was pride, but this didn't feel like pride. On the other hand, how did he feel about her own so-called negligence that had allowed Grace to be kidnapped? If that had been him, he knew that he'd never have forgiven himself, would have seen it as further proof of his failings. Yet it had never once occurred to him to blame Nora for her role in allowing Grace to be taken. And it still didn't. What she did was perfectly innocent, perfectly reasonable given the situation.

Was this "different standard," as she called it, that he held himself to truly an outgrowth of the worst kind of pride?

For the first time since it had happened, he willingly recalled the events of that long-ago night. He felt again the stifling heat of that garret room, felt again the bone-deep weariness he experienced from working all day in the factory and trying to keep himself awake at night to watch Tommy. He crossed the room to get a dipper of tepid water from the bucket on the table. Tommy's laughter made him smile and he turned just in time to see the boy run to catch the moth. He could still feel the splash of the water as the dipper fell from his hands, could hear his voice yelling for Tommy to stop, could still feel the pounding of his pulse as he tried to get across the room in time. But Tommy was too enthralled to listen and Cam's own reflexes were too slow for him to stop what was happening.

Cam shook his head, trying to push the nightmare away, but his brain refused to let him. And suddenly he pictured Nora in that same scene. He stood in the corner of the room and watched as she took his place. He saw her face twist in horror and grief as the final scene played out and what he felt for her was compassion and a soul-deep desire to comfort her and wipe away her tears. There was no trace of condemnation or recrimination for her.

He pictured that twelve-year-old boy as someone else and his perception of what had happened shifted, changed. No one could be everywhere at once. Sometimes terrible things happened without being anyone's fault.

Tommy's death had been horrifying and tragic, yes. But it had also been an accident. He would carry the painful memory of what had happened with him all of his

life, he knew that. And that was as it should be. It was the
burden he had to bear for his part in what had happened.

But that memory had lost its power over him. It was no
longer a poison that was killing any chance he had at true
joy. It had become more of a warning beacon, a reminder
of what could happen when he dropped his vigilance.

Cam closed his eyes and offered up a silent prayer
of thanksgiving. He felt freer, lighter than he had in a
very long time.

Then he stood and headed down the beach. There was
something very important that he had to do.

Chapter Twenty-Five

Nora stepped off the back porch and headed for the garden. Mollie was giving Grace her bottle and Nora was feeling restless. Had she done the right thing by confronting Cam the way she had? It was so hard to know how much to push and how much to let him work out on his own.

But she'd never been the patient type.

She paused in front of the bench, running a hand across the now smooth, sturdy arm of the thing. Cam had put so much of himself into this place. She could barely look around without seeing evidence of his handiwork.

"Hello again."

Nora whirled around to see Cam watching her, a strangely intense light in his eyes. She swallowed, trying to moisten her suddenly dry throat. "You seem to have made it your mission to come upon me unawares today."

"I did as you asked."

"Oh?" Something about the way he was looking at her was making her pulse flutter.

"Yes." His lips curved in a crooked half smile. "I find it's often in my best interest to heed your advice."

She smiled back at him, wondering at his strange mood.

"Oh, yes. I looked out over the ocean and thought about all your nonsense talk of sinful pride and different standards, and I finally came to one very important conclusion."

"What was that?" She was finding it difficult to breathe normally.

He stepped forward and took her hands in his. "That it was not nonsense talk after all."

She searched his face, trying to discern his meaning. Could he really have taken her words to heart?

"I'm ready to put it behind me now. And I have you to thank for that."

She squeezed his hands, heart swelling with happiness for him. "Oh, Cam, that's wonderful. But all I did was show you the truth that was already in front of you."

"You did so much more than that. You are amazing and generous and beautiful. And I love you."

Her heart actually stuttered at those words. But she didn't hesitate. "Oh, Cam, I love you, too. I have for quite some time."

He led her to the bench and sat down next to her. "I want to build a life with you, Nora honey. I can't give you a big fine house like Will and Flynn gave your sisters, but I can love you with every fiber of my being, every day of my life. Say you'll marry me and I promise to do my best to see that you never have cause to regret it."

She loved it when he called her "Nora honey" in that tender way he seemed to reserve just for her. "Oh, Cam, I don't need a big house, I just need you by my side. Yes, yes, yes, I'll marry you and count myself blessed to do it."

Cam pulled her into a fierce embrace. "Nora honey," he said, his voice low and husky, "unless you have any serious objections, I'm going to give you the kiss I've wanted to give you since you first came into my life and this time I intend to do it proper."

He'd wanted to kiss her even then? She smiled and raised her face. "I thought you'd never ask."

With a strangled laugh, Cam did just as he'd promised.

Epilogue

~~~~

Faith Glen, Massachusetts, June 1851

Nora and Cam stepped out on the ribbon-bedecked terrace at Mrs. Fitzwilliam's home. Nora's eyes immediately locked on the adorable toddler with the golden curls and sparkling blue eyes who was holding court at the far end of the terrace.

The little girl spotted Nora at about the same time and her face lit up. She lifted her arms and took a few shaky steps forward. "Na-wa!"

"Grace." Nora took a few quick steps, then halted when a familiar arm looped around her waist.

"Whoa there, Mrs. Long. No mad dashes for you, remember?"

She rolled her eyes as she turned to face her husband. "That was *not* a mad dash."

He tucked her hand on his arm. "No point taking any chances. Now, let's not keep Ladybug waiting."

Together they crossed the terrace at a much-too-sedate pace for Nora's liking. Finally reaching her target, she stooped to give Grace a hug. "Happy birthday, sweetheart. You're looking so pretty today."

Grace returned Nora's hug and gave her a loud, sloppy kiss. Then she turned to Mollie who was seated at her side, snatched something from her lap, and held it out to Nora. "Bee-bee"

Nora admired the rag doll. "Yes, baby. Very nice."

Grace giggled and snatched back her doll, then toddled over to Gavin, demanding he pick her up.

Before Nora could rise, she felt Cam's hand under her elbow. She allowed him to help her up, then put her fists on her hips. "Cam, you're hovering. Why don't you go join that group of men over there while I find Maeve and Bridget?"

"Maybe I should stay—"

"I want a word alone with my sisters," she said firmly.

He nodded reluctantly. "Of course. I know you've been fair to bursting to talk to them, but promise me you won't go haring off and that you'll be careful on the stairs."

Nora rolled her eyes again. If he was going to be like this for the next seven months it would drive her plumb crazy. Then again, it was nice to have someone who cared this much about her. More than nice. "I promise."

Cam dropped a lingering kiss on her cheek, then stepped back. "I'll be right over there with Will and Flynn if you need me."

She smiled. "I will always need you."

His eyes darkened at that and she laughed. "Now run on so I can find Maeve and Bridget."

But before she'd taken more than two steps, Mrs. Fitzwilliam found her. "Nora, I'm so glad you could come."

Nora smiled. The woman had softened considerably

over the past year. "Thanks for inviting me. Everything looks lovely."

"Goodness, we couldn't have Grace's party without her Aunt Nora. Oh, and that birthday cake you made for her is marvelous. Thank you for sending it."

"It was my pleasure."

Mrs. Fitzwilliam patted Nora's arm. "You just run along and enjoy yourself. I believe I saw your sisters strolling on the lawn."

"Thank you." Nora descended the terrace steps, stopping to greet a number of friends and neighbors, trying not to let her impatience show. Where *were* Maeve and Bridget?

She finally spotted them sitting on a stone bench in the formal garden. No doubt their current state had them tiring more easily then normal.

She moved toward them, reined into a walk by her promise to Cam.

"Nora." Bridget saw her first and started to get up.

Nora waved her back down. "Please don't get up on my account." To her amusement, Maeve didn't even attempt to stand.

She came to a halt in front of the bench and smiled down at them. Both sisters were glowing with health and happiness, and both sisters were very obviously with child. Maeve was due to deliver next month and Bridget two months later.

"We were wondering when you'd get here," Bridget said. "It's not like you to be late, especially when Grace is involved."

Nora hugged her secret close for a few more minutes. "Cam and I had something to take care of first."

Maeve sighed. "Can you believe it—Grace is one year old today."

Nora smiled fondly. "It seems like she's learned something new each time I see her."

"You know what this birthday means, don't you?" Bridget asked.

Nora nodded. "It's an anniversary of sorts for us, as well. One year ago today we were just setting out on our voyage to this country."

Maeve rubbed her very round tummy. "How could we have ever imagined what this past year would bring? New homes, wonderful husbands, loving families."

"Blessings beyond measure," Nora agreed. Then she clasped her hands in front of her. "I have a question for the two of you. Have your husbands been treating you with a ridiculous amount of extra care since you each found out you were going to have a baby?"

Bridget laughed. "Oh my goodness, yes. Will wanted to move us into a bedchamber on the first floor so I wouldn't have to climb the stairs."

Maeve shook her head. "My normally pragmatic husband has decided he will only take emergency cases from now until the time I deliver so that he can watch over me. I'm surprised he isn't here with us now." She shifted as if trying to get more comfortable. "I do believe every husband on the planet turns into a mother hen when his wife is expecting."

Bridget patted her little sister's hand. "True, but I find it can be quite nice to be so cherished." She laughed. "When it's not annoyingly smothering."

Nora smiled. "It's good to know that Cam is not the only one who is taking the news that way."

Maeve understood the implication of her words first

and let out a loud squeal. "Oh my goodness, Nora, you're expecting, too!"

"What!" Bridget did stand now. "Nora, why didn't you say something when you first walked up? When are you due?"

"We're thinking we'll have a Christmas baby."

She sat down next to Maeve, and Bridget sat beside her. Nora put an arm around both of her sisters and let the joy of the moment wash over her. "As I said, blessings beyond measure."

* * * * *

THE PROPER WIFE

And let us consider one another
to provoke unto love and to good works.
—*Hebrews* 10:24

To my dear friends Connie Cox and Amy Talley, who helped me brainstorm, provided critiques and generally listened to me moan when I got stuck or needed to talk through the sticky parts.

Chapter One

May 1893
Knotty Pine, Texas

He needed a wife and he needed one soon.

Eli Reynolds strode through town, ignoring the intermittent drizzle as he pondered his current situation. According to the workmen he'd hired, the renovations to his newly acquired home would be ready by the end of next week. Once that was done he and Penny would no longer have a legitimate reason to remain at the boardinghouse.

Which meant his time was running out.

Because no matter what the cost, he was determined to be married, or at least have wedding plans, before he moved himself and his nine-year-old half sister into that house. Mrs. Collins, the widow who ran the boardinghouse where he and Penny were staying, was doing a good job of watching over his sister for the time being. But leaving an impressionable young girl like Penny in the care of a housekeeper or governess every day while he went to his office at the bank was an unacceptable option for the long-term.

Trusting a servant with such a precious duty had already resulted in one tragedy. He wouldn't make such a costly mistake twice.

This business of finding a proper wife should have already been settled, *would have already been settled,* if he hadn't so badly misjudged his field of candidates. He thought he'd found the right woman in Myra Willows. She appeared intelligent, mature, of good character, competent in the domestic arts—all the characteristics he was looking for. He'd actually been on the point of declaring his intentions yesterday when he'd been pulled up short by a bit of gossip.

He'd overheard a couple of bank clerks speculating that Miss Willows might possibly be the person behind that ridiculous pseudonym of Temperance Trulove, the very woman who penned the ridiculous and highly melodramatic bit of drivel titled *The Amazing Adventures of Annabel Adams* for *The Weekly Gazette.*

Eli didn't quite credit that the rumor could be true— Miss Willows seemed much too reserved and sensible a female to indulge in such nonsense. But at this point he wasn't willing to risk being wrong, not with his sister's upbringing hanging in the balance.

So he'd been forced to regroup, to review the remaining names on his list and chose another bride.

Eli turned his collar up against the weather as a spurt of water fell on him from the eaves of the nearby storefront. What a day! He wasn't just damp, he was beat. Bone-deep, soul-achingly beat.

Truth to tell, the turn his life had taken two months ago, and the nonstop effort he'd put into building a new life for himself and Penny since then, was beginning to wear on him. But soon it would be done and he could relax a bit. Until then, he would continue pressing on toward his goal.

"Looks like you could use yourself a rain slicker." Sheriff Hammond lounged against the doorpost of his office, whittling on a stick.

Eli moved closer to the building to take advantage of the meager shelter from the shower. "A bit of rain never hurt anyone." He winced as he felt a trickle of water make its way down his back. "Then again, I may have to look into getting myself one of those slickers if this weather continues."

The sheriff grinned in sympathy. "Spring showers tend to be unpredictable in these parts." Then he went back to whittling. "How's Mrs. Collins's arm doing?"

The boardinghouse proprietress had fallen and hurt her arm about a week ago. She seemed to be bearing her injury well, but having her out of commission had put the entire boardinghouse in disarray. And the arrival of her friend, purportedly to 'help out', had only served to add to the problem rather than alleviate it. Sadie Lassiter had breezed in from whatever distant cattle ranch she called home with all the grace and finesse of a brown-eyed, auburn-haired dust devil.

He pulled his thoughts back to the sheriff's question. "The doctor says she should refrain from using it for another week or so. But she seems impatient to be back at work."

Sheriff Hammond nodded. "That's Cora Beth for you. The woman can't stand to sit idle." He tipped his hat back with the point of his blade. "How's Miss Lassiter working out?"

It would be ungentlemanly of him to speak his true

feelings on the matter. "She is trying," he temporized. "And I'm sure she's good company for Mrs. Collins."

Sheriff Hammond grinned. "As bad as all that, is she?"

Eli merely spread his hands.

"Ah well, Cora Beth's shoes would be hard for anyone to fill." He shaved another curl of wood from his stick. "By the way, mind giving Mrs. Collins a message for me?"

"Be glad to."

"Tell her I'm heading out to the Martins' place in the morning and I'll be happy to carry a food basket for the Ladies' Auxiliary if she still wants me to."

"Will do." Apparently part of the sheriff's duty in these parts was to periodically look in on the various families on the outlying farms and ranches.

With a wave, Eli moved along the wet sidewalk again, eager to reach the boardinghouse where he could dry out and get something filling to eat. Too bad it wouldn't be one of Mrs. Collins's always excellent meals. If he was lucky it would be more edible than the scorched roast Miss Lassiter had served last night.

Eli had barely taken a half dozen steps, however, when he found himself hailed again. One of the benefits—and hazards—of small town life he supposed.

Mrs. Danvers, who ran the mercantile with her husband, stood in the doorway of her store. Swallowing the urge to keep walking, he tipped his hat. "Good day, ma'am. Is there something I can help you with?"

"It's such a dreary day that I thought you might want to come in out of the weather for a bit." She gave him an ingratiating smile. "I'm sure Imogene would be happy to fix you a hot cup of tea while you dry off by the stove."

The woman would be better served to focus her matchmaking schemes elsewhere. Eli had scratched Imogene Danvers off his potential-bride-list early on. She was too timid, too much under her mother's thumb to provide the kind of oversight he wanted for his sister. And having an overbearing, meddlesome woman for a mother-in-law was not something he was inclined to look favorably on either. "That's very kind of you, but the weather doesn't show signs of letting up any time soon and I need to see to my sister."

A flicker of disappointment flashed in her eyes and then she rallied. "Such a thoughtful brother you are. Perhaps another time."

"Perhaps." He tipped his hat again and moved on.

And yet another reason for him to find a wife soon. He was well aware that his wealth and newcomer-to-the-area status had made him the target of every matchmaking momma and marriage-minded female in the area. Time to take himself off the market.

Which brought him back to making his selection. He'd given the matter careful consideration most of the day and had decided that the widow Collins was now the obvious choice. The only reason she hadn't been his first choice was the fact that she had three children of her own and a younger brother to raise. But while this meant Penny wouldn't have her undivided attention, perhaps it would be offset by the fact that Penny would have other children in the house to play with.

As for appearance, she wasn't an eye-catching beauty, but with her light brown hair, bright green eyes and ready smile there was a sweetness to her appearance that was quite pleasant.

Yes, this might work out for the best after all.

Eli finally reached the boardinghouse and sprinted up the steps, pausing under the shelter of the front porch roof to shed his wet hat and brush the drops of water from his coat.

After stomping his boots on the porch, he stepped inside and hung his hat on the hat tree in the entry. His attention was almost immediately caught by the sound of unruly giggles coming from the dining room.

Apparently the weather-confined children had found some sort of amusement indoors. There were five other youngsters besides Penny currently in residence here. Mrs. Collins's three girls, Audrey, Pippa and Lottie, and her young brother Danny were, of course, permanent residents.

The other child, Mrs. Collins's niece Viola, had moved in just last week. The child's parents were currently on a trip out of the country. Viola, it turns out, was also Miss Lassiter's niece since Miss Lassiter's brother Ry was married to Mrs. Collins's sister Josie. From what he could tell, that nebulous relationship was the only thing the two women had in common.

It seemed odd that a woman who professed to have grown up on a cattle ranch would be so inept at cooking and housework. Since Miss Lassiter's arrival, routines had gone out the window, the meals had been barely palatable and housework seemed to be handled with a less-than-impressive 'lick and a promise' approach.

About the best one could say for her in the way of domestic skills was that she had a way with children. In fact, his normally reticent sister had taken a keen liking to the flibbertigibbet of a woman. Then again, Miss Lassiter acted as if she were little more than an overgrown child herself. It was probably just as well he'd be moving Penny away from her unfortunate influence soon.

Speaking of which, was that Miss Lassiter's voice mingled in with the children's laughter?

Sadie, blinded by the cloth wrapped around her head, felt a half dozen hands turning her this way and that, leaving her completely disoriented. The sound of laughter blended with that of the rain pattering against the windows.

"Enough, enough," she protested, "I'm getting dizzy." *Please, Heavenly Father, help me get through this without showing signs of panic.*

"One more turn," replied one of her tormenters. It sounded like Audrey, who, though only seven, was often the ringleader of any mischief the group got into.

Finally the hands fell away and Sadie was left standing with no point of reference to tell her which direction she faced. She took a deep breath, keeping the smile planted firmly on her face. "All right, you little imps, look out 'cause here I come."

Because of her fear of small, dark spaces, blindman's bluff had never been one of her favorite games. She'd promised Cora Beth to keep the restless children occupied for an hour or two, though, and she'd made the mistake of letting the children pick the activity.

Really, this wasn't so bad. Even though she was blindfolded, there was lots of room to move around. It wasn't like her nightmare of being trapped in a closet or chest.

Muffled giggles, from Pippa and Lottie this time, cued her that the five-year-old twins were located to her left. She already felt a touch of anxiety thudding in her chest at the prolonged darkness, but she resisted the urge to go after the two youngest and instead turned to her right.

Holding her hands out in front of her at chest level reassured her that there was lots of room to move around and Sadie took a couple of tentative steps before she made contact with the sideboard. Ah-ha! A point of reference. The sound of footsteps scampering away to her left brought a smile to her face.

"Remember, you can't leave the dining room," she warned with mock sternness.

Something brushed against her ankle, startling a squeak from her. A moment later her heart returned to normal rhythm as she realized who the culprit was. "Does it count if I catch Daffy?" she called out.

"Cats can't play."

So, Viola was straight ahead. Her eight-year-old niece hadn't been 'it' yet. Sadie took a couple of confident steps, straining to catch any sound that might indicate her target was on the move.

Then she caught the sound of a heavier footstep, coming from the direction of what she judged to be the hallway. It wasn't Cora Beth. Uncle Grover, then. *Thank you, Father.*

All she had to do was tempt the good-humored older gentleman to enter the room and she'd have an easy capture. And the sooner she could remove this blindfold, the easier she'd breathe.

Moving as quickly as she dared under the circumstances, Sadie headed in the direction of the hallway. "Would you step in the dining room for a moment," she called out in her sweetest tone.

Sadie's hand connected with a sleeve and she latched onto her quarry's arm with an iron grip. "Gotcha!" She smiled in relief. "Sorry, Uncle Grover, but I caught you fair and square."

Why was his sleeve wet?

"Not exactly."

Uh-oh. She recognized that stern tone at about the same time she realized the arm beneath her grip was much too firm and muscled to be Uncle Grover's.

Sadie released his arm as if it were a snake, then yanked off her blindfold. She looked up into the disapproving gray eyes of the much too proper Mr. Eli Reynolds. His censuring stare made her feel smaller than her five-foot-three height.

The man disapproved of her—for the life of her she couldn't figure out why—but this was no doubt going to add another entry to his list of her shortcomings. "I'm so sorry." The heat climbed in her cheeks. "I thought you were Cora Beth's Uncle Grover."

"So I gathered." He didn't raise his voice and his tone was conversational. So why did she feel as if she were being scolded?

"You've obviously found an enjoyable way to pass the afternoon," he continued. "Much more enjoyable than, say, chores would be."

Oh yes, there was definitely a barb buried in that smooth-as-corn silk tone. "Most of the chores are done," she said. "The kids and I were just having a bit of fun while supper simmers on the stove."

"How pleasant." He gave her a pointed look. "I wonder how Mrs. Collins is faring? Perhaps I should send Penny to check on her."

And to think she'd thought him interesting and in need of a friend when she'd first met him a week ago. "Cora

Beth is resting at the moment." Not that she owed him an explanation.

Then a smile twitched her lips as an impudent idea took root. "But it *is* time for me to check on things in the kitchen." She handed the blindfold to Audrey. "Looks like Mr. Reynolds is 'it' now. Y'all have fun."

With that, she swished past the suddenly disconcerted gentleman and headed toward the kitchen.

That should give the too-stuffy-for-his-own-good Eli Reynolds something new to frown over.

Chapter Two

Sadie felt quite pleased with herself—for all of about five seconds. Putting him on the spot that way had been a petty move on her part. No matter what his demeanor, she was convinced his intentions were good and he didn't deserve such treatment. But the man really did have a way of getting her back up. Did he even know *how* to have fun?

Poor Penny. What would that little girl's life be like once she moved out of the boardinghouse and had only her brother for company?

Shaking off that thought, Sadie pushed open the kitchen door and immediately forgot the Reynolds siblings.

"Goodness, Cora Beth, what do you think you're doing? You're supposed to be resting." Sadie had come here a week ago to lend a hand while her brother's sister-in-law recuperated. Though she'd only met Cora Beth twice before, she'd jumped at the opportunity to do this. Not because she'd felt charitable, but because she'd been feeling restless and purposeless of late. Coming here and pitching in was supposed to make her feel useful, but so far things hadn't exactly worked out as planned.

Cora Beth was too polite to say anything, but Sadie knew her domestic skills had not lived up to the challenge of running a boardinghouse. Rather than trying to lend a hand herself, she would have done better to have hired some competent help. In fact, Sadie was beginning to wonder if she'd ever find a place where she served a real purpose.

Cora Beth smiled over her shoulder. "I'm tired of resting. Thought I'd check on the stew."

Sadie pushed her much-too-maudlin thoughts aside and marched across the room, glad Eli Reynolds wasn't here to see that his fears were well-founded. "Dr. Whitman said you weren't to use that hand any more than you had to for another week."

"It only takes one hand to stir a pot."

"Still, that's my job for the time being. I may not be able to cook as well as you, but I can make do. And I didn't travel eighty miles just to watch you defy doctor's orders." Sadie held her hand out for the spoon. When Cora Beth hesitated, she added "We may not know each other well, but you should've learned enough about me by now to understand I can be downright stubborn when I've a mind to have my way." Having been raised on a cattle ranch in a mainly masculine household, Sadie had spent most of her life surrounded by folks who tended to either underestimate her abilities or treat her as if she were still a child.

One thing this trip had accomplished was to give her an opportunity to show her mettle among these relative strangers and she aimed to take full advantage of that.

Cora Beth held onto the spoon a moment longer but Sadie stood firm.

"Oh, very well." Cora Beth surrendered the spoon and moved away from the stove. She gave Sadie an exasperated look. "And there's nothing wrong with your cooking."

Sadie gave her an unconcerned smile, deciding to be gracious in victory. "There's no need for you to sugarcoat things—I know my shortcomings as well as my talents. Out at Hawk's Creek the kitchen has always been Inez's domain and I'm happy to leave her to it. About the best you can say for my cooking is that it's edible. But we'll all muddle through for the next few days while you take care of yourself."

Heavenly Father, please let me do well enough not to embarrass Cora Beth in front of her boarders again. I'm asking not for myself, You understand, but for the folks who have to eat my cooking. Sadie struggled with her conscience a moment, then added a postscript to her silent prayer. *All right, it would also save me a bit of embarrassment, as well.*

"A commendable attitude."

It took Sadie a moment to realize Cora Beth was responding to her comment—not her silent prayer.

"Did I hear Mr. Reynolds come in?" Cora Beth added.

Sadie tried to keep her tone light. "Yep. Walked smack-dab into the middle of our blindman's bluff game." Funny, though, that even when she was irritated with the man she could notice how the rain had darkened his pecan-brown hair a couple of shades and caused it to curl up slightly at the ends.

"Oh dear." Cora Beth gave a rueful smile. "I take it he didn't approve."

An understatement. Sadie sighed. "I don't know what I did to curdle that man's cream but it's plain to see he doesn't think much of me." It was a shame, really. *Her* first impression of *him* had been positive, and it wasn't just because she liked the lean, broad-shouldered look of him. He was a bit too somber, perhaps, but he had a certain air of quiet confidence mixed with respect for others that she admired. What had really drawn her to him, though, was the hint of suppressed sadness she thought she'd sensed in him.

Of course, she'd been known to be wrong before.

"I'm sure it's not as bad as all that." Cora Beth's words drew her back to the present. "He just needs to get to know you a little better is all. He's really a very nice man."

Nice, yes—he just didn't approve of her. Which was a new experience for Sadie. She might still be treated as something of a child at home, but folks tended to like her. And as one of the Lassiter siblings and part owner of the Hawk's Creek Ranch, Sadie was used to her name, at least, commanding a certain degree of respect.

"You have to agree, though," Cora Beth said, "a man who takes such good care of a younger sister the way Mr. Reynolds does must have a lot to recommend him."

Sadie refrained from comment. Was Cora Beth forming an interest in the newest resident of the boarding-house? She wouldn't blame her if she had—still, for some reason, that thought didn't sit well.

Best to change the subject. "Now, get yourself on out of here. If you don't want to lie down, why don't you find a book to read or something quiet to do with the kids?"

"Don't you want some company?"

Sadie knew if Cora Beth stayed she'd try to lend a

hand. The woman just didn't know how to take it easy. "That's not—"

The door eased open just then, and Penny stood there, hesitating as if unsure of her welcome.

Sadie smiled at the young girl. "Hi there, princess, come on in." Then she arched a brow Cora Beth's way. "Seems I have someone to keep me company, after all. And since I intend to teach her all my kitchen secrets, you'll just have to run along."

Cora Beth looked from one to the other of them, then smiled. "Very well. I think I'll see what Uncle Grover's been up to today."

As soon as she'd left, Penny looked up at Sadie. "Are you really going to teach me secrets?"

Sadie tapped the little girl on the nose. "Actually, my biggest secret is that I'm not very good in the kitchen. But if you'd like to help, maybe between the two of us we can pull off something acceptable. What do you say?"

Penny's buckskin-colored pigtails danced as she nodded.

"Good. Now, let's find you an apron." Sadie hummed as she bustled around the kitchen, glad of the girl's company. She'd taken a real liking to the quiet nine-year-old this past week. And it really warmed her heart to see that the feeling was returned. With Penny she never felt judged or that she had to prove herself. The little girl just seemed to enjoy being with her.

Once she'd tied the oversized apron on Penny, Sadie put a finger to her chin. "Now, let's see. The stew is doing fine and the bread is already done." She'd even managed not to overcook or undercook it this time. "I guess we're ready to work on dessert."

Penny smiled, luring forth the rare appearance of her dimple. "I like dessert."

"So do I. Cora Beth helped me with a pound cake this morning, but I thought we might try to make a sauce to pour over it. Inez, the cook over at our ranch, makes a really scrumptious honey sauce that I think I can duplicate." At least she hoped she could. "Why don't you get the honey from the pantry while I get the butter and the cream?"

Penny nodded and headed off to do just that.

Sadie placed the butter and cream on the table then paused when she spied a neatly folded copy of this week's *Gazette* on the counter. At least one thing had gone right since her trip here. Mr. Chalmers had agreed to run her story and it had met with gratifying success. She might not be a good cook, but it seemed she could spin a fine yarn. The thought of accomplishing something like this entirely on her own boosted her spirits again.

"Here's the honey."

Sadie glanced at the crock in the girl's hands and gave her an apologetic smile. "Sorry, princess, that's the wrong container." Cora Beth had taken pains to explain to her that *that* particular jar contained a special honey that she used exclusively for her fruitcakes. Apparently it took on a special flavor because of the flowers that grew near the hard-to-find hive. "There's a blue crock on the same shelf where you found that one—it has the store-bought honey."

Penny nodded and turned back. But before she'd taken more than a step, she dropped the crock.

Sadie gazed down in horrified fascination at the sticky shards of crockery and gooey splatters. Cora Beth was not going to be happy.

"I'm so sorry. I didn't mean to—"

Penny's cracked-voice apology snapped Sadie out of her thoughts and she gave the girl a bright smile. "That's okay, princess, it was an accident. Don't you worry any more about it. Goodness knows I've had more than my fair share the past few days."

"Is Mrs. Collins going to be very upset?"

Sadie flipped her hand dismissively. "Oh, not at all. I'll just get her some fresh honey and she'll be happy as a hog in a wallow."

Penny wrinkled her nose as she smiled. "You say the funniest things."

"That I do." She gave the girl's shoulder a pat. "Now, you fetch the mop while I get a pail of water to clean this up. And watch your step."

Worried that the little girl might cut herself on the shards, Sadie fetched the other crock of honey and placed it on the table with the butter and cream. "Do you mind working on the honey sauce while I clean the floor? It would really be a big help."

Penny's shoulders drew back and her chest puffed out a bit, obviously proud of being given such a 'big girl' responsibility. "I can do that."

Hiding a smile, Sadie got her started, pouring the ingredients into a large bowl in what looked to be the correct proportions. "Now you just stir that up until it's all mixed together and the lumps are gone." She gave the girl a challenging look. "It may take a while to get it just right. Think you're up to it?"

"Oh yes. You can count on me."

Sadie gave her a big smile. "I know I can. You and I make a pretty good team."

Rolling up her sleeves, Sadie stepped over to the splatter and got down on her knees. At least *this* chore was one she was confident she could accomplish well.

A few minutes later she dropped the last of the larger shards into the trash pail and wiped the back of her hand across her forehead. "How's it coming?" she asked Penny.

"There's still a few lumps, but I'm getting close."

"Good. Guess I'd better check on the stew before I finish up here." She certainly didn't want to scorch supper the way she had last night. Who knew a roast could go from pink to charred so fast?

She put her hands on her thighs, prepared to stand. But her shoe caught on the hem of her skirt and she came down hard, landing on her backside with a jarring thud.

"Oh!" Penny's exclamation rang with anxiety.

But before Sadie could tell her she was okay, the door pushed open and Eli Reynolds stepped through. Sadie groaned inwardly. Of all times for her biggest critic to show up.

"Have you seen—" Penny's brother halted mid-sentence, his expression turning to a mix of surprise and something else she couldn't quite identify from this distance.

Then he crossed the room, bearing down on her with long, quick strides that took her aback.

"Sadie fell," Penny proclaimed worriedly. "I don't know if she's hurt."

"I'm fine." Even if she hadn't been, Sadie would never have hinted otherwise. She ignored the urge to rub her now-tender backside. If only he would just go away and leave her to recover her wounded dignity in private.

She stared up from her less-than-dignified position as he knelt beside her, waiting for the inevitable censure.

Instead, he met her gaze with a concern that took her completely by surprise. "Are you sure you're not hurt?"

She blinked, not quite certain how to react to this softer side of the man. "Yes, I mean, there's no need—"

Why in the world was she stammering? She took a deep breath then offered a self-mocking smile. "The only thing smarting at the moment is my pride."

He studied her a moment longer, then offered a hand. "In that case, here, let me help you up."

She allowed him to take her elbow, liking the feel of his strong, protective grip. When he placed his other hand at her back to steady her, she decided, that yes, she liked this very much indeed.

"You're bleeding!"

Penny, her complexion ashen, was pointing to Sadie's hand.

Sadie stared at the thin ribbon of blood running from her palm as if it belonged to someone else. Then she turned back to Penny. "It's all right, princess. I must have put my hand on a bit of crockery when I fell. But it doesn't hurt. Truly."

Mr. Reynolds intervened. "Just to be certain, let's clean it up and have a look."

"Oh, that's not necess—"

He caught her gaze and tilted his head ever so slightly toward Penny. "I think everyone will feel better if I do."

Penny nodded. "You don't have to worry, Aunt Sadie. Eli's real good at making boo-boos feel better."

She saw his brow go up at Penny's use of 'Aunt Sadie' but he let it pass without comment. Warmed by the thought that he took time to address his sister's 'boo-boos', she allowed him to steer her towards the sink.

Even as she followed docilely along, though, Sadie

again tried to make light of her injury. "Truly, it's just a little cut."

"Best to be safe." He carefully extended her hand over the sink, filled a dipper with water, then looked up. "Ready?"

Seeing reassurance instead of disapproval in those cool gray eyes of his was a new experience for Sadie, one she found she rather enjoyed. Then she realized he was waiting for her response. "Ready," she answered.

He gave her an approving smile, then slowly poured the water over the cut. It was strange to feel him holding her hand like this. His own hand was smoother than those of the ranch hands she was used to, but not soft in a namby-pamby way. She sensed strength there and an unexpected protectiveness.

"Looks like there's a sliver embedded in your palm." He glanced up and met her gaze again. "This might hurt a bit. I'll make it quick."

She nodded. Staring at his bent head, she noticed the way his hair tended to curl around his ear, how his brow wrinkled slightly when he was concentrating. His expression shifted and she saw the flicker of concern as he caught hold of the offending sliver, then the small spurt of triumph mixed with relief as he pulled it free.

"Sorry."

She blinked and it took her moment to realize he was apologizing for any discomfort his actions had caused her. "I hardly felt a thing." Which was the absolute truth as far as the cut was concerned.

Penny held out a bit of cloth. Sadie had been so riveted by Eli that she hadn't noticed Penny had crossed the room. "You can use this for a bandage," she said to her brother.

"Of course." He took the cloth from her and again his touch was gentle and sure as he wrapped her palm in the makeshift bandage.

"Thank you." Was that soft voice hers?

He cradled her hand a moment longer as his gaze caught on hers.

And held.

For several long, breath-stealing moments.

Chapter Three

"Wild wiggly worms, what happened in here?"

At the sound of Danny's horrified question, Eli abruptly released Miss Lassiter's hand and they both spun around.

He straightened his cuffs, trying to regain his composure. Surely Cora Beth's brother didn't think—

A heartbeat later he realized Danny was staring, not at the two of them, but at the mess on the floor.

"Just a little accident with the honey crock," Miss Lassiter explained. "Nothing to get all excited about."

"Who—"

"It doesn't really matter who dropped it. What's done is done."

Eli raised a brow at her hasty interruption. Did she have trouble admitting when she'd made a mistake?

Danny didn't seem inclined to let the matter drop. "But that was the last of Cora Beth's fruitcake honey."

Fruitcake honey? What was that?

Miss Lassiter, however, seemed to have no trouble understanding the significance. "I know, and that's unfortunate. But don't worry, I'll make it up to her."

Eli took himself in hand while Danny and Miss Lassiter babbled on about the honey. No doubt his uncomfortable, off balance feeling of a moment ago was caused by sympathy for Miss Lassiter's injury, nothing more. After all, it was quite natural for a gentleman to feel some concern for a lady in distress. Especially a petite little thing like Miss Lassiter.

It was time he set his mind to more important matters. Like pressing his suit with Mrs. Collins. He'd set a few pieces in motion this evening and then lay his case before her tomorrow.

No doubt she would think his proposal sudden, but Mrs. Collins struck him as a sensible woman, one not given to fanciful notions. And since his offer of marriage would afford her an opportunity to finally shed the onerous workload she bore as proprietress of this boardinghouse, he was confident she would view his suit most favorably.

He spared a glance for Miss Lassiter. She'd moved back to the table with Penny and the two of them were stirring something in a large bowl. They looked so comfortable together, as if they were old friends. How did she manage to coax that sweet smile from his sister so often?

He shook his head to clear it from those stray thoughts. This waffling was unlike him—he preferred an orderly, calculated approach to decision making. Cora Beth Collins was the logical choice and she would make a wonderful mother figure for Penny.

And after tomorrow it would be settled.

The evening meal passed pleasantly enough. The food, while not up to Mrs. Collins's standards, was passable. And Miss Lassiter made a point of giving credit to Penny for making the dessert sauce. While his sister reddened under the attention, she also seemed pleased by it, as well. He would have to remember to thank Miss Lassiter for her consideration.

He was also pleased with the progress he'd made with Mrs. Collins. Earlier he'd sought her out and asked for her help with the selection of a cook-housekeeper for his new home. He'd solicited her opinion on what qualities he should look for, then asked for suggestions on which local women might be suitable. He'd been impressed with her thought processes—another signal that he'd selected the right woman. In the end, he'd convinced her to allow each of the three women she'd recommended to take a day and cook the meals here at the boardinghouse so she could help him evaluate their performances.

He'd dropped a few hints about how dearly he valued her opinion and how he hoped to find a woman 'just like her' to preside in his home. He'd been subtle, as propriety dictated, but he was confident she would not be completely surprised when he proposed tomorrow.

Once the meal ended, Eli stood, ready to make his exit with the other boarders so the family would have the freedom to clear the dining room, but Mrs. Collins detained him with a comment. "I understand the work is almost complete on your new home," she stated.

Eli nodded, taking it as a positive sign that she had singled him out. "Yes. Unfortunately that means we'll soon have to say good-bye to the wonderful hospitality we've enjoyed here at your fine establishment." Of course, if things worked according to plan, she would soon be enjoying the relative ease that came with presiding over *his* household.

"As pleased as we've been to have you and Penny

with us," she replied, "I'm certain you'll be happy to be settled into your own home."

Eli found himself momentarily distracted by the sound of Miss Lassiter's laughter. It was a sound he'd heard quite a bit during the past week, though rarely when he was in her immediate presence. Not a polite titter or girlish giggle, hers tended to be a robust laugh, full of merriment and outright enjoyment. Hard to believe all of that exuberance could be contained in such a petite frame. A second later he had to school his expression as he realized he'd smiled in response.

"At any rate," Mrs. Collins continued, "it's good to see the old Thompson place all spruced up. It was so sad the way it got so run down after Mrs. Thompson passed away last winter."

Audrey approached them with Viola and Penny in tow. "Momma, is it true we have to wait until next week to find out what happens to Annabel Adams?"

"Afraid so, girls."

Audrey's lower lip poked out. "But that's such a long time."

"Which means you'll have an opportunity to practice patience. Now back to clearing the table."

Audrey didn't seem at all happy with that answer, but she nodded and moved toward the table.

Eli, however, was more focused on his sister. "Penny, am I to understand you've actually read this nonsense?"

She responded with a guilty smile. "Aunt Sadie read it to us this afternoon." Her expression turned earnest. "And it's not nonsense, Eli. Annabel Adams is so brave and good-hearted."

Miss Lassiter, was it? He should have known. He'd

have a word with her on the subject, but he wasn't such an oaf that he'd dress her down in front of her friends.

As Penny moved away, Mrs. Collins offered him a smile. "It really is quite harmless and entertaining, you know. Everyone's been talking about *The Amazing Adventures of Annabel Adams* ever since it appeared in the *Gazette* this week. Printing it was certainly a smart move on Fred Chalmers' part. I reckon there'll be a whole lot more folks than usual lined up for his paper next week."

Eli supposed from a business perspective it did make sense. But that didn't mean he approved of his sister reading such drivel. "Any idea who this Temperance Trulove really is?"

"No and Fred Chalmers isn't talking."

Why should he? Keeping the author's identity a secret only piqued the subscribers' interest all the more.

Time to change the subject. "I'm in the market for a carriage and a horse. Do you know where I might find something of quality?"

"Danny would be more able to help you with that than me." They moved toward the boy, who was gathering up an armload of dirty dishes.

Once Eli explained what he needed, Danny nodded. "There's a couple of rigs whose owners would likely part with them for the right price. What kind are you looking for?"

Eli was surprised at how grown up the eleven-year-old suddenly appeared. Apparently he was all business when it came to the livery stable. "Something suitable for getting around town and for short excursions. With enough room to seat three or four comfortably."

"Mr. Anderson's buggy is your best bet then. It's extra roomy and still in fine shape, but now that his kids are moved on he wants to replace it with something that has less seating and more room to haul goods. As for horses—"

"My brother runs Kestrel Stables," Miss Lassiter interjected. "He raises the finest horses in these parts. He and Josie are away right now, but I'd be glad to show you his stock."

That's right, Miss Lassiter's brother was married to Mrs. Collins's sister—that's how the two came to know each other. He'd met Ryland and Josie Lassiter once when they'd visited Mrs. Collins. Ryland seemed like a fine man, much more levelheaded and grounded than his sister.

"She's right," Danny offered. "Ry and Josie raise some mighty fine mounts. It's where I'd go if I was looking to make a purchase."

Eli met Miss Lassiter's gaze. "And can you make deals on his behalf?"

She lifted her chin as if taking offense. "Of course. Ry was the one who taught me most of what I know about horses, so he trusts me. And Henry, Ry's foreman, will know which animals are for sale and which are not."

Something flashed in her expression, there and gone so quickly he didn't quite make it out. "In fact, since Cora Beth mentioned that we'll have someone else in to do the cooking tomorrow, I was thinking I might take a trip out to the ranch. You're welcome to accompany me to look over the stock if you like."

Eli hesitated. Something about her smile made him a trifle uneasy. On the other hand, a horse was an important purchase and he wasn't inclined to wait the month or so until her brother returned from his trip.

Besides, if she was up to something, he was certain

he could handle it. "Thank you for your kind offer. Just let me know what time you wish to depart."

Sadie placed the hamper next to the sack Mr. Reynolds had already loaded in the back of the buggy for her. As she stepped back she noticed him eyeing her suspiciously.

"Are you making deliveries to the ranch?"

She allowed him to take her hand and help her up. "You could say that. Kestrel is Viola's home, remember? She wanted to send gifts to her friends there and Cora Beth let her raid the pantry. There are a couple of pears to feed to her pony, a few jars of preserves for the cook, a jug of apple cider for Henry—that sort of thing." No point mentioning the items she herself had packed just yet.

She cast around for a change of subject as he climbed up beside her and decided the weather was as good a topic as any. She waved a hand to draw his attention to the clouds scattered against the dark blue field of sky. "Looks like we're in luck weather-wise. If we *are* in for more rain today, it's several hours out."

He nodded as he picked up the reins. "I agree. We should be back in town well before any foul weather sets in."

After that the conversation lagged. Sadie tried not to fidget as she wondered when and how she should broach her plans for her little side trip with him.

Dear Father above, help me find the right words. This all felt like the right thing to do last night when I planned it, but I'm just not certain he's going to see it that way.

After about five minutes, Mr. Reynolds finally broke the silence. "There is something I wish to speak to you about."

"Oh?" From his tone, this did *not* sound like a conversation she was likely to enjoy.

"In case it has escaped your notice, my sister is young and very impressionable. As are the other children in Mrs. Collins's household. I think it would be best if you refrain from reading that weekly serial to them in the future."

His words took her completely by surprise. "Why ever not? The children enjoy it and it seems harmless enough."

He raised a brow at that. "Do you truly think it appropriate reading material for children?"

"I wouldn't have read it to them if I didn't." Did he think her so irresponsible? And what would he think if he knew *she* was the author? "The heroine exhibits high morals, healthy curiosity and steadfast courage. Have you even *read* the story?"

He brushed her question aside. "I didn't need to. I've seen its ilk before. It's a frivolous piece of work, one that is liable to put notions in innocent young minds that are at best nonsensical, and at worse dangerous."

How dare he! She shifted in her seat to face him more fully. Did the man realize how pompous he sounded? "Dangerous? That's a bit melodramatic, don't you think? I suppose you'd prefer that I read to them from school books or perhaps morality plays."

He didn't seem at all ruffled by her sarcasm. "If you must read to them at all I will be happy to furnish you with copies of suitable material." He glanced her way with a stern look. "Penny is my sister, and I must insist that you accede to my wishes in this matter."

Sadie took a deep breath. As much as his criticisms stung, and as much as she disagreed with his perspective, he *was* Penny's brother and guardian. It was not her place to argue with him about her upbringing.

I'll trust in You to look out for the girl, Father. Goodness knows she'll need some sort of intervention if she's to be allowed any fun at all in her brother's household.

"Very well." Sadie was proud of the calm tone she managed. "I won't read to her about Annabel Adams's adventures without your permission." Besides, it wasn't as if she'd have much opportunity anyway. The installments came out once a week and he'd be moved into his new home soon. And she'd be headed back to Hawk's Creek before long, putting even more distance between them.

Hoping to lighten the mood, she changed the subject. "So tell me about where you and Penny come from. That's definitely not a Texas accent you speak with."

"We come from Almega, New York, a city about thirty miles southeast of Albany. It's much bigger than Knotty Pine with a nice variety of theaters, museums, fine restaurants, and even a hospital. All of the latest modern conveniences are available there and you can find more shops on one street than there are houses in Knotty Pine."

She supposed she should be impressed, but it all sounded terribly crowded to her. "So what made you leave such a fine place to come out here?"

A muscle in his jaw twitched. She was probably being too nosy again.

"I thought the change would be good for Penny," he finally said. "And the bank here was a good investment opportunity."

He'd done all this for his sister? He must care a great deal for her. "Penny sure is a sweet girl and bright as all get-out. I know Cora Beth's kids and Viola are all quite taken with her. She seems a mite shy, though."

He stiffened. "She's just naturally quiet."

Sadie heard the note of defensiveness in his voice. "Of course. I didn't mean to imply I thought there was anything wrong with her." She smiled. "Any more than there's anything wrong with Audrey for her natural chattiness."

He seemed to relax at that, and his lips twitched in a smile. "True—no one would ever accuse Audrey of being a wallflower."

Oh my, he really should smile more often. Then she caught site of an oak with a double trunk and a twisted branch. "You need to turn on that road off to the left up ahead."

When he followed her directions without question, Sadie felt a twinge of guilt. She'd wait just a few minutes more, she told herself. Once they were off the main road a piece, she'd fill him in.

She kept up a stream of chatter hoping to keep him distracted from his surroundings as she watched for the milestones Danny had told her about.

Fifteen minutes later, he interrupted her mid-sentence. "Miss Lassiter, are you certain this is the right way? I haven't seen any farmhouse or other sign of civilization for a while."

"Oh, we're going in the right direction—I'm sure of it."

"Your brother's ranch is out this way?"

Okay, time to come clean. "Not exactly."

That brought the expected frown. "Explain, please."

She winced at the frostiness of his tone. Perhaps she really should have let him in on her plans sooner. "I have an errand to run for Cora Beth and thought we'd handle that bit of business first."

"An errand?"

Did she detect a note of suspicion in his question? "Yes. I need to fetch something she needs." Oh dear, was he slowing the horse? "I assure you it's important. We just need to go a little further down this road."

He pursed his lips as if unhappy with the unplanned detour, so she quickly added, "And I promise you, Cora Beth will be *very* grateful."

Finally he nodded, and to her relief he allowed the horse to resume its earlier pace. "I suppose, if Mrs. Collins asked you to do this, it's the least we could do. But I hadn't expected to be gone all day."

"You won't be."

A few minutes later he cut her another sideways glance. "I'm beginning to feel like we took a wrong turn. Are you certain you know where we're going?"

"Absolutely. I asked Danny to run through the directions twice and I've seen several of the landmarks he gave me. It should be just a little farther along."

He didn't seem reassured. "Exactly what is the nature of this errand you are running for Mrs. Collins?"

Sadie took a deep breath and then offered him her brightest smile.

He was *not* going to like the answer to that question.

Chapter Four

"Actually, I'm looking for Josie's honey tree."

Eli thought for a moment he'd misheard. "You're what?"

"Looking for Josie's honey tree." She made the statement as if it were nothing out of the ordinary. "I want to replace the honey that spilled out on the floor yesterday."

He pulled the buggy to a stop and set the brake. He couldn't believe he'd gone all this way down a rutted-pig's-trail-of-a-road on such a fool's errand. When he turned to speak to her again it was all he could do not to growl. "And Mrs. Collins asked you to do this?"

"Actually, I intended it as a surprise." Before he could say anything she rushed on. "I never said Cora Beth asked me. I just said we were fetching something for her. Which we are." She grimaced, then sat up straighter. "I'm sorry. I *do* know that a lie by omission is still a lie. You're right to be angry. I should have been more up-front with you."

Her honesty was disarming but it still didn't make him any fonder of the current situation. "If you felt the need to replace the honey you ruined, why couldn't you just purchase a jar at the mercantile?"

A flash of some strong emotion crossed her face, but then she shook it off. "Because that honey was special." Her tone was earnest but he noticed the way she clasped and unclasped her hands in her lap. "It was the last of a batch of wild honey that has a unique flavor. Cora Beth uses it to make those wonderful fruitcakes that she sells. She didn't say anything but I know she's worried about missing some of her regular delivery dates, what with her hurt arm. And now this. She counts on the income from those cakes to help her make ends meet."

Something she would have no need to do once she became his wife. Not that he could say that to Miss Lassiter.

"The location of the hive is supposed to be secret," she continued, her voice a nervous babble, "but I had a suspicion Danny would know where it might be." Her expression turned smug. "I grew up with two brothers of my own and they weren't likely to let a secret like that get the better of them. Sure enough, when I questioned Danny he admitted he followed Josie, all sneaky-like, on one of her trips. He couldn't get real close—seems he swells up something awful when he gets stung, but he got close enough to spot the general vicinity."

That was it? That was what she'd based this ill thought-out expedition on? "I'm going to find a place to turn this buggy around and we're going to head right back to the main road."

Dismay clouded her expression. "You can't, not when we've already come this far. Look, right over there is the turtle back rock Danny told me about. We're close, I know it."

"Miss Lassiter, I don't—"

She placed a hand on his arm. "Please. If not for me, do it for Cora Beth. This would mean a great deal to her."

Her action, as well as the touch of desperation in her tone, startled him.

As if seeing him weaken, she pressed her case. "Give it just ten more minutes. If we haven't found the hive by then, I'll go without complaint." She gave him a cajoling smile. "Besides, who doesn't like the idea of a treasure hunt?"

He had to bite back a smile at that—the woman really was incorrigible. "Oh very well—ten minutes." He hoped he didn't regret the decision. "What's the next landmark we're looking for?"

She released his arm and settled back into her seat. "Thank you. There should be a small cabin of some sort just a little way farther along. Then we'll need to go the rest of the way by foot."

Of course they would. But he absolutely drew the line at wondering through the woods. If it wasn't in easy sight of the trail he would most definitely put an end to her quest. "If Danny didn't set eyes on the hive itself, how do you know you can find it?"

"He says he got close enough to hear her working. Don't worry, I'll find it."

The small cabin turned out to be a one room building that looked as if it would topple over with the next good wind that blew by.

Eli tied the horse to a bit of brush, then paused as he considered a possible flaw in her plan. "Do you even know how to collect honey?"

But she nodded confidently. "I've done it a time or two—remember, I have two brothers and I grew up on a ranch." She smiled as he took her hand to help her down. "How about you?"

"I have not yet had that pleasure."

His sarcasm seemed lost on her. "Don't worry, I'll show you how. I have some netting and gloves for the two of us so we shouldn't have to worry much about getting stung. And I also have some oil-soaked rags for smoking the little critters, along with a bucket to collect the honey comb in."

He'd wondered why she'd packed so many provisions to deliver to her brother's ranch. "Sounds like you came prepared."

"Of course. Actually, I don't know how Josie managed it on her own. I've always thought of this as a two-person job. Come to think of it, it'll be interesting to see how she managed to not destroy the hive while she was at it."

He stepped forward to assist as she reached behind the seat of the buggy to collect her supplies. He was irritated with her, yes, but he was still a gentleman.

Miss Lassiter studied the brush beside the road and finally pointed toward a narrow space between two scraggly saplings. "There's a trail here, just like Danny said. But it's overgrown and looks to be marshy in spots, so watch your step."

He stepped forward. "I'd better take the lead." He wasn't going to risk her getting them lost or wandering too far afield.

Saying the trail was overgrown was an understatement. Within minutes Eli began to wonder if this was actually a trail at all. When his left shoe sunk into a muddy patch a few moments later, he was ready to call the whole thing off. "I'm sorry, Miss Lassiter, but I think—"

"Look, there it is."

Eli glanced to his left where she was pointing and sure enough the brush gave way to a small flower-bedecked clearing. And right at the edge of it was a crudely constructed man-made hive.

Without waiting for his lead, she moved toward the clearing. "Why Josie, you clever girl. So this is how you were able to harvest honey from the same hive time after time." She glanced over her shoulder at Eli. "Normally, when you harvest honey from a natural hive, you end up destroying the hive itself or killing the queen. But Josie's created a cleverly designed artificial hive using this log. This way, you can get at the honey with minimal disruption to the bees." Then she looked around. "Oh my—no wonder the honey has such a distinctive flavor. I see honeysuckle vines, wild roses and larkspur, but I don't even know what half of these other flowers are."

Eli was struck by the way her face fairly glowed with pleasure as she took it all in. That simple joy made her look even more childlike than usual.

Then she turned back to him and her expression immediately sobered. "Sorry. I know you're in a hurry to get this over with."

Oddly moved by the loss of her smile, he almost felt as if he should apologize to her for having dampened her mood.

She waved toward the bag he carried. "You can set that here." As soon as he'd set it down, she dug around inside and withdrew two pair of gloves and netting.

She turned and handed him a large piece of the netting. "Place this around your head and tuck it securely into the collar of your shirt. It'll keep the bees from getting to your face and neck. Then put these gloves on to protect your hands."

Eli studied the material uncertainly. He hadn't really expected them to find the hive, hadn't considered that he might actually have to assist in the harvesting. Where was his backup plan when he needed one?

But it seemed he was committed to this project now. With a mental sigh he did as she'd instructed.

Despite his misgivings, he actually found himself intrigued by the whole honey-gathering experience. Miss Lassiter spent some time exploring the setup of the hive and the implements Mrs. Collins's sister had left on site, all carefully wrapped in oilcloth and stored off the ground to keep them from rotting or rusting. His companion seemed delighted with each new discovery and her explanations were filled with superlatives. When she finally set to work, she patiently explained everything she did and everything she needed him to do in great detail, from how to gently waft the smoke into the hive to how to slice the comb as she lifted the frames.

Her bubbly enthusiasm and childlike pleasure in the task puzzled him. The woman seemed to tackle every job she undertook as an adventure to be savored. Which, while naive and inefficient, was also an intriguing novelty. One, he was certain, would become tiresome over time. And surprisingly she seemed much more confidant and capable than she had with her duties at the boardinghouse.

Once they'd finally collected enough honey to satisfy her they moved a safe distance from the hive with their treasure. She set her burdens down and removed the netting from her head, losing a few hairpins in the process. "Now aren't you glad we came?" she asked as she tucked the cloth into the sack. "You had a chance to experience something new, and Cora Beth will be so pleased with the honey."

He added his netting and gloves to the sack and then glanced up at the sky as he picked it up. "Let's just try to make it to your brother's ranch before that rain starts."

She seemed disappointed with his staid response, but nodded. "You have the sack, so I'll take—"

They both reached for the bucket of honey at the same time, their hands overlapping on the handle. He studied her small, delicate hand next to his larger, coarser one and felt that same something strange that had jangled through him in the boarding-house kitchen yesterday.

He forced his gaze up to meet hers and was surprised by the soft warmth in those sorrel-brown depths. Shaking off his momentary disquiet, Eli released the bucket and straightened. "We'd best hurry."

He preceded her as they marched toward the road, wondering what had gotten into him lately. Perhaps all the events of the past few months were finally starting to have an effect on him. He—

A movement on the ground in front of him caught his attention and he halted mid-step. His pulse quickened as he recognized the coiled form. He *hated* snakes!

His companion bumped into him and he took firm hold of her arm. "I don't want to alarm you, but there's a snake directly in our path. Move back." He tried to keep his voice calm, to ignore the sweat trickling down his back. She would no doubt count on him to keep her safe.

The snake lifted its head and flicked its tongue in their direction. Fighting his own visceral reaction, Eli tried to tug Miss Lassiter back with him. Problem was, she didn't seem to feel the same sense of urgency.

Blabbering some nonsense about the snake being

harmless, she tried to pull away from him. Concerned for her safety he held onto her all the harder and tried to pull her away from the snake's proximity.

And then it happened. He caught his left foot on something and a sharp pain in the vicinity of his ankle drove him to his knees.

Chapter Five

Sadie's heart thudded in her chest as she dropped to her knees beside him. "What's wrong? Are you all right?" *Please God, let it just be a stumble.*

His expression was contorted, a sure sign he was in pain, but he still tried to get up. "The snake. Where—"

"Gone." She placed a hand on his shoulder to keep him down. "But like I tried to tell you, it was just a harmless king snake."

He went very still, his expression closing off. Then he nodded stiffly. "My apologies for the overreaction. It seems I made a bit of a fool of myself."

Sounded like it was his pride that was injured. Growing up with two older brothers, she'd dealt with her fair share of *that* ailment over the years and knew how prickly it could make a fella. "I'm sure the snakes in this part of the country look different than those do where you come from." She offered a reassuring smile. "And when in doubt it's always wise to give the critters a wide berth."

Her words didn't seem to ease his stiffness any. Ah well, he'd get over his wounded pride soon enough. Right now they had other things to worry about.

"Can you walk? 'Cause we probably ought to get a move on. Collecting that honey took a little longer than I expected and from the looks of those clouds up there the rain is going to come in sooner than we expected."

He glanced up toward the sky and nodded.

Sadie bit her lip as she studied him. He seemed to be okay but the fact that he'd made no move yet to stand was making her uneasy.

She could almost see him gather his strength before he started to push himself up, and her stomach knotted.

"You *are* hurt." It wasn't a question.

"I think I twisted my ankle," he admitted. "I'll be fine once I get back to the buggy. If you can find me a stout stick to use for leverage—"

"Take my arm and I'll help you up."

His look was dismissive. "I appreciate the offer, but you can't support my weight."

Now he *did* sound like her brothers. "I'm stronger than I look."

She saw the stubborn glint in his eye—probably that pride thing again. Before he could protest further she gave him a stern look of her own. "Look, I don't see any stout sticks nearby and I sure don't intend to waste time looking for one while we wait for the bottom to fall out of those clouds. So just take my arm."

His irritation was plain, but after a second he nodded. "Very well." He took the arm she offered and gingerly stood, while carefully avoiding putting any weight on his left foot.

She gave him a minute to steady himself. "Okay. Now put your arm around my shoulder and we'll get you to the buggy."

Without a word, Mr. Reynolds set his hand gingerly on her nearest shoulder.

The man was exasperating. "That'll never work. I assure you I won't break and I won't swoon. For the next few minutes I will simply think of you as one of my brothers and you are free to think of me as a sister. Now, put your arm around me to my other shoulder so you can get proper support and we can get out of here."

His lips compressed, but he did as she'd com-manded.

As they picked their way along the overgrown trail, Sadie was acutely aware of his arm around her, of his weight against her—warm, heavy, vital.

So much for thinking of him like a brother.

By the time they finally made it back to the road, the first drops of rain had begun to fall. It was intermittent, but the fat drops, suddenly darkened sky and oppressive air promised worse to come.

Once at the wagon, he released her and used the frame of the buggy to leverage himself up onto the seat. At least they'd made it to the relative shelter of the buggy before the worst of the weather blew in.

"I apologize for not being able to hand you up," he said as he settled in, "but—"

"Don't give it another thought." She resisted the urge to rub away the tingle that lingered where his arm had been.

"If I can impose on you to untether the horse, we'll get on our way."

She could tell that simple request had not been easy for him. "Of course. Just as soon as I fetch that pail of honey."

"But the rain—"

"Oh, a little rain never hurt anyone. After all the trouble we put into collecting it, I don't intend to leave even a drop behind if I can help it."

Before he could protest further, she hiked her skirts up to her ankles and dashed back into the thicket. She grabbed both the honey and the supplies just as the rain began to fall in earnest. Encumbered by her bulky burdens, she made slower progress on the return trip and by the time she was ready to scramble onto the seat beside him she was more than a little damp.

But it had been worth it.

She ignored Mr. Reynolds's censoring glance and laughed as she tried to shake some of the water from her skirts. "I haven't played in the rain since I was a schoolgirl—I'd forgotten how fun it was."

Of course, it would be a lot more fun if her companion wasn't so stodgy. She wished there was some way she could get him to relax and see the joy in the little things.

Eli resisted the urge to roll his eyes. How could she make light of her sodden state? She had to be uncomfortable. And even on this warm May day, there was a real chance of her catching a cold if she didn't find something dry to change into soon. He had to get her back to town.

Then she sat up straighter. "Would you like me to take the reins?"

Some of his sympathy evaporated as he gritted his teeth and released the brake. "It's my ankle that's hurt, not my hands." Just because he'd overreacted when he spied the snake was no reason for her to try to molly-coddle him.

Using the small clearing in front of the ramshackle cabin, he turned the wagon around and headed back the way they'd come.

There, that should show her he could still handle the buggy. He gave her a sideways glance. "Given the weather and the condition of my ankle, I think it best we return to town rather than proceed to your brother's ranch."

"Yes, of course. We need to get the doctor to look at your ankle as soon as possible." She rubbed her hand over her arm as she stared out at the downpour.

Had she already taken a chill? He shrugged out of his relatively dry jacket. "Here, put this on."

"But—"

"No arguments. You're soaked through and the last thing we need is for you to get sick." He tried gentling his tone. "After all, Mrs. Collins is counting on you."

She chewed her lip a moment as he held her gaze and slowly nodded. "Thank you."

His coat swallowed her up, making her appear even smaller than normal. Several tendrils had escaped the confines of their pins and hung, damp and forlorn, down her neck. His hand moved, almost of its own accord, to brush her cheek in reassurance. At the last moment he came to his senses and flicked the reins instead, hoping she hadn't noticed his lapse of control.

They rode along in silence for a while as he tried to maneuver the overgrown trail in the rain. The throbbing in his ankle was getting worse and his mood was going downhill with it as a bright flash of lightning lit the sky just then, almost immediately followed by a much-too-close clap of thunder. His companion jumped, but Eli had no time to reassure her. It took all of his focus to steady the horse. Even so, he couldn't help but notice how tightly she grabbed the seat.

"That sounded like it was close." She didn't sound quite so carefree now.

"It was probably further away than it seemed." Why this sudden urge to comfort her?

A moment later they rounded a corner in the trail and Eli pulled back on the reins. "Whoa."

Up ahead, a tree was down, completely blocking the road. The char marks on the trunk left no doubt as to what had happened.

Miss Lassiter leaned forward, trying to get a better view through the driving rain. "Do you see any way around it?"

He could tell from her tone that she already knew the answer. "Afraid not."

She sighed as she settled back in her seat. "What now?"

What now indeed? Under other circumstances he might have tried to find a way to hitch the horse to the trunk and move the blamed thing, at least enough to allow the buggy through. Or left the carriage behind and rode out on the horse alone to find help. But between the worsening storm and his throbbing ankle there was no way he could make the attempt now. They needed a fall-back plan. And there was only one option.

"Now we go back to that cabin and wait out the storm." He used his most decisive tone. "Once the weather clears I'll find a way to get us out of here." To add to their problems, he had no idea what kind of shelter that miserable looking cabin was going to afford them when they arrived. He fervently hoped it was more solid than it appeared, but with the luck he was having lately he wouldn't be surprised if it leaked like a sieve.

It took a bit of maneuvering to get the buggy turned

around on the narrow, overgrown road. By the time they were headed back toward the cabin, Eli could feel the tenseness in his shoulders and jaw. Hearing her sneeze only added to his worries about what the rest of this day might hold. What a mess!

She shifted on the seat, glancing his way from the corner of her eye. "I'm sorry I got us into this fix. I suppose I should have thought this whole thing through a little better."

He agreed, but it would be churlish to say so. Besides, he could have put an end to this as soon as he discovered what she was about. He'd examine his reasons for not doing so later. "I don't think there is any value to be had in either assigning or assuming blame." He tried to ease his foot into a more comfortable position. "Our efforts would be better focused on trying to find shelter from this rain."

It didn't take long to make their way back to the cabin, but this time they were headed against the wind. Spray from the rain peppered their faces, dampened their clothes. Eli pulled the buggy up as close to the door as possible. Not that it mattered. A person could only get so wet.

Before he could even set the brake, Miss Lassiter had scrambled down and raced around to his side of the buggy.

The woman was already soaking wet.

"Come along, let me help you inside."

He held onto the frame of the buggy again as he climbed down, but then gingerly placed his arm around her shoulder. There was no time for another argument over the proprieties.

He did his best to help her open the door of the cabin,

taking out some of his frustration on the stubborn hinges. Once inside, it took a few minutes for his eyes to adjust. There were four windows with shutters, one set on each wall. Since most of the shutters were broken or askew, enough daylight had pushed through so that it wasn't entirely gloomy.

It might have been better had it not revealed quite so much.

A thick coat of dust covered everything. 'Everything' being a generous term. Very little furniture remained. And it wasn't just dust—leaves and other debris from outside had made their way inside, as well.

The cabin consisted of one large open area, with an alcove to their right—probably for sleeping—and a fireplace to their left. Fortunately, the roof seemed relatively sound. There was one steady drip in the alcove area and one near what must be the back door. Other than that, the place appeared dry.

He glanced his companion's way, expecting to see dismay, and perhaps something stronger. Instead she was looking around with interest, seeming pleased by what she saw. "God was definitely looking out for us," she said cheerily. "We ought to be able to wait out the storm in relative comfort here."

A sudden rustling from across the room snagged his attention. Before he could do more than stiffen, a squirrel shot out of a far corner. His companion, who'd merely shrugged her shoulders at the sight of that snake earlier, jumped. The animal, tail flickering in agitation, disappeared through a half-shuttered window, apparently preferring the rain to their company.

Miss Lassiter gave him a sheepish look. "Sorry. Hope I didn't jar you. The squirrel startled me."

"I'm fine." He released her shoulder and braced his arm against the wall. To be honest her reaction made him feel slightly better about his own reaction to the snake.

A few other skittering noises came from the vicinity of the alcove, but he told himself they were caused by the wind coming in, not mice or other vermin.

Besides, there were more pressing things to worry about at the moment. Like, was that a working fireplace? A fire would go a long way to helping them dry out.

"Will you be all right for a few minutes?" she asked, reclaiming his attention.

Eli eyed her suspiciously. "Of course. But where do you think you're going?"

"I need to unhitch and tether the horse. And while I'm out there I intend to fetch whatever I can find in the buggy that we can use to make us more comfortable in here."

All things *he* should be taking care of. "That can all wait until the storm—

She held a hand up, palm out. "I can't get any wetter than I already am. And it would be cruel to leave the horse standing out there for who knows how long hitched to the buggy. Besides, we can't risk him getting spooked by the storm and running off."

She was right, of course. But that didn't make him like it any better. "At least take this." He pulled his hat off. "That scrap you've got on your head is no protection in this weather." And from the looks of it, it probably wouldn't ever be fit for use again.

She nodded and untied the ribbon that secured the soggy bit of frippery. He placed his more sensible hat on her head and found himself brushing the hair off her forehead to tuck it under the brim. The wisps tickled his fingers, as if even her hair was prone to playfulness.

He moved back and studied the picture she made in his too-big-for-her coat and hat. They swallowed her up, making her look like a child playing dress up. But she was covered except for the bottom half of her skirt.

As if reading his thoughts she gave him a reassuring smile. "Thanks, this is much better. And don't worry, I shouldn't be long."

He watched her head back out into the weather, feeling frustrated at his enforced uselessness. Then he looked around, taking stock of their temporary shelter. The least he could do was get to work doing what he could to make the place as comfortable as possible. Even though he was certain that thanks to Miss Lassiter, this would be one of the most uncomfortable afternoons he'd spent in quite some time.

Arms full, Sadie shoved the door of the cabin open with her shoulder. The load was bulky and awkward to manage but she hadn't cared for the idea of making a second trip to the buggy in this weather.

Stepping inside, she found Mr. Reynolds sitting on the low hearth, working on cleaning out the fireplace. Even with damp clothes and smudges on his sleeve, the always-dapper banker was still quite handsome.

He looked up and caught her staring so she looked away, setting the hamper and the covered bucket of honey just inside the door.

"I feel sorry for the mare," she said to cover her embarrassment. "She's a good horse and deserves a nice dry barn to wait out the storm in."

"Hopefully this will blow over soon."

Sadie refrained from comment, but she'd seen this kind of storm before. She doubted it would be over "soon."

"So what did you find in the buggy?" He eyed the hamper with interest. "Any food?"

"Hungry, are you?" She grinned as she folded the blanket into a smaller square. Then she set it down on top of the hamper and bucket, taking care to not let it touch the dirty floor.

"Not starving," he answered. "But I wouldn't turn down a bite to eat." He gave her a challenging smile. "Not that I'm worried we'll starve. There's always that honey you have there."

"Bite your tongue—that's for Cora Beth." She doffed the hat he'd loaned her and bumped it against her skirts to shake some of the water off. "Besides, I don't think it'll come to that." She removed the coat and gave it the same treatment. No point trailing water all through the place—all this dirt and dust would turn into a muddy mess. "The hamper has all of the stuff Cora Beth helped Viola pack for the folks at the ranch. I think they'll forgive us if we help ourselves." She tried to jab a few stray hairpins more securely on her head. "I know it's nothing fancy but we can always pretend we're on a picnic."

"Picnic fare sounds good. Given the situation, I'd say we're lucky to have it."

"I'd say, rather, that the Good Lord was looking out for us." She opened the sack and began digging around. "As far as other supplies, I found an old picnic blanket under the wagon seat, and I also have this sack of honey-gathering tools, including—" she straightened "this flint."

His eyes lit up at that. "Good. Because as far as I can tell the chimney is clear, and I think the first order of business should be to get a fire started so we can try to dry out."

"I agree." She looked around as she crossed the room. "And there certainly seems to be a lot of material laying around that we can use for firewood. That old stool and those rickety benches both seem to be fit for nothing else. And the shutter on that window is already hanging by one rusty hinge."

He nodded, only glancing up briefly before resuming his work at the fireplace. "There's a few pieces of actual firewood the last squatters left behind in the hearth. But we could really use some kindling. If you see any twigs or other bits of debris that would serve the purpose gather them up."

She took in the layers of dirt and debris surrounding them and wrinkled her nose. "That shouldn't be a problem."

Once he took the flint from her, she hung his hat and coat on two of the half dozen nails jutting from the mantel. The garments would fare much better there than on any of the dusty surfaces the cabin had to offer.

In short order she had collected a goodly number of twigs, pecan husks and other flammable-looking bits and carried them to the hearth.

She tamped down the urge to offer to lend a hand as she watched him arrange the kindling and bits of wood. Instead, she stood and surveyed the cabin. "If we're going to be stuck here for a while, we might as well try to make it more comfortable. I don't suppose you saw a broom anywhere?"

He glanced up with a surprised expression, then shrugged. "Afraid not." He looked at the floor with a grimace. "Too bad."

"Then I'll just have to improvise. A leafy branch or bit of brush will work just about as well—bound to be lots of those handy. If you'll loan me your pocketknife I'll see what I can find."

He paused and frowned up at her. "You're *not* going back out in that storm."

His commanding tone took her aback, but she kept her own tone light. "Don't worry. I figure with the way things are grown up around here, there'll be something right out the back door."

"Distance won't matter in this downpour. You'll be soaked as soon as you step outside."

So he was worried about her. Why did everyone think she couldn't fend for herself? She spread her arms. "Can't get much wetter than I already am. And you'll have that fire going soon so I can dry out when I get back." She shrugged and added a touch of firmness to her voice. "Besides, I've got to do something to keep busy."

He gave her a long, considering look, then apparently decided to let it go. "At least put the hat and coat back on."

"Of course."

It took some time, and quite a bit of shoving to get the back door opened, but when she looked at the rain-shrouded grounds behind the cabin Sadie gave a little crow of pleasure.

"What is it?"

She smiled over her shoulder. "I've found a real treasure back here. There's a whole tangle of dewberry vines growing right up against the wall, and they're ripe for the picking."

He sat up straighter. "Need some help?"

"No, I can get them. Besides, you have your hands

full getting that fire going and I plan to take full advantage of it when I get done."

Sadie snaked a hand toward the nearest vine. "I love dewberries." She plucked two of the plump berries and popped them one after the other into her mouth. Savoring the way the juice exploded between her teeth, she scanned the overgrown patch of ground, trying to spy a likely bit of brush to use as her makeshift broom. No point heading into the weather until she had her quarry in sight.

There! That one should work. She sprinted out into the rain and made quick work of breaking off the targeted bit of brush. In the process she caught sight of a stout stick on the ground. Scooping it up, she headed back to the house. Leaning her brush-broom against the inside wall, she shook out her skirts, then reached back to pluck a few more berries.

Crossing the room with her two offerings, she smiled at the sight of the crackling flames. "Oh good, you've got the fire going."

"The chimney is clear enough to draw the smoke, thank goodness."

She held out the stout branch. "Look what I found. I thought you might be able to use it as a walking stick."

The relief and approval on his face sent an answering warmth through her.

"Thanks." He took the stick and used it to leverage himself up. Placing his weight on it, he took a couple of hobbling steps to test it out. "Perfect."

"Good. Now here, try some of these."

He stared at the berries she held out but didn't make a move to take them. "You picked them, you eat them."

She waved away his concern. "Oh, don't be silly—

I've already had a handful." From the look on his face she reckoned he didn't get called silly often. "There are lots more on those vines. This is just a little snack to keep our strength up. I plan to pick a whole passel more once I've gotten some of the cleanup done." She raised her hand a bit closer to his face and slid the berries back and forth under his nose.

After rolling his eyes, he took half of the berries and popped one into his mouth. "Delicious."

"Nothing like berries fresh from the vine. Here take the rest so I can get to work." She held up her other hand, palm out.

With a nod and a thank you, he accepted the rest of her offering.

That was better. The man just needed someone to stand up to him occasionally. And this afternoon was as good a time as any.

Chapter Six

Eli watched Sadie energetically swish her rustic but surprisingly effective broom across the floor, chafing at the fact that he couldn't be of more help. Thank goodness she'd found the walking stick for him, at least he could get around a little better now. Even though his foot throbbed enough to make his teeth ache, the renewed mobility made him feel a little more in control of the situation.

While she swept and cleaned he hobbled around, determined to do what he could. He shoved the heavier bits out of her way, gathered up whatever scraps of wood he could find to stack by the fireplace and tossed some of the rest of the junk in a far corner. The woodpile grew surprisingly large and while he hoped they wouldn't be here long enough to need it all, his gut told him that there was a good chance they would be.

Not that he had any intention of letting Miss Lassiter see his concern. He wasn't sure how she would feel about being trapped out here for an extended period and he didn't relish the idea of having a hysterical female on his hands on top of everything else.

As the minutes ticked away, however, her energy and continued positive attitude surprised him. He hadn't noticed her being this industrious back at the boardinghouse. Her fervor with the broom coupled with the sodden, muddy hem of her skirt and damp, disheveled hair should have given her the appearance of a scullery maid.

But somehow it didn't.

He wasn't sure if it was the cheery smile she wore, or her soft humming as she worked or something that went deeper, but she looked both softer and more competent than before.

She kicked up enough dust with her efforts to set them both to sneezing, but she maintained her good humor, treating it more as a game than a chore. In short order she had the area in front of the hearth as clean as she could make it given the tools on hand.

Finally setting aside her broom, she fetched the blanket and spread it in front of the fireplace. "There now, why don't you sit and rest that foot of yours?"

That did sound good. "Ladies first."

Rather than showing appreciation for his manners, she looked exasperated. "Oh for goodness sake, this isn't Cora Beth's parlor. Given the situation, I think we can put those sort of niceties aside."

He clenched his jaw. Didn't she realize that, "given the situation," they should make every effort to maintain whatever decorum they could? "Good manners are always in order, no matter the circumstances."

She waved a hand dismissively. "You know what I mean. You're hurt and I've got berries to collect. Now, do you need help getting situated before I head back out?"

Her question set his teeth on edge. He wasn't entirely helpless. "I'll manage."

She studied him uncertainly. "Your foot—"

"Is better off inside my boot where the pressure will keep the swelling down."

"But what if it's a break?"

"It's not." And even if it was, there was nothing she could do about it.

She nodded, then looked around. "Now, what can I put the berries in?"

"Are you sure you want to do that now? The rain hasn't slacked off yet."

She shrugged and gave him a playful smile. "I'd rather be wet than hungry."

He started to point out that they had other things to eat, but then decided there was no point. Her mind seemed to be made up. "In that case I think the hamper is probably our best bet."

"Of course." She knelt and quickly emptied the contents. Reaching for the hat and coat, she nodded toward the blanket. "Set yourself down and I'll be back in no time."

"I'm coming with you."

She paused with one arm in a coat sleeve and one not. "I can handle this. You should get off that foot—"

He ignored her protest. "It doesn't take legs to pick berries. And, since I'll be sharing in the fruits, literally, I should also share in the labor." He grabbed up the hamper, tightened his grip on his cane and headed for the door. She could follow or not as she liked.

A heartbeat later he heard her scurrying to catch up. "You are one of the stubbornest men I've ever come across. And if you'd met my brothers you'd know that was saying something." She flounced past him, pushed the door open, then turned back to face him. "You stand here with the hamper and I'll pick the berries." Before he could argue she held up a hand. "You're almost dry so no point in getting yourself soaked again. Besides, if you insist on going out there I'll feel obliged to give you back your coat and hat and how gentlemanly of you would that be?"

Speak of stubborn! He stared at the downpour. "Perhaps we should just wait to see if this lets up soon."

"It's not coming down quite as hard as it was earlier. And what if it doesn't stop? I'd just as soon get to it while I'm still wet. Once I get dry I'm not going to be quite so eager to step outside again."

He supposed that made sense. But the woman was never going to dry out at this rate.

Without waiting for his response, she drew the collar of his jacket up higher and stepped out into the storm.

Several minutes later, as she dumped yet another handful of berries in the hamper, he took her wrist and drew her out of the rain. "Time to come back inside. We have plenty enough to hold us for a while."

As if not quite trusting him, she peered into the hamper. "I suppose that'll do for now."

Eli turned, glad that he could finally get off his feet. He hadn't taken more than two steps, though, when he realized she'd stepped back out in the rain. What was she up to now?

Ignoring the throbbing in his foot, he set the hamper on the floor and limped back toward the door. "Miss Lassiter?"

"I'll be there in a minute." Her voice was muffled but he could tell she hadn't gone far.

It was several long minutes later before she reappeared inside the doorway. Not surprisingly, she wasn't empty-handed.

"Look what I found," she said nodding to the four large pieces of firewood and two stout sticks in her arms. "There's a chopping block out back. There's more but the other pieces hadn't been split yet and they were too heavy to carry. Anyway, I thought these might come in handy for the fire."

Hadn't she seen the small pile he'd stacked by the fireplace? Or, like him, was she worried about how long they'd be stranded here? "It was a good thought, but these pieces are soaking wet."

"I know, but if we place the pieces just inside the fire-place around the fire, they'll dry out faster. Then if we get down to where we need them, we'll have a better shot at getting them to burn."

While she crossed the room with her burden, he fol-lowed more slowly with the hamper. The woman had a sensible head on her shoulders after all, it seemed. Had he been wrong about her in other ways?

Once she'd arranged the damp wood to her satisfac-tion, Miss Lassiter stood and rolled her shoulders. Then she shed the garments he'd loaned her and hung them back on the make-do coat pegs.

"Thanks for the use of your hat and coat." She studied them with a wince. "I'm afraid they're showing signs of what I put them through."

He shrugged. "They can be replaced."

She made no move to approach the blanket and her face wore a slightly embarrassed look. Surely she wasn't worried that he would—

"I've got water in my shoes," she blurted out. "I was

thinking I'd take them and my stockings off and set them by the fire to dry. If it won't offend you, that is."

Was that all? "Of course."

She nodded and hesitated. Realizing her dilemma, he busied himself with studying the items she'd pulled from the hamper earlier, keeping his gaze averted to allow her what privacy he could while she removed her footgear.

A few moments later she carefully arranged her shoes and stockings on the uneven hearth.

"Ready to eat?" Wanting to put her at ease, he kept his tone conversational.

She nodded. "As soon as we give thanks."

Give thanks? She saw something in this situation to be thankful for? But he supposed keeping to normal rituals in such an otherwise unusual situation gave her comfort and perhaps some sense of normalcy. So he would go along with her request. And since she seemed to be waiting for him to lead the blessing, he dutifully bowed his head. "For the food we have before us, Lord, we give You thanks and ask that You continue to bless our respective families and our endeavors. Amen."

Miss Lassiter echoed his "Amen", then nodded toward the cluster of food items. "I'll take one of those pears if you don't mind."

He nodded and reached for the fruit. To his surprise, she remained standing as he handed it up to her. What now?

As she accepted the pear from him, he noticed the red marks on her wrist and frowned. "What happened?"

She followed the direction of his gaze, then gave a sheepish smile. "I got a little careless. Dewberry vines have lots of nasty little thorns and I tangled with a few when reaching for the plumper berries." Before he could offer sympathy, she shrugged. "Don't worry, though, I've gotten much worse on other berry-picking expeditions."

She took a bite out of the pear, and his gaze was captured by a little dribble of juice that found its way to her chin. He couldn't seem to look away, until she used her sleeve to wipe it away.

Giving his head a mental shake, he turned his focus to the food, grabbing the jug of apple cider to moisten his unaccountably dry throat.

Miss Lassiter appeared not to have noticed anything out of the ordinary. She was staring at one of the windows, her head cocked to the side. "Sounds like the rain's coming down even harder now. Good thing we picked those berries when we did. We may be in for a long afternoon."

Eli merely nodded. No point in adding to her worries. Fact was, even if the rain stopped in the next few minutes, he had no idea how in the world they were going to get around that fallen tree. His only hope right now was that they'd be missed before long and someone would be out looking for them.

"Did you tell Danny you were planning to come out here?" He kept his tone casual.

"Not specifically. It was supposed to be a surprise."

So much for that idea. No one would know where to look even if they realized the two of them were missing. Miss Lassiter had definitely not thought things through this morning.

"You might as well sit," he said. "There's plenty of room here."

She shook her head. "My skirts are soaked." She wrinkled her nose. "Sitting would be uncomfortable right now. I thought I'd stand in front of the fire for just a bit to try to speed the drying process."

Which was sensible but it put him in the position of lounging on the floor while she remained standing. He wasn't doing very well in the gentleman department.

They ate in silence for a while, Eli trying hard not to stare at her bare feet and trim ankles peeking out from the hem of her skirt.

An explosive sneeze, quickly followed by a second, jerked his gaze up to her face. "Are you okay?" Had she caught a chill?

But she dismissed his worries. "I'm fine. I think it's just all the dust we kicked up when we were cleaning earlier."

Eli grabbed the jug of cider. "Would you care for some of this?"

She nodded and set the core of the pear in the fireplace. Wiping her hands on her gown with the indifference of a child, she took the proffered cider.

"I'm afraid you'll have to drink straight from the jug—I didn't see any drinking glasses."

The caveat didn't seem to bother her. "I'll manage."

As Miss Lassiter drank, Eli studied her closely for other signs that she might be taking ill, but she seemed remarkably robust.

After a couple of deep swallows, she absently handed the jug back to him while she studied the room. "I wonder what kind of history this place has. I mean, I know it's not much to look at today, but now that we've cleaned it up a bit, I can picture how it might have looked back when it was new. It would have made a cozy little home for some farmer and his wife."

Eli looked around skeptically. Even though it was midafternoon, the dark-lidded sky and semi-shuttered windows left the one room cabin in shadow except for the area here by the fireplace. No matter how hard he tried, he couldn't picture this place as anything but a hovel.

"Whatever its history, apparently it didn't suit," he said diplomatically. "It appears to have been abandoned for some time."

"Yes, but aren't you at all curious about why? Maybe there was some great tragedy, where the farmer or his wife died and the one left behind could no longer bear to be here. Or maybe they headed farther west looking for adventure. Or maybe the farmer who lived here married a woman who preferred life in a big city." She had a faraway, dreamy look. "There are so many stories a place like this could tell."

What in the world was she going on about? "Speculating over such things seems like a pointless exercise."

She studied him as if he had somehow disappointed her. "Don't you like imagining things? I mean, don't you ever do things like make up stories to tell Penny?"

He shifted, feeling her opinion of him had just dropped a few points. "I read to her from time to time." It was hard to keep the defensiveness from his tone.

"Not quite the same, but it's a start."

A start? A start on what?

She bent down and scooped up some of the berries. "I think my back is dry enough." She fanned her skirt out with her free hand. "Time to dry the front." And with that she turned to face the fire.

Eli placed his palms behind him on the blanket and leaned back as he studied her back. She was definitely a puzzle to him. How could a woman be so sensible one moment and so fanciful the next? And why was Penny so taken with her? His half sister had been so quiet and withdrawn since the tragedy. But around Miss Lassiter she seemed more lighthearted than she had since he'd assumed guardianship.

Truth be known, while he'd hoped it was just a matter of giving Penny time to grieve, he'd worried that she'd been permanently scarred by everything that had happened. Yet she seemed to really come alive around Miss Lassiter. And while he was relieved to see the old Penny come back, he couldn't help but be curious as to the reason.

He studied the coiled tendrils that had escaped his companion's pins, listened to her soft humming as she held her skirt out to the fire. And wondered again if perhaps he'd misjudged her.

Sadie studied the flames as she absently munched on the berries. How very sad and lonely to live without the occasional daydream, without letting the imagination have reign from time to time. Had he always been that way? Or had something in his life hardened him? Maybe he just needed someone to teach him how.

For Penny's sake, of course.

She wiped her hands together as she finished the berries. Her skirts were still damp, but they were dry enough to sit now.

Sadie turned and knelt down across from him on the quilt and reached for the sack.

"What are you looking for?"

"Just seeing what we have to work with." She emptied the sack, dumping the contents between them. There were the gloves and large pieces of net they'd used to protect themselves from the bees. Some rags. A ball of twine she'd brought just in case.

Mr. Reynolds didn't appear impressed. "Doesn't look like there's much that'll be of any use to us."

His lack of imagination was showing again. "All depends on how long we'll be stuck out here."

"Hopefully it won't be longer than another hour or so."

Sadie nodded, but she wasn't feeling very confident. The rain was still pounding pretty hard and not showing any signs of letting up. "So, what do we do now?"

"What do you mean?"

"Well, we can't just sit here staring at each other all afternoon."

He raised a brow. "I'm open to suggestions."

Was he now? "Do you know any games?"

There went that eyebrow again. "You mean like chess?"

She grinned and shifted to a sitting position. "Afraid we don't have a board and pieces handy. How's your memory?"

"Better than average."

"Then let's put it to the test with a word game called *I Packed My Suitcase*. The rules are pretty simple."

For the next hour they occupied themselves with simple word and memory games. It took a while, but once Mr. Reynolds relaxed, he seemed to get into the spirit of the challenge. He turned out to be quite competitive, but no more so than her brothers.

But unlike her brothers, he didn't tease or throw the occasional game her way. It was refreshing to know he considered her a proper opponent.

Finally, he reached for his makeshift cane. "I'd better feed the fire again before it goes out."

She popped up to a kneeling position. "You should stay off that foot. I can take care of it."

He gave her a reproving look. "I'll manage."

Sadie sat back down on her heels. So much for the easy camaraderie they'd shared a moment ago.

She watched him stir the coals and lay additional chunks of wood just so. "You're pretty good with a fire. Have you ever been out camping?"

"No, but I've tended my share of fireplaces."

"Too bad. There's nothing like sleeping out under the stars on a clear night." Not that she expected him to understand such a simple pleasure.

Eli frowned, not certain he'd understood her properly. "I would imagine it would be uncomfortable, what with having to deal with the hard ground and the elements and the insects." Sort of like what they would be faced with if the rain continued for much longer.

"Oh but if you've got a proper bedroll the ground doesn't feel so hard and if by the elements you mean the fresh air, the stars and moonlight, the scent of trees and grass and saddle leather, then it's really quite pleasant. As for the insects, I like the sound of their nightly chirping but yes, the mosquitoes and such can be a problem. A bit like the thorns on a rose, you put up with taking a little extra care in order to enjoy the beauty of the flower."

The woman was an incurable romantic. She always seemed to try to paint things in the most positive light. Why couldn't she accept that not every cloud had a silver lining?

He pushed himself up, leaning heavily on his make-shift cane. "Well, to each his own, I suppose."

She tried to brush a stray tendril off her forehead. "So, what shall we do now? I can come up with another word game if you like."

He was tired of word games. "Why don't you tell me about your family."

"All right." She gave him a cheeky grin. "I like to think we're a pretty special lot, but I suppose I'm a bit biased. My father comes from a long line of cattle ranchers. His grandfather built Hawk's Creek and it's grown to be one of the biggest and most respected cattle ranches in northeast Texas. Mother came from a prominent Philadelphia family, a real socialite. But when she met my dad she was ready to give up everything to be with him, just like in a fairy tale. She married him and settled quite happily into life as a cattle rancher's wife. Unfortunately, she died when I was eight, so for most of my life it's been me and my two brothers and my dad. I spent a good part of my growing up years trying to keep up with my brothers, while they spent theirs trying to treat me like a baby sister."

Something about the way she said that last part caught his attention. Almost as if she had mixed feelings about the role they'd cast her in. His curiosity got the better of him. "Tell me about your brothers."

She smiled in obvious affection. "Ry and Griff are the best brothers a girl could ask for, bar none. But they're as different from each other as the moon is from the sun."

"How so?"

"Ry is five years older than me. He's the one who taught me to ride a horse, how to climb a tree and how to fish. But over the past dozen years he's spent as much time in Philadelphia as he has at Hawk's Creek—maybe more. He got himself some big city polish and a college education and eventually became a lawyer."

"Actually, I met him just before he and Mrs. Collins's sister set out on their trip. I didn't spend much time with him but he seemed to have a well thought-out approach to things."

"Yep, that's Ry. He seemed a little lost for a while— sort of torn between his life in Philadelphia and his life on the ranch. But he met Josie last year and Viola became his ward about the same time. Those two were the saving of him. He's settled down and found a way to make his west-meets-east background work for him."

"And your other brother?"

"Griff's three years older than me and there's not a lick of ambivalence in him. Just like our pa, Griff's a cattle rancher through and through. His life is tied to Hawk's Creek like a tree to the earth. He seems to know just about everything there is to know about cattle, and a lot of it he got on his own." Her smile took on a reminiscent quality. "When I was still in pigtails he taught me to throw a rope and to build a fire and skip stones." She stared into the fire. "Since our dad died three years ago it's been just him and me running the ranch."

"Sounds to me like they haven't babied you at all. On the contrary it seems they've taken pains to teach you to be much more independent than is normal in a young lady." Perhaps her hoydenish tendencies were a result of her upbringing in an all male household.

She laughed. "Oh they taught me all kinds of useful skills. It's just…"

"Just what?" he prompted.

"They never stopped seeing me as the baby sister.

Someone to be humored, teased and then patted on the head while the menfolk took care of things. They still call me 'Sadie girl', same as they did when I was six."

"Sounds more of an endearment than a judgment."

She laughed self-consciously. "Oh, you're probably right. I don't know why I even mentioned it. My brothers love and respect me. Same as I do them."

He eased himself back down on the blanket. "So, your brother Ry likes to work with horses and do a bit of lawyering on the side, and your brother Griff has ranching in his blood. What do you want out of life?"

She seemed uncomfortable with that question. "I'm still trying to figure that out."

Then she brushed her hands and hugged her knees. "My turn. What about you? Do you have any family besides Penny?"

Eli shifted. He shouldn't have started this line of talk. "It's just Penny and me now."

Before he could turn the subject to something less personal, she made an observation. "Penny's so much younger than you—I guess you were really an only child growing up."

He nodded. He'd been on his own for what seemed most of his life. But not any longer. He hesitated a moment, then decided it wouldn't hurt to share just a little of his history. After all, she probably was hungry for a bit of a distraction from their current situation. "Like you, my mother passed on when I was young—six in my case—and it was just me and Father until he remarried when I was seventeen. Penny was born a few years later. I'd moved out shortly after so I'm afraid I didn't know her as well as a brother should until I recently became her guardian." He hadn't done all those things for his sister that her brothers had done for her.

"I can tell you care for her a great deal. She's lucky to have you."

Penny probably didn't share that sentiment. But he fully intended to make up for that lack, as well. With the proper wife by his side, his little sister would get the attention and discipline she needed to grow into a confident, genteel young lady.

Afraid he'd revealed too much, Eli cast around for another kind of distraction. "You know, I imagine I can use my knife to scratch a checkerboard into the floor. If I pull the tacks out from some of those old shutters waiting for the fire that'll give us one set of pieces and we can break some of twigs into bits to make the other set. I think we can actually try to make a game of it."

She nodded agreement and moved to the woodpile. Eli studied her for a moment, wondering how she could say with such authority that Penny was lucky to have him for a brother. She barely knew either him or his sister so her feelings on the matter were meaningless. So it was altogether strange that he'd felt that uncharacteristic shot of pleasure at her declaration and smile of approval.

Not that he was seeking her approval. No, it was more likely just a sign of how tired he was.

Eli sat on the uneven hearth, staring moodily into the night-darkened room. If pressed he'd guess it was probably sometime around midnight, but he wasn't curious enough to pull out his pocket watch. He shifted, trying to get comfortable. Not easy since his foot was throbbing unmercifully.

Sadie slept nearby, her soft breathing keeping a steady

rhythm that seemed to be in tune with his own pulse beat. He'd insisted she place his folded coat inside the sack and use it for a pillow, so hopefully she was relatively comfortable. Perhaps not quite as comfortable as she would be if she'd had one of those proper bedrolls she'd mentioned earlier.

He studied her in the faint light afforded by the glow from the fireplace. Curled up on her side, with her bare feet and ankles peeking out from her modestly arranged skirts, she looked both peaceful and oddly vulnerable. She was such a petite thing—he really couldn't blame her brothers for wanting to coddle and protect her.

But if they still considered her a child they were off the mark. She'd surprised him today. There'd been no hand-wringing, no hysterics, no sitting back while she waited to be rescued. All things he would have expected from most of the well brought up women of his acquaintance.

In fact, Miss Lassiter had proven herself to be both resilient and industrious. She'd tended to the horses, cleaned, picked berries in the rain, collected firewood, and when insects became a problem as the light began to fade, she was the one who'd come up with the idea of using the netting to cover the windows. And she'd done all of that without any prompting or expectations from him.

Just as surprising, however, was her generosity of spirit. She'd been quick to share the bounty of the berries, making sure he had some before she ate her fill. And she'd gone out of her way to find him the walking stick in the pouring rain. He absently picked up the stick, resting his hands on the knobby end. She probably didn't realize how having this had made him feel a bit more useful, a bit more in control.

Or had she?

He listened to the sound of frogs and insects playing counterpoint to the occasional drip-drip-drip of water falling from the eaves. The rain had finally tapered off to an intermittent drizzle about forty minutes ago—with luck it would be entirely gone by morning.

Then what? Hopefully he could use the harness to hook the horse to the tree and drag it far enough for the buggy to squeeze by. If that didn't work he could always ride out on the horse and go for help.

But it wouldn't change any of the facts regarding their current situation. He stared again at her peacefully slumbering form.

Somehow he didn't think she'd realized yet that both of their lives were about to change.

Chapter Seven

Sadie stretched, wincing at the stiffness of her muscles. A moment later she remembered where she was and sat bolt upright.

Eli—hard to think of him as Mr. Reynolds after what they'd shared the last twenty hours—was over by the fireplace, placing another chunk of wood on the embers.

"Good morning."

He glanced over his shoulder. "Good morning."

The lines on his face seemed more deeply etched this morning. "Did you get any sleep at all?"

"Some."

Liar. Then she realized how quiet it was. "The rain stopped."

"So it seems." The thought didn't seem to cheer him up any. He nodded toward the hamper. "I prepared breakfast." His voice held a hint of dry humor.

She scooted over and peeked inside. "You picked more berries. But your foot—"

"I managed."

"Thanks." She studied his profile. Something was bothering him. Was it his foot? Or was he concerned about how they were going to move that tree? Or was it something else?

Whatever was on his mind, the least she could do was try not to add to his worries. She got to her feet with as much dignity as she could muster. "I think I'll step outside for a few moments before I eat."

"Of course."

She pulled her stockings and shoes back on, noticing he kept his gaze averted. As she headed out the back door, she thought again about what a meticulous gentleman he was, despite his brusqueness. He knew how to make her feel comfortable and safe without being obvious or condescending about it. Such consideration was both comforting and refreshing.

Sadie found herself humming as she stepped outside into the fresh morning air. *Heavenly Father, thank You for this glorious day. And thank You for getting us through all the trials of yesterday relatively unscathed. Help me to remember, at least for this day, to think before I speak and act, to not be so impulsive.*

When she returned several minutes later, Eli was poking at the fire with a stick—one that looked suspiciously like the remnants of her makeshift broom. He glanced up but almost immediately went back to studying the fire. She rubbed her arm as gooseflesh pebbled her skin. What had put that somber look on his face?

Sadie finger combed her hair as best she could, then twisted it in a bun at the back of her head. She had no illusions that it looked even remotely smooth and stylish, but at least it was out of her face.

She knelt beside the hamper and scooped up a half dozen or so berries. "Aren't you going to eat, too?"

"I ate while I was picking them."

Still not feeling particularly talkative it seemed. This time she let the silence draw out as she munched on the berries. But she watched him closely from the corner of her eye.

Soon this little adventure of theirs would be at an end. In a strange way she was kind of sorry. She was surprised to realize she'd actually enjoyed spending time with him, especially since he'd lost that disapproving frown somewhere along the way.

After her second handful of berries she decided to try to draw him out. "So what's the plan for this morning?"

For a moment it appeared he was going to ignore her question. But he finally turned and settled on the hearth, facing her. "We need to talk."

She slowly placed the stopper back in the jug of apple cider and folded her hands in her lap, steeling herself for whatever bad news he wanted to impart. "All right. What about?"

He raked a hand through his hair, as if trying to gather his thoughts.

"If you're worried about that tree across the road," she offered, "I'm pretty sure we'll be able to move it. And even if we can't, we've likely been missed and folks will be looking."

If anything, his expression grew more sober.

He leaned forward, giving her a probing stare. "I'm not worried about the tree." He waved a hand dismissively. "Or at least that's not what I want to discuss with you at the moment."

Now she was *really* getting worried.

He rubbed the stubble on his jaw. "I've been debating with myself since first light about whether to have this discussion now or after we get back to town. And

I've come to the conclusion that it's better to discuss this while we have a bit of privacy."

All this hemming and hawing was starting to irritate her. "Then out with it."

"What you said a moment ago, about us having been missed by now—"

When he paused she clasped her hand around her knees. "I know you're concerned that Penny's been worried to distraction about you. But I've been thinking on that. Since no one knew we were making this little side trip, Cora Beth probably figured we decided to hole up at Ry's place to wait the storm out. Course, that means they probably won't send anyone to look for us for a while yet. But—"

He made an impatient movement with his hand. "That's not the point I was trying to make."

"Oh." This time she decided to keep quiet until he had his say. No matter how long he took getting to the point.

"There's no way to broach this without being indelicate, so I'll just be direct."

About time.

"We spent the night alone here last night. And we're not going to be able to hide that fact."

Sadie felt the heat rise in her face. What was he saying? "But—" She swallowed then tried again. "But nothing happened. I mean, you were the perfect gentleman—" She couldn't finish that sentence.

He gave her a sympathetic look. "I want you to know that you're not to worry about any of this. I'm prepared to do the right thing by you. As soon as we get back to town we can announce our intention to get married."

Married! She scrambled to her feet—hang dignity. "Mr. Reynolds! You're making too much of this."

But his expression never wavered. "I know this is not ideal, not for either of us, but I see no other option."

If she wasn't so angry at his high-handedness she'd be mortified by his obvious lack of enthusiasm for what he was proposing. "Then you aren't looking hard enough because *I* sure see other options." Her mind scrambled to come up with something. "For one, we can just go about our lives as if nothing happened—because *nothing did*. And I'll be heading back to Hawk's Creek in a week or two anyway."

"Miss Lassiter, I refuse to believe you care so little for your reputation." He stood and clasped his hands behind his back. "You're in shock I suppose. Understandable. I've had a little more time to reconcile myself to the inevitable, but you haven't had that luxury. Once you've had an opportunity to think things through, you'll see that marriage is the only possible option—for either of us. Believe me I've given this considerable thought."

The fact that he seemed so reluctantly resigned didn't do much to warm her to his plan. She'd be hanged if she'd marry some man who not only proposed to her out of a sense of duty, but who had, up until yesterday, shown such disregard for her as a person.

She tilted up her chin. "I think it says something about your upbringing that you'd regard the townsfolk with such cynicism. I don't know about where you come from, but the people around here are not such self-righteous, judgmental gossips that we should be shamed into marrying just to appease them."

He'd stiffened. "It has been my observation that people are pretty much the same wherever you go. But be that as it may, it's not so much that people will gossip— which they will—but that there are certain conventions within civilized society that we are expected to meet. These conventions are there for a reason and to flout them is to risk ostracism and criticism. Not to mention the sorry example this would set for Penny."

"Penny is nine years old. She won't even notice any improprieties unless we make an issue of it."

He looked like a man who was having trouble controlling his temper. "Miss Lassiter—"

She held up a hand to interrupt whatever other argument he was prepared to deliver. "Save your breath. Nothing you can say will change my mind. Perhaps we should concentrate on getting back to town."

His lips tightened. "Very well. But this conversation is *not* over."

She repented slightly as she noted the way he was favoring his hurt foot. In the heat of their argument she'd forgotten about his ankle. "You're still limping. Maybe we should just wait here until help comes."

"There's nothing that guarantees help is coming anytime soon. Or at all, as you noted a few moments ago. And I'd prefer not to spend yet another night in this cabin. I'll manage."

"But Danny will figure it out—"

"I'm sure he will—eventually. I just don't intend to sit here and twiddle my thumbs hoping it's sooner rather than later. That storm will have washed away any sign of our passing and the searchers might not bother to go past that tree until they've checked out the easier-to-get-to places. Besides," he gave her a crooked grin, "it'll be better than just sitting here and continuing this conversation."

Good point. She gave a short nod. "Agreed. If you

think you can get started packing up our stuff, I'll go hitch the horse to the buggy."

She had another reason for wanting to get back to town as soon as possible. She was worried about his ankle. The sooner Dr. Whitman had a look at it, the better she'd feel.

As she stepped outside, though, some of her assurance slipped away. Surely he was making too much of their situation? He had to be wrong about the sort of reception they'd receive when they got back to town. Oh, she didn't doubt that a few loose tongues would wag, but it would blow over soon enough. There was absolutely no need to do anything so rash as rush to the altar as if they were guilty of something.

By the time she returned inside, Eli had all the supplies packed and the fire damped. She suspected it had been a matter of pride for him to not have to ask for help.

She picked up the honey and the sack while he grabbed the hamper and the blanket. Without a word they exited the cabin. At the doorway she turned and took a final look back. Even with all that had happened, she'd enjoyed their time here yesterday. The two of them had worked together well. Sure, she'd had to overcome his initial tendency to underestimate her, but once she'd elbowed her way past that, she'd felt like a true partner in their adventure, felt her contributions were worthwhile and valued. In fact, it said something for how far they'd come that he hadn't tried to talk her out of tending to the horse and buggy.

Realizing Eli had continued on to the buggy, Sadie hurried after him. He seemed to be leaning heavily on the walking stick, but otherwise fine. If she wasn't so annoyed with him, she could almost wish he would lean on her shoulder again.

Sadie told herself it was concern over his safety on the uneven ground that prompted the thought, not the miss of his touch on her shoulder.

As he set the hamper in the back of the buggy, she watched him for signs of pain and fatigue. He should have looked a sorry sight—his clothes were wrinkled and covered with smudges from the dirt and ashes, he needed a shave and his limp was pronounced. Not to mention her suspicion that he hadn't gotten much, if any, sleep last night.

So why did he look so appealing, so heroic?

On the other hand, she had no illusions that, with her muddy skirt, hair that hadn't seen a brush in over twenty-four hours and thorn-scratched hands and wrists, she looked like anything more presentable than a scruffy ragamuffin.

Sometimes, life just didn't seem fair. *I know, Lord, I shouldn't be so self-centered and vain. But this man sure knows how to scramble my thinking.*

Once she had settled into the buggy, Eli gave the reins a flick to get the horse moving. Sadie didn't even bother to offer to take the reins this time. She understood him much better now than she had when they set out on this trip—was it really less than twenty-four hours ago?

But this whole issue of marriage had spoiled things. The air practically thrummed with the tension between them and she didn't know how to ease it. How could he believe she would seriously contemplate marriage—they hardly knew each other.

Was he right about the reception they would receive?

Would people really think they had, well, had been…
indiscreet?

No! And even if they did, it didn't matter what everyone thought. Marriage was a sacred institution, instituted and blessed by God. She refused to marry simply because he couldn't face a bunch of gossips. He might be ready to buckle under but her faith was stronger than that. Besides, she'd always expected to marry someone she loved and who loved her in return. The kind of marriage her parents had had. The kind of marriage her brother Ry had found. She refused to settle for anything less.

And, no matter how much the oh-so-proper Mr. Reynolds postured and argued, he couldn't force her. Because she knew deep down that he didn't really *want* to marry her—his tone and his choice of words had made that abundantly, humiliatingly clear.

Still, she couldn't stop her mind from wondering what it would be like to have him propose to her under other circumstances…

Dear God, I freely admit to being confused. Please help me to discern Your will in this and please give me the strength to follow wherever that might lead.

Eli kept going over this morning's conversation in his mind, wondering if he could have handled things differently, could have presented his case more persuasively. She was undoubtedly one of those females with romantic sensibilities when it came to marriage—he should have realized that. But there seemed to be a sensible streak in her, too. Surely she understood that, under the circumstances, there hadn't been time for flowery speeches and heartfelt declarations—not that he was given to such things anyway.

And regardless of how much she protested, he found it hard to believe she cared so little for what other people thought of her. Most other females faced with such public censure would have been relieved to have him step up with such alacrity. She just needed more time to accept the inevitable, as he had. She would come around, and the sooner the better.

But it would cause less talk if they were of one accord from the outset. There would be enough tawdry gossip as it was, no point adding additional fuel to the fire. He had to make her see reason before they reached town.

Eli halted the buggy a few feet from the fallen tree. Miss Lassiter hopped down almost before he'd tied off the reins. She went to work unhitching the horse without a word, her silence after her chattiness of the day before an obvious testament to her high emotions.

He stepped down from the wagon as well, though much more deliberately. He might not be able to do the entire job himself, but he'd be hanged if he'd sit by and watch her do it alone.

Before he'd joined her, however, Eli heard a rider approaching.

"Someone's coming," Sadie said, echoing his own thoughts. "I knew Cora Beth would send help."

The relief in her voice stiffened his shoulders. Didn't she think him capable of getting them out of this fix?

They both moved toward the tree to get a better look and a second later the rider came into view.

"Sheriff Hammond!" Miss Lassiter's hail sounded like that of a long-marooned sailor who'd spied a sail.

The new arrival reined in his horse just short of the tree. "You folks okay?"

"We are now." She pushed the hair back off her face. "You sure are a sight for sore eyes."

Eli felt a flash of annoyance. Did she really think so little of his ability to get them out of this?

The sheriff's gaze came to rest on Eli's cane. "What happened to you?"

"Twisted my ankle. I'll be okay."

The new arrival leaned back in the saddle, one arm draped casually over the pommel. "I reckon you don't look too much the worse for wear."

"How'd you find us?" Miss Lassiter asked.

"Cora Beth asked me to make sure you'd weathered the storm over at Ry and Josie's place and hadn't got caught out in it." Sheriff Hammond dismounted. "I'll admit I got a mite worried when Miss Dotty told me you never showed up."

"Sorry you had to make a trip all the way out there for nothing." She waved an arm to encompass the scene. "As you can see we took a little detour. How did you know where to find us?"

"Danny pulled me aside and told me about you questioning him on the location of the beehive. He thought you might have been tempted to try to find it."

"He told you where it was?"

The lawman grinned. "Only after swearing me to secrecy."

"We found the hive and gathered the honey, sort of as a surprise for Cora Beth. But then Mr. Reynolds hurt his ankle, and the storm came and the tree fell blocking the road. It was all quite dramatic—a real-life adventure."

Was that a grin the sheriff was trying to hide? "Looks like y'all managed to find a dry place to hole up."

Sadie nodded. "There's a cabin back there a way. Kept

us from the worst of the storm and we even managed to get a fire going in the fireplace."

"Oh, the old Dubberly place. Still standing is it?"

"Just barely."

Sheriff Hammond finally turned his focus to Eli. "Glad y'all had a safe place to spend the night."

Eli didn't miss the look or the question behind it. Should he announce the wedding plans now to set the man's mind at ease?

But Sadie reclaimed the sheriff's attention, chattering on about the honey and lightning strike and the dewberries. He was relieved that she glossed over the episode with the snake.

The sheriff finally tipped his hat back. "Well it sounds like you two had quite an adventure. Miss Lassiter, why don't you get back in the buggy and off this muddy road while Mr. Reynolds and I take care of moving the tree?"

Eli was not surprised to see her forehead wrinkle in protest.

"But I can help—"

"I'm sure you can," Sheriff Hammond's tone was genial, "but I'm also sure you wouldn't want to deprive us menfolk of the opportunity to show off our hero potential for a pretty lady such as yourself. Besides, Cora Beth would have my hide if she knew I allowed you to lend a hand with this."

Eli was impressed, and just a tiny bit jealous, of how easily the man maneuvered Sadie into returning to the buggy without wiping the smile from her face. But, at least now he wouldn't have to watch her do what should be his job.

As the two men tied the horse to the fallen tree, Eli felt Sheriff Hammond's assessing gaze on him once more.

"I want you to know, sheriff, that I'm quite aware of my duty. I have every intention of doing what I can to protect Miss Lassiter's reputation. To that end, we will be announcing our engagement very soon."

The sheriff's expression relaxed a bit. "Then I suppose congratulations are in order."

"I'll ask that you don't extend any felicitations to Miss Lassiter just yet. She's not taking to the idea very well."

"I see." He glanced her way then back at Eli. "Then of course I'll wait until the more public announcement is made." He was silent for a moment as he worked with the traces. He glanced back up. "I assume I won't have long to wait."

Eli certainly hoped not. "We'll make the announcement as soon as Miss Lassiter gives me leave."

That seemed to satisfy the man and he turned his focus back on the job at hand.

Thirty minutes later the tree had been moved just enough to allow the buggy to slip by. Once Eli maneuvered the buggy around the obstacle, Sheriff Hammond remounted and they set off, with the sheriff riding alongside the buggy.

For a while, Sadie kept the conversation going with light, inconsequential talk. Not that she fooled him for a minute. Was the sheriff as aware of the strained undercurrents as he was?

Finally Miss Lassiter turned to the sheriff. "Would you mind riding on ahead and letting Dr. Whitman know about Mr. Reynolds' injury? I think it's important that he have it tended to as soon as possible."

"Of course." Sheriff Hammond gave Eli a sympathetically amused look, then tipped his hat to Sadie and rode off.

Sadie turned to Eli with an 'I told you so' look. "Sheriff Hammond didn't seem at all inclined to think poorly of us. I knew you were worried for nothing. And I'm sure the other folks in Knotty Pine will be just as understanding, just you wait and see."

"You're wrong." He kept his tone even. "Sheriff Hammond was quite aware of the situation, he was just too much of a gentleman to let it show in front of you. The only reason he seemed so equitable is because I assured him we would be announcing our engagement soon."

"You did *what?*" Her voice rose several octaves. "You had no right—"

"Please compose yourself. I did what was necessary to make certain your reputation did not suffer further damage."

His explanation did not seem to appease her. If anything her chin tilted higher. "My reputation is my business. You don't—"

"Miss Lassiter, just because you speak with such conviction doesn't make what you're saying fact."

She clamped her lips shut at that and tossed her head. The rest of the trip was accomplished in prickly silence.

When they arrived in town, Danny was waiting for them. "Cora Beth said y'all are to head straight for the boardinghouse. I'm gonna fetch Doc Whitman to meet you there and then I'll bring the buggy back to the livery for you."

Eli nodded and turned the buggy toward the boardinghouse. It seemed Cora Beth had already figured out that Sadie needed to be protected from prying eyes. Why couldn't Sadie herself see that?

A few women stood outside the mercantile, watching as they made their way toward the boardinghouse.

From the corner of his eye he saw one of them lean over to whisper in her companion's ear.

So it begins, he thought.

Chapter Eight

Sadie tried to ignore the looks cast their way, tried to convince herself that the glances signified nothing more than idle curiosity. Still, the back of her neck prickled uncomfortably.

When they arrived at the boardinghouse, even before the buggy came to a halt, Cora Beth came rushing down the front steps to meet them, closely followed by Uncle Grover. "Sheriff Hammond told me what happened," she said. "I've been worried to no end about you since that storm rolled in yesterday."

Sadie scrambled down from the buggy. "I'm so sorry to have worried everyone like this. It was all my fault." Still feeling the weight of those glances, she felt compelled to add, "But Mr. Reynolds was a perfect gentleman the whole time."

Cora Beth gave her a quick one-armed hug, patting her back at the same time. "I'm sure he was." Then she pushed away and studied Sadie's face. "Are you sure you're all right? You look so pale."

"I'm fine, truly. Mr. Reynolds is the one who's hurt."

Cora Beth turned back to Eli as if just remembering

him. "Oh my, yes, of course. Bless your heart, Sheriff Hammond told me about your foot. Let Uncle Grover help you down and then we'll get you into the downstairs chamber and make you comfortable while you wait for Dr. Whitman."

Sadie wondered if she was the only one who saw the flicker of annoyance on Mr. Reynolds's face. No doubt about it, the man did *not* like to be thought of as weak in any way.

"No need to worry over me." His tone was mild, reflecting no hint of the annoyance she knew he was feeling. "I'll manage fine with the use of this walking stick."

"No need to be stubborn, my boy," Uncle Grover observed. "There's no shame in allowing others to help you now and then." He held the walking stick while Eli climbed down, then handed it back to him. "Sturdy piece of oak you've got there but it's a bit rough. I'll fetch you one of my own to use as soon as we get you settled in."

The words had barely left the older man's lips when Dr. Whitman came strolling up the walk.

Ten minutes later, Cora Beth stepped out into the hallway and turned to Sadie. "We'll just leave him in Dr. Whitman's capable hands for the time being. Uncle Grover can assist if need be. Now, you come along with me and I'll prepare you a nice bath."

Sadie nodded. "Actually, that sounds wonderful."

"You go find a change of clothes and I'll fetch the kettle of water that's been heating on the stove."

Sadie halted and turned back. "Oh no, don't you be trying to fill that tub on your own—I'll be back down in a minute." She placed a fist on her hip. "Promise me."

Cora Beth rolled her eyes but nodded and made a cross-my-heart sign over her chest.

Satisfied, Sadie plodded up the stairs. Her limbs felt heavy and there was an uncomfortable throbbing at her temples. She was suddenly so very, very weary. How could the events of one day have so completely turned her world upside down?

When she stepped inside her bedchamber she glanced in the mirror and gaped at her appearance. No wonder Cora Beth was in such a hurry to get her into a bath. And no wonder those folks in town had been staring. She looked a bedraggled mess. Her mud-splattered and forlornly wrinkled dress, her mussed hair, her smudged hands and face—she definitely didn't look like a lady who'd waited out the storm in the comfort of her brother's home.

Turning her back on the much-too-revealing mirror, she quickly gathered up a fresh change of clothes and a few other necessities, then headed back downstairs. When she stepped into the bathing room, Cora Beth was pouring something into an already full bathtub. An empty kettle sat on the floor next to her.

She glanced up with a smile. "There you are. I hope you don't mind but I added some of the fancy bath salts Josie got for me when she was in Philadelphia this past winter. I thought you could use some pampering after what you've been through."

Just what did Cora Beth think had happened while they were gone? She pushed that thought aside. "I thought you promised not to fool with that kettle on your own."

"I didn't. Nettie Dauber is cooking for us today—interviewing to be Mr. Reynolds's new cook—and she very kindly took care of it for me."

"Oh." So there was an outsider in the house. Would the woman go carrying tales as to what went on here today?

Better not think about that for now either. "And thank
you for the bath salts, but it wasn't necessary."

Cora Beth waved off her comment. "Don't you worry
about that—I wanted to do it. Now, I've laid out several
thick towels for you to use and the water is nice and
steamy, so you can soak as long as you like."

"Thank you. For everything." Sadie set her clean
clothes on a nearby bench and started pulling pins from
her hair—what few pins remained, that was. "Any word
from Dr. Whitman on Mr. Reynolds' condition?"

"Not yet." Cora Beth moved toward the folding screen
that was pushed against the far wall. "As soon as Doc's
done with the examination I'll let you know."

"Here, let me do that." Sadie took one end of the
screen and the two of them arranged it in front of the
tub. When it was placed to their satisfaction Sadie stood
uncertainly for a moment. She felt the need to explain.
Problem was, she wasn't sure just *what* she wanted to
explain. "Cora Beth, I feel just awful for putting you
through all this trouble and worry."

"Pish-posh. I'm just relieved you're both okay."

Sadie chewed at her lip for a moment then tried again.
"Mr. Reynolds is concerned that there might be some
talk around town."

"Is he now?"

Cora Beth's tone was carefully neutral and Sadie
wasn't having much luck reading her expression either.
"Yes. I told him he was overreacting."

"And how did he respond?"

Still no hint of how she felt. "He asked me to marry
him." The words hung in the air between them, almost
as a living thing. Sadie hurried to take away some of
their power. "Isn't that the silliest thing you ever heard?"

But Cora Beth shook her head. "I don't see anything silly about it at all."

Not the response she'd hoped for. "Oh, for goodness' sake. To marry simply to avoid gossip—it's ridiculous."

"People have married for less compelling reasons."

Did Cora Beth really believe what she was implying? "Compelling? Aren't you giving too much influence to idle gossip?"

"Perception and appearances can be very powerful forces."

"So can the truth and self-assurance."

Cora Beth smiled. "You're right, of course. And I will support you no matter what you decide. You just need to think seriously about the long-term implications of whatever decision you *do* make." Cora Beth kept a steady hold on her gaze.

"But nothing improper happened." The words came out almost as a wail.

"Oh Sadie, I don't doubt that for a minute. But that doesn't change the fact that the two of you *did* spend the night alone together in an isolated cabin. The folks here in Knotty Pine are good, fair-minded people for the most part, but the rules of acceptable conduct among *any* Christian community are very unforgiving in such matters."

Sadie couldn't dredge up a direct response to Cora Beth's logic, so fell back on her own emotions. "But marriage is a sacred institution. No matter what the circumstances, I could never make those vows lightly."

Cora Beth straightened and made a shooing motion, indicating Sadie should step behind the screen. "For goodness' sake, here we go nattering on while your bath is getting cold. Get out of those dirty clothes so I can wash them and you can get your soak."

As Sadie complied, Cora Beth continued. "I wouldn't expect you to make this decision lightly. Nor does Mr. Reynolds strike me as a man who would enter into marriage frivolously."

"Then you understand my position." Sadie tossed her skirt over the screen.

"I truly admire your scruples," Cora Beth continued after a moment, "But there are times when we must set our personal wishes aside. Do you think you can face the whispers and stares?"

Sadie tossed the remainder of her clothing over the screen. "I'm not so fainthearted that I can't face down a gaggle of gossipers."

"When it comes down to it," Cora Beth continued, "would marrying Mr. Reynolds be such a terrible fate?"

Sadie was glad she was behind the screen so Cora Beth couldn't see the heat rising in her cheeks. Sure, Mr. Reynolds was a nice-looking man, and there was something about him that tugged at her more than she cared to admit. But looks and honorable intentions weren't everything. And when she'd daydreamed about the man she might one day marry, he wasn't some straightlaced city fella and he sure wasn't some dour banker. No, she was looking for a rancher, someone who wasn't afraid to get his hands dirty and who would want to set down roots at Hawk's Creek, to help her turn her share of the place into something they could manage and take pleasure in together.

Realizing she'd been silent for far too long, Sadie covered her lack of response by making a bit of noise and she eased herself into the still-warm water of the tub.

Cora Beth cleared her throat. "Well, you just clear your mind of all of this for now and have a nice long soak before your water gets cold. There'll be time enough to think and pray over this after you're rested."

Once Cora Beth was gone Sadie settled herself more comfortably, letting the water envelope her. It felt wonderful.

But the niggling thought that this was the last moment of peace she would have for quite some time wouldn't allow her to totally relax.

Alone at last. Eli lay in the unfamiliar room they'd ushered him into and stared at the ceiling. First, his unexpected role as guardian, then the tragedy with his stepsister, Susan, and now this. It seemed that for the past year, no matter how meticulously he planned, no matter how good his intentions, no matter how certain his path, some unseen force had been playing fruit basket turnover with his life.

He had to get a better handle on things, had to put himself more firmly in control of his future, of Penny's future.

But for now, he needed to get this matter under control. If he didn't, all of his careful planning to ensure that his and Penny's new life here was above reproach would be for naught. Somehow he had to gain Miss Lassiter's cooperation. Because he wasn't about to let himself be defeated by the vagaries of circumstance. He'd just get busy figuring out how to turn this set of circumstances to his advantage.

The first order of business, of course, was making certain Miss Lassiter came to her senses and accepted the inevitable outcome, just as he had. Since he knew his strengths as a negotiator, he was confident he could make that happen in the next day or two. Once he had her agreement in hand, he'd salvage a portion of his original plan, with a few adjustments for the woman now irrevocably cast as the leading lady.

At least picking Miss Lassiter for a wife provided the advantage of his knowing from the outset that Penny would approve.

She wasn't the woman he would have chosen for the role, of course. He'd been looking for someone with more maturity and decorum. But he was willing to set aside his own preferences given the situation. Besides, though he still had some reservations about her suitability to take on the role of Penny's caregiver, perhaps Miss Lassiter wasn't as big a flibbertigibbet as he'd first thought.

Yes, she undoubtedly was spontaneous and unorthodox—two characteristics he had little appreciation for. But she'd shown surprising spirit during their ordeal. The fact that she hadn't uttered a word of complaint, fallen apart or given much thought to her appearance spoke well of her.

Perhaps she was one of those people who was at her best in a crisis. Which had both its good and bad points. Good in that she wouldn't fall apart when faced with problems. Bad in that, since they wouldn't be in a constant state of crisis, would she revert back to her flighty ways?

He let his mind dwell on the idea of being married to Sadie Lassiter. Surprisingly, he wasn't as upset by that thought as he would have been just twenty-four hours ago. With the right man to teach her the proper way to go about things, she could be the proper sort of wife he was looking for. And the idea of being the one to teach her, of taming her spirit just enough to take her place beside him, was actually quite intriguing.

Growing up without a mother, being raised by her father and brothers and a bunch of ranch hands—it was no wonder she was more than a little hoydenish. She had it in her to be level-headed and responsible, he could see that now. She just needed the right person to draw that out, to help her emphasize her better qualities and tame the less desirable ones.

And he was just the man for the job.

The next day was Sunday and Sadie carefully studied the dresses she'd brought with her to Knotty Pine. She usually wasn't one to fuss over her clothes overmuch, but what she wore for her first appearance in public since her and Mr. Reynolds's return to town yesterday somehow seemed a matter of great importance this morning. After much consideration, she settled on her simplest, most modest dress.

Cora Beth had kept her busy inside the boardinghouse with simple tasks all day yesterday, but there was no way she was going to remain indoors today. *Father, I'm determined to visit Your house this morning, no matter what—I truly need to show Cora Beth's neighbors that I don't feel the need to cower in private as if I'm guilty of something. But I'd take it kindly if You could keep the townsfolk's stares and whispers to a minimum.*

She hadn't seen much of Mr. Reynolds since they'd arrived back at the boardinghouse yesterday. According to Cora Beth, Dr. Whitman had verified that his foot wasn't broken, thank goodness. But the physician had also made it clear the ankle would need several days to heal.

It was strange, but she was both looking forward to

seeing him this morning and dreading it. The warring emotions were making her jittery, leaving her with an off balance feeling that she didn't much care for.

Would he be joining them for the church service or would he stay in his room with his foot carefully propped up on pillows? She wasn't even sure which she hoped for more.

When she headed downstairs, Cora Beth stood at the foot of the stairs, almost as if she'd been waiting for her to come down. "Are you sure you don't want to stay here and rest this morning?" she asked. "I know everyone would understand, what with the ordeal you had—"

"I'm perfectly okay—not the least bit tired." There was no way she would cower in her room. The best way to show everyone that her conscience was clear was to walk into church with her head high. "This is a fine Sunday morning and I need to be in the Lord's house giving thanks that He watched over me and Mr. Reynolds during that storm."

Cora Beth touched the locket at her throat. "You know you don't need to be in the Lord's house to give Him thanks. Still, if you've set your mind on going then I won't try to talk you out of it."

Mr. Reynolds stepped into the hallway just then and Sadie felt her pulse kick up a notch. His gaze locked onto hers with a determined glint. Would he bring up that silly notion of their need to marry?

But he broke eye contact and glanced around at the others who had started to gather downstairs. Sadie took in his Sunday-best garb and realized he was planning to go to church service this morning, as well. His foot must be better.

She noticed he was still using the stout branch she'd

found for him even though she'd heard Uncle Grover offer one of his own. It probably didn't mean anything, but it still gave her a warm feeling inside.

Cora Beth greeted him as he approached and Sadie dropped her gaze, guiltily aware that she'd been staring.

"I hope you don't mind," Cora Beth said, "but I took the liberty of asking Danny to fetch the buggy for you. I figured you'd want to ride to church this morning rather than walk."

Sadie saw that telltale twitch near the corner of his mouth and thought he was going to protest, then something seemed to flash between him and Cora Beth. To her surprise, he nodded, gave Cora Beth a "thank you," then turned to her. "Miss Lassiter, would you do me the honor of accompanying me and my sister in the carriage?"

Being alone with him would definitely *not* be a good idea, not with her emotions all swirling chaotically and this marriage business between them. "Thank you, but—"

Cora Beth stepped forward. "Go along now, Sadie. I'm sure Mr. Reynolds could use the company and the support."

Before she could protest again, Mr. Reynolds cleared his throat. "I would be most grateful."

She narrowed her eyes. It wasn't like him to sound so humble. But to refuse now in front of the others would seem churlish. Feeling outmaneuvered, she nodded and moved toward the front door.

A little later, as they rode through town, Sadie was grateful that Penny was seated between them. She served as a much needed buffer.

Yesterday, once Penny had assured herself that Sadie and Eli were okay, she'd begun comparing the whole misadventure to the exploits of Annabel Adams. While Sadie had been amused, Eli most definitely had not. And she supposed she could understand his viewpoint in this particular case.

As the carriage slowed to a halt in front of the church, Sadie felt the prickles of dozens of eyes studying the two of them, saw the speculative glances and knowing nods rippling through the clusters of townsfolk. She thought she'd been prepared, but she could feel the heat climbing up in her cheeks.

Sheriff Hammond stepped forward to hand her and Penny down. "Good morning, ladies. You're both looking mighty fine this morning." He glanced Eli's way. "Glad to see your ankle isn't keeping you down."

Eli carefully descended from the buggy. "Dr. Whitman is of the opinion I should be as good as new in a few days."

"I believe he said a week or two," Sadie corrected, ignoring his frown. "And that was assuming you stay off it."

The group from the boardinghouse strolled up just then.

"Hello, sheriff," Cora Beth greeted him with a friendly smile. "I want to apologize again for imposing on you yesterday."

The sheriff tipped his hat. "No problem, ma'am. All part of the job."

Somehow, as they prepared to enter the church, Sadie found herself flanked by Cora Beth on one side and the sheriff on the other. Eli was right behind them, surrounded by the children and Uncle Grover.

When they slid into the pew, however, Sadie somehow ended up seated between Penny and her brother. All through the service, Sadie kept her eyes focused forward, not daring to meet anyone's gaze but the preacher's. His sermon, one based on Jeremiah 29:11, touched her. It was comforting to be reminded that God had plans for each of them and that those plans were for their good. Still, when she stood at the end of the service she realized she'd heard very little of the sermon itself.

Forgive me, Father, for being so self-centered. Sometimes I need reminding that the only being whose opinion of me really matters is You.

As they exited the church, Reverend Ludlow clasped one of her hands between both of his. "I heard about the ordeal you and Mr. Reynolds endured during our recent storm. I'm thankful that the Good Lord saw fit to keep you both safe."

She was pleased to see there was no trace of censure on the man's face. "Thank you, Reverend. And you're right, God was definitely watching out for us."

She moved on to make way for others exiting the church, and found herself without a companion for the first time this morning. Strange that instead of relief she felt suddenly vulnerable.

"Good morning, Sadie dear."

She turned to find one of the older ladies of the community at her elbow. The face was familiar, but who was she? Oh yes—the lady who ran the mercantile with her husband. "Mrs. Danvers, good morning. It's a beautiful day, isn't it."

"Oh yes. It must be especially refreshing after that ordeal you went through during Friday's storm. I must say I admire how calm you are considering what you've been through. I confess I would be prostrate with hysteria."

Sadie gave a half smile, unsure of how that was meant.

"Thank you for your concern, ma'am, but I assure you I am quite well—comes from having a clear conscience, I suppose. Since I suffered nothing more than some minor inconveniences, there's nothing heroic about my current calm."

"Minor inconveniences." There was a note of incredulity in the woman's tone. "How admirable of you to put such a brave face on it. Still, a less…*adventurous* lady would undoubtedly be more strongly affected."

Sadie got the distinct impression that Mrs. Danvers did not think being adventurous was something to be proud of. But she kept her smile firmly in place, refusing to let the woman's words rattle her.

Eli took one look at Miss Lassiter and realized immediately that something was amiss. Not that she gave any overt signs. But still, he saw something in her stance…

He took a closer look, identifying her companion. Ah, Mrs. Danvers—so that explained it. Undoubtedly the less-than-subtle matchmaker was not happy to find her hopes for landing her daughter a match with this particular well-to-do bachelor had been so soundly crushed.

He excused himself from Sheriff Hammond and moved to Sadie's side. "Good day, Mrs. Danvers. Reverend Ludlow gave a mighty fine sermon this morning, don't you think?" He didn't miss the flash of relief that crossed Sadie's face. So, she was not as immune to censure as she had tried to have him believe.

The old biddy, however, gave him a decidedly frosty smile. "Quite fine, yes. I was just complimenting Miss Lassiter on how well she weathered that little adventure the other day."

"Yes, she is a remarkable woman, isn't she? Now, I

do hope you will excuse us but I have strict orders from Dr. Whitman to stay off this foot as much as possible."

"Of course. Good day to you."

Eli saw Myra Willows stroll past. Was it just this past Thursday that he'd scratched her off his potential-bride list because of the mere possibility that she could have been the woman hiding behind the name Temperance Trulove? That seemed such a trivial thing compared to his current situation.

As he handed first Penny and then Sadie up into the buggy, he took note of the whispers exchanged behind hands and the eyes that were quickly averted.

He had to convince Sadie it was time to put an end to the gossip and speculation before both of their reputations were beyond salvaging. For Penny's sake, if not their own.

As Eli escorted Sadie into the boardinghouse, the rest of their party strolled up the walk.

Viola skipped up to them ahead of the others and looked up at his companion. "Aunt Sadie, what's a reputation?"

Eli sensed the sudden tension in Sadie, felt an echo of it in himself. The mere fact that the child was raising the issue could only mean she'd overheard some talk.

"It's the way other people think of you," she said. He was surprised at how calm her tone and demeanor were. "For instance," she continued, "your daddy has a reputation for being a good horse breeder and an honest person, your aunt Cora Beth is known for making the best fruitcakes in the county, and Mr. Reynolds here has the reputation for being an honest businessman."

Is that how she viewed him?

The six-year-old seemed confused by the explanation. "Oh. I thought it must be a dress or pair of shoes."

"Why?"

"Because I heard Mrs. Franklin say it was a shame that yours was all soiled."

Eli stiffened, reflexively putting a hand at Sadie's back in support. He wanted to take away some of the sting she must be feeling, but wasn't sure how to do it. Then again, perhaps if she felt the full brunt of this *now* it would serve to shorten the time it took her to come to her senses.

Luckily Viola seemed to lose interest in the conversation, and skipped back to rejoin Audrey and Penny without pressing for further explanation.

"Are you all right?" Eli pitched his voice so that only she could hear him.

"Yes." But she didn't sound quite as confident as she had before.

He took advantage of the situation to press his case again. "Are you convinced now?"

"That there will be wagging tongues? Yes. I had hoped for better but I suppose it was inevitable."

He made an impatient gesture. Why did she insist on not seeing what was so obvious to everyone else? "You know that wasn't what I meant. And I would appreciate it if you wouldn't make light of the situation. We need to announce our engagement as soon as possible."

He could tell by her expression he'd gotten her back up again.

"And I would appreciate it if you would respect my wishes and stop pestering me with your talk of marriage." She raised her chin. "This talk will blow over soon, you'll see. And once I'm back at Hawk's Creek, that will be the end of it."

Was she just being stubborn, or was the idea of marrying him so abhorrent to her? "Perhaps as far as you are concerned, though I somehow doubt that. But what about the rest of us? What about me and Penny and even Viola, who all make our home here?"

He saw the argument forming on her lips and held up a hand to forestall her. "Very well," he said. "I will hold my peace for now. But we *will* talk of this again." With a short bow, he left her and headed to his room.

He paused in the doorway as he realized Penny had followed him, with something obviously on her mind. Had she heard any of the gossip?

"Did you need something?" He mentally held his breath, preparing himself for an uncomfortable discussion.

"Is your foot feeling better today?"

He relaxed. She was only worried about his injury. "Some. Don't you worry. I'll be as good as new before you know it."

She sat in a nearby chair and started swinging her legs. "Why were you and Sadie out there in the woods?"

A trickier question. "We were trying to replace the honey Miss Lassiter spilled the other night. There's a special place out there Mrs. Collins gets it from."

Penny's nose wrinkled. "Sadie didn't spill that honey, Eli. I did."

Eli stilled, staring down at his sister. "You did? But I saw Miss Lassiter..." He hadn't actually seen her spill it, just trying to clean up the mess.

He sat down hard on the bed. He'd made the wrong assumption and the maddeningly stubborn woman hadn't bothered to correct him.

Seems he wronged her yet again.

* * *

Sadie sighed in frustration as she climbed the stairs to her room. The man just didn't know when to let it go.

She'd found herself watching as he hobbled down the hallway. It was amazing how, even with his limp, he could make a dignified exit.

But as she entered her room, Sadie felt her determination waver just a bit. She'd faced condescension and criticism before, but never this questioning of her very character. Perhaps she should talk about cutting her visit short. If push came to shove, she'd find a way to make Cora Beth accept her offer to hire help to take her place. The thought of not seeing Penny again, though, saddened her to no end.

She refused to think about how the thought of not seeing Penny's brother again made her feel.

Chapter Nine

"Sadie, I feel responsible." Cora Beth, stood at the counter while Sadie washed the lunch dishes, looking genuinely contrite. "If you hadn't come here to help—"

Sadie raised a wet hand before Cora Beth could say more. "This is *not* your fault. Coming to Knotty Pine was entirely my idea, not yours. And taking that detour to collect the honey Friday was *also* my idea. My very ill-conceived idea as it turns out." How in the world could she have anticipated that what seemed nothing more than a quick side trip to help a friend would land her in this mess?

"Have you reconsidered Mr. Reynolds's offer?"

Actually, she'd thought of very little else since he'd so matter-of-factly proposed Saturday morning. Not that she'd changed her mind. "Like I told you before, I can't—"

Before Sadie could finish the sentence, the door flew open and a familiar figure came striding in.

"Griff!" She quickly dried her hands on her apron. "What are you doing here?"

Her brother crossed the room in ground-eating strides

and grasped her by her shoulders. He looked deep into her eyes, his expression tense, worried. "I heard what happened. Are you all right, Sadie girl?"

Sadie shot Cora Beth an accusing glance then turned back to her brother. "I'm fine, really. There was no need for anyone to worry you with this silly kerfuffle. And certainly no need for you to come hightailin' it out here to check on me." Why did her brothers continue to treat her like a helpless schoolgirl? Even their pet name for her, Sadie girl, made her feel relegated to the status of a child.

Cora Beth stepped toward the doorway. "I'd best go see what the twins are up to."

Griff barely acknowledged her exit as he continued to study Sadie. "You don't look fine to me."

He was too perceptive by half. She pretended indignation. "Griffith Michael Lassiter, I might be your little sister but that doesn't give you call to insult me like that."

But he wasn't to be sidetracked. "You know what I mean. I can tell this whole thing's not sitting right with you."

"Of course it's not. Getting caught out in that storm was more than a little inconvenient and unexpected. And yes, I might be a little worse for wear, but I truly am fine. In fact, now that it's over, I'm looking back on the whole thing as a great adventure."

Griff relaxed enough to smile at that. "Sadie girl, I do believe you could see a barn on fire and spin it into a yarn of high adventure."

"Nothing wrong with looking for the positive in things."

Griff turned serious again. "Is this Eli Reynolds fellow around?"

Sadie didn't like the way he said Eli's name, as if he

planned to dislike him on sight. "Not right now." She tried again to deflect his focus. "Anyway, who's keeping an eye on the ranch while you're here playing overprotective big brother? Aren't you in the middle of spring branding?"

Griff shrugged. "Red can handle things for now." He stepped back and crossed his arms over his chest. "So where is he? I'd like to have a word or two with him."

Uh-oh, that had an ominous sound to it. "Don't you go doing anything rash. Mr. Reynolds feels bad enough for what happened as it is, even though it was more my fault than his. He even offered to marry me." As soon as the words were out of her mouth, Sadie wished them back. But it was too late.

Griff got very, very still, like a predator just before it pounced. "He did, did he? And just why did he do that, Sadie girl?"

Sadie mentally groaned. Sometimes her brother's temper was too short by half. "Griff—*nothing happened.* He made the offer because he's a gentleman with misguided notions of what his duty is."

He studied her, his eyes lidded. "And did you accept?"

"No! Of course not."

At her protest, Griff's eyebrows went way up.

Had she been just a mite too emphatic?

"Are you sure nothing happened?" her brother asked.

"Positive." This time she managed to keep her tone conversational. "What I meant was, I refuse to marry *anyone* simply because circumstances beyond our control might give rise to a bit of gossip. Besides, he doesn't really want to marry me." Yet another admission she wished she could call back. What was wrong with her today?

Naturally Griff caught her slip—she could tell by the way his eyes narrowed. "Let me ask you again, where is Eli Reynolds?"

She didn't like the measured steel in his tone. "Before I tell you, you need to promise me you won't do anything rash."

Griff spread his hands in a semblance of innocence. "I just want to talk to him."

She sighed, knowing if she didn't tell him he'd find out some other way. "He's probably over at that house he's having renovated. I'll take you there."

"No thank you—just tell me the way. I think this conversation is one that should be kept just between him and me."

Sadie rolled her eyes. Whatever Griff and Eli had to say to each other, she sincerely hoped they could get past the posturing. It wouldn't do to have her husband and her brother at each other's throats.

Eli studied the new banister on the main stairway, but to be honest, his mind was not on the task at hand. The reaction of the townspeople to what had happened was just as he'd expected. Seems he'd left one scandal behind in New York just to land him and Penny in the middle of another one. If he didn't get the stubborn Miss Lassiter to see reason soon he might as well pull up stakes again and find another town to settle in.

A sound drew his gaze to the entryway and he saw a man with an intense, none-too-friendly expression studying him from the front doorway. Was he one of the workmen?

"Eli Reynolds?"

Something in the man's tone alerted Eli that he did not

consider himself an employee. "Yes?" A moment later he took in the familiar features and realized who this must be. The man's next words confirmed his suspicion.

"I'm Griff Lassiter—Sadie's brother." The man's demeanor remained assessing, suspicious.

"Mr. Lassiter, I'm glad you're here." At least from a something-that-needs-to-be-done standpoint. "Let's step into the parlor. The furniture is already set up there and we might as well make ourselves comfortable. I believe you and I have quite a few things to discuss."

With a stiff nod, Sadie's brother let him lead the way.

As soon as they'd taken their seats, Eli tried to take control of the conversation. "First, I want to assure you that absolutely nothing of an improper nature occurred while your sister and I were stranded in the woods. It was an awkward situation but your sister maintained her composure and I treated her with every respect."

"So Sadie says." He didn't sound entirely convinced.

Eli pressed on. "That being said, however, I know my duty and am prepared to do it."

"Sadie says she doesn't want to marry you. In fact she was quite emphatic about it."

Eli mentally winced at the implication behind those very blunt words. "Your sister has not yet fully realized the gravity of the situation. Surely you, as her brother, understand that we have no choice."

"As her brother," Griff repeated with a flinty steadiness, "what I *understand* is that my sister has both a tender heart and a hard head. If she says she doesn't want to marry you, then there's no way that you or anyone else is going to force her." The man's eyes could have bored through granite. "And to even try, you're gonna have to come through me."

Eli understood the strong protective instincts that drove him to defend his sister, emotions he'd gotten all too familiar with in the days leading up to his and Penny's departure from New York.

He had to make Sadie's brother see that he had her best interests at heart. "Mr. Lassiter, I assure you my intentions toward your sister are entirely honorable. Surely you understand that, through no one's fault, her reputation has been tarnished. I am merely trying to put the best face that I can on the situation and lend her the protection of my name."

That only deepened the man's frown. "The protection of the Lassiter name has always been more than enough to carry her and I don't see that changing. I intend to take my sister back to Hawk's Creek with me in the morning."

It appeared stubbornness ran in the Lassiter family. "I understand how you feel, she's your sister and you'd do anything to protect her." Oh yes, he knew the feeling well. "But I believe spiriting her away so precipitously would be a grave mistake." He refused to consider that that was exactly what he'd done with Penny. His reasoning, however, had been based not on an emotional knee-jerk reaction but on a carefully controlled assessment.

He leaned forward, trying again to find common ground with Sadie's brother—his future brother-in-law if things worked out as planned. "At least stay here long enough to give your sister sufficient time to think this through. Once she realizes the extent of the situation I think she'll begin to see reason."

"Give you enough time to coerce her into marrying you, you mean."

Did the man *know* his sister? "You're giving me way too much credit if you think I can convince your sister to do something she doesn't want to." Eli had spoken without thinking, but he noted the slight twitch to his visitor's lips and felt hope flicker back to life. "Besides," he used his most persuasive tone, "you'll be right here to make certain everything is handled as it should be."

Griff's expression hardened again. "You can sure as this morning's sunrise count on that."

Did that mean he planned to stay after all? Eli held his peace. And his breath.

"If Sadie has no objections," Griff said slowly, "I suppose I can stick around until Friday." Then he gave Eli a hard look. "But the moment she says she's had enough, we're on the first train headed north."

"Your brother came to see me today."

Sadie mentally winced. Eli's tone was conversational but she could read the undercurrents. They were standing on the front porch of the boardinghouse, watching the first stars of the evening make an appearance. The others had diplomatically stayed inside, though it had taken a stern look from her to stop Griff from joining them.

She inhaled the scent of roses from the nearby bushes. That scent always reminded her of her mother. "I apologize if Griff was overbearing. He can be very single-minded sometimes."

"A family trait perhaps?"

Sadie smiled, glad that he could find some humor in the situation.

Then he waved aside her concerns. "But there's no need to apologize. He was worried about you, and rightly so. I don't think he's ready to believe that he can't protect you from this. Naturally he's determined to stand by you, whatever decision you make."

She found herself pinned by his stare and decided to let him do most of the talking.

"I think his brotherly devotion is blinding him to the gravity of the situation," Eli said evenly. "If word of this incident were to follow you to your hometown, and it almost certainly will, even your prominent family name won't shield you from the wagging tongues. More importantly, it will put your chances of eventually finding a more desirable match in serious jeopardy."

She almost protested the idea of there being a 'more desirable match', but caught herself just in time. "Are you trying to frighten me into marrying you?" she asked instead.

He didn't rise to the bait. "Just trying to help you face facts. Perhaps I was less than sensitive back there at the cabin when I made my case for the need for us to marry."

What an understatement! But that wasn't the sticking point. "Admit it," she said, going on the offensive, "you don't want this marriage any more than I do."

He didn't try to deny it. "That's beside the point. But if it makes you feel any better, it's been my intention since I arrived in Knotty Pine to seek out a proper wife, one with whom I can build my new life."

That *did* surprise her. Of course, she doubted he considered her 'proper wife' material. "Part of furnishing your household?" She wished the harsh words back as soon as she uttered them.

Something flickered in his expression, but he covered it quickly. "Let's say, rather, that it's an effort to *complete* my household. Penny is at an impressionable age where she needs a maternal influence."

"Then hire a nanny. A marriage should be based on mutual caring and respect."

She saw the muscles in his jaw tighten. "I'm sorry if what I'm offering doesn't meet your notions of what a marriage should be, but it has of necessity become my measuring stick."

It must make for such a joyless life to be so analytical about *all* aspects of one's existence. "So, are you saying you see me as someone who could provide that maternal influence to your sister?"

He shifted slightly before he answered. Which was, she supposed, in itself an answer. For a moment the only sound was that of the insects welcoming the darkness.

"You *could* be," he finally said. "Naturally we would need to come to an understanding of the sort of routine and discipline to be maintained in our household."

His main focus was *discipline?* Surely she'd misunderstood. "Those things are important, of course. But surely you're also looking out for what will make her feel loved, encouraged, supported?"

He tugged on the cuff of his shirt. "Sound discipline and a steadfast routine are required to produce true harmony in a home. Harmony, in turn, leads to contentment. Those other, more sentimental notions, can be deceptive, even harmful, if not tempered with a rational approach. Naturally I wish Penny to be happy, but not at the expense of providing a proper upbringing and considering her ultimate well-being."

"Ultimate well-being comes from God alone."

"Of course. But we must do our part, as well. And I'm determined to do everything in my power—including finding her a mother figure to provide the proper example."

Actually, it sounded like he wasn't looking for a motherly influence for his sister, he was looking for a warden.

Which meant he needed to look elsewhere—she most definitely would not fit the bill. But poor Penny.

She straightened. "Mr. Reynolds, while I appreciate that you're attempting to be gallant, I will assure you again that I'll survive this brouhaha without resorting to a hasty, unwanted marriage. Especially given that you and I have such different notions of what we want in a spouse."

He brushed at a moth flitting nearby, his frustration evident in his expression. Then he seemed to come to a decision. "I think you're under the impression that I'm doing this entirely for your benefit, and I'll confess that I allowed you to believe that. But that's not entirely true."

She eyed him suspiciously. Was this another ploy to get her to agree to his proposal?

"It isn't just *your* reputation at stake. I was there too, remember?"

What was he getting at? "But surely, I mean, you're a man."

"Yes. But do you think any woman of character will want to marry me if the perception is that you and I were…indiscreet? And that I refused to do right by you afterwards? Not to mention how this might affect Penny."

Surely none of this would affect that sweet, innocent little girl? "You're being overly dramatic again." But she felt her determination waver. What if there was some truth to what he was saying? She'd never forgive herself if Penny felt the sting from any nasty gossip.

He leaned a hip against the porch rail. "Oh, perhaps someday I might shake the stigma, but not anytime soon. And I need someone to help me care for Penny now."

Sadie started to repeat her earlier refusal, but something in his expression caught her attention. Beneath his logic and confidence, she saw another emotion flicker in his expression, something that looked very much like *need*.

It had to be her imagination. Still, it stopped her for a moment. "For someone who doesn't care much for melodrama, you seem to be quite adept at it."

His lips twisted in a wry grin. "This does seem very much like our own version of the Adventures of Annabel Adams, doesn't it?"

Had Penny planted that idea or had he come up with it on his own?

"Still, I'm asking you to think about what I just said, to take into consideration what it will mean to how Penny and I are accepted here in Knotty Pine, before you make your final decision."

She could tell that hadn't been an easy request for him to make. Did he truly *need* her? The thought confused her, set her mind spinning in a different direction. Perhaps she *had* been too hasty in making her decision. *Heavenly Father, I've been guilty of not seeking Your guidance in this matter. Guess it's time I started to do a little more listening and a little less deciding.*

"Maybe you're right," she finally said. Then she quickly held up a hand as victory flashed in his expression. "I only mean that I agree I hadn't considered how all this might affect you and Penny and that I do need to give it more thought and do some praying about it."

"Quite reasonable," he said magnanimously. "Take a few days if you need them."

She turned toward the front door, then had another thought. "Would you mind, I mean, perhaps we could pray together for heavenly guidance."

He gave her a startled look, then nodded. "Of course."

"You can start." She bowed her head and closed her eyes.

There were a few seconds of silence and then, "Lord, please give Miss Lassiter the clarity of vision to see that marriage is the only logical solution to this unanticipated situation and then give us both the wisdom to conduct our lives with honor and dignity."

She glanced up, slightly shocked. She'd never heard anyone pray in that manner—*telling* God what the outcome should be rather than seeking His will. It seemed so, well, so presumptuous.

But it wasn't for her to judge.

She bowed her head again, and added her own prayer to his. "Heavenly Father, we give You thanks for Your wonderful gift of grace, a gift You extend to us daily. And we thank You again for watching over us during that storm and providing us with the comfort of food and shelter. Those berries were especially nice. We acknowledge that You are all-knowing, all-powerful, ever-present and all-loving. Which means You already know about the pickle Mr. Reynolds and I find ourselves in. We are of two different minds on what we should do about this and are sorely in need of Your guidance. Please provide us with the wisdom to understand Your will and the courage and good sense to follow it, no matter our reservations or desires. Amen."

She opened her eyes to find him studying her with a slightly puzzled look in his face. What was he thinking? No matter, she needed to have some time to herself. "Thank you for praying with me. Now, if you'll excuse me, I think I'll retire to my room."

He straightened. "Of course. I hope you have a good

night's rest and I look forward to hearing your decision soon."

"You'll be the first person I discuss it with." She stepped back, strangely reluctant to leave him.

As soon as she entered the boardinghouse, Griff stepped out of the parlor. "Anything we need to talk about?"

Sometimes she could do with a little less big-brothering. "Not on my account. I'm going up to my room." She ignored his concerned frown and headed for the stairs.

But she was waylaid once more before reaching her destination. Penny met her at the top of the landing, an anxious expression on her face. "Are you going to marry my brother?"

Penny obviously felt strongly about this—but which way? "I haven't decided yet." She studied the little girl, trying to read her reaction. "How would you feel about it if I did?"

The child's cheeks pinkened, but her expression lost none of its earnestness. "It would be nice to have someone else in the house with us. And I like you—you smile a lot."

Now that was a telling statement. Did her brother not "smile a lot" when they were alone? "Thank you—I like you, too. And you have a very pretty smile that brightens up the room when you choose to share it with us."

"So you'll come live with us?"

She brushed a lock of hair off the girl's forehead. "I need to pray about it before I know my answer to that. And I'd appreciate your prayers, as well." She stooped down to give Penny a hug. "But whatever I decide, you know that you and I will always be special friends, don't you?"

Penny nodded.

She gave the girl a light pat on her backside. "Now scoot. I need to go to my room and I think Audrey and Viola were looking for you."

Sadie watched Penny head down the stairs, then turned to her room. The thing about this whole situation was that there was a part of her that *wanted* to tell him yes. But even that traitorous part of her wanted it only if he was going into this willingly, happily. Not because he felt he had no other choice.

Then again, was he right about how her continued refusal would affect his and Penny's standing in the community? And if he was, was that a burden she was willing to carry, that she even had a right to carry?

Heavenly Father, I'm so confused—please let me see Your will in this. It occurs to me that I've been imploring You to help me find a place where I can feel truly useful and of value, but I never imagined it might lead to this. Is this marriage truly Your will? Or should I stand firm in my refusal?

Sadie lay awake far into the night, no more sure of what answer she would give Eli than when she'd left his company.

Eli lay with his arm behind his head, staring up at the ceiling in the moonlit bedchamber.

He tried to tell himself that she would give him the answer he sought, but he wasn't quite so confident. His admission that he needed her had chipped away at her stubborn stand, but had it been enough to convince her? He devoutly hoped so, because the idea that he hadn't would mean his and Penny's position in this town was in serious jeopardy.

The strangely personal prayer she'd uttered this evening still echoed through his mind. Naturally he believed in the civilizing influence of religion. He said grace at every meal, attended church on Sundays, gave a portion of his income to the church. He took pains to make certain his sister was raised to understand moral and spiritual concepts.

But he'd never heard anyone speak so intimately and familiarly to God as Miss Lassiter had out there on the porch. It was as if the deity was not only real to her but was a close friend. As if when she asked for guidance she was confidant she would receive it. As if she had *faith,* not logic.

After the first few words he'd opened his eyes and watched her, studying her face, trying to understand what drove her. Her eyes had remained closed for a few moments after the "Amen," then she'd opened them and met his gaze with a soft smile. A smile that had made him momentarily forget all the reasons why she hadn't been his first choice for a wife.

But his head had cleared quickly. And now he was back to making certain he had things well in hand. Assuming she did agree to marry him, because the alternative was not worth considering, he needed to adjust his plans accordingly. He was confident that, give the opportunity, he could make this work.

If she could learn to control some of her exuberance and spontaneity, to think before she acted and to conduct herself with more decorum, then they would get along quite well indeed.

But that was a whole lot of "ifs."

* * *

As Eli rose from the breakfast table the next morning, Miss Lassiter cleared her throat and met his gaze.

"Before you head for the bank," she said, "I'd like to have a word with you."

Thank goodness. She'd been a little late joining them in the dining room and he hadn't been able to read anything in her expression. In fact, he'd begun to think he'd have to be the one to initiate the conversation.

She cut a quick glance toward her brother. "In private."

Eli ignored the frown on Griff's face and kept his focus on Sadie. "Of course. If Mrs. Collins would allow us the use of the family parlor?"

At Cora Beth's nod he swept out his arm, indicating Miss Lassiter should precede him. This was it, he could tell from the determined set of her back that she'd reached a decision. What would he do if her answer was still no? For that matter, what would he do if her answer was yes?

They entered the parlor without another word. Eli pulled the door to, making sure it did not close entirely.

Miss Lassiter eyed the gap, but made no comment. "Before I give you my answer," she began, "there are a couple of things we need to discuss."

He leaned back, trying not to show signs of the relief flooding through him. Surely if she was going to say no she would have come right out with it. Given the circumstances, if what she wanted was assurances, he was prepared to give them to her. "So let's discuss."

"How do you feel about dogs?"

Not the turn he expected the discussion to take. But

he would follow her lead. "I have no objections to the animals in general."

"I have a dog. His name is Skeeter and I've raised him from a pup. Were I to move, I would expect to take him with me." She gave him a challenging look. "You should understand, he's used to having the run of the house."

Was that all? While he wasn't particularly enamored with the idea of giving a dog the run of his new home, and he found pampered lapdogs irritating, it was a small concession to make to get her to the altar. Besides, he could set some boundaries once they were married. "Of course. In fact, I'm sure Penny would enjoy having a pet around."

She nodded, as if his acquiescence had been a forgone conclusion.

He felt a flicker of irritation at her presumptuousness, but let it go. "So, are you prepared to give me your answer now?" Time to get on with it.

"There's one other matter we need to discuss first."

He certainly hoped this next issue was as innocuous as the first. "I'm listening."

She took a deep breath, as if fortifying herself. "I'm Temperance Trulove."

Chapter Ten

Eli felt his jaw tighten as the tolerant smile on his face froze. Of *course* she was the author of that bit of nonsense. He should have realized it before. Not only was the timing right but it was exactly the sort of thing he would expect of her.

It was several heartbeats before he could trust himself to break the crackling silence. "I see. I suppose it was harmless enough as a way to pass the time. But as my wife you will have other responsibilities to keep you busy so of course you'll give that up. I mean, there will hardly be time—"

She held up a hand. "Make no mistake, I fully intend to continue. Not only did I make a commitment to Mr. Chalmers at the *Gazette,* but I find I really enjoy writing the stories. Mr. Chalmers already has the next two installments and I had planned five more to finish off Annabel's adventures."

"Miss Lassiter, I simply cannot allow a wife of mine to devote time to such a frivolous undertaking."

She stood. "Then you have your answer, sir. We have nothing more to discuss."

Irritation and frustration warred with his desire to gain her agreement to his marriage proposal. "Wait."

She raised her brow and he realized there'd been more than a touch of command in his voice.

He tried to moderate his tone. "Please, sit back down." Looked like it was his turn to make a hard-to-swallow compromise.

The "please" mollified Sadie somewhat. And she belatedly remembered the decision she'd made this morning, and more importantly, why she'd made it. But that didn't mean she was going to just let him stampede over her on this.

"I assure you I'm quite determined."

"Perhaps we can strike a compromise. My main concern is that you don't present an improper example for my sister. If I go along with this, I would need to have your word that you won't let Penny know you are the author of that—" he caught himself "that story."

Her chin tilted up at his continued autocratic pronouncements and she mentally counted to ten. *Heavenly Father, You're going to have to help me find patience if we're going to make this work.* "I won't lie to her if she asks." She finally replied. "But I will agree not to offer up the information on my own."

He didn't seem particularly pleased with her response, but after a moment, he nodded. "Agreed." Then he leaned back. His pose was relaxed but she sensed an underlying tension. "Does this mean you are now prepared to accept my proposal?"

Was she really ready to do this? There'd be no going back if she said yes. But hadn't she already reached that point?

She squared her shoulders, said a quick mental prayer and then met his gaze. "Yes, I suppose it does."

A quickly suppressed flicker of relief was his only reaction. She hadn't expected any deep emotional response to her acceptance of his proposal, but still...

"Good." He tugged on the points of his vest. "Now that we're in agreement on that point, there are a few additional details to be worked out. First, there's picking a date for the wedding. Since time is of the essence, I trust holding the ceremony on Saturday will give you enough time to do whatever planning is necessary."

This Saturday? "But that's only five days away." She clasped her hands together in front of her. "I mean, won't such haste seem almost an admission of guilt?"

He didn't seem to share her concern. "Actually, I think the sooner we put this whole situation behind us the better it will be all the way around."

How romantic.

"Besides," he continued "I assume your brother can't stay here indefinitely. And having his presence at the ceremony will serve two purposes. First, I assume you want to have family present for obvious personal reasons and second, it would add an additional air of normalcy to have his visible seal of approval."

"Yes, of course." He'd definitely been giving every aspect of this a lot of thought. Did the man ever act spontaneously?

He smiled approvingly. "The house will be ready by then, too. It'll be a smoother transition for all of us if you can join Penny and me when we move in and immediately step into the role of lady of the house."

She took a mental breath and nodded. "Of course. I guess I just hadn't expected things to move quite so fast."

Goodness, by the end of the week she would be Mrs. Eli Reynolds. Was she ready for that? She tucked a strand of hair behind her ear, feeling unaccountably nervous.

More importantly, was *he* really ready for that?

Eli was oddly touched by the hint of vulnerability in Sadie's expression. "I know this is all a bit disconcerting and will take some getting used to, but I'll be right here to help you get through it." He chose his next words carefully "And I won't rush you into anything you're not ready for." Did she understand his meaning? From the slight blush on her cheeks, it appeared she did.

"Now, I've already spoken to Reverend Ludlow," Eli continued, "and he's prepared to perform the ceremony whenever I give him the word."

Her eyebrow went up. "Taking my agreement for granted, were you?"

The touch of dry humor in her expression was a good sign. "Not at all, though I was definitely hoping. And I wanted to make certain everything was in order in case you did, um, agree." He'd almost said *come to your senses.*

"Then I suppose there's no reason to delay. Saturday it is."

And just like that, it was settled. Eli took a moment to absorb that he was truly engaged to the woman seated before him. There was a touch of unreality to the whole situation.

As they stepped out of the parlor, he wasn't at all surprised to find Griff Lassiter standing nearby. The man didn't make any effort to hide the fact that he didn't trust Eli where his sister was concerned.

"You can be the first to congratulate us, Griff." Sadie's smile was perhaps a bit too bright. "Mr. Reynolds and I are engaged to be married."

But her brother didn't look as if he were eager to hand out congratulations. He shot a suspicious glance Eli's way, then turned to his sister. "Are you sure, Sadie girl?" His voice was surprisingly tender.

"Quite." She placed a hand on her brother's arm. "Don't worry. I've prayed long and hard and I've decided this is not only what I *need* to do, but it is what I *want* to do." She gave his arm a squeeze. "Truly."

Her words surprised Eli and pleased him at the same time. Did she mean it? Or was it just a way to appease her brother?

He waited while Griff studied Sadie, as if looking for some sign of duress or unhappiness.

Then Griff turned his stare back his way. "Make sure you do everything in your power to take care of her." Then, without a backward glance, he marched up the stairs to his room.

When Sadie finally turned back to him, her smile seemed a bit forced. "How do you suggest we spread the word?"

"Don't worry, that will happen quite naturally. For now, I thought perhaps it would be a good idea for me to give you a tour of the new house."

"Right now?"

He'd expected a little more enthusiasm. "If it's not too inconvenient. After all, it will soon be your home as well and you've never set foot inside. This will give you an opportunity to look things over and see if there's anything you want to change."

"You would let me make changes?"

The speculative way she asked the question gave him

pause. Was she already planning something? But now was not the time to second-guess himself. "Within reason, of course. I want you to be comfortable and feel at home there."

"Don't you think you ought to let Penny know about our decision before we make any announcements?"

He should have been the one to think of that. He knew Penny liked Miss Lassiter, but how would she feel about having her as part of their household? "We'll tell her together. In fact, let's invite her to tour the house with us. She hasn't seen the latest changes."

"Doesn't she have school this morning?"

"We'll call a special holiday—it's not every day her brother gets engaged." And it would probably be best to have her with them while they were touring the house. He planned to bend over backwards to follow the very letter of propriety between now and the wedding.

He was pleased to see Penny's broad smile when they delivered news of their upcoming nuptials. Sadie, with the impulsiveness he was becoming resigned to, stooped down and scooped the girl up in a tight hug. Whatever her feelings about him, Sadie seemed to have no reservations about his sister.

He studied the picture they made with their bright smiles and two heads bent together. There was a feeling of rightness there, as if they were already on the road to becoming a proper family.

When they separated, he cleared his throat. "I'm going to show Miss Lassiter our new house this morning. Would you care to join us?"

Penny's eyes grew large. "But what about school?"

"I think it will be okay if you miss just one day. What do you say?"

Penny nodded quickly. "Let me just tell the others to go ahead without me." And she raced off down the hall.

"Since she's telling the kids," Sadie said, "perhaps we should tell Cora Beth and Uncle Grover."

Cora Beth was predictably delighted and promised to help Sadie with all the planning and preparation that went into a wedding. Uncle Grover offered congratulations and announced his intent to make them a "special gift." Since the man was an entomologist, Eli had some concerns, but decided to not add that to his current list of worries.

Later, as the three of them made their way down the street, Eli set a leisurely pace. They hadn't gone far from the boardinghouse when he spied a familiar figure. Mrs. Van Halsen—perfect.

He tipped his hat. "Mrs. Van Halsen, beautiful day isn't it?"

She paused but her smile was merely tepid. "Why, yes it is. I hope your injury is not paining you overmuch."

"It's healing quite nicely, thank you. Besides, it would take more than a twisted ankle to bother me today."

That seemed to pique her interest. "Oh?"

"Yes. In fact, I want you to be among the first to know—Miss Lassiter has done me the honor of agreeing to be my wife."

The woman's demeanor thawed immediately. "How marvelous. Have you set a date yet?"

"We want to start our married life together in our new home. So we'll speak our vows this coming Saturday. Everyone in town is invited, of course."

"Does that mean you'll be married here instead of your hometown, Miss Lassiter?"

An unanticipated question. Eli started to step into the breach, but Sadie spoke up first.

"Cora Beth still needs my help, so yes, we decided to be married here." Her voice was conversational, her expression polite. "That's why my brother will be here through Sunday, so he can walk me down the aisle."

"It's a shame you can't wait for Josie and your other brother to return from their trip."

"Yes, it is." Sadie placed a hand on Penny's shoulder, directing the woman's gaze that direction. "But Eli, I mean Mr. Reynolds, and I thought settling into our new family roles as soon as possible would be best for everyone. I know a caring mother such as yourself will understand why."

Mrs. Van Halsen looked at Penny, then back at Sadie and nodded meaningfully. "Of course, you're right as rain on that point. A mother's role is very important. I see now that it was a very wise decision on your part."

She gave a smile that took them all in. "My felicitations on your happy news and you can count on me to be there to see you wed." With another nod, she continued on her way.

Eli watched as the woman entered the mercantile and hurried over to the cluster of women gathered near the counter. The news of their upcoming nuptials would be all over town within the hour.

He turned back to Sadie. "Well done."

She gave him a smile and a shrug. "All I did was tell the truth." Then she glanced toward the mercantile. "The news will spread naturally, did you say?"

He smiled, feeling just a tad smug. "These things have a way of taking care of themselves."

After two more such encounters, they finally reached

their destination. Eli opened the gate to the front walk and waved Penny and Sadie on ahead of him. He was quite proud of the work that had been done, almost as if he'd done it with his own two hands. He had, after all, directed every step of the way.

He was pleased to see the approving smile on her face as she climbed up the wide front steps to the wraparound porch that fronted the soft yellow facade. This was probably a far cry from the ranch house she was brought up in.

He opened the tall double doors that served as the entrance and waved Sadie and Penny inside.

The new wallpaper had been hung just two days ago and added an elegant touch to the entryway.

Sadie touched the paper, tracing the design. "This is lovely."

Pleased by her response, Eli turned to his sister. "Why don't we show Miss Lassiter the dining room first?"

"You know, back at Hawk's Creek we didn't stand on ceremony much, especially in how we addressed each other. Since we're engaged now, I'd take it kindly if you'd please call me Sadie."

Her words took him by surprise. But her request was logical. "If you wish."

"And may I call you Eli?"

He should have offered sooner. "Yes, of course."

"What about me?" Penny asked.

"Why, you must call me Sadie, as well. After all, we're going to be sisters." She smiled. "I've always wanted a sister—it'll be nice to finally have my wish come true."

Eli saw a shadow flit across Penny's expression. And wondered if Miss Las—Sadie, caught it, as well.

Hoping to distract Penny, he quickly led them through

a door to their left. "This is the dining room. All of the furnishings come from our previous home in New York."

She looked around without a word. Was she overwhelmed by it all? Not that he would blame her if she was. He hadn't seen any furnishings of this quality since he'd arrived.

Once they'd looked their fill, he led them across the hall to the parlor.

"The doors on this room and the dining room are extra wide and made to fold away. When they're opened it makes for a large area, perfect for entertaining large groups. In fact, if you're agreeable, I thought it would be a good idea to combine the wedding reception with an open house here after the ceremony."

That should make her happy. He hadn't met a woman yet who didn't like to throw a party.

Host a large party? She could do that. She'd played hostess at the ranch a number of times. But she'd always had Inez to help with the details. Sadie squared her shoulders. She'd just have to get used to getting along without Inez's help from now on. Scary thought.

Then she realized he was waiting for her answer. "It sounds like a fine idea. It'll put us on a good footing with our new neighbors."

He nodded his approval. "Exactly."

"A party." Penny gazed up at her brother. "Can I come, too?"

Sadie didn't wait for Eli's response. "Of course you can, princess. After all, this is your house and you should help show it off, too."

After they'd admired the parlor sufficiently, Eli led them down the hall to another room. But Sadie's mind was only partly on the little tour he was giving them. The thought of her upcoming nuptials kept turning over and over in her mind. She thought she'd made peace with the idea. But now that she'd given her word, she found herself second-guessing the decision. And goodness, what had he meant when he said he'd "give her some time?"

Heavenly Father, please help me find peace with this new role I'm going to be taking on.

He strode down the hall and opened another door. "This was originally a bedchamber, but I had it turned into a library."

Sadie pulled her thoughts back to the present and gave her future husband—that thought still rattled her—her attention. She stepped inside and gaped. Three of the four walls were completely lined with floor to ceiling bookshelves. And the shelves were stocked with hundreds of books, all neatly arranged and organized. "My goodness. I thought we had a large library at Hawk's Creek, but I've never seen so many books in one place in my whole life."

She moved close enough to read some of the titles. There were texts on subjects from botany to history, from medicine to law. There were bound atlases, biographies and collected sermons. Books of poetry and music. She saw titles by Shakespeare and Dickens and Hawthorne. And so many authors that she didn't recognize. "This is a treasure trove. Have you read all of these yourself?"

He shrugged. "Most of them, but not all. Some of these were acquired by my grandfather or by my father."

What about the females in the family—didn't they like books?

"You can feel free to read any of these any time you

wish," he continued. "After all, they will be yours as well as mine once we're married."

So the man had no problem with literature as a rule. It was just her penning stories that he disapproved of.

The next room he led them to was his study. Another dark somber room full of heavy, solid furniture. "It suits you."

"Thank you." Then he gave her another glance, as if suspicious of her meaning. "And how do you like what you've seen so far?"

"Everything seems very solid and formal."

He seemed pleased by her response, as if formal was exactly the effect he'd wanted to achieve.

"Did you pick out all these things yourself?"

He moved toward the massive desk that dominated the room. "Most of these pieces were taken from either my former town house or my father's country estate. Some of them are relatively new and some have a rich history with my family. This desk, for instance," he said as he ran his hand lightly across the intricately carved rosewood piece, "was imported by my great-grandfather from England. The dining room table was commissioned by my father as a gift to my mother on the first anniversary of their wedding. That tapestry that hangs in the library was begun by my maternal grandmother and finished by my mother shortly before she died."

That did put the furnishings in a different light. She still believed, though, that the home would benefit from the addition of some whimsical touches to lighten the atmosphere. But she kept that opinion to herself.

Eli spread his hands. "Of course, if there are any personal pieces of your own that you wish to add, we'll most certainly find a place for them."

She mentally reviewed several of the items from Hawk's Creek she was most attached to and just as quickly rejected them. "Most of the furnishings at the ranch *belong* at the ranch." She paused a moment, thinking about what he'd just said, about the furnishings representing bits of his family history and tradition. Those things *were* important. "Then again, there *are* one or two pieces I might consider asking Griff to send back when he returns home." She mentally winced, wondering if he'd caught her slip. Hard *not* to think of Hawk's Creek as home.

"As I said earlier, since this will be your *new* home I want you to feel free to add whatever touches you like—to put your stamp on our home, as well."

So he *had* heard her slip. At least he didn't seem particularly put out by it. And his referring to this as "our home" warmed her heart all over again.

Before he could quiz her, she moved down the hall to the next room. This one was slightly smaller and the walls lighter in color.

He stepped up behind her. "This sitting room can be reserved for your personal use."

She nodded as she looked around. "I'd like to furnish it myself, if you don't mind."

"Not at all. Feel free to equip it as you like."

Ten minutes later they had reached the back part of the house. "The kitchen is through here," Eli said. "I believe you're already aware that I plan to hire a cook and housekeeper, so you don't have to worry yourself with having to spend much time in here."

Was that a comment on her cooking skills? "Back at Hawk's Creek the kitchen was one of the brightest spots in the house."

"But this isn't Hawk's Creek." He seemed to realize how abrupt that had sounded and moderated his tone. "What I mean is, there will be other, more appropriate, places here for us to gather as a family."

"Of course."

"Naturally, as the soon-to-be lady of the house I'll leave it to you to hire the woman who best meets your own requirements for a cook and housekeeper. I've already interviewed the three ladies Mrs. Collins recommended, but if you want to broaden the search, that's your prerogative. However, given that we'll be moving in on Saturday, I suggest you hire someone as soon as possible. It would probably also be a good idea to hire a couple of other women to help with the preparations for the wedding reception."

Goodness, so many responsibilities, and she wasn't even married to him yet. What would life be like after the wedding? Her cheeks warmed and her mind quickly shied away from that thought. "I trust Cora Beth so there's no need to broaden the search. I'll have a decision by tomorrow."

That won her a look of approval.

He waved a hand. "In the meantime, if there's anything not to your liking in here, let me know and I'll take care of it."

The kitchen was roomier than Cora Beth's and nearly as large as the one at the ranch. The stove looked brand-spanking-new and the worktable situated in the center of the room had a rack hanging above it that held a number of implements Sadie was completely unfamiliar with. She walked to one of the cabinets and opened it, noting it was well stocked.

"All of the dishes, utensils, pots and such were shipped

from the kitchen in Almega. If there is something else you need, though, just let me know."

He'd been thorough, she'd give him that. Not that she was likely to know if there was anything lacking. Other than the obvious, she had no idea what an experienced cook would expect to have on hand.

She felt a tug on her skirts and looked down to see Penny staring up at her expectantly. "Can we cook together in here sometimes like we do at the boarding-house?"

Before she could answer, Eli stepped forward. "I'm sure Sadie will be happy to teach you all that a lady of the house should know. But you wouldn't want to get in the way of our new cook, would you?"

Penny slowly shook her head.

Sadie gave the girl's shoulder a light squeeze. "But don't you worry. You and I are going to find lots of other things to do together." She snapped a finger. "Oh, and did I mention that my dog Skeeter is going to come live with us as well?"

Penny's expression brightened immediately. "Really?"

"Uh-huh. You're going to love Skeeter." She tweaked one of the girls braids. "And I know he's going to take to you like a new sprout takes to sunshine."

Penny giggled.

Still smiling, Sadie glanced up at Eli and was caught off guard by the expression on his face. It was almost… wistful. But it was there and gone so quickly she decided she had been mistaken.

"If we're done in here," he said as he turned back toward the hallway, "why don't I show you around up-stairs?"

She glanced at his walking stick. "But—"

He waved off her concern. "I won't be running any races in the next day or two, but I'm definitely up to climbing a set of stairs."

Sadie almost smiled at that—she couldn't imagine the dignified Eli Reynolds running a race under *any* circumstances.

As they climbed the stairs, Penny skipped ahead to the room at the far end of the landing. "This one is mine," she called out. "Eli let me pick it myself." She opened the door and then waited for the grown-ups to join her.

Sadie cut him an approving smile for giving his sister that much control, then joined Penny and looked around. "I must say, you made a very fine choice."

Penny grabbed Sadie's hand and tugged her to the window. "You can see both the big oak tree and the street in front of the house from here."

"That *is* a nice feature. We'll have to frame this window with some really special curtains. Do you have a favorite color?"

Penny nodded. "Yellow."

"Then yellow it is," Sadie said. "Would you like to go with me to the mercantile tomorrow to pick out the fabric?"

Penny nodded enthusiastically, obviously pleased to be included in the decision making. Then she cocked her head to one side. "So which room is going to be yours?"

The child's innocently voiced question caught Sadie by surprise and raised questions she herself had avoided dwelling on. Eli had mentioned giving her time to adjust, but what exactly did he mean? And how much time?

Surely as husband and wife they would share a room. Or would they?

At what point did Mr. Reynolds expect them to live

together as man and wife? And more importantly, what did *she* want?

Sadie studiously avoided looking directly at her soon-to-be husband as the heat rose in her cheeks.

To her relief, Eli's gaze remained on his sister. Almost as if he was avoiding looking at her, as well. "Why don't we let Miss Lassiter look at all of the rooms before she makes her pick?"

So, he *didn't* intend for them to share a room. Surprisingly, her relief was tinged with just the slightest touch of disappointment.

Penny took her hand again. "Come on, I'll show them to you."

"Besides Penny's room, there are four other bedrooms," Eli said as they moved into the hall. "The master suite, which is there across the landing, is the roomiest. You are, of course, welcome to claim that one—I can be quite comfortable in one of the others. If that's not to your liking, however, there is this one next to Penny's and two at the head of the stairs. They are basically the same with a few differences in view and wallpaper."

Sadie dutifully looked into each of the rooms, though she had to force herself to concentrate on what was in front of her when she could feel Eli's presence so close behind her.

The master bedchamber, as he'd said, was the roomiest of the bunch. It was furnished with the heavy pieces that he seemed to favor, but that she found much too oppressive.

She finally settled on one of the two rooms at the head of the stairs. It faced east, the same as her room at the ranch, and was papered with a cheery floral and striped pattern in pastel shades of green and rose. "This will do nicely."

"Are you certain you wouldn't rather have the larger master suite?"

Did he think she was just being polite? "No, this is definitely the one I want."

"All right then. Shall I have someone bring over your things from the boardinghouse?"

Since she'd only planned for her trip to Knotty Pine to last a few weeks, the only things she'd brought with her from Hawk's Creek were clothes and a few personal items. She supposed she'd have to get Griff to pack up and ship the rest of her belongings once he returned home.

Home—she had to remember that *this* place was home now. She hadn't realized when she left Hawk's Creek ten days ago that she wouldn't be returning to it, except as a visitor, ever again.

Sadie felt a stinging behind her eyes. Then she lifted her chin. No! She'd already made her decision, had felt this was the path God wanted her to follow, and she would *not* allow herself to grow maudlin over it. This would work out, all she needed was a little bit of courage. And faith.

She moved to the window to see what kind of view she would have and her spirits immediately rose. "You have a stable."

"A small one, yes. It will house up to three horses and a buggy. I suppose you have a mount at Hawk's Creek."

"Yes, Calliope. She's a sweet little mare I raised from a foal."

"Then by all means you should send for her."

Surely, once she had Skeeter and Calliope here with her, this would begin to feel much more like home.

Eli followed Penny and Sadie down the stairs, calling himself all kinds of a fool for not discussing sleeping arrangements beforehand. He and his soon-to-be bride needed to have a discussion, indelicate as it might be, before their wedding day.

As they strolled back to the boardinghouse, the two adults let Penny filled the silence with her excited chatter, mostly questions for Sadie about how they would decorate her room.

Eli listened to the easy way Penny chatted with Sadie, saw the frequent smiles on her lips and lightness in her tone, and wondered how Sadie managed to draw her out. Why hadn't he already known his sister's favorite color or why she had picked that particular room for her own? Why hadn't he even thought to ask?

When they finally reached the front porch of the boardinghouse, Eli turned to his sister. "Why don't you go on inside and see how Mrs. Collins is feeling this morning? I need to have a few words with Mis—with Sadie in private."

"Okay Eli."

He turned to Sadie. "Would you stroll with me?"

"Of course."

He led them away from the busier part of town, taking a few minutes to gather his thoughts. He wasn't certain how she would react to the subject matter he needed to broach. "It occurs to me that we should discuss our expectations for, well, for how we will conduct the more personal aspect of our marriage." Yes, that was a sensible way to approach the topic.

He raked a hand through his hair, keeping his gaze focused straight ahead. "I mean, naturally, as husband and wife, there is a certain, um, intimacy that is normally expected."

Why didn't she say anything? Surely she understood—

He suddenly remembered she'd said her mother had passed away when she was nine—Penny's age—and that she'd been raised by her father and brothers. It was possible that there'd been no one to take on the duty of preparing her for her wedding night. The thought of taking on that duty himself made a cold sweat break out on his forehead. Perhaps he was mistaken.

"Miss Lassiter, that is, Sadie, how much, I mean, what do you know of—" he cut a glance her way.

Her expression had a gently puzzled look. "How much do I what?"

He cleared his throat and shifted his gaze forward again. She was more of an innocent than he'd expected. But if this had to be done, then best to get it over with quickly. "How much do you know about what goes on between a man and a woman once they are married?"

She bent slightly to pick a bit of lint from her skirt. "Since I've never been married myself I naturally have no firsthand knowledge."

Firsthand knowledge—good grief he should hope not! "That is how it should be. I was speaking of a more intellectual knowledge, perhaps relayed to you by a married woman of your acquaintance."

She shook her head sadly. "There are very few married women on the ranch and none that I've had that sort of conversation with."

Eli felt his collar tighten. Perhaps this was a conversation best left to Mrs. Collins. "I see. Then perhaps you can inquire of Mrs. Collins just what—"

Her laugh cut him off. "Oh Eli, I'm sorry. I know I shouldn't tease you but I couldn't help myself. I grew up on a ranch, remember? I have a pretty good idea of what you mean by *intimacies*."

His relief was tempered by a touch of annoyance. This was not a subject to make light of. At least she'd had the grace to blush on that last part. "Very well. Then, to get back to my earlier point, I'm aware that you and I are not well acquainted and that it's only natural for you to want a period of time to adjust to the idea of our being married."

"Very considerate of you."

There was a certain dryness to her tone that made him uneasy. "Of course, the current arrangement won't last forever. Eventually, that is to say, well…" Aware that he'd moved into indelicate territory, Eli wrestled himself back under control. "I want to have children of my own one day," he said matter-of-factly.

"I see." She finally smiled. "Then it's fortunate you and I are in agreement on that point."

Eli breathed a mental sigh of relief. She was not going to be coy or unduly missish over this. He found himself hoping she would not take too long to "adjust."

Sadie climbed the stairs to her room, wanting a few moments to herself before checking to see if Cora Beth needed her for anything. Fortunately Griff was nowhere to be seen. She didn't think she could deal with him right now.

She wasn't certain how to react to that unorthodox conversation they'd just shared. It had been fun, though, watching the always-in-control Mr. Reynolds squirm for a change.

Was he truly being considerate of her feelings, or just putting off what he saw as a duty to be dispatched at some point? So how did they decide the time was right? And who made that decision? Was she supposed to give him some signal? Her face grew red-hot at the thought.

Dear Lord, please see me through this.

A knock at the door provided a welcome interruption to her jumbled thoughts. "Come in."

Cora Beth opened the door and hesitated on the threshold.

Sadie popped up from her perch on the edge of her bed. "Oh, I'm so sorry. I should be downstairs helping with the cooking. I—"

Cora Beth waved her back down. "You've had a very eventful day—the chores can wait a bit." She crossed the room as she spoke and pulled the chair away from the vanity table. Turning it to face Sadie, she sat and folded her hands in her lap. "I know you had reservations about accepting Mr. Reynolds's proposal. Are you at peace with your decision now?"

Was she? "I'd be lying if I said I haven't had second thoughts. But I've been praying about it and I've come to believe this is the course I'm meant to take." She tucked an unruly strand back behind her ear. "Heaven help us both."

Cora Beth's lips twitched. "You are to be commended on your honesty at least." Then she turned serious again. "I've been praying over this, as well. Praying that God will grant you both the discernment to go forward with open minds and open hearts."

Sadie nodded. "Thank you." Then she added, "as for

open hearts, I don't think the man has a romantic bone in his body."

"I think in time you'll come to think differently." Cora Beth took on a wise-woman aura. "Most men guard their more tender feelings from the world—some more so than others. But I've seen the way Mr. Reynolds looks at you."

That piqued Sadie's interest. What did she mean—the way he looked at her? Was there something—

But Cora Beth didn't give her an opening to ask. "Do you have any questions? About married life, I mean."

Had Eli asked Cora Beth to talk to her? Or did everyone think she was so uninformed? Then she straightened. "As a matter of fact, I do." She leaned forward. "How do I make sure I'm a good wife?"

"Well, there are certain, um, behaviors, between a man and a woman, that may seem a bit awkward at first glance, but that are really quite—"

Sadie stopped her before she could go any further. "That's not what I meant. I know all about *that*." At Cora Beth's shocked expression, she quickly added. "I mean, I've lived on a ranch my whole life. I've seen cows and horses and other animals mate so I understand the basics." Though she preferred not to think about doing *that* with Eli.

Cora Beth smiled. "Oh my goodness. No wonder you have that rather-not-know expression on your face. It's not quite the same between a man and a woman. Especially when they care for each other."

Sadie was caught off guard by her words. "It's not?"

Cora Beth shook her head, then shifted as if searching for the right words. "Farm animals act instinctually and pretty much indiscriminately. For people, it's different. While it may take a bit of getting used to, it's a beautiful, loving act, meant to draw two people who care for each other even closer together and prepare them to create and nourish the family God meant for them to have."

The image Cora Beth's words conjured up sparked Sadie's imagination. It sounded so...so wonderful. Would she and Eli ever...

She shook off that thought. Better not to get sidetracked thinking like *that*. "What I meant was, how do *I* make a good wife in other aspects of our life. I mean, we both know I'm no good at cooking and sewing and all those domestic tasks that normally fall to a wife. How do I learn?"

Cora Beth nodded. "I'll let you in on a little secret my momma taught me. A wife's true role in the home is to be its heart. Love and selflessness and a focus on pleasing God make for a happy home, and it'll be your job to make sure your home has that. While many women display those qualities through the way they perform household chores, that isn't the only way, or even necessarily the best way to add heart to a home."

Did Cora Beth truly believe that? Or was she just trying make her feel better. "Still, it would be a good idea for me to learn some of the basics."

"If you like. But remember, a cook or housekeeper can take care of the basic chores. The true role of a wife is to be all those things I said before and to give her husband a haven where he can feel comfortable just being himself."

She reached forward and took both of Sadie's hands. "You, my dear, are a special person and you have so much heart. Just be yourself. You can bring joy and warmth and love to that house, all the important things that make a house a home."

Sadie wished she could be as sure of that as Cora Beth seemed to be. But, with God's help, she'd sure give it her all.

Strolling through town on her own the next afternoon was an interesting experience for Sadie. Several folks stopped to offer congratulations on her upcoming nuptials. Most had sounded genuinely happy for her, some merely intrigued.

After interviewing the three women who were in the running for the job of cook, she happily settled on Nettie Dauber. The widow, who was old enough to be Sadie's mother, was plainspoken, seemed very capable and was willing to take direction or take control—whichever was required.

Feeling good about the first decision she'd made for her new life, Sadie couldn't wait until she could tell Eli about it.

When she stepped inside the boardinghouse, Sadie saw Griff waiting for her, a big grin on his face. And he wasn't alone.

"Inez!" She flew across the distance separating them. "You came."

Inez returned her hug. "Of course I came. You don't think I'd let you get married without me here to witness it, do you, Sadie girl?"

"But Red and the others—"

"Can eat Grady's cooking for a week." Inez gave her a cheeky grin. "It'll make them appreciate me all the more when I get back."

Sadie laughed. "As if they don't already appreciate you."

"Oh, our baby girl's going to be a bride." Inez put her

calloused hands on Sadie's face. "Ry is going to be so sorry he couldn't be here."

Sadie bit her lip. "There are reasons we can't—"

"I know." Inez smiled softly and gave her cheeks a couple of quick pats before dropping her hands. "Now, introduce me to this young man of yours."

"Eli is still at work. You can meet him when the bank closes."

Inez nodded. "Griff told me he's a banker. Always figured you for a rancher's wife, but you never were one to take the expected path."

What did she mean by that?

Inez stepped back. "Now, tell me what kind of reception you're wanting and how many folks will be there."

Sadie shook her head. "Oh no you don't. You're my guest. I want you at the church, witnessing my wedding, not working in the kitchen."

"Wild horses couldn't keep me away from that church when the time comes. But that doesn't mean I can't get things organized for your celebration, too. You just leave everything to me, Sadie girl."

Sadie hooked her arm through Inez's. "Well come along into the kitchen. I promised Cora Beth she could help with the planning, as well. It looks like you ladies are going to get me organized in spite of myself."

Griff shook his head. "Sounds like this is no place for a man right now. Think I'll take a ride out to Ry's place and see how things are going over there."

Griff's words reminded Sadie of her own fateful trip down that road just a few short days ago. It also brought to mind a bit of unfinished business. "If you don't mind, I'd like you to do a favor for me while you're there."

If things worked out the way she hoped, her wedding present to Eli would be truly memorable. Perhaps it would, in some small way, make up for his having had to settle for something less than that proper wife he'd hoped to find.

Chapter Eleven

Sadie set her pen down and gently blew on the paper. She'd thought, what with all the commotion happening in her life, she might have had trouble continuing her chronicle of Annabel Adams's adventures. Surprisingly, that hadn't been the case. In fact, for the last hour the words had practically flowed out of her and she'd barely looked up from her scribbling. It had been a relief to escape her world for the comparatively safe confines of Annabel's. When she finally stopped, she'd left poor Annabel in yet another tight situation and would need to think on how to get her out of it before she continued.

She was glad Eli had finally backed down on wanting her to give it up, though she was surprised he hadn't put up more of a fight. Had he seen how important it was to her? Or had he merely been trying to finally get her to the altar?

Whatever the case, she wasn't sure she could have given it up. What had started out as just a lark to pass the time while she was here in Knotty Pine had fast become a creative outlet that she couldn't imagine living without again. The story was the first thing that was wholly hers. And people actually liked it. Not merely tolerated it or viewed it as a nice little pastime for her to amuse herself with, but genuinely liked it and eagerly looked forward to seeing more. The speculation around who was behind the stories was tinged with an admiration she found guiltily exhilarating.

Sadie stood and drew her elbows back, trying to get the kinks out, then crossed to the window. It still stung a bit that Eli looked down on her work the way he did.

Not that she required his approval.

The man was still a puzzle to her—so formal and analytical in his approach to life in general. Yet there was that hint of suppressed emotion in him, as if one ever got past his defenses, one would find a deeply passionate individual.

After Inez met Eli and Penny yesterday evening, she'd given it as her opinion that Sadie had made a fine match. Sadie hadn't realized until then how concerned she'd been that Inez, the woman who'd been like a mother to her, would have reservations.

Sadie glanced at the small watch pinned to her bodice. "Oh my goodness!" Dinner preparations should have been started thirty minutes ago. She turned and rushed to the door. Hopefully she could make up some time and not be late getting the meal on the table.

When she stepped into the kitchen, however, she found Cora Beth and Inez there ahead of her. "I'm so sorry. I lost track of time."

Inez waved her away. "No worries. We have it all well in hand."

"But I'm supposed to be—"

"It's okay," Cora Beth motioned for her to take a chair.

"You should be thinking about your wedding, not doing my chores."

"That's right." Inez tapped the spoon against the pot and then set it down. "I was just telling Cora Beth here that I'm willing to stay on a few days after the wedding and help her around here since you'll have your own place to tend to. Don't see any reason why I can't start now."

Sadie closed her eyes for a moment. *Father, I know they mean well. So why do I feel like such a failure right now?*

Cora Beth motioned for Sadie to take a seat at the table beside her. "So tell me, have you thought about what dress you'll be wearing for your wedding?"

Not until just now. She feigned indifference. "It won't be a hard choice to make. Since I wasn't planning on a wedding when I left home, I only have two dresses with me that would be suitable."

"Oh my goodness, where's my head?" Inez set the cook spoon down. "I brought your mother's wedding gown with me. Thought you might want to wear it on your special day."

Sadie was taken aback. "Oh Inez, that was so thoughtful of you. But there's no way that dress would fit me." And the elegant style definitely doesn't suit me.

Her mother had been a graceful, delicately-built woman—several inches taller and much trimmer than Sadie. And that dress—ah that beautiful, frothy dress. Covered with yards and yards of lace and enough beadwork to make it sparkle when it moved, the dress had filled her with awe when she was a little girl. And she'd dreamed of one day wearing it herself.

Right up until the day she'd realized that she was not

the striking, elegant person her mother was, and on her the dress would look laughably inappropriate.

But Inez was not to be denied. "You're just a mite shorter than your mother but we can take care of that with a new hem. And if we need to let out a seam or two, well, that's easy enough to do, as well."

Oh there would definitely be need. Sadie's mind was working furiously trying to come up with some convincing reason to give Inez for not wearing that dress.

"Don't you worry about a thing," Inez said. "It'll be my wedding present to you."

Sadie saw the pleased, expectant expression on the woman's face and knew she was defeated. She stepped up and gave her a big hug. "Thank you so much. It's a lovely gift."

As they were pushing away from the table that evening, Griff took Sadie aside. "I'd like to have a word with you."

"About what?"

"It has to do with finances."

"Then Eli should be included."

"I don't think—"

"Nonsense. He's going to be my husband and I don't intend for us to have any secrets from each other." Before he could protest further, Sadie took matters into her own hands. She crossed the room and touched Eli's sleeve. "Griff has something he wishes to speak to us about."

"Oh." Eli glanced across the room toward her brother. A brow went up as he no doubt made note of the glower, but he nodded. "Of course. I'm at your disposal."

Once they were seated in the parlor, Griff got straight to business. To his credit he made an effort to make Eli a part of the conversation. "This concerns Sadie's interest in Hawk's Creek. I'm prepared to make her the same offer I made Ry when he got married and put down roots here." He turned back to Sadie. "I can buy your portion of the ranch, or you can continue as a long-distance partner and I'll send you payments every quarter for whatever your share of the profits might be."

Sadie, who was as aware of the financial state of the ranch as Griff was, knew it would be stretching matters pretty thin for him to buy her out. He'd more than likely have to take out a loan and she didn't want to put him in that position. Besides, she wasn't ready to give up her share of Hawk's Creek just yet.

But it wasn't just her opinion that mattered. She glanced Eli's way. Finance was his business, after all. Did he have a preference? "What do you think?"

He met her gaze with a steady one of his own. "Your brother is right. This is your decision. And whatever you decide to do, I'll support you."

He was being gentlemanly again, not a bad quality in a husband. "But I'd like to hear your thoughts on the matter."

"Very well." Eli leaned forward. "Thinking about this objectively, if you were a bank customer asking for advice, I'd want to know much more about the operation, perhaps even have a look at it myself."

But I'm not a bank customer, she wanted to say, I'm your soon-to-be-wife.

Griff, however, seemed to see nothing wrong with Eli's statement. "I can tell Jackson, the manager over at the bank I do business with, to answer any questions you might have on the finances. And you're welcome to have a look at the place any time you've a mind to."

"That's a wonderful idea," Sadie said.

"What?" Eli looked puzzled.

"Going to Hawk's Creek for a visit after we're married."

"I don't know. I won't be able to go right away. There are some things at the bank—"

Griff stood. "No problem. This is a big decision and I really didn't expect an answer today. Hawk's Creek isn't going anywhere and my offer stands indefinitely. Discuss it together, plan a trip out there if you like. Pray about it. And in the meantime Sadie retains partial ownership, same as before."

Griff was wrong—nothing was the same as before. She might remain partial owner of Hawk's Creek, but it would no longer be her home. How strange to think about living in town permanently, about living among folks she barely knew.

If nothing else, experiencing this unsettling, set-adrift-in-unknown-waters feeling for herself made her even more sympathetic toward Penny. Whether Eli knew it or not, she was going to be a very good big sister for Penny.

Eli watched Griff leave the room. It was edifying to know that his independent-minded fiancée not only welcomed but actually sought his opinion, on this matter at least. Was it because she was finally beginning to recognize the value in his analytical approach to decision making? Or because it was how he made his profession? Or rather, was it because, now that they were engaged, she was ready to show him just a bit of deference? He could live with any of those answers.

But whatever the case, he was determined not to disappoint her. "Your brother seems a fair man."

"As fair and honest as they come. He doesn't know any other way to be."

What it would be like to have her speak of him with such admiration and certainty? He shook off that non-sensical thought. "I appreciate your asking for my input in this."

"We're going to be married. It's only right we share in making these decisions. And that we pray over them together."

This tendency she had to want to pray over every decision left him uncomfortable. Isn't that what God gave man a brain for—to reason things out and make decisions? But maybe it was just her way of organizing her thoughts.

He spread his hands. "Of course. But getting back to the current question, just to make sure I understand the situation, when faced with the same choice, your brother Ry sold his interest in the ranch when he married Mrs. Collins's sister, is that correct."

"Yes, but you can't really go by that. Ry is the owner of his own ranch now. And he took a piece of Hawk's Creek with him, in the form of his prize stallion and a string of mares."

There was something she wasn't saying but he was having trouble figuring out just what was going on in that unpredictable mind of hers. "So, if we sold your interest to Griff, is there some element of Hawk's Creek you'd want to take with you?"

She chewed her lip for a moment. "I hadn't really thought of it that way before, but no, I don't think so."

Still he could sense something was bothering her. Then he remembered how sentimental she was.

On impulse, he leaned forward and placed a hand over

hers. Doing his best to ignore the sudden and very un-characteristic urge to lift that hand to his lips, he stared straight into her eyes. "Sadie, I realize this is your home we're talking about. You must have strong feelings about which way you want this to go. Tell me."

Her hand, so small and fragile-seeming under his own, continued to stir protective instincts in him.

Her gaze dropped to his hand and she stared, as if mesmerized. Finally she looked up again, but there was an endearing hint of distraction now. She nodded. "Hawk's Creek. Yes." Her focus sharpened. "Of course I do. Hawk's Creek is the only home I've ever known. The thought of selling off my piece of it, even if it's to Griff, seems as unthinkable as selling off a piece of my arm." She took a deep breath. "I'm not saying what Ry did was wrong, but it was different for him. He'd already found other things to tug him away, other places to call home."

Would Sadie find those other things, other places that she could comfortably set down new roots? Would what he could offer her be enough?

But she was right. He supposed, for an emotional woman such as her, such attachments were important. If she wanted to hold on to a piece of her childhood home, who was he to say nay? "If it means so much to you, then there's no need for me to perform any sort of analysis. Of course you should maintain your interest in Hawk's Creek."

The smile she gave him made his small gesture worthwhile. Then she straightened. "I hope this doesn't mean you don't want to visit Hawk's Creek now. I'd really enjoy showing you around the place."

"Of course. But as I told your brother, not right away. I've only just taken over the reins at the bank and I wouldn't feel right being gone for an extended period right now."

Her smile dimmed for only a heartbeat and then she rallied. "I understand. After all, school won't let out for a few more weeks and we'd want to take Penny with us."

She knew good and well that wasn't his reason. Was she lying just trying to save face? That uncharitable thought was quickly followed by a sharp jab of guilt. After all, even if it had been for her own good, he'd all but forced this wedding on her. And he wasn't allowing any time for a honeymoon trip. Perhaps, once they were settled in and school was out, he'd suggest she and Penny take a trip to Hawk's Creek without him. That should cheer her up. After all, given their relationship, she wasn't likely to really care that much if he was along or not.

And, strangely, that thought bothered him much more than he'd expected it to.

The days leading up to the wedding passed more quickly than Sadie would have thought possible. It seemed every time she turned around she was either being asked to make a decision or being asked to approve a decision someone else had already made.

The highlight, for her, was looking over the trio of horses Griff brought over from Ry's ranch. She had no trouble at all picking out the one she wanted, a lively brown mare with strong lines and a sassy spark in her eyes.

At least she was keeping too busy to worry over what her new life would be like. Except when she lay awake at night, staring up at the ceiling. Was Eli feeling the same sense of unreality, of rushing headlong into something before either of them was ready?

She awoke Saturday morning to an absolutely perfect day for a wedding. Gone were the storms of the previous week. Instead, the sky was bright and sunny with a few fluffy clouds scattered across the blue expanse, a slight breeze wafted in to keep the heat from being overbearing, flowers bloomed everywhere—it was everything a bride could ask for.

By one o'clock, Sadie stood at the back of the church, wearing her mother's wedding gown, feeling like a little girl playing dress up. At least she'd managed to convince Inez to simplify the dress a bit, explaining that the church in Knotty Pine was not a magnificent cathedral and the people who would be in attendance were not Philadelphia's social elite. Still, she felt out of place, like a magpie pretending to be a hawk.

She had thought that by now it would all have felt right. But this lacey confection was not right for her, this ceremony was not being held at her home church as she'd always imagined it would be, and most calamitous of all, the groom waiting for her at the altar did not love her.

Heavenly Father, I know that not every path You lead us down is a comfortable one, and I know Your hand is on us always. But right now I can't see the rightness of this, so I need Your blessed assurance more than ever.

She took a deep breath and willed herself to have only positive thoughts. *I'm going to make Eli the best wife I possibly can. I'm going to make certain Penny has a house filled with as much joy and love as I can manage. And, dear Lord, I'm going to make sure You are a part of this family, too. As Cora Beth said, I'm going to strive*

to be the heart of our home. These two people need me,
whether they know it or not.

Her stomach settled and her smile relaxed. It was time.

Sadie turned to her brother, who stood waiting for her
to give the signal that she was ready.

Griff tugged at his shirt collar. He looked mighty fine
in his Sunday suit, but the concern on his face was entirely unsuitable for a wedding. "Are you sure this is what
you want?" he asked. "It's still not too late to back out."

She knew without a doubt that if she asked him to,
Griff would escort her out of the church and purchase a
ticket on the next train headed north. He'd always looked
out for her, had always been there when she needed him.
With Ry spending so much time in Philadelphia, it had
been just her and Griff for the most part after her father died.

And for the first time it struck her that this marriage
signaled a change for him, too. He would be alone now.
The last Lassiter left standing at Hawk's Creek. Would
he miss her company? She put a hand on his arm and
looked deep into his eyes. Seeing the concern and love
there, she felt a deep, bittersweet ache. "Eli and Penny
need me, Griff." Those words went a long way toward
settling her own nerves.

He stared at her a moment longer, as if trying to peer
into her heart, and finally nodded, as if satisfied with
what he saw there. "I want you to know you always have
a place at Hawk's Creek. You can come back any time,
for however long you need to, no questions asked."

She reached up and smoothed his collar. "I know, and
that's a lovely, comforting thought. But this *will* work
out. I'm sure of it."

She moved her hand back to his arm. "Now, walk me

down that aisle and make all the female hearts go pitter-patter at the sight of you."

With a grin, Griff tapped her nose and then placed a hand over hers where it rested on his arm, straightened and faced forward. Sadie did likewise.

As they took the long walk down the aisle, Sadie studied Eli's face. Was he feeling any qualms or doubts, was he disappointed that he'd wound up with her instead of the "perfect wife" he'd hoped for?

But she saw no sign of regret or resignation on his face. In fact, if she didn't know better, she'd almost believe it was satisfaction and encouragement. He'd quit using the walking stick on Thursday, though she noticed he still favored his left leg ever so slightly when he walked.

Just before Griff placed her hand in Eli's, her brother bent down and kissed her forehead. Then he stepped back and joined Uncle Grover, Inez and the children in the front pew.

A moment later she was standing before the preacher, her soon-to-be husband at her side.

Cora Beth stood at her left and Sheriff Hammond stood beside Eli. But the only person her senses could take in was Eli. Standing tall and straight, his broad shoulders set off by his dark suit, the comforting feel of her hand in his, the subtle clean scent of bay rum and leather and masculine spices that seemed to be uniquely his—this man was to be her husband, hers to learn to love and cherish the rest of her days. The thought almost overwhelmed her.

When it came time for them to speak their vows, Eli held both of her hands in his, his gaze holding hers just as securely. She felt strength and promise and approval in there.

And her heart seemed to swell until it filled her chest. For the first time she felt genuine hope that perhaps they could be happy together—not merely accepting or okay, but genuinely happy.

When he placed the ring on her finger, Sadie stared at the sparkling bauble. It was a lovely thing—a diamond and two sapphires mounted on a gold band.

"You may now kiss the bride."

Reverend Ludlow's words caught Sadie off guard. Her gaze flew to Eli's, trying to gauge his reaction. This could get very awkward.

She saw a heartbeat of hesitation flash in his expression. Then he seemed to collect himself and with a reassuring smile he leaned down, apparently intent on following the preacher's suggestion.

Sadie had a split second to anticipate, and then their lips touched. Her eyes closed and she opened herself up to the sensation. There was an unexpected gentleness and warmth there, and a touch of something else, something that took her by surprise and left her slightly breathless. But before she could quite figure out what that something was, or get her fill of it, he pulled away.

Her eyes remained closed for a few seconds longer and she could still feel the tingle of his lips on hers. Then she opened her eyes and was pleased to see the same bemused surprise on his face, as well. Then he smiled and there was a touch of satisfaction and a totally masculine cockiness to it.

A moment later he seemed to pull himself together and turned to face the congregation with his usual businesslike demeanor. But as he escorted her down the aisle, she was pleased to note how securely he kept her arm tucked in his.

It was done. Eli felt a sense of elation. Sadie was his wife now and there was no going back. Not that he wanted to go back.

When she'd stepped into the church on her brother's arm, he'd been astounded. Her wedding dress had transformed her from a hoyden to a lady. She'd sought out his gaze and latched onto it as if wanting to find shelter from a storm. And he'd found himself more than ready to offer her that protection.

And that kiss they'd sealed their vows with. She'd responded with such sweetness, such trust, it had taken him completely by surprise. His hand involuntarily tightened its hold on her arm at just the thought.

When they stepped outside, Danny stood on the church lawn, holding the lead of a sleek brown mare, and grinning at the two of them like a generous uncle bearing gifts. Eli paused, staring at the lovely animal as she tossed her head, obviously aware she was on display.

"Her name is Cocoa," Sadie said. "Do you like her?"

"She seems a fine animal. Is she yours?"

"No, she's yours." Sadie colored slightly, but her face wore a wide grin. "It's my wedding gift to you."

Eli didn't know what to say. He was well aware that she'd entered into this marriage reluctantly, that he'd backed her into a corner. And still she'd taken the time to find a gift that would be both thoughtful and meaningful to him. He was oddly touched.

Sadie's smile faltered and he realized he'd been silent

way too long. "If she's not what you had in mind, we can select another—"

He rushed to reassure her. "No. That is, I like her very much. It's just that I wasn't expecting—" He stopped, taking a moment to collect his thoughts. "Thank you."

He didn't have anything to give her. How could he have forgotten a bride gift?

"I know it's not as fine as what you gave me."

What was she talking about? Then he noticed her gazing down at the ring on her left hand, the one that had belonged to his mother. He covered her hand with his. "It's the perfect gift. In fact, I couldn't have asked for anything finer."

He turned back to Danny. "Can you take her to my stable. And see that she has enough to eat."

Then he patted Sadie's hand. "Shall we find Penny, then lead the way to our new home and prepare to greet our guests, *Mrs. Reynolds?*"

He saw the pink creep into her cheeks and the sparkle in her eyes and suddenly felt several inches taller.

A few minutes later Eli stood inside the foyer of his new home, between his wife and sister, greeting wedding guests and accepting their well wishes. He decided that standing between the two ladies in his life was a very comfortable place to be.

The conversation flowed over him like a stream over stones.

"The ceremony was just beautiful."

"Mr. Reynolds, you've done a wonderful job restoring this old place. It looks even better than it did when it was brand new."

"Sadie, my dear, we're so tickled to welcome you as a permanent resident of Knotty Pine."

And so on.

Sadie was radiant. He would have liked to have her more genteelly reserved, but somehow her informality worked. Today was a special day, after all. Time enough for subtle grooming later.

And people seemed to take to her quite well, smiling tolerantly at her fulsome laughter and occasional faux pas. Penny, too, seemed to be enjoying herself.

When the last of the guests had been formally received, he allowed Penny to go in search of Audrey and Viola while he and Sadie separated to mingle with their guests.

The women Sadie had hired to prepare the food had done a good job. Even though it seemed every citizen of Knotty Pine was here, there was plenty of food to go around, and he was pleased to see that his home was up to the task of accommodating everyone. The guests seemed equally impressed with the reception and with the viewing of the now completed house.

At some point Sadie slipped upstairs to change out of the elegant wedding gown and into another, no doubt more comfortable dress.

As he mingled, Eli found his gaze returning time and again to Sadie. She was animated and the smile never seemed to leave her face. Her laugh was not the gentle, ladylike titter he was accustomed to hearing from females. Rather, it was delightfully infectious. Once, when her gaze met his, she sent a soft, intimate smile his way that warmed him through and through.

Sadie watched as Griff approached her. With the exception of family and near-family from the boardinghouse, the last of the guests had departed for their own homes, and evening was approaching.

Her brother stopped in front of her and leaned back on the balls of his feet. "Well, Sadie girl, it's done. You're a married lady now with a fine new home and a fine new family. I'm very proud of you." Then he took her hand and said softly "But then, I always have been."

His words both surprised and touched her. "Oh, Griff." She launched herself into her brother's arms, doing her best not to cry. "You're the best big brother a girl could ask for.

He laughed. "Why don't you say that sometime when Ry's around? He could stand to be taken down a peg or two."

She stepped back with a laugh. "You know I love Ry, too." Then she gave him an arch look. "Besides, I rather enjoy letting you two fight for my affections."

He laughed and tapped her nose. "Tease." Then he sobered. "Just don't ever forget where you came from."

"How could I? I'll always be one of the Hawk's Creek Lassiters, no matter where I am."

He nodded and shoved his hands in his pockets. "Guess I'll be saying my good-byes now. I plan to head back to Hawk's Creek on tomorrow's train."

Sadie gave him another bear hug, then abruptly released him. "Just a minute—I almost forgot." She raced up the stairs and returned, clutching a piece of paper. "Here. Inez knows about the clothing and such, but this is a list of the other things I'd like to have packed up and sent here. Would you mind handling it for me?"

Griff glanced at the list and his eyebrow went up. "Are you sure?" He looked around, as if gauging where she would be placing her things.

"Oh yes." She gave him her most demure smile. "Eli told me I could add some of my own things to this place if I wanted to and I plan to take him up on it."

Griff's answering grin had a devilish edge to it. "If there weren't so many chores waiting for me back at the ranch I'd be tempted to deliver these things personally."

"I'm sure I have no idea what you're talking about," she said airily. Then she laughed. "And, once he gets used to my lighter additions to his st—*solid* furnishings, I'm sure he'll appreciate them." She'd caught herself just in time. It wouldn't do to describe Eli's efforts as stuffy to Griff.

Griff looked skeptical. "If you say so." Then he gave her an awkward, big-brother hug. "I hope that husband of yours knows what a lucky man he is." His voice was suspiciously gruff.

He stepped back and jammed his hands back in his pockets. "Now, I'd better go take my leave of your husband."

Inez came up next, her eyes misty as she took both of Sadie's hands. "You made such a beautiful bride, Sadie girl. Your daddy and dear momma would have been so proud."

"Thank you. And thanks for everything you did to make this reception, this day, so wonderful."

Inez waved off her thanks, then gave her hands another squeeze. "I'm just pleased to see that you have yourself a lovely home and a lovely new family. I never would have pictured you as a city girl but I think you're going to do just fine here."

She most sincerely hoped so. "I agree. But I'm glad you think so, too."

Inez stepped back. "Oh and I like Nettie Dauber. I

think she's going to do a fine job for you as cook and housekeeper."

"With that kind of endorsement, I know I have nothing to worry about." She glanced up and saw her brother watching them. "I think Griff is ready to escort you back to the boardinghouse. But I'll see you again before you head back to Hawk's Creek on Wednesday."

Inez nodded. "She insists she'll be back to full strength by then. I think she's rushing it a bit, just like that man of yours did with his cane."

That man of yours. Sadie glanced toward her new husband and found him watching her, as well. Their guests would all be gone soon, Penny would be tucked into bed, and they would be alone. What then?

Sadie watched as Eli closed the door behind Griff and Inez. Cora Beth had taken her children home earlier, most of the cleaning up had been done, and what was left could wait until morning.

"Well, Mrs. Reynolds, I think the party went well."

Did he use her married name because he liked the sound of it as much as she did or was he just trying to get accustomed to having a wife? She decided to focus on the first reason. "Thanks to Mrs. Dauber and Inez."

"Yes, well, I'm certain you had a lot of input into the planning."

She found his attempt to praise her both endearing and encouraging. Another hint that he was willing to make the effort to ensure this arrangement would work out, after all. She felt a definite bounce to her step as she moved toward Penny, who was curled up on one end of the sofa. "Come along, princess, time to get you to bed."

She stroked the child's hair. "Would you like me to tuck you in and hear your prayers?"

Penny nodded and placed her hand in Sadie's as she stood. Sadie felt her heart do a flip-flop, oddly touched by the trusting gesture. It didn't matter what Eli had to say about routine and discipline, she was going to make sure this little girl had lots of reasons to smile.

As she climbed the stairs, she could feel Eli's gaze tracking her progress.

And that set her heart flip-flopping in an altogether different manner.

Eli watched until Penny and Sadie reached the top of the stairs, then turned sharply and stepped out on the front porch. His first night in his new house. With his new wife.

Where was the sense of accomplishment, of pleasure at the culmination of all his plans? Why did he feel this restless energy instead?

But there was a sense of anticipation, of better yet to come, as well. Eli leaned against the porch rail and stared out at the night sky.

Seeing her with Penny just now had driven home the fact that, no matter how he'd arrived at it, this had been a good choice for his sister. Not perfect, perhaps, but good nonetheless.

He could sense the potential in Sadie even stronger now, could see where this match could really work with just the right bit of guidance from him. Yes, with his gentle coaching, she could become a lady fine enough to grace the halls of society ballrooms.

The three of them would become valued members of this town, Penny would grow up protected and happy, and ready to face the world with assurance and confidence.

He was startled out of his thoughts by the sound of the door opening. He turned to see Sadie standing there, silhouetted like a cameo in a broach.

"Penny's asleep," she said, joining him at the porch rail.

"She's had a long day."

"We all have." She hooked an arm around one of the support posts and sighed. "But it was lovely."

Eli leaned his elbow on the railing again, but surreptitiously studied her. "I'm glad you think so. A bride should have fine memories of her wedding day." Why had she joined him out here? Was there something she wanted?

She smiled as if he'd just said something exceedingly clever. "Memories are wonderful things, aren't they? Especially when you can share them with others." She lifted her face to the stars. "I think the three of us are going to make some wonderful memories in this house."

That didn't seem to require an answer.

She finally looked at him and there was a curious mix of vulnerability and determination in her expression. "I know I'm not the wife you wanted, Eli, but I promise to try to make you a good one." She gave him a crooked smile. "No promises as to how successful I'll be at it though." With that she lifted up on her toes, kissed his cheek and scurried back inside the house.

Eli stood there a bit longer, staring at the door and stroking his cheek where her lips had been. He could still feel the petal-soft warmth of that kiss, could detect the faintest hint of the floral scent she'd worn.

His thoughts shifted of their own accord to the kiss

they'd shared earlier, at the wedding ceremony. The sweetness of her response, the bemused softness of her expression afterwards had tightened his chest, had made him want to live up to the trust he saw in her eyes.

This kiss, though, had been different. While a bit more chaste, it had been sweet and spontaneous, and more significantly, she had initiated it. It was as if she'd given him a very special, aching, filled-with-promise kind of gift.

He wasn't certain exactly what to make of it. But, all in all, it seemed a very promising beginning to their married life.

Chapter Twelve

Eli escorted his sister and new wife into church the next morning. This time they were greeted with warm smiles and felicitations. Eli settled into the pew feeling as if all was finally right with the world again.

After the service, Penny raced off to join Audrey and Viola, Sadie stopped to chat with a group of women which included Inez and Mrs. Collins, and Sheriff Hammond drew him into a small circle of men who were discussing the latest news on national politics. It was edifying to discover the men listened attentively to his opinions. His hard work to make himself a valuable member of the community was beginning to bear fruit.

He found his gaze drawn to his new wife. Her expression was bright and animated. Yes, she still had a bit of a childlike look about her, but instead of putting him off, he was beginning to see it as an asset.

Last night, when he'd stepped into his room, alone, he'd found himself wondering how long she would need to come to terms with their being married, to be ready to join him in the marriage bed.

Had it been a mistake to hold off? She professed to

understand that aspect of marital relations, but how did she feel about it? Living up to his word might be more of a challenge than he'd expected.

A question from Horace Danvers forced his focus back to the conversation at hand. But not for long. When he finally excused himself, there were several knowing glances that passed between the men, but he ignored them. After all, from an appearances standpoint, he was newly married and it was normal to want to spend time with his bride.

Sadie entered the library, looking for something she could read to Penny. Once they'd eaten lunch, Eli had gone to his study, leaving her and Penny to amuse themselves as they saw fit.

She searched the titles and quickly discovered there was not much material designed to capture and hold a child's interest. Thank goodness that was one of the things she'd put on the list for Griff to send her—copies of her own childhood favorites. Many of them were sadly dog-eared, but the words were still as entertaining and spellbinding as ever.

Perhaps they could do something else. She looked around—the house felt so formal, so stiff, as if it were a sour schoolmarm who forbade anything resembling horseplay in her classroom. She missed the casual, comfortable atmosphere of the house at Hawk's Creek, the feeling that it was okay to laugh, to get a bit rowdy, to really spread out. Maybe, once her things arrived, it would feel a bit more like home around here.

In the meantime, she decided to take advantage of the large piano in the parlor and she convinced Penny to play a number of duets with her. Apparently, Penny felt repressed by her surroundings as well, but once Sadie was able to get the girl to relax and not take things so seriously, they had a grand time improvising with both tempo and melody.

Later, she glanced out the window and spied the stable. Spinning back around she smiled at Penny. "I think I'll go down and check on Cocoa. Want to come?"

"All right."

"Good. And since I plan for us to get good and dirty, we probably ought to change into our oldest clothes." She crouched slightly, as if at a starting line. "I'll race you to see who can get changed and make it back down here first."

With a giggle, Penny made a mad dash for the stairs.

Sadie changed into one of her older dresses, then waited until she heard Penny's footsteps race past her door before stepping out of her room.

Penny stood at the bottom of the stairs grinning smugly as she watched Sadie descend.

Sadie had never before felt this good about losing a race. It would be fun finding new ways to make this little girl smile.

Distracted by the sound of clattering footsteps and feminine laughter, Eli stepped out of his office. And came face to face with two breathless females. Their laughter stopped abruptly and they faced him with identically sheepish expressions.

"Oh, sorry if we disturbed you." Sadie's expression was that of a kid on a lark. "Penny and I are headed out to check on Cocoa. Want to join us?"

He waved a hand toward his desk. "I've got some paperwork that needs my attention."

"Penny tells me she's never learned to ride a horse. Do you mind if I teach her?"

He looked at his sister. "Do you *want* to learn?" His stepmother had always frowned on the practice, deeming it unfeminine.

"Oh yes. Sadie says it's quite fun and zilerating."

He smiled at her mispronunciation. "She does, does she?"

Penny nodded.

Sadie gave him a reassuring smile. "Don't worry. I've been riding since I was five years old and I'm much more graceful on a horse than on foot. She'll be safe with me."

"Please, Eli?"

He was no proof against the two of them. "Very well. But take it slow."

Penny skipped forward and gave him a hug around his waist. "Thanks."

He stroked her hair, then rested his hand lightly against her back. When he looked up, he found Sadie studying the two of them with a soft smile. He'd give a pretty penny to know what she was thinking.

Then his sister stepped back and took hold of Sadie's hand. "I'm ready. Let's go."

He frowned. "You're not going to teach her right now, are you?"

Sadie shook her head. "Today, we're going to work on how to groom a horse. We'll move on to riding lessons in another day or two."

Good. That would give him time to find Penny a suitable mount. Eli watched the two of them move toward the rear entrance and for a moment was tempted to join them.

After breakfast the next morning Eli headed to the bank and Sadie walked Penny as far as Danvers's Mercantile, where she met up with a group of children on their way to the schoolhouse.

Sadie headed back home, wondering what she was going to do with herself all day. Feeling at something of a loss, she drifted into the kitchen where Mrs. Dauber was already at work chopping vegetables. The woman glanced up at Sadie. "Will Mr. Reynolds be home for lunch?"

Would he? Sadie perked up. Of course he would. He'd always returned to the boardinghouse, after all. "Yes, he'll be here."

"Then I'll make certain I fix enough for two."

After a bit more discussion about the menu, the conversation dragged and Sadie wandered out to the stable. She saddled up Cocoa and rode her at a sedate pace round and round the tiny paddock. She would have to talk to Eli about providing proper exercise for the mare. A nice long ride across the countryside sounded very appealing right now.

She cleaned up, then headed to the library where she found an interesting-looking book and curled up on the window seat to read. Fifteen minutes later she found herself too restless to continue.

So what now? If she'd been at the ranch she'd have gone for a ride in the south pasture or checked on Dusty's new foal or maybe even seen if Clem needed help mending tack.

Had Griff had time to get her things together yet? If she was lucky, maybe they would arrive in the next few days. Cocoa was a fine animal but she missed Calliope. Perhaps, when Calliope arrived, she and Eli could go riding together.

And there were all those furnishings and ornamental

pieces, too. Normally she didn't pay much attention to how a house was decorated, but in this case she couldn't wait to add a few touches of Hawk's Creek to this place.

Sadie decided to walk down to the boardinghouse and visit with Cora Beth and Inez. Perhaps Cora Beth could clue her in as to what the womenfolk did around these parts.

By the time Eli returned for lunch, she was full of news about what she'd learned.

"Cora Beth invited me to join the Ladies's Auxiliary. They help with keeping the church clean and tidy, and they fix food baskets and do chores for folks who are ailing and need a bit of help." He should be happy as a tic on a hound that she was finding ways to get involved with the community. It's one of the things he'd wanted in his "perfect wife" after all.

"Sounds like a worthy cause."

She ignored the hint of condescension in his tone. "Of course, I'm not good at cooking or sewing, but I can clean as well as the next person and there's all kinds of chores I can do like milking cows and caring for livestock. And, since I'm not as busy as most of the other ladies around here, I can deliver things, as well."

He frowned at that. "I'm not certain it's appropriate for you to go traipsing around the countryside on your own."

Not appropriate? "I did it all the time at Hawk's Creek. Rode all over the six hundred acres of the ranch and the half dozen or more miles it took to visit some of our neighbors."

"This is not Hawk's Creek."

"And I'm not your little sister. I'm a grown woman."

They glared at each other for several long seconds before Sadie backed down. He was only worried about her.

"I'm sorry. It's just that I'm not used to having to check with someone before I do something."

Some of his stiffness eased. "I apologize, as well. It's just that now you are in my care, and you are part of my family. I'm responsible for keeping you safe."

Sadie felt a stab of disappointment. Appearances and duty again. He'd been worried about how it would look, not about her well-being. "If I need to make deliveries that are very far from town, I'll find someone to go with me." "Very far" being a relative term. "Griff will be sending over Calliope, my horse, when he sends Skeeter. I trust you have no objections to me riding alone."

He gave her a long look. "As long as you're not going far."

By mid-morning on Tuesday Sadie was getting cabin fever. She'd already written a long letter for Inez to deliver to Griff, and The Ladies's Auxiliary didn't meet until tomorrow, so she was at loose ends. To top it off, Eli had said not to expect him for lunch—he was scheduled to look at a farmhouse a local was wanting to borrow money on.

What was she supposed to do with herself all day? She was pretty far ahead on Annabel Adams's story, but perhaps she would do some more writing just the same. She actually had an idea for a new story that had fired her interest and now might be the time to experiment with it a bit.

Before she could get started though, a knock at the door brought a welcome distraction. Calling out to Mrs. Dauber that she would get it, Sadie headed for the door, hoping whoever it was had come for a long visit.

Then she heard a familiar bark and raced forward,

throwing open the door. As soon as she did, she was nearly knocked over by fifty pounds of barking dog. "Skeeter!" She knelt so that her ecstatic pet could have access to lick her face, which he did with great enthusiasm. "Oh, I missed you too, boy." She laughed and finally held him back.

Then she looked up to belatedly greet the man who'd accompanied her pet. "Hello, Red."

The weathered ranch foreman tipped his hat. "Hi Miss Sadie. Or should I say Mrs. Reynolds?"

"Sadie will do just fine. Thanks so much for bringing Skeeter to me."

Red grinned. "He was moping so much it was an act of charity."

"Well, come on in and rest yourself a spell."

Red pulled off his hat and entered the foyer. "Thanks, but there's a whole lot more to deliver. Griff sent everything you had on that list of yours. They're over at the train station, waiting on transport."

"Everything?"

Red Grinned. "Calliope is already stabled at the livery."

Sadie felt a flutter of excitement in her chest. It had been so long since she'd had herself a good gallop—she hadn't realized until just now how much she missed it.

"Did she make the trip okay?"

"Like a trouper. Almost like she knew you were at the end of the line. She's been fretting for you ever since you left. She'll be mighty glad to see you." He tilted his hat back. "I suppose you're just as eager to see her. So get your hat and let's go."

It was tempting, but she knew Red had had a long day.

"Time enough for that in a bit. Come on into the kitchen and get yourself something to eat first."

She ruffled Skeeter's fur one more time for good measure, then led the way down the hall.

Mrs. Dauber took one look at Skeeter and crossed her arms over her chest. "Animals don't have no place in my kitchen—especially not one as big and rambunctious at that one." The woman seemed adamant, but with some cajoling on Sadie's part she reluctantly allowed it "just this once." Sadie did notice, however, that within ten minutes the cook was slipping Skeeter little tidbits of food.

After Red had a chance to eat and refresh himself, Sadie, with Skeeter at her heels, allowed him to escort her to the livery. Knowing Calliope was waiting, it was all Sadie could do to maintain a sedate pace. Along the way, she recruited a couple of strapping youths, Harry and Wilbur Browder, to help Red with the loading and unloading.

Once they'd arranged for a wagon and horse to transport Sadie's possessions, Red and the boys headed for the train depot while Sadie spent time with Calliope. Borrowing a set of brushes, Sadie spent the next thirty minutes happily grooming her horse and chatting away about all that had happened, just as if the animal could understand her every word. She paused occasionally to say something to Cocoa who was in the next stall.

Red sent Wilbur to fetch her once the wagon was loaded, and Sadie reluctantly left. But as she headed home she was surprised by the tingle of anticipation. Who'd have thought she would get so all fired up about decorating a house?

By the time she reached the house, the men were al-

ready unloading the first of the items. There were several
trunks that no doubt contained her clothing and personal
items. But it was the crates she was more interested in.

She couldn't wait to get everything unloaded. Sadie
had the Browder brothers carry her trunks up to her
room, absently directing them to stack them as best they
could. But she had the rest of the items placed in the foyer
where she could inspect them herself. As soon as the last
of the crates were brought in she had them opened up.
With the men's help she unpacked every item and laid
them out where she could see them all. Then she started
grouping them based on which room she thought each
should go in.

For her sitting room she set aside the brocade wingback chair and small writing desk that had graced her
own mother's sitting room—she thought of it that way
even now—as well as a small table that had stood in a
corner near the main stairwell.

For the front parlor she quickly grouped the rug, the
painting, the lamp and the chess set.

The two pottery bowls and the hawk came next—
where would they look best? She finally settled on placing the bowls on the sideboard in the dining room and
the hawk on the table in the entry.

The books, of course, would go in the library.

That only left the pair of porcelain figurines. She finally decided to put those in her sitting room, as well.

Skeeter trotted at her heels wherever she went, as if
determined to never let her out of his sight again.

When the work was finally done, Sadie stepped back
and admired her efforts. The eclectic, colorful pieces
she'd selected had gone a long way toward brightening
up the formerly somber parlor. She bent down and rubbed

Skeeter's head. "What do you think, boy? Do you think Eli will appreciate the change?"

Then she snapped her fingers. "That's right, you don't know Eli. It's okay. He takes a bit of warming up to but I promise you it's worth the effort. And you're really going to like Penny. She's sweeter than buttermilk pie and cute as a bunny in clover."

"You always talk to that mutt as if he can understand you."

Sadie smiled at Red over her shoulder. "That's because he can."

She heard the front door open and Skeeter's ears went up. They stepped out into the hall in time to see Penny shut the door behind her.

The little girl halted in her tracks, her eyes widening as her gaze latched on to Skeeter.

"Is that your dog?" she asked without glancing up.

"Yep, this is Skeeter. Come on over and get acquainted."

Penny set her books down on the entry table, only sparing a quick, surprised look at the hawk, then approached the dog cautiously.

"Hold out your hand and let him sniff it."

Penny bravely did as she was bid, and stood with a stoic expression while Skeeter licked her hand.

"I can see he likes you."

"He does?"

"Absolutely. Go ahead, pet him if you like."

She watched as Penny gingerly smoothed a hand across the dog's head and nape. When Skeeter gave an encouraging woof and started wagging his tail, at first she looked startled, then grinned.

"He *does* like me."

"I told you."

Penny knelt down and giggled as Skeeter attempted to wash her face with his tongue.

Sadie couldn't help but smile at the picture they made. Skeeter liked children as much as she did. She only hoped Eli took to her pet as well as Penny had.

Penny finally looked up from the dog and pointed to the entry table. "Did that bird come from your ranch, too?"

"Uh-huh. Do you like it?"

Penny stared at the hawk. "It's different. What's it made from?"

"It's made from the horn of a bull. Would you like to hear the story that goes with it?"

"There's a story?"

Sadie smiled. "Of course. Most everything has at least one story to go with it. We just don't always know what that story is."

"Then yes, I want to hear the story that goes with your bull horn bird."

Sadie grinned at her descriptive. "Ok. And afterwards I'll show you all the rest of the pieces that came from my old home."

"Do you know their stories, too?

"Of course. That's why they're each special to me. And I promise to tell you each and every one."

Eli strode into the house and halted on the threshold. Penny sat on the floor like a scullery maid, playing with an oversized, rough-looking dog of questionable breeding. He'd already gotten word of the shipment that had arrived from Hawk's Creek. Was *this* Sadie's pet? With a name like Skeeter he'd been expecting a lap dog whose biggest drawback would be an annoying yip. This animal was large, well-muscled and must weigh at least fifty pounds. Its short-haired coat was gray with black spots, and its tongue seemed as long as Eli's hand and wrist. He couldn't tell what breed it was—seemed to be a touch of collie, a touch of greyhound and a touch of who-knows-what-else in the animal.

Where was Sadie and why wasn't she supervising? Was it really safe for his sister to be behaving so familiarly with the beast? "Penny, what are you doing down on the floor with that animal?"

Penny, however, seemed oblivious to any danger the animal might pose. "Look Eli, Skeeter's here. Isn't he great?"

Great was *not* the word he'd use. "I had expected something…smaller."

Sadie stepped out of the parlor. "Skeeter isn't a 'something'—he's a dog."

From the bristle in her tone he could tell he'd gotten her back up. "My apologies. It's just, I thought your pet was a lapdog. This looks more like a guard animal."

Her frown deepened. "I never said anything about him being a lapdog—he comes from working stock."

A strange man appeared from the vicinity of the kitchen just then. "Miss Sadie, I— Oh, sorry, didn't realize you had company."

"Red, this is my husband, Eli Reynolds."

Before the man could do more than nod, she turned and completed the introductions. "Eli, this is Red Hannigan from Hawk's Creek. He was kind enough to bring Skeeter and most of my belongings here for me."

Eli extended a hand. "Mr. Hannigan, Sadie and I thank you for your trouble."

The man pumped Eli's hand with what seemed unnecessary force. Mr. Hannigan seemed to be sizing him up. "It's just Red. And no need for thanks—it wasn't any trouble. Fact of the matter is, I had to arm wrestle three other hands for the chance to come down here and check out the fella who managed to capture Miss Sadie's fancy."

Did the man think this was a love match? Eli wasn't certain what he thought of that.

"Red's going to be staying the night at the boarding-house and escorting Inez back to Hawk's Creek in the morning."

"Mrs. Collins runs a clean, comfortable place."

"So I've heard." Red turned back to Sadie. "If you don't need me to help you arrange any more of your things I think I'll be heading on over to the boarding-house now."

What "things" had he been helping her arrange?

"You're free to do as you please, Red, you know that. I appreciate all your help today. Let Inez know I'll come by to see you both off at the train station tomorrow."

He nodded. "Will do." Then he tipped his hat Eli's way. "Nice meeting you, Mr. Reynolds. You take care of our Miss Sadie now."

As Eli watched Red head out the front door, his gaze was caught by a carving on the entry table. What was that? A closer look showed it to be the head of a bird—hawk maybe—carved out of what seemed to be an animal horn and mounted on a block of polished wood. He moved closer to get a better look, not believing what he was seeing.

"It's a hawk," Sadie said. "It sat in my father's study for as long as I can remember. Do you like it?"

So this had sentimental value to her. He just wished

she had found a less prominent place to display it. "I've never seen another quite like it," he said diplomatically.

Her bright smile told him she hadn't picked up any undercurrents in his statement. "Yes, it's very special." She waved him forward. "Come on in the parlor and I'll show you some of the other pieces I had sent over."

"Other pieces?" Eli braced himself. Surely it wasn't more of the same.

Penny stood, dusting her skirts. "Oh, just wait until you see all of the other things she's brought, Eli. They're absolutely splendid."

His sister's words did little to reassure him. Nor did the fact that Sadie's "pet" seemed even larger now that it was standing.

Sadie was happily chatting as she led the way into the parlor. "I made a list for Griff so he'd know just what items to send. And they look even better than I imagined they would."

"You should have waited until I got home so I could've helped you unload and set out your things." And perhaps influenced *where* they were set.

"Red helped. He's a very handy fellow. Besides, I wanted it to be a surprise."

He was surprised all right. With some trepidation Eli moved to the parlor. And stopped on the threshold to stare at the transformation she'd wrought.

A bearskin rug now lay in brutish state in front of the fireplace. A colorful but amateurish picture of a ranch house hung on the bit of wall that separated the two tall windows on the far side of the room. A hobnail cranberry glass lantern presided over the small table next to the sofa, replacing the more traditional, elegant lamp that had been there this morning. And a rustically carved chess set occupied the table near the piano.

"What do you think?"

Eli tried to pull his thoughts together. Did *all* of these items have sentimental value? "You've certainly put your stamp on this room."

"That was the plan," she said happily. "Isn't it wonderful the way your things and my things go so well together even though they're so very different?"

She thought these items went well with his furnishings? He hadn't realized her taste was so underdeveloped. "Is this everything?" Please say it is.

"Oh, no. I wanted to spread things around a bit. I put some things in the dining room and in the library and in my sitting room. Come on, I'll show you the rest."

Eli studied the two bowls that now anchored each end of the sideboard. They were crafted of glazed pottery, painted in a bold shade of blue and decorated with flowers—one had two roses and the other had five lilies.

The bright colors were a jarring note in the otherwise elegantly-appointed room.

"I thought these would brighten up the room a bit. My mother had a whole collection of these—sixteen in all. The daisies and lilies were always my favorite though." He supposed he should be grateful she hadn't had the entire collection brought in.

Next she led the way to the library where his gaze was immediately drawn to two porcelain figurines situated on the low table that fronted the fireplace. At least these were finely crafted pieces, but they were badly cracked and chipped.

Sadie, however, fingered them as if they were priceless treasures. "I used to play with these when I was a little girl."

Another sentimental attachment. He supposed he should be thankful she hadn't *all* her playthings with her.

He expected to find a whole trove of her "treasures" when they moved to her sitting room, but he was surprised to find it still woefully under furnished—a tasteful wingback chair, a delicately constructed writing desk and chair and a table that had seen better days but were obviously of good quality. These furnishings were a bit delicate for his taste but were of a quality and workmanship much more refined than the pieces she'd placed in the more public areas of the house. Why couldn't she have swapped the placements?

"Why so sparse?"

She shrugged. "I don't really need a lot right now." She ran her fingers lovingly along the top of the chair back. "These pieces came from my mother's study and I didn't want to strip it bare."

Too bad her taste didn't mirror her mother's.

"I figure I'll do what she did," Sadie continued. "Find pieces over time that I like and make it more of a personal haven."

He mentally winced at the thought of just what her personal taste in furnishings would do to this room if the other items she'd brought into the house were a reflection.

As they returned to the parlor, Sadie spun around to face him. "So, what do you think of my additions?"

Hearing the note of worry in her voice, Eli did his best to answer diplomatically. "The pieces certainly are colorful."

Her eyes lit up. "Exactly! They brighten up the rooms and give them character."

Changed their character more like. From elegant and sophisticated, to a mishmash of unmatched styles and garish colors.

All through the evening meal, the gaudy blue bowls taunted him, set his teeth on edge. Afterwards, as they sat in the parlor, he was acutely conscious of the bear-skin rug. How could they possibly entertain guests with that atrocity sitting there? But how could he broach the matter to Sadie without hurting her feelings?

Chapter Thirteen

The next morning Eli came downstairs prepared to deal with her tasteless additions. Perhaps some of the less egregious items could stay, but items like the bearskin rug and carved hawk would need to find new homes. He'd pondered the situation as he lay in bed last night and finally decided the best course of action was to try to be subtle but firm.

Once breakfast was served, he cleared his throat. "About those things you had delivered from Hawk's Creek."

Sadie glanced up. "Yes?"

"I was just thinking, I mean since the pieces are all so special to you, and since your sitting room seems so bare, maybe you'd like to move them there, where you can surround yourself with familiar objects."

"Oh, but I like having them scattered around where we can all enjoy them. And I don't mind sharing."

She wasn't making this easy on him. "That's quite generous of you, but perhaps the colors are a bit *too* bright…"

Her smile slowly faded. She stared at him for a long

moment, then her chin came up. "You don't care for them." The words were flat, emotionless.

He tried to smooth things over. "I didn't say that. I only meant they don't match—"

She brushed his words aside as if he hadn't spoken. "So you didn't really want me to put my stamp on the entire house, just my isolated, private portion of it that neither you nor our guests will have to be bothered with."

"You're twisting my words."

"Am I?"

He set his fork down in exasperation. "Yes, you are. I was just thinking that it might be better if perhaps we shop for some new pieces together, pieces that we can both enjoy and maybe build new memories around." Sentimental memories seemed to be important to her.

But she wasn't appeased. "I see. Does that mean we will be replacing your desk or your grandfather clock."

He frowned. "Those are family heirlooms."

"And mine are mere bric-a-brac. Don't worry, I'll have everything moved to my sitting room and bedroom as soon as possible." She set her napkin on the table.

"Feel free to hire whatever help you need."

"Of course. Because money is the answer to everything." She stood. "Now if you'll excuse me, I need to speak to Mrs. Dauber about today's meals."

Eli stared at her back as she turned and marched stiffly out of the room. That didn't go quite as he'd hoped.

"That wasn't very nice, Eli."

He'd forgotten his sister was even present. "Come now, Penny, she might be a bit put out right now, but she'll be fine once she thinks on it. Perhaps I was a bit too straightforward, but I'll help her pick out new things that both she and I like."

Penny's gaze still condemned him. "But it won't be the same."

He certainly hoped not.

"These are her *story pieces*." Penny said that as if it explained everything.

"Story pieces?"

Penny nodded. "That's what she calls them. I asked her why she chose these things out of all the things in her house, and she said it's because there's a story she can tell about each of them." Penny crossed her arms. "Sadie likes stories."

A bit too much perhaps. "Stories are fine for children, but grown-ups must learn to set make-believe behind them and deal with the real world."

"Why?"

"Because when you're an adult you have adult responsibilities, you have people depending on you and you can't just pretend things are something that they're not. You'd never get anything done if all you cared about was fun and make-believe."

"But Sadie has fun and she gets things done." Penny tilted up her chin. A gesture she'd no doubt picked up from Sadie. "When I grow up, I want to be like Sadie." She stood up from the table. "May I be excused, please?"

"Yes. Collect your books and head out for school."

Penny paused next to her brother and placed a hand on the arm of his chair. "Eli," she looked at him with a surprisingly adult disappointment, "I know her things are different from yours, but I like them, and you would, too, if you heard her stories. I think you should ask her to tell them to you."

"We'll see."

Eli rose from the table and straightened his cuff. He refused to feel guilty. It was important that Sadie learn good taste so that Penny would also grow up with an appreciation for the finer things. Some things he could overlook, but bearskin rugs and carvings made from bull horns—no. He knew he was in the right here.

So why did he suddenly feel so wrong?

Sadie managed to keep her emotions under control through most of the morning. She walked Penny to the mercantile as usual. The little girl's sympathy and obvious outrage at her brother's actions forced Sadie to defend Eli—not an easy task with her emotions still roiling around. But by the time they parted, they both agreed that Eli had a right to his own opinion, and his was no more right or wrong than theirs.

Then she met Red and Inez at the train station to see them off. Inez took one good look at her and knew something was wrong. Sadie waved off her concerns with a laughing comment about adjusting to life in the city.

When she was finally alone, she headed straight for the stable. She fed Cocoa a bit of extra grain and promised to exercise her later. The she saddled Calliope and mounted up. She rode sedately until she was well out of town. But as soon as the last of the buildings were behind her she let the horse have her head.

For several minutes she just let everything else go except the exhilaration of galloping across the long stretch of flat, open road. The feel of the sun on her skin, the wind on her face, the smell of dust and grass and wildflowers, the sound of crows and jays and pounding hooves—if she closed her eyes she could almost imagine herself back at Hawk's Creek. When she passed a buggy headed into town she finally slowed her horse to a walk.

And allowed her emotions to come flooding to the front. Anger, frustration, disappointment, hurt—all the wasplike, hurtful emotions that prick and sting. She should have known better than to think Eli would appreciate her additions to their home. The man was too set in his ways, too focused on appearances.

His disregard for her feelings *was* hurtful, but she could deal with that. What bothered her more was the thought that this might be an indication of how he felt about her personally. Was he ashamed of her? Did he see her as an embarrassment, as someone to keep out of sight as much as possible? After all, he'd only pressed his suit with her because he'd felt honor bound.

He'd admitted he'd been seeking a wife, a *proper* wife, before their "little incident" forced his hand. Perhaps he'd already set his sights, his affections, on someone else here in Knotty Pine. Oh—what if he was nursing tender affections for another woman? Jealousy added its own sting.

She tried to forcibly put that from her mind. Whatever the case, she and Eli were married now. So it was up to the two of them to make the marriage work. For Penny's sake, if not their own.

As Cora Beth had said, as Eli's wife, it was up to her to bring the heart to their home. Perhaps, in time, he would come to value her viewpoint. For now, it was enough that he seemed to at least be trying to be kind.

She tugged on the reins, turning Calliope back toward town. "Come on, girl. I have some things to take care of back at home."

* * *

By the time Eli returned home for lunch, all traces of Sadie's additions to the household furnishings had been removed from at least casual view. And Sadie herself seemed calm and relaxed. There was no mention of this morning's conversation, no mention of where her things had gone.

He waffled for a minute about whether to ask what she'd done with the missing pieces, but finally decided to not ruffle the feathers.

She chatted with him about seeing Red and Inez off at the train station, about her morning ride and about the upcoming Ladies's Auxiliary meeting. "Cora Beth tells me the ladies alternate which home they meet in," she told Eli. "They're meeting at Mrs. Danvers home this afternoon and at the boardinghouse next week. I thought I would volunteer to have it here the following week."

"That sounds like a fine idea."

The conversation lagged for a few minutes, then she broached a new topic. "Do you ever do much riding?"

"When I have someplace to go. And more often than not it's by carriage."

"But don't you ever ride horseback just for the pure enjoyment of it?"

"Pure enjoyment?" Where was she going with this?

"Yes. You know—the exhilaration you get from galloping across the countryside, letting the wind whip at you and the sun warm you, knowing you can control the powerful animal beneath you with just a touch."

Was she worried he didn't appreciate her wedding gift to him? "Cocoa is a beautiful mare. I think she'll make a good carriage horse but you're right, it might be enjoyable to ride horseback occasionally. Perhaps, once we have a suitable mount for Penny, we can ride as a family."

Sadie nodded, smiling as if he'd given her a gift. "That would be nice. In the meantime, I'll alternate my daily rides between Cocoa and Calliope so they both get exercised."

Was *that* the point she'd been trying to make. "I can hire someone to exercise them if you like."

"No, please don't. Riding is something I've always done and always loved. It would be foolish to hire someone else to do it."

Not her point then. "As you wish."

Her smile was his reward. Yes, she seemed as cheerful and carefree as always with no lingering resentments. It appeared he'd been right when he told Penny she would get over her hurt feelings quickly. She seemed to have a fleeting attention span—moving from one emotion to another as easily as she moved from one topic to another.

He'd been right to speak his mind earlier. His worry about hurting her feelings had been entirely unfounded.

When Eli stepped through the front door that afternoon, he was greeted by the sound of Penny's laughter. He followed the sound to Sadie's sitting room and stood in the doorway staring at the transformation she'd made. Here were all of the items that had come from Hawk's Creek.

"Oh Eli, isn't this the most amazing room?" Penny exclaimed.

Sadie glanced his way with a smile. "I took your suggestion and brought all my things from Hawk's Creek in here. You were right, they make this room into something special."

The hodgepodge of items was startling when brought together. The colors clashed, the styles were all over the place. The elegant little table with the knick on it held the hobnail lamp and stood right beside the bearskin rug. The cracked porcelain figurines overlooked the chess set and hawk's head carving. The blue bowls sat in garish splendor on the mantle, flanking either side of her watercolor. And so on around the room.

Yet somehow it all looked like it belonged together. As did Sadie, Penny and Skeeter.

Where did that leave him? "There was no need for you to bring it all in here. If you want to leave a few things, like the lamp and the figurines—"

"No, no, you were right, these pieces belong together." She stood. "Penny, I believe you have some homework to do. And Eli, if you'd like to relax in your study, I'll check with Mrs. Dauber and see when we can expect her to serve supper."

Within seconds he was left standing alone. Even her dog had followed Penny out. He moved slowly toward his study trying to figure out why he felt this sudden restlessness.

This was what he'd been hoping for. A wife who would run his household and take her place in the community beside him. Someone who would not just take care of his sister but who would come to love her, who would give her the attention and discipline she needed, while at the same time keep her happy and entertained.

And Sadie was well on her way to providing all of that.

Even though she'd gone off in a bit of a huff this morning—and no matter how his conscience tweaked he would not allow himself to feel any guilt for that—she had come to her senses and was behaving quite decorously this evening.

So why wasn't he feeling more pleased with the way things were shaping up?

Chapter Fourteen

"And how was the Ladies's Auxiliary meeting?" Eli was hoping to draw Sadie out a bit as they sat around the dining table.

"Mrs. Danvers put me on the broom brigade," she said proudly.

"The broom brigade?"

"Yes. We're divided into three groups—the sewing brigade which mends the altar cloths and curtains and anything else around the church that needs that kind of attention. Then there's the polishing brigade which, of course, polishes the pews and other woodwork. And us, the broom brigade which takes care of the floors." She waved her fork in a tight circle. "Mrs. Van Halsen was a member of that group but she's moved over to the sewing brigade so they needed a new person."

"And that's where they put you—sweeping floors."

Sadie nodded. "It's work that needs doing and I don't mind. But that's just the once-a-week work. We do other things, as well. There's some folks here in town who need someone to check in on them occasionally and I volunteered to help out with that, too. After all, I'm not as busy as some of the other ladies."

Eli nodded, pleased to hear she was finding her place here. Charitable undertakings were an important part of community life.

The subject of Sadie's things was not broached again. Eli watched her closely for signs of unhappiness or discontent over the couple of days, but saw none. Her disposition remained sunny and open.

He wasn't sure whether to be pleased or concerned.

He *did* notice that she and Penny spent a great deal of time in her sitting room rather than the parlor. And for some reason that made him feel left out. Not that he wasn't welcome there. He just didn't feel quite comfortable there.

It was almost as if her things were frowning at him. That highly fanciful notion was so unlike him that he found himself feeling even more out of sorts.

Friday, Charlie Jamison stopped by the bank to make a deposit. He stuck his head in Eli's office. "Just wanted to let you know how much we appreciate that missus of yours."

Eli leaned back in his chair. "Is that so?"

"Yep. My pa has been real down since he hurt his hip last month. He's not one to take to just sitting around. But Miss Sadie, she didn't just drop off a meal. She cheered him up real good yesterday with her checker playing and reading to him. Tickled him to no end when that little slip of a thing beat him two games out of three."

"You don't say."

"I do. Hadn't seen pa this lively since his accident."

After Charlie left, Eli set his pen down. So, Sadie was

doing more than delivering food baskets, was she? Why hadn't she said anything? He couldn't remember—had he asked her about her day yesterday?

An hour later, Bart Dugan stepped in his office. "I suppose you already know this, but that's one fine woman you married, Mr. Reynolds. She brought a bowl of soup to my Martha this afternoon and stayed to take care of our young'ens. First chance I've had to come to town and get supplies since Martha got sick."

Later, when he headed home, Mrs. Nelson stopped him. "Please tell Sadie how much we appreciate her visit to Granny Lawrence this morning. Having someone to listen to her reminiscences and read to her just cheered her up so much. She's missed getting around on her own since her sight got so bad."

His wife had certainly been busy.

"So how did your day go today?" Eli asked as he passed the platter of bread at supper that evening.

"Oh, nothing much." Sadie took a slab of bread and passed the platter to Penny. "I took a ride on Calliope, enjoyed the fresh air, visited with a few folks."

Eli took his own seat at the table. "Anyone I'd know?"

"I met Mrs. Nelson today. Do you know her?"

"I don't believe I've had the pleasure."

"A wonderful character, full of salt and vinegar. She's nearly blind but that doesn't stop her from speaking her mind. We had a great conversation about how she used to play the fiddle when she was a girl."

Eli listened to her chatter on about Mrs. Nelson and then Mrs. Dugan and her kids. Not once did she mention or even imply that she'd paid a charity call on any of her new friends. Instead she made it sound as if she'd had interesting encounters with intriguing people who were their neighbors.

And her stories were full of humor and wit, but always kind. The only person to come off in a bad light was herself. He could see why Penny enjoyed listening to her so much.

And he was beginning to understand just how complex a person she was. But he couldn't decide if that was a good or bad thing to have in a wife.

Saturday morning, Sadie and Penny were out at the stable, grooming the horses. Sadie was working with Calliope and Penny was imitating her every move as she worked with Cocoa.

Sadie had just batted a horsefly away, when she looked up and spied Eli headed toward them. "Oh, hello. Finished with that stuffy old paperwork?"

"Thought I'd take a break and see what you two are up to."

"Just working with the horses." She glanced toward Penny. "That sister of yours is really taking to it. I think we'll be able to move on to riding lessons soon."

Penny's face lit up. "Really?" She turned to her brother. "Oh Eli, can I? I promise to be really careful and do everything Sadie tells me."

"Not today," he said, "but soon."

Sadie mentally winced as she saw Penny's expression droop. She should have waited to talk to Eli before speaking up. When would she learn to think before she acted?"

"I have an idea for something almost as good, though."

Penny stared at him dubiously.

"Why don't we go for a ride?"

The little girl's eyes grew large. "All of us?"

"Of course all of us. You can ride up on my horse with me."

Sadie stared at him. Her sweet-but-stuffy husband was offering to go horseback riding with them? Then she gave her head a mental shake. Whatever had gotten in to him, best take him up on the offer before he found an excuse to change his mind. "You heard your brother—let's get changed and saddle up."

"Can we race to the house?"

Sadie took a quick glance Eli's way and decided not to press her luck. "I have a better idea. Let's show your brother what perfect ladies we can be when we set our minds to it, what do you say?"

Thirty minutes later they were setting off at an easy walk to the edge of town. Though they rode side by side, Sadie let Eli set their course. She watched Penny and Eli riding together, saw the happy look in Penny's eyes and wanted to sigh in contentment. This was just what that little girl needed. More time and attention from her brother. Did Eli realize how much his sister loved him, how desperately she craved his approval?

They were on their way back to the house when Penny brought up the subject of Hawk's Creek.

"While we were grooming Cocoa and Calliope today, Sadie told me all about Hawk's Creek," she told Eli.

"Did she now?"

Sadie laughed. "Not *all* about it princess, that would take much longer than one afternoon."

Her eyes widened. "There's more?"

"There certainly is. I saved some of the best parts for another day. And I'll bet Viola could tell you some stories about it, too. She's been up to visit a half dozen times."

"Can *we* go visit?"

Sadie cast a quick look Eli's way before answering. "Of course we can. But we'll have to sit down and figure out a good time. Your brother is very busy with his job right now."

"Couldn't we go without him?" Penny looked up at her brother. "You wouldn't mind, Eli, would you? I mean, you don't care about tadpoles and fishing holes and cows and tree swings, do you?"

Was that a wince that crossed Eli's face? It was there and gone so quickly Sadie couldn't be sure.

"Actually, I might be able to get away for a little while," he said slowly. "If we left on a Friday morning and came back on Monday I'd just be away from the bank for two days."

Sadie couldn't believe she'd heard right. First this horseback ride and now an offer to travel to Hawk's Creek. Was he finally trying to meet her halfway?

Penny had no trouble believing him. She was practically bouncing in the saddle. "Do you mean tomorrow?"

He laughed. "No. But Wednesday is the last day of school for the summer so maybe we can plan for next week." He looked over at Sadie. "What do you say? Is that time enough to plan a trip?"

"Absolutely. I'll send a telegram to Griff on Monday to let him know to expect us."

She turned to Penny. "In the meantime, young lady, we need to work on your riding lessons. You'll want to be able to ride a horse on your own when we get there."

Sadie felt the bubble of happiness in her chest expand until she was certain it was visible on her face. Could it be that Eli was making a true effort to do something to please her? If so, he'd found a great way to do just that.

Did he know that she cherished the effort every bit as much as the end result?

Sadie leaned forward to get a look at the passing landscape. She and Eli sat in the backseat of the buggy with Penny between them, while Skeeter got the place of honor up front with Manny. For the past several minutes the road they were traveling had been cutting through a corner of the rolling green hills of Hawk's Creek ranch. It had been nearly a month since she'd left the place but right now it seemed as if she'd been gone forever.

Once they made it over the next rise, the house itself would come into view. Sadie leaned forward a bit more, as if that would help her see it faster.

Sure enough, as soon as they topped the hill, the arched ironwork gateway sign guarding the drive came into view and there was the house itself, with the barn and other outbuildings behind it.

"There it is!" She couldn't keep the note of pride from her voice. There was nowhere else like Hawk's Creek, and no matter how many times she left or how far she traveled, returning here always felt like returning home.

"Look Eli," Penny said. "It's kind of like Amberleigh."

Sadie turned back to her. "What's Amberleigh?"

"It's where we lived before we came to live with Eli."

"We?"

Penny's expression sobered. "Susan and me."

Confused, Sadie started to ask who Susan was. Then she caught sight of Eli who gave a slight shake of his head and mouthed the word *Later* before taking the conversation on a tangent.

"Amberleigh was built along a much different style," he said. "But it did have a lot of open ground like this place and a large stable area."

Penny seemed to have rallied a bit. "I wish we'd brought Cocoa and Calliope with us so we could go horseback riding again while we're here."

Sadie laughed. "Don't worry, princess. There are plenty of horses here—I'm sure we'll find some we can borrow."

As soon as the buggy rolled under the arched Hawk's Creek sign, Skeeter bounded off the wagon seat and raced on ahead. By the time the buggy came to a stop in front of the house, Griff was waiting to greet them.

He stepped over to Sadie's side and grabbed her by the waist to swing her down. "Glad to see you remembered your way back to the place."

Manny set the brake and handed a slip of paper to Griff. "Curtis asked me to deliver this telegram that came for you."

Griff opened the paper and his face split into a smile.

"Ry and Josie are back in the States. They want me to meet them in Tyler when the train comes through on Wednesday for a short visit because they don't plan to delay getting back to Viola and their place a moment longer than they have to."

Sadie smiled as Eli handed her down. "Viola will be so happy to hear that. I know she's been missing them something awful."

Griff waved them toward the house. "Y'all come on inside. I know you'll want to freshen up after that long trip."

Manny followed them into the house with their bags. "Where do you want me to put these?"

"I put you and Eli in Mother and Dad's old room, and Penny in your room, Sadie."

Sadie stilled. She hadn't thought far enough ahead to realize this would be an issue. Of course Griff would expect them to share a room. She cut a quick glance Eli's way.

Griff, sensing something was wrong, frowned slightly. "If that's a problem, we can shuffle things around a bit. Just let me know what arrangements you'd prefer."

Eli saw the panicked look in Sadie's eye. Was she worried what her brother would think if she asked for separate rooms? Or what he would think if she didn't? He decided to take the burden of replying off her shoulders. "I'm sure the arrangements you've made will work just fine."

He was rewarded with a quick look of gratitude from Sadie, closely followed by a telltale pinkening of her cheeks as she looked away.

"Yes, of course," she said. "Sorry, I hadn't thought far enough ahead to wonder about the sleeping arrangements." She turned to Eli and Penny. "I'll show you the way and we can all get freshened up before we say hi to Inez."

Griff laughed. "She's been cooking all morning. Think I saw some of her special pot roast and smothered potatoes on the stove."

"Ummm—my mouth is watering already." Sadie placed her hand at Penny's back. "Come along, you two, our rooms are this way."

Eli waited in the room Sadie had pointed out to him while she got Penny settled in. It was spacious, with a large bed, a large armoire, a chest, a dressing table and several chairs scattered about. A folding screen discreetly guarded one corner of the room and a hat stand and boot-jack sat in another.

He'd just picked up the picture of a lovely woman that sat on a bedside table when Sadie walked in.

"That's my mother." She crossed the room and touched the frame. "Dad never quite got over her loss."

"You look a bit like her."

She shook her head, then dropped her hands. "I'm sorry about the room assignments. It never occurred to me—"

"No need to apologize. I should have thought ahead, as well. But it's just for a few nights." He could tell she was still agitated. "I'm sorry if this makes you uncomfortable. I promise to be a gentleman. But we can make an excuse for you to sleep with Penny, if you prefer."

"No. I'll be fine."

Her answer pleased him. Not only had he not been looking forward to facing Griff's inquisitive looks if they asked to sleep apart, but he didn't like to think that she feared him, or worse, was repulsed by the idea of them sharing a room.

In fact, this might be just the thing to ease her into the idea of sharing a room with him permanently.

Several minutes later, as they headed down the stairs with Penny between them, Eli took the opportunity to look around. He'd been too focused on what she might be feeling earlier to focus on anything else. And surprisingly there were more than a few touches of elegance amongst the expected rustic trappings. The first thing he noticed was the intricate stained glass window, a match for anything he'd seen in the grand estates of Almega, that let colorful patches of sunlight into the landing.

A fine crystal chandelier graced the front entryway. Of course, just below it was a plain braided rug covering a large area of the polished oak floors.

Still, the juxtaposition of the elegant and the rustic seemed to create a comfortable, inviting environment.

When they reached the bottom of the stairs, Sadie waved a hand to her right. "We better step into the kitchen and tell Inez hello or I'll never hear the end of it."

The kitchen was a large open room with lots of windows and counter space. Not only did they find Inez there, but Griff as well, munching on a piece of pecan pie.

Inez immediately set down her rolling pin, wiped her hands on her apron and bustled over to greet them. After welcoming Eli with a smile and Sadie with a hug, she turned her full attention to Penny. "My goodness, don't you just look sweeter than molasses in sugar."

Penny grinned. "You talk just like Sadie."

"Well I should think so," Inez answered. "I practically raised the gal."

After Inez had plied them with cookies, Sadie led them away, proclaiming it was her turn to play tour guide.

As she led them from room to room, Eli again noted the little touches of refinement and sophistication mixed in with the more functional items.

When they reached the sitting room, he was struck by the subtle elegance of the furnishings.

"This was my mother's special place," Sadie said. "I can see her in just about every piece in here." Sadie moved to a colorful globe that was stuck over in a corner of the room. "Her father gave her this as a wedding present when she left Philadelphia. He told her he wanted to make sure she knew how to find her way back home if she ever tired of married life out in this 'uncivilized territory.'" Sadie gave the globe a dismissive spin. "I never saw her look at the thing, even when she told me that story."

"But she brought some of her former home with her, didn't she?" Eli asked. "I mean I see touches that could only have come from New England or abroad."

Sadie laughed. "Oh yes. Mother always liked to surround herself with pretty things. But she wasn't obsessive about it. She always said she held to the notion that beauty was in the eye of the beholder. She was just as pleased with a drawing one of us kids did for her as she was with an expensive painting." She pointed to a crude drawing of a horse that had been framed and prominently displayed on a sofa table. "See here? Ry drew this and gave it to her one year for her birthday. Even when he got older and was embarrassed by it and wanted her to hide it away, she refused. Said it was her favorite piece."

So, she got her sentimental streak from her mother.

"My father's taste was quite different," she continued. "But he always tried to get her pretty things to make her smile."

"Like the blue bowls," Penny said.

Sadie gave her a quick smile. "That's right."

"Can we see the rest of them?" Penny asked.

She took Penny's hand. "Of course. Come on, they're in the parlor."

Eli was left to follow behind them.

Sadie crossed the room and pointed to a glass-fronted curio cabinet that reached nearly to the ceiling. "Here they are."

Eli found himself staring at a dozen or so bowls, the exact same shade of blue as the ones Sadie had had delivered to Knotty Pine. Why these bowls? Why not the beautiful crystal bowl or china vase he could see displayed elsewhere in the room.

"One rose, two petunias, four calla lilies..." Penny called out the design on each of the bowls.

Was there some significance he was missing here?

Griff joined them just then. "Ah, showing off the infamous anniversary bowls, I see."

"Anniversary bowls?" Eli repeated.

"Don't tell me Sadie never told you the story?"

Eli glanced Sadie's way. "No."

Griff laughed. "I'll let Sadie tell it to you when she's ready. She does a much better job of it than I do."

Penny tugged on Sadie's skirt. "Can I play on your swing now?"

"Of course you can, princess." Sadie glanced up at her brother. "And I'll just bet your Uncle Griff would be glad to give you the same big old pushes he used to give me."

Griff shot her a puzzled look before he turned to Penny. "Come on, buttercup, let's let these two sit here all lazy-like while we see if that old swing still works."

Taking hold of Griff's outstretched hand, she let him lead her from the room, Skeeter at their heels.

As soon as they were gone, Sadie turned and Eli braced himself for the question he knew was coming.

"Who is Susan?"

Chapter Fifteen

Sadie saw the slight tensing of his jaw, saw the shadow of grief and something else darken his eyes.

"Susan was our sister," he answered

Was? Her heart immediately went out to both him and Penny. "Oh Eli, I'm so sorry. What happened to her?"

"My father married Adelle, my stepmother, when I was seventeen. Adelle was a widow and already had one daughter at the time—Susan. Penny came along a few years later."

So he'd had a stepsister and a half-sister. Yet she could tell he'd loved them both.

He raked a hand through his hair. "Father passed away six years ago. I had already moved out by then—I inherited a house in town from my maternal grandparents that suited my needs much better than my father's country estate. While my stepmother relied on me to take care of her financial affairs after she was again widowed, she and my sisters spent most of their time at Amberleigh, and I stayed close to my business interests in the city. Then Adelle passed on several months ago and I suddenly found myself the guardian of two girls, my own sisters, whom I hardly knew at all."

She could imagine how that must have thrown his orderly world upside down.

"Susan was fifteen at the time," he said, "and Penny had just turned nine. I hired a well-recommended nanny and moved them all into my house, turning the third floor entirely over to them."

His jaw tightened. "Adelle had mentioned to me once that Susan had been found walking in her sleep on a few occasions, so I asked the nanny to be particularly watchful. And I checked on her in the evenings before I turned in, as well. There was no sign that she'd resumed her sleepwalking."

He was silent for so long that Sadie wondered if he had decided not to finish. Then he inhaled deeply. "I came home from a late meeting one evening about ten weeks ago and found Susan's body on the flagstone terrace, just below her third story window."

Sadie's hand flew to her throat. "Oh, how awful! But, Eli, please don't tell me you blame yourself. I'm sure you took every reasonable precaution."

She saw his hands fist at his sides. "She was my responsibility. And I let her down." His voice was tight, almost raw. "I don't intend to make the same mistake with Penny."

"Of course you won't." This explained so much about him, about his drive to find a suitable wife, about his inordinate concern over her and Penny's welfare.

"Penny had nightmares for weeks afterwards," he added. "But once we moved here, and she was able to put some distance between herself and all the reminders, she seemed ready to move on."

"Poor little sweetheart. To lose so many loved ones at such a young age—it's amazing she's come through it all with such a sunny disposition. She's lucky to have a brother like you."

"That's a matter of perspective."

"I won't let you talk about yourself like that."

That earned her a startled glance, then he gave a crooked smile. "Loyal and forthright as always."

Sadie placed her hand on his arm. "I promise you I will help you protect and cherish Penny," she said fiercely. "And ask the Good Lord to help us to know how best to guide her." She gave his arm a light squeeze. "Thank you for sharing that with me. I know it wasn't easy. But now you have someone to share that burden with."

He looked slightly uncomfortable. Was it her praise or her offer to share his burden that bothered him?

"Speaking of Penny," he said, obviously ready to change the subject, "perhaps we should see how she's doing."

"Don't worry, she's in good hands with Griff. But come on, I'm ready to get outside, too."

As they stepped outside, Sadie offered up a silent prayer. *I know why You put me in this position now, Lord. They're both hurting and grieving, and I'll do everything I can, everything You show me to do, to help them heal.*

When Griff caught sight of them, he stopped pushing and the swing gradually slowed to a stop.

"Hey you two," Sadie called out, "we're headed out to the stable to take a look at the horses. Want to come along or are you having too much fun?"

"Can we go for a ride?" Penny asked.

"Not today. We've been traveling all day and I'm

ready to just relax for now. But tomorrow I can show y'all around the place all good and proper."

"The fishing hole and the lightning tree and the new barn."

Sadie laughed. "All of it."

Griff shook his head. "Sounds like someone has been spinning stories again."

"Sadie tells the best stories ever." Penny's tone dared anyone to dispute her statement.

"That she does, buttercup. Been doing it almost since the day she started talking. Hadn't been able to shush her since."

"Is that so, Mr. Too-Big-for-his-Britches Lassiter?"

Griff raised his hands in surrender. "Hey, I was just stating facts. I never said it was a bad thing."

He turned to Penny. "Someday you need to get my little sister to tell you the story about how Ry and I tricked her into sitting smack dab in the middle of a mud hole."

Penny immediately turned to Sadie and clamored for the story.

"Come along," Sadie said with a martyred sigh, "I'll tell you about my dastardly brothers while we walk to the stable."

That evening, Sadie didn't intend to linger long over the nightly ritual of hearing Penny's prayers and then tucking her in. Eli had diplomatically let her know that he would wait a bit to follow her upstairs. She just wasn't certain how long "a bit" was. But Penny was full of talk about the new experiences and it was several minutes before her yawns finally overcame her chatter.

Sadie made quick work of changing into her bed-clothes, but she was still at her mother's dressing table, pulling a brush through her hair, when a soft knock signaled Eli's presence. Fighting the urge to scamper across the room and dive under the shelter of the bedcovers, Sadie took a deep breath. "Come in."

Eli opened the door and stopped in his tracks. Rather than lying under the covers, his wife sat there, robed in a dark green dressing gown, brushing her hair. And what hair! For all that they had been married two weeks now, this was the first time he'd seen it down.

She looked softer this way, more feminine. Not like a child—no, not at all. Like a woman, a gentle, beautiful woman. His wife.

But he'd promised her he wouldn't make this uncomfortable for her. "I'm sorry. If you need more time I can—"

"No, don't be silly. I'll be done in a minute."

He sat in a chair by the window and began pulling off his boots. But he couldn't take his eyes from her. He was mesmerized by the rhythmic motion of her hairbrush as it slid through her hair, by the way the auburn tresses shimmered in the glow of the lamplight, by the fluid motion of her free hand as it separated the locks and held them away from her head for the brush to caress.

What would it be like to take the brush from her hand and perform that service himself? To bury his face in the silky tresses? To— With a mental oath he forced himself to look away.

When he heard her set the brush down, he looked back up, just in time to see her rise. Her hair was braided now and his fingers itched to set it free again. Then he noticed the color in her cheeks. Was she merely embarrassed at the thought that they would share a room tonight or was she worried that he would break his word? That thought splashed cold water on his runaway imagination.

She waved a hand toward the large folding screen that guarded one corner of the room. "There's clean cloths on the stand and fresh water in the ewer." Her hand fluttered in an uncharacteristically nervous gesture. "If you should need anything else—"

"I'll be fine.

She nodded and turned down the bedcovers. He deliberately turned his back before she could shrug out of her robe.

When he stepped from behind the screen he found her under the covers but still wide awake. His nightshirt should be enough to keep from embarrassing her, but still, crossing the room under her silent scrutiny was almost his undoing. He might be a gentleman, but he was also a man. And the woman in that bed was his wife.

But how could he know if she was ready? If only she would give him the least little sign—

Then he remembered that this was her parents' bed. And her brother was sleeping right down the hall. This was perhaps not the best time to try to woo his wife.

He turned down the one lamp in the room she'd left lit, then slid into bed, careful not to do anything to alarm her. As he let his eyes grow accustomed to the dark, he could hear her breathing, could tell she was trying to regulate it and was failing. And the sudden overwhelming urge to protect her, to put her fears at rest, swept over him and overtook his other, less altruistic urges.

"Good night, Sadie," he said softly. Then he rolled over, turning his back not so much on her as on his own desires.

* * *

Sadie stared at Eli's back. She'd thought for sure tonight he would make her fully his wife. She'd saw the look in his eye when he first walked in and spotted her at the dressing table. She'd watched surreptitiously in the mirror as he'd stared at her brushing her hair. There'd been something there, something that called to her in a visceral way.

She'd been tingling with anticipation, wondering what it would be like, remembering what Cora Beth had said *"...it's a beautiful, loving act, meant to draw two people who care for each other even closer together and prepare them to create and nourish the family God meant for them to have."* Those words had painted such a deeply touching image, had planted the seed of want inside her, that Sadie found herself yearning to experience it, to become truly one with her husband.

Why didn't he seem to want that as well?

Chapter Sixteen

By the time Eli reached the dining room for breakfast the next morning, Sadie and Penny were already seated and attacking their plates. He hadn't slept well last night, lying awake long after Sadie's breathing evened into the steady rhythm of sleep, and when he had finally dozed off he'd woken twice when his sleeping wife rolled over against him. He wasn't certain he could take another night of such sweet torture.

His mood hadn't improved any when he woke to discover Sadie already up and gone from their room. Apparently *she* hadn't had any trouble sleeping. He should have been pleased to know she trusted him so fully, but somehow that hadn't been his primary emotion.

Sadie looked up and saw him just then. "Good morning, sleepyhead."

Penny gave him a worried look. "I told Sadie you must be ill because you *never* sleep this late but she said you were probably just tired because you always work so hard."

The door opened and Inez stepped through with a

plate piled high with eggs, biscuits and steak. "Hope you woke up hungry."

"I'm fine," Eli addressed Penny's fears first as he took his place across from Sadie. Then he smiled up at Inez. "Thank you, it smells delicious."

"Griff is already out checking on the herd." Sadie slathered jelly on her biscuit. "Said for us to entertain ourselves today and he'll see us this afternoon." She plopped the two halves of her biscuit together. "I thought this morning might be a good time for us to ride out over the place and let me show you some of my favorite spots."

"Can I ride my own horse?" Penny asked.

Eli was pleased to see Sadie looked to him to answer Penny's question. "You've been coming along really well, but riding across an open field is a bit trickier than riding in a paddock or on a hard-packed road."

Penny's face fell.

"But," he continued, "if Sadie can find us an easy-tempered horse and we take it nice and slow, I might see my way toward allowing it."

His sister's expression immediately brightened, as did Sadie's.

"Oh, please say you have an easy-tempered horse, Sadie."

"I know just the one. Buttermilk is as gentle as they come."

"Can we go now?"

Sadie laughed one of those infectious laughs he was learning to appreciate. "Let's give your brother a chance to eat his breakfast first, what do you say?"

"And here's the pond I told you about."

Eli studied Sadie's happy smile. It was obvious how

much she loved this place. Did she resent that he'd been the cause of her having to leave it?

"It's so big." Penny turned to him. "This is where Sadie's father taught her how to fish, and where her brother Ry taught her how to swim and where her brother Griff taught her how to skip stones."

It seemed Sadie had shared a lot of her history with his sister that she hadn't with him. But then again, he'd never shown any interest in hearing about it. "Sounds like a special spot."

"Sadie has lots of stories about this place." Penny sat up taller. "Like the time she pushed her brother in because he was teasing her about getting mud in her hair. And—"

Sadie laughed. "I'm sure your brother isn't interested in those stories right now." She prepared to dismount. "Why don't we let the horses drink and graze a bit while we get down and try some of that lunch Inez packed for us?"

Eli quickly dismounted as well and went to help Penny down. It was amazing how quickly she'd taken to riding horseback. He suspected part of it was because she wanted to emulate Sadie.

"This place is ever so much bigger than Amberleigh."

"That it is."

Sadie had taken them over acres and acres of open land earlier. At one point they'd topped a rise and were able to see a large herd of cattle contentedly grazing some distance away. "That's the main herd. Griff is over a bit east of here, culling out some of the young bulls."

She'd taken them to a large structure she called the north barn, which she proudly declared Griff had designed himself and gone into detail about just why his design was so superior to others. In fact, everywhere they went she had personal anecdotes to relate. She told how the charred tree they'd passed about thirty minutes ago had been struck by lightning just one day after she'd picnicked in that very spot. And how the creek they were crossing had flooded one spring and washed out a long string of fences. And so many more tales, all of them told with her signature humor and vividness.

"Well looky here." Sadie had already spread the picnic blanket and was on her knees digging through the sack of food Inez had provided. "We're in for a real treat. Inez packed us up some of her best-you-ever-tasted fried chicken and biscuits. Looks like there's some of her pecan cookies, too." She glanced up at them. "Anybody hungry besides me?"

"I am." Penny plopped down on the blanket beside Sadie.

Thirty minutes later Penny was off gathering flowers to braid into a crown and Sadie sat with her arms propped behind her, staring dreamily at nothing in particular.

Eli settled down beside her. "I can see how much you love this place."

She gave him a curious look, then smiled. "Of course I do. It's where I grew up. Don't you feel the same about Amberleigh?"

He shrugged. "I suppose, but perhaps not as intensely." He doubted he felt *anything* as intensely as Sadie. "Just like I liked my house in the city and I like my—our— new home in Knotty Pine. They are merely places and are what you make of them."

She slowly nodded. "In a way I suppose that is true. Because when it comes down to it, it's the memories you have about something that make it feel special. So much of a person's childhood is filled with wonder and discovery and the feeling that we are safe and so can be as adventurous as we like. And where you grow up is all tied up in those feelings."

Is that what her childhood had been like? He reached over and pulled a leaf from her hair.

Before he could coax her into saying more, Penny was back.

Sadie sat up straighter. "What a lovely crown you're wearing. You look just like a woodland princess."

Her praise made Penny laugh and preen a bit. "Can you teach me to skip a stone across the pond?"

To his surprise, she didn't jump right up. "Why don't you ask your brother if he will?" she said instead.

Penny turned to Eli uncertainly. "Do you know how to skip stones?"

Unaccountably pleased to be asked, Eli stood. "I most certainly do. I'll have you know I once had a stone skip five times before it sunk."

Penny's eyes widened. "You did?"

"Come along young lady, and I'll see if I still have it in me."

Eli sat in the backseat of the buggy next to Sadie while Penny sat up front with Griff. They were headed to Sunday morning service, at a church that was apparently some distance away from the ranch. While Penny chattered on to her captive listener, Eli tried not to let himself fall asleep in the morning sunshine.

Last night he'd waited over an hour after Sadie went up to bed before joining her. Her soft breathing when he entered the room had let him know she was sleeping and he'd gone to great pains to make certain he didn't wake her up. Unfortunately, while she slept, he hadn't gotten much sleep at all. Good thing there was just one more night of this. Perhaps, once they returned to Knotty Pine where he wasn't so conscious of being in her parents' room and of her older brother sleeping—or not—right down the hall, he could talk to her about—

"We're here!"

Eli peered across the way at the whitewashed country church which, he'd learned, was built on a small corner of Lassiter property. There were an amazing number of wagons and horses tethered nearby and the churchyard seemed to be filled with simply-dressed folks mingling and visiting with each other. He imagined in rural communities such as this the Sunday service was the one time of the week when neighbors saw each other.

As soon as she dismounted, Sadie was surrounded by the folks there, all welcoming her back and wanting to congratulate her on her wedding. The women oohed and aahed over her ring and made a fuss over her new status. The single men all proclaimed themselves to have had their hopes dashed and their hearts broken, and the others just generally welcomed her home.

In short order Eli and Penny were pulled into the crowd, as well. Penny, who shyly clung to Sadie's skirts, was fussed over. Eli received a number of slaps on the back and congratulatory comments for his good fortune in marrying Sadie.

Watching her amongst her friends and neighbors, Eli was struck again by how much she'd given up to become his wife. Here, among these people, she was obviously well loved. Her family was both prominent and respected. In Knotty Pine she'd had to start over, to try to build relationships with people she barely knew. Building a new life there had been his choice, but not hers. No wonder she'd held out so long.

If he were to return to Almega tomorrow would there be anyone to make a fuss over him this way? He sincerely doubted it.

As they entered the church Sadie paused to greet an elderly, bespectacled gentleman. "Reverend Martin, it's so good to see you again."

The man took both her hands in his own. "And you too, Sadie my dear. I hear felicitations are in order."

"Thank you. Let me introduce you to my new family." She placed a hand on Penny's shoulder. "This is Penny, my pretty new sister."

"Hi there little lady, welcome to Everlasting Love Church."

"Thank you very much, sir."

"And this is my husband, Eli Reynolds."

Eli took the minister's hand and found his grip surprisingly strong.

"It's an honor to meet the man who claimed our Sadie's heart."

Eli mentally winced at the reverend's turn of phrase. Claiming Sadie's heart was not something he could boast of having achieved. "A pleasure to meet you as well, Reverend."

He cast Eli a severe look over the top of his spectacles. "Young man, I hope you know what a treasure has been given into your keeping."

Sadie rescued him from having to answer. "Goodness gracious, Reverend Martin, enough of that. You're going to embarrass me." She linked her arm through Eli's and took Penny's hand. "Now, we are going to find our pew. I look forward to hearing another of your rousing sermons."

Eli could hear the man of the cloth chuckling behind them as they walked up the aisle.

By Monday evening they were back home in Knotty Pine. And to Sadie's surprise, it did indeed feel like coming home. Amazing how quickly a place could grow on a person. She suspected, though, in spite of what she'd said to Eli, that it had more to do with the people in a place than the place itself.

She had enjoyed her trip back to Hawk's Creek though. Showing Eli and Penny around had been fun, but more than that, it had been a chance to say a proper good-bye to her childhood home, the chance she hadn't had before her wedding.

That chapter of her life was closed now, and she was looking forward to seeing what this new chapter held for her.

Eli knocked on the door of the sitting room and stepped inside to find Sadie at her writing desk. "Am I interrupting?"

"Not at all. I'm ready for a little break."

"Where's Penny?"

"We just came in from making sure Buttermilk was settled in nicely."

Griff had given the horse to Penny, saying it was a welcome-to-the-Lassiter-family gift and that she'd spoiled the horse for other riders anyway. Penny had been thrilled to finally have her very own mount. However Eli wasn't quite sure how he felt about it yet. But he couldn't bring himself to say no.

"She's in the kitchen with Mrs. Dauber now," Sadie continued. "Trying to talk her into making a cherry cobbler for supper I believe."

Good. It would give him a chance to speak to Sadie alone. He crossed the room until he was standing nose to toe with the head of the bearskin rug. He still couldn't figure out what she saw in the thing, but he was ready to find out. If he'd learned anything the past few days it was that Sadie usually had a reason for the things she did. And most of the time, it was a very good reason. "Penny tells me these pieces you had shipped here from Hawk's Creek are what you call story pieces."

She gave him a startled look. "They are."

"I imagine the story that goes with this rug is a good one."

"It is."

For a normally chatty person she was being frustratingly terse at the moment. "Mind sharing it with me?"

She stood and crossed the room to stand beside him. "Well, the rug itself is from the pelt of a bear killed by my grandfather. He shot the critter when it was trying to make dinner out of one of his prize cows. But that's not the reason it's special to me." She stooped down and softly stroked the fur. "When I was little, this rug lay on the floor of my father's study. One of my earliest memories is of my mother laying on the floor beside me on this very rug, next to the fireplace, reading from a book."

She straightened. "It was just her and me and I can still remember the sound of her voice though I don't remember the words. And I can picture the dress she was wearing that day just as clear as if it were here in front of me. It was lavender with little yellow flowers and had a narrow ribbon of lace all around the bodice. And I remember feeling that I had the most wonderful mother in the world."

She smiled self-consciously. "Of course, I'm sure every child feels that way about her mother. It's just that the memory is so clear and perfect, and every time I see that rug, I get a little bit of that feeling back."

Definitely a strong sentimental attachment, especially if it could evoke such emotions. Did all her pieces have strong emotions tied to them? "And this picture?" he asked, waving to the framed watercolor above the mantel. "I can see now that it's a depiction of Hawk's Creek. Did you know the artist?"

She nodded. "My mother painted it. She wasn't very happy with the way it turned out but Pa insisted on hanging it in his study. Said he'd rather have something she'd created than anything he could find in a museum. Mother pouted a bit that he wouldn't let her burn it like she wanted, but just to tease him. She then said she'd let him keep it only if he made something for her." She pointed to the chess set. "That's why he carved that chess set, as a gift to her." She sighed. "They were so in love."

It seems that the romantic streak in her went deeper than he'd imagined. And that she came by it honestly.

"How about that table over there?" He figured it was a safe guess that the cracked and badly-repaired leg was going to be part of its "story."

She eyed him suspiciously. "Now you're just being nice."

He grinned. "And is that such a novel idea?"

She tossed her head. "At times like this it is. But if you really want to hear the story…"

He followed as she drifted closer to the table.

"Do you see that broken place on one of the legs?" she asked.

He felt a smug satisfaction that he'd guessed correctly.

"It happened one rainy day when I was six years old," she continued. "The weather was near as bad as that storm you and I got caught out in, and Ry, Griff and I were playing tag in the house—something we weren't supposed to be doing. We ended up knocking over that table and busting the leg. The three of us found some nails and tried to fix it ourselves—or at least my brothers did while they set me to be the lookout. Of course Pa noticed it right off and we had to come clean. We were given extra chores for a week."

"And that's a *good* memory?"

Her smile turned wistful. "The three of us were having a good time up until the accident. My brothers were even treating me as if I wouldn't break if I got rowdy right along with them." She traced the edge of the table with a finger. "It's the last clear memory I have of the three of us being so carefree before Mother passed. Then afterwards, Ry went off to visit Grandfather in Philadelphia and the three musketeers were never quite the same."

Eli touched her arm in sympathy. "I'm sorry."

She refocused on him. "Thanks. But it's okay to sometimes remember the sad things in our past as well as the happy. Gives us perspective."

Always reaching for the silver lining. "You know, if you wanted to move one or two of these pieces into other parts of the house, like the parlor or library, that would be all right with me."

"Thank you, but I think I like them all together this

way." She gave him a sassy look. "But that doesn't mean I won't pick up new things from time to time to brighten those other rooms." Her smile softened. "I'm ready to make some new memories."

Eli bolted straight up in bed, awakened by the sound of terror-filled cries. Penny! Her nightmares must have returned.

Within seconds he was tearing down the hall headed for his sister's room. He'd nearly passed Sadie's door when he realized the cries were coming from her, not Penny. He threw open her door to find her buried under her bedcovers, flailing in an attempt to find her way out, crying about not being able to breathe. He rushed to her side, trying to talk to her, to reassure her that he would help her, but he couldn't seem to get through her hysteria and the more she flailed the more tangled she became. It was several eternal seconds later before he finally freed her and she fell against his chest, sobbing. He held her close, rocking her and making soothing sounds, the way he'd done with his sister so many times before. But this did *not* feel like his sister.

"What's the matter with Sadie?" Penny's fear-shaken voice came from just inside the doorway.

Sadie still clung to him as if he were a lifeline and her whole body trembled with alarming force, but Eli tried to keep his voice calm and reassuring. "She's just had a bad dream." At least he devoutly hoped that's all it was.

"Is she going to be okay?"

Both of his girls needed him. Sadie was still trembling, but not so violently now, and her breathing had eased somewhat. He loosened his hold just enough to motion Penny forward.

She ran into the room as if afraid he'd change his mind and stood beside the bed staring at the two of them with wide, frightened eyes.

He took one of her hands. "Do you remember those bad dreams you used to have?"

She nodded.

"It was scary and very upsetting, but afterwards, when you woke up and realized it was all a dream, you were okay, weren't you?"

She nodded. "Because you stayed with me and made me feel better."

His heart hitched at her trust in him. "And just like with you, Sadie will be okay soon, too. She just needs a few minutes to let the dream fade."

He felt Sadie take a deep shuddering breath, then she pushed back enough to meet Penny's gaze. Even in the shadowy room he could see the effort she made to pull herself together. "I'm so sorry I woke you up, princess. But I'm okay now." Her voice was husky, but she managed to smile.

"Do you want me to stay with you?" The little girl still wore a worried frown.

Sadie managed another smile at that. "That's very sweet of you, but I'm fine, truly."

Eli squeezed his sister's hand. "Don't worry, I'll stay with her until she falls back asleep. Just like I did for you. Okay?"

Penny nodded. "Okay." She turned to Sadie. "Eli helps keep the bad dreams away."

"I'm sure he does."

Once they heard Penny's door close again, Eli pulled Sadie's cheek back against his chest. He brushed the hair from her damp forehead and then rested his chin on her head. "Would you like to tell me about it?"

She shook her head. "It's nothing really. Just a bad dream."

"It didn't sound like nothing. It sounded like you were terrified of something." He couldn't imagine what it would take to make his brave spitfire react with such terror. "It might make it less overwhelming if you talk about it."

She picked at her sleeve. "I guess I got tangled under the covers somehow while I was sleeping. That must be what brought it on."

He held his peace, hoping she'd say more.

"It's just that, I can't bear to be in a crowded, dark, enclosed space."

He gave her shoulders a squeeze. "Most folks would feel the same."

She shook her head. "You don't understand. Whenever it happens, I panic and succumb to all-out, screaming, crying, uncontrollable hysteria. It's all so silly and embarrassing, but I can't seem to control it."

Again he brushed the hair from her face, trying to calm her with his touch. "Some things we just can't control."

"The first time it happened was when I was six years old. Inez asked me to fetch her something out of the root cellar. I didn't really want to go, the root cellar always made me uncomfortable, but Griff and Ry had refused to let me join them in one of their games earlier, claiming I was too little, and I wasn't about to admit that I was scared."

So she'd been defiant even at six.

"Anyway, somehow the door shut behind me and I

couldn't get out. The fall crops had just come in so the root cellar was full—someone had stacked the potatoes so high they blocked the one window so it was pitch-black. I suddenly felt as if the walls were closing in on me and that I couldn't breathe—almost like being buried alive. I don't think I was down there very long but by the time someone found me I was screaming and sobbing hysterically.

She shuddered. "Ever since then, I have to force myself just to go into a pantry or small storeroom, and I always double-check that I can't get locked in." She gave a self-conscious laugh. "I told you—silly. A grown woman, panicking at being trapped under her bedcovers."

"No more silly than a grown man twisting his ankle trying to scramble away from a harmless king snake."

"That was different."

"No, it wasn't and I only wish I'd had the courage to be as honest about it at the time as you are tonight."

She gave him a trembly smile. "Thank you for trying to salve my pride. You, Eli Reynolds, are a very kind man."

He reached up and with one of his thumbs wiped a tear from her cheek. "No, I'm not," he said softly. "But you make me want to be."

Surprise and then something else warmed her eyes. Her lips curled into a soft smile and her eyes closed as she turned her face into his hand.

The gesture was so tender, so trusting, that almost before he realized what he was doing, Eli had lowered his lips to hers.

He'd wanted to do this ever since that first kiss they'd exchanged to seal their vows. She was so sweet, so soft, so giving—he wanted to protect her from nightmares and from dark places and from hurtful things. He wanted to always be the one she turned to, whatever her need.

She seemed ready to return his fervor. The tension eased from her muscles and she seemed to melt against him. Her hand reached up to stroke his cheek. And her kiss tasted of sweetness and trust and joy.

When he finally broke it off, Eli drew her head gently against his chest and stroked his hand across her head while he tried to get his own suddenly ragged breathing back under control. Her nightmare struggles had partially loosened her braid and he decided to finish the job. Using his fingers to comb through the tangles, he watched the tresses tumble free.

"Eli?"

Her soft question echoed pleasantly against his chest. "Yes?"

"Do you love me?"

His hand stilled. It seemed she still clung to those romantic notions of hers. Love was the stuff of make-believe and fairy tales, an ideal that was mostly unattainable. "You are very dear to me, Sadie," he said carefully. "I admire you a great deal. And I would protect you with my own life if need be."

"I see." She drew back, her expression reflecting disappointment and brittle dignity. She folded her hands in her lap and met his gaze head-on. "Thank you for being so kind and patient with me tonight. I'm sorry I woke you and that I upset Penny." She attempted a smile. "I think I'll be able to sleep now."

She was dismissing him? Didn't she realize that he was offering her something much more substantial than some fleeting emotion? But she sat there, composed and utterly determined.

He stood. "Then I will wish you a good night." He almost reached a hand out to brush her cheek but stopped himself just in time. With a nod, he turned and took a seat in a chair across the room.

She frowned. "That's not necessary. There won't be a repeat of my nightmare, I assure you."

He crossed his legs. "I told Penny I'd stay with you until you fell asleep. I pride myself on being a man of my word."

She stared at him for a long minute, then finally nodded. Carefully folding the covers back, she lay down on top of them and curled on her side with her back to him.

There was something almost forlorn about the way she lay there, something that made him ache to comfort her, to promise her whatever it was she needed.

But she'd asked for the one thing he wasn't able to give her.

It was a long time before he heard her breath even out into a sleeper's rhythm, saw her form relax into the numbness of sleep. Still he stayed there, watching her. Longing to hold her.

He could almost wish he shared that special relationship she seemed to have with their Maker. Maybe if he did, he could ask God to give him some insights how to win her back.

Because something told him he was not going to be able to accomplish it on his own.

Chapter Seventeen

When Sadie woke the next morning she knew even before she opened her eyes that Eli was no longer in her room. She'd felt his presence last night, strong and brooding, until she'd finally fallen asleep. And while she'd lain there, there'd been something comforting in his presence as well, a sense that no harm could get to her with him standing guard.

Why had she spoiled the mood with her question? After that achingly sweet, utterly wonderful kiss. And he'd been so kind to her, so gentle and understanding about her irrational fears. She'd felt safe and secure in his arms, as if nothing bad could reach her there. And more than that, she'd felt *cherished,* had felt as if she'd finally found where she was meant to be. Why couldn't she just be satisfied with that?

Because she deserved to be loved, that's why. The way her parents had loved each other. The way Ry and Josie obviously loved each other.

But more than even that, Eli had to learn how to express love. If not to her, than to Penny. He felt it, she was certain of it. He just hadn't learned how to show it yet.

*Heavenly Father, please don't let me make a mess of
this. For Eli's and Penny's sakes, let me help him find
his way.*

Before she could get out of bed, her door inched open
and Penny stuck her head inside. "Good morning." It was
more of a question than a statement.

Sadie sat up and gave Penny her brightest smile.
"Good morning, princess. Sleep well? After I woke you,
I mean."

Penny nodded. "How are you feeling?"

Sadie patted the bed and Penny rushed over and
scrambled up bedside her. "I'm feeling just fine. I'm so
sorry if I scared you last night."

"That's okay. I get bad dreams sometimes, too."

Sadie pulled the girl against her and stroked her hair.
"They're not very fun, are they?"

Penny shook her head. "Did Eli hold your hand and
make you feel not so scared?"

"He did."

"And stay with you until you fell asleep?"

"Uh-huh. And I didn't have any other bad dreams the
rest of the night."

Penny nodded in satisfaction. "That's what he always
did for me too. Sometimes he was still there when I woke
up the next morning."

Not so with her. But what did she expect, after the
way she'd pushed him away last night. "We're very lucky
to have your brother to look out for us. He does a very
good job of keeping us safe." She gave the girl one last
squeeze, then straightened.

Her stomach rumbled and Penny giggled.

"You think that's funny, do you?" Sadie asked with
mock-sternness. "I'll have you know bad dreams at night

always make me hungry in the morning." She grimaced. "Of course good dreams leave me hungry, too."

Penny giggled again and Sadie made a shooing motion with her hand. "Now scoot. I'm hungrier than a plow horse after a long day in the field. Time for me to get up and get dressed. And after breakfast we can plan what we're going to do today while Eli is at work."

"Okay." Penny gave Sadie an impulsive hug around the neck, then scooted off the bed and crossed the room with much lighter steps than she'd had when she entered.

There was one Reynolds, at least, who didn't have trouble expressing love.

When Sadie came downstairs, Eli was already finished with his breakfast and preparing to leave.

Was something wrong? "I hadn't realized I was so late."

"You're not. I just decided to go to the bank a bit early this morning. I'm sure there are several matters requiring my attention since I've been away for a couple of days."

Was that really the case or was he running away from her? "Of course. We'll see you at lunch then."

He shook his head. "Probably not. I had Mrs. Dauber fix me something to take with me."

"I see." She forced a smile. "Then we'll see you this afternoon."

As he shrugged into his coat, she remembered how her father and mother had never parted without a quick peck-of-a-kiss good-bye. What would Eli think if she initiated the same practice?

Only one way to find out. Impulsively she stepped forward. "Eli?"

"Yes?"

She reached up to straighten his collar. "There, that's

better." Then, before her courage could abandon her altogether, she placed a hand on his chest, popped up on
her very tippy-toes and gave him a quick peck on the side
of his chin, which was the best she could do given the
difference in their heights. Then she stepped back and
smiled, pretending she didn't see his startled expression.
"Don't work too hard."

Eli strolled down the sidewalk, ignoring the urge
to reach up and stroke the spot that she'd kissed. What
was with the woman? Was she deliberately sending him
mixed signals? Pushing him away last night after a kiss
that he'd considered next to perfect. Then, just when
he'd accepted that she wanted nothing to do with him,
popping up out of the blue to kiss him good-bye. She
couldn't have it both ways. And if she kept trying it
would drive him mad.

No, he needed to regain control of the situation. He'd
let his emotions get the better of him. But no more. He
would speak to her tonight and make certain she understood.

"We went exploring today and found a great spot for a
picnic." Penny said to him. "It's a secret place that's not
easy to find. We just came on it all accidental-like. Sadie
says that's 'cause God wanted to show it to us. Of course
it wasn't like the fishing pond at Hawk's Creek but Sadie
said it was time to find some new memory places. Oh
and you should have seen Skeeter. He chased a rabbit and
jumped in the creek and when he ran out he shook himself all over and sprayed my dress and hair. But I didn't
mind because it was a hot day and it felt kind of good."

Her chatter seemed to be liberally sprinkled with the

phrase "Sadie said." "Sounds like the two of you had quite a day."

"Oh and we saw a possum up in a tree and watched a hawk catch a field mouse. And we even tried to fish with a string and a bent hairpin, just like Annabel Adams."

He stiffened. "Penny, have you been reading that story after I told you not to."

"Yes." Her lip poked out in a pout. "But I don't see why you don't like it."

Eli was well aware of Sadie's presence in the room, but continued to focus on his sister. "I just think there are more uplifting stories for you to focus your mind on. Fairy tales and silly make-believe just fill your head with romantic notions that bear no resemblance to real life." Was Sadie paying attention to what he'd said?

"But it's a fine story, Eli. Annabel Adams is a sure enough heroine." She spun around, looking for support. "Tell him Sadie."

To her credit, Sadie showed no sign of being torn. "I'm sorry, Penny, but Eli is your brother. If he feels this strongly about it, then I'm sure we can find lots of other stories to read that will meet with his approval."

"But if he knew you wrote it—" Penny slapped a hand over her mouth.

Eli went very still. "What's this?"

But Penny was staring at Sadie with wide liquid eyes. "I'm sorry. I didn't mean to tell your secret."

So Sadie had told Penny about being the creator of Annabel Adams. "I thought we had an agreement."

"We did." She held up a hand as he started to say more. "Not now, Eli. Can't you see she's upset?"

She turned back to Penny. "Hush now, princess, it's all right. Eli already knew, so you see you really didn't let the cat out of the bag, after all. And a family shouldn't keep secrets from each other anyway."

Penny spun back around. "You already knew Sadie was Temperance Trulove? Then why are you so against it?"

Eli didn't like the accusatory way his sister was staring at him. "It doesn't matter who writes the stories, Penny. I don't think they are appropriate reading for little girls. Now, I think you should go up to your room while I have a little talk with Sadie."

"Please don't fuss at her, Eli. I won't read about Annabel any more, I promise."

"Penny, please—"

"It's okay, princess. Your brother won't scold, the two of us are just going to have a chat about what is best for you. Because that is what we both really want. You just go on along to your room, and take Skeeter with you."

Penny looked from one to the other of them, then with dragging feet, left the room.

As soon as she was gone, Sadie turned to him. "Eli, I assure you I kept my word. I did *not* tell Penny that I wrote the Annabel Adams story."

He wasn't buying it. "Perhaps not directly, but I can see how it would be tempting to brag a bit. After all the two of you have become quite close and she enjoys the tales. If she somehow saw a bit of your work laying around then you would be free to bask in her praise."

Red flags appeared in each of her cheeks. "How dare you? Do you think I prize my word so little that I would skirt around it in such a way? And for your information, Penny and I have many other activities we can enjoy together. I've no need to seek her praise in this way."

"Whatever the case, by accident or design, it seems

you not only let your little secret get out, but the example you've set for her has taken a biddable girl and made her outright rebellious."

Sadie stood and fisted her hands on her hips. "Eli, she's not rebellious. Yes, she has a mind of her own and is learning to express it, but you don't want her to be a silent twit, do you? And she would *never* disobey you or do anything to hurt you, you must know that."

"It's your culpability we're talking about, not Penny's."

"My—" She took a deep breath. "Eli you're acting irrationally and that's not like you. Would you please tell me what it is you find so distasteful about my story?"

"They fill little girls's heads with romantic nonsense. With tails of heroes and heroines, of romantic love and happily ever afters."

"And is that so terrible?"

"You like stories? Let me tell you some. My mother was a romantic. So much so that when it became obvious my father didn't share her tender feelings she let it cripple her emotionally. She took to her bed and became a semi-invalid until the day she died. Her two sisters, Aunt Sophie and Aunt Genevieve, were the same. Aunt Sophie gave up everything to marry a man beneath her station and he ended up abandoning her and leaving her heartbroken. Aunt Genevieve never married because the man she considered her one true love died before they were wed. And Susan—"

He stopped himself before he said too much. "Well at any rate, romantic notions are nothing but trouble and I won't have you filling Penny's head with them. Better that she learn to be sensible, that she look at the world in a rational, no-nonsense manner. That's the way for her to find security and happiness."

Her expression had softened. "Deep, abiding love does exist, Eli. Not everyone finds it, and I'm sorry for your mother and your aunts. But I saw it in my parents. I see it in Ry and Josie. It's there if you are but brave enough to reach for it."

"I'll thank you not to put such notions in Penny's head." He collected himself. "And now that your secret is out, perhaps it would be best if Temperance Trulove retired."

"I suppose I could write the next story under my real name."

"You know that's not what I meant. And what do you mean—next story?"

"I've already turned in the last installment of Annabel Adams's story. I talked to Mr. Chalmers about starting a new one once that one is out."

"Tell him you've changed your mind."

"But I haven't." She gave him a hard look. "What if I asked you to stop working at the bank because I had an aversion to bankers? Would you do it?"

"That's entirely different. Your writing is merely a hobby. I work at the bank to support our family."

"Poppycock!"

"What?"

"You heard me, Poppycock. Balderdash. Hogwash. Piffle. Horsefeathers. Pick your favorite—they all mean one thing. You don't work at that bank because you need to. You admitted yourself that you're already as rich as Midas. You work at that bank because you want to and because it gives you a sense of purpose. I'm not saying that's a bad thing—after all, they do say idle hands are the devil's workshop—but don't you stand there all righteous and tell me you have to work to support us. And I'm saying that's the same as writing is to me."

"Has nothing I said made an impression on you?"

"*Everything* you said made an impression on me, Eli. You think romantic notions are bad for a girl just because things turned out badly, in your estimation, for your mother and your aunts. And you think my writing my stories is going to fill Penny's head with romantic nonsense and that she'll end up just like they did."

"That's an edited version, but that's the gist of it, yes."

"So you see, I heard you. I just happen to disagree is all." Her expression asked for his understanding. "You can't protect a person from all of life's heartaches no matter how much you might want to. And you sure as springtime can't tell them how to feel and who to love. Childhood is a time for make-believe and daydreams and carefree play—don't take that away from your sister. Penny is a smart girl and she has you and me to guide her along the way, to teach her to turn to God when she has tough decisions to make, and to know that we will always stand behind her, no matter what. That's what's going to shape her life more than anything else. So trust her to make the right choices when the time comes. And trust yourself to know when to let go."

"I'll let go when she is safely married and under her husband's care."

"I know you care for her, Eli, but you've got to do more to show it or she may never realize just how much she means to you."

If Sadie only knew how much he'd done to protect his sister she wouldn't speak to him like that. "Of course I care for her."

"Then show her. Spend time with her. Talk to her. Better yet, listen to her. Let her know the small milestones of her life are important to you, as well. Help her build happy memories that include you."

"Fine words, but you've never had responsibility for a young child before, have you?"

The bitterness in his voice startled Sadie. Was he referring to Susan? Her death had been tragic, but what did it have to do with the matter at hand? "Why, no, I haven't, but surely—"

"Then I will ask you to defer to me in this matter." His expression softened just a bit. "Sadie, I know that you believe all you just said to be true, and for you perhaps it is. But look where your carefree tendencies landed you—compromised and forced into a marriage not of your choosing."

Sadie winced. Is that how he saw her role in this marriage?

"And you're an adult. Yes, when she is grown up she will make her own choices, find a fine young man to marry and I will have to let her go. But in the meantime it's up to me to lay the proper foundation, to protect her from herself if need be, so that she can grow up to be the fine young woman you see in her already."

"But—"

"Penny is my sister and I'm asking you to trust that I know what is best for her."

But did he really? Or was he blinded by his own experiences? "I'll think on what you've said and pray about it."

His fist came down on the arm of his chair. "Hang it all, Sadie! Not every decision requires prayerful consideration. Some are simple enough for us to make on our own."

This time his words shocked her. Did he truly feel that way?

He seemed to collect himself and he raked a hand through his hair. "I'm sorry, I shouldn't have done that. But this is not some question of what you happen to think might give her fleeting pleasure. I'm looking at the bigger picture."

"I'm sorry, Eli, but I disagree with what you said a moment ago. We should always turn to God to help us make the right choices." She clasped her hands in front of her, as much to keep them from trembling as anything else. "I can see now how strongly you feel about this and I understand how your first thoughts must always be for Penny. But please, understand that I care about her just as much and right now I'm confused. I need time to sort this out to make sure I know what truly is best for her."

He nodded stiffly. "Looks like we are at an impasse. It's time for supper. I'll fetch Penny while you let Mrs. Dauber know we're ready."

After he left, Sadie sat back down, her heart weighing heavily in her chest.

Heavenly Father, every fiber of my being tells me he's wrong, that if he hedges Penny around too tightly he'll lose her. But is my writing the stand I need to take? Or should I let this go and find some other way to help him see the right path?

Supper that evening was a subdued affair. Eli said very little and Penny kept glancing from her to him, as if looking for some sign that things were returning to normal. Sadie did her best to keep the conversation light, talking to Penny about Buttermilk and about Ry and Josie's imminent return when Eli proved uncommunicative.

Later, when it was time to tuck Penny in, she lingered a while, trying to place the little girl more at ease.

When it was finally time to go, Sadie leaned forward and kissed Penny's forehead. "Sweet dreams, princess."

"It's all my fault that Eli's angry."

Sadie took Penny's hand. "It's not anyone's fault and Eli is not angry. We just need to work a few things out between us." She slipped Penny's hand under the covers. "Now, I don't want you to give any more thought to all this folderol. Tomorrow, you and I are going to go to the train station and meet my brother Ry and his wife when they come back from their trip to Egypt. And we're going to listen to them tell us all about the grand adventures they had. Won't that be fun?"

Penny nodded her head.

Sadie tapped her nose. "So make sure you get lots of sleep because you'll want to be wide awake to hear every bit of what they have to say."

With another nod, Penny rolled over on her side and closed her eyes. Sadie watched her for another minute, then made her exit. She stood on the landing, chewing at her lip. What now? It was too early to retire. But she knew Eli was not ready to talk to her yet.

Perhaps she'd find herself something to read. The lamps in the hallway were still lit, which meant Eli was still up. The sliver of light escaping from under his closed study door told her exactly where he was. She paused. Should she go in, try to talk to him again and see if they could work out their differences?

Her shoulders drooped as she turned toward the library. Perhaps it would be best for them to both get a good night's sleep first.

She circled the room, looking at the books, trying to find something to take her mind off the tangle she and Eli had gotten themselves into. She spied an atlas and pulled it down, carrying it to a nearby table. She figured looking up some of the locations Ry and Josie had been to would be a good way to pass the time. It would be good to see Ry again. And since they would be seeing Griff first, he and Josie would already be forewarned about her newly-married status. She was grateful she wouldn't have to deal with that at any rate.

Sadie closed the atlas and returned it to its place on the shelf. Then her eye was caught by an old leather bound volume on a stand in the far corner of the room. Curious, she strolled over and discovered it was a bible. Opening it, she found a family history recorded in the front. The entries ended with Eli's birth. Why wasn't Penny listed? Then she looked more closely at the names and realized it was Eli's maternal ancestry, so Penny would not be part of the line.

She looked at the entry for Eli again and blinked. My goodness. His birthday was coming up soon—Saturday. Perhaps she and Penny could plan a small family celebration. It would be something fun to take Penny's mind off the current tension in the house and might in fact go a long way toward easing that tension.

Feeling considerably better about things herself, Sadie closed the bible and decided she was finally ready for bed. She glanced at the clock in the hall and realized it had been over an hour since she'd tucked Penny in. And the light still shone in the study. Did Eli really have that much paperwork to do?

She climbed the stairs, still feeling buoyed by the thought of planning a birthday surprise for Eli, when a sound caught her attention. At first she thought Skeeter was whining to get out, but as soon as she opened Penny's door she realized it was Penny herself. Rushing over to the bedside she sat and gathered the girl in her arms. "What is it, princess? Did you have a bad dream?"

Muffling her sobs against Sadie's chest, Penny nodded.

"Well I'm here now. You just cry all you want to until you get it all out. Then we'll talk, okay?"

Penny took her at her word, crying with wracking sobs for a good while longer, before she finally began to calm down. The most terrible thing about it was that she tried to cry quietly, as if something terrible would happen if her crying was overheard.

When the crying finally stopped, Sadie gently pushed her far enough away to look into her eyes. "Feeling better now?" she asked as she brushed the hair off her forehead.

Penny nodded but Sadie could still see the haunted look in her eyes. "Do you want to tell me about it?"

This time Penny shook her head.

"Should I get Eli for you?"

Penny's hand tightened on her arm. "No, please."

The vehemence of her response startled Sadie. "Sweetheart, you need to talk to someone about this."

"It was just a bad dream."

"And what was this bad dream about?"

The little girl hunched her shoulders and refused to look Sadie in the eye. "You'll think I'm a bad person if I tell you."

Sadie gave her a fierce hug. "Penny, I could *never, ever* think of you as a bad person. Whatever it is, tell me and we'll figure out how to make it right together."

"I dreamed about the terrible thing I did. And nothing can ever make it right."

What in the world had happened to so wound this child? Perhaps she should get Eli? But Penny had been so insistent...

"Just tell me. I promise you'll feel better once you do."

Penny took a deep breath, then let it out in a rush. "It's my fault Susan died."

Chapter Eighteen

"I didn't mean to, I promise. I would never hurt Susan on purpose."

"Oh baby, of course you wouldn't. Tell me what happened." Sadie was horrified that Penny had borne all this inside her and was trying desperately to make sure she said the right thing. Oh, why hadn't she gotten Eli?

"It was right after we got back from a visit to Amberleigh. Susan was so sad and she didn't look well at all. I wanted to tell Nanny to fetch the doctor but Susan said I mustn't bother her or Eli, that she was certain everything would be better by morning. It was very stuffy and she asked me to open her window, so I did, even though Eli said we were not to. She just looked so pale."

The sobbing started again and Sadie rocked her in her arms.

"She hadn't gone sleepwalking since we moved in with Eli," Penny continued between sobs, "so I thought it would be all right. Only it wasn't. She fell out of the window and it's all my fault."

Her voice broke on those last words and Sadie gently cupped her chin and forced her gaze up. "Listen to me,

Penny, this is not your fault. No one could have foreseen what would happen. If she hadn't fallen out the window she might have fallen down the stairs or off the landing."

She held the girl's face between her hands. "Look at me. You are *not* to blame yourself for this. Susan fell, pure and simple. Yes, it's an awful thing to have happened, but no one is at fault."

"But—"

Sadie put a finger to the girl's lips. "No buts. I don't care how that window got opened, it was *not* your fault. Understand?" She had to convince the child, had to ease what must be an overwhelming sense of guilt.

Penny finally nodded.

"Have you told Eli about this?"

"No!" She grew agitated again. "He would hate me."

"He most certainly would not. Eli loves you, princess."

"But only because he doesn't know—"

"It doesn't matter. He loves you because you're you. And nothing you can do will change that."

She seemed reluctant to believe that. Then she gave a big yawn. Her hand snaked out and took hold of Sadie's. "Thank you for being so nice to me."

"How about we say a little prayer together? Would that be okay?"

Penny nodded.

Sadie took her hand, then bowed her head. "Heavenly Father, we ask that you bring healing to this sweet little girl's heart. Let her know that You love her and cherish her and will always be there to comfort her in her times of trouble. Bring her that promised peace that passes all understanding. And let her dreams always be filled with light and laughter. Amen."

Penny echoed her amen, then snuggled deeper under the covers.

"Do you want me to sit with you until you fall asleep?"

Penny seemed to think about that for a minute, then she shook her head. "I'm okay now. And I have Skeeter with me." She gave Sadie a conspiratorial smile. "Don't tell, Eli, but sometimes Skeeter jumps up in bed with me."

"It'll be our little secret."

Penny yawned again and Sadie patted her through the covers. "Sweet dreams, princess."

"Sweet dreams, Sadie."

Had she done enough to ease Penny's burden of guilt? Would the child be able to rest easier now? What a tremendous burden for such a little girl to be carrying. How could Eli not have known?

As she closed Penny's door she caught sight of Eli climbing up the stairs. Good, it would save her the trouble of seeking him out. She waited for him at the top of the stairs, arms crossed.

Eli was two-thirds of the way up the stairs when he saw Sadie waiting for him at the top. He paused. "Sadie. What—"

She put a finger to her lips and pointed to Penny's door.

He clamped his mouth shut. What now? He was tired and not up to another confrontation with her.

As soon as he stepped off the top stair she whispered, "We need to talk."

At this hour? She was carrying her penchant for melodrama just a little too far. "If you want to rehash—"

"No." She put her finger to her lips again. "Not here."

She marched to his bedchamber and waited for him to open the door.

She definitely had his interest piqued now.

Eli stepped past her, opened the door and waved her inside. Once he'd closed the door behind him, he waved her to a chair, which she refused.

"Do you mind telling me what this is all about?"

"It's about Penny. She had another nightmare tonight."

He came fully alert, every muscle tensing. "Is she all right? I should probably go to her."

"She's fine for now and she doesn't want to see you."

He froze as her words sunk in. Penny didn't want to see him? Had she completely lost faith in him? All because of his aversion to Sadie's stories?

Sadie's expression softened a fraction. "That came out wrong. She still loves you and craves your approval. She just—oh hang it all Eli, have you ever really talked to her about what happened to Susan and how she felt about it?"

Why wouldn't she sit down so he could as well? Her words weren't making a lot of sense to him. "Yes, I mean no, I mean, well naturally she was grieving. She was really broken up about it. She thought the world of Susan and her mother had passed on only a couple of months earlier."

He tried to pull his thoughts together. "Is that what her nightmare was about, Susan's fall? I assure you I never let her see the body." It was enough that he'd seen the mangled remains of his once-lovely stepsister. He could never have subjected Penny to that horror. But had she somehow seen it before he had the body covered?

"Eli, she thinks Susan's death was her fault."

Everything in Eli went still. "That's impossible. Penny had nothing to do with what happened."

"Of course she didn't. But it's her you need to convince, not me. Penny was the one who opened Susan's window that night. Apparently, Susan was feeling sickly and Penny thought the fresh air might help make her feel better. So now she thinks if she hadn't left the window open, Susan would never have fallen."

Bile and self-recrimination rose in his throat. How could he not have realized what Penny was feeling all this time, how could he have let his young, innocent little sister carry such an undeserved burden of guilt? "Why didn't she tell me?"

"Apparently, you'd warned them not to leave any windows open. She was afraid you wouldn't love her any more if she admitted what she'd done."

The words sliced through Eli like a knife. He felt blindly for the mattress that he knew was behind him and sat down hard. "How could she think that?"

Sadie stood in front of him and crossed her arms again. "She's nine years old, she felt guilty, and you were the only person left in her world. She didn't want to risk losing you, too."

Eli heard the thing she'd left unsaid just as clearly as if she'd shouted it. He'd never told Penny he loved her, never given her reason to believe he would stand by her. "I have to go talk to her."

"Of course. But do you know what you're going to say?"

Eli eased back down. What indeed? "I can't tell her the truth."

Sadie frowned. "Why not?"

"Because I'm not sure she's old enough to understand. And because it might tarnish her memory of her sister. I could never do that to her."

He was surprised when she didn't ask him to explain. Glancing up he saw only concern and patience. He took a deep breath. "I suppose I owe you the rest of the story."

"Only if you want to tell me."

Surprisingly he did. "I told you I came home that evening to find Susan's body on the flagstones below her window. What I didn't tell you was that she jumped out of the window of her own accord."

There was a sharp intake of breath and then Sadie was sitting beside him, taking his hands in both of hers. "Oh Eli, how horrible. Are you certain?"

"She left a note." Sadie's hands gave his a squeeze and he squeezed back, comforted by her touch. It was such a relief to finally share the story, the horror of that discovery, with someone, someone he could trust to hold it close to her heart.

"I should have realized what was happening, should have seen there was more than grief eating at Susan. It turns out that before her mother's death she had been… intimate with one of the servants at Amberleigh. It was only after I moved them to the city with me that she realized she was with child." Had he shocked her, repulsed her?

But again there was only sympathy. "She must have been terrified."

"She was convinced that if she could just talk to the bas—fellow, he would do right by her. Of course I never knew any of this until I read her note. I took her constant begging to visit to Amberleigh to be mere homesickness."

"Eli, you were doing the best you could."

He wished he could believe that. But he knew better. "When I finally did take the girls back to the country for a short visit, the man in question apparently refused to take responsibility and was gone from the property the next morning. The first night of our return is when she jumped from her window."

"It must have been horrid for you to have to go through this alone. And then to shield Penny as you did. That's why you sold everything and moved here, isn't it?"

How had she known? "I did my best to put it forth as an accident. But some ugly rumors began to surface almost at once. I couldn't let Penny grow up in the shadow of that. I couldn't."

"Of course you couldn't." She lifted a hand to his cheek. "You were incredibly strong and generous and someday Penny will understand all that you've done for her." Her expression softened. "But for now you'll just have to make do with the understanding that *I* know and I think you are the most selfless, heroic man I've ever met."

Her words were like a balm to his soul. He captured her hand and held it against his cheek. "Ah, Sadie, what did I ever do to deserve you?"

She gave him a gentle, teasing grin. "You helped me harvest some honey."

That surprised a chuckle out of him. "That I did." He sobered almost immediately. "I can't tell Penny any of this."

"Perhaps someday, but you're right, this might be just as hard for her to deal with." She touched his arm with her free hand. "The most important thing is to let her know that you know what she did and that you don't blame her, that you still love her unconditionally. That'll go a long way to easing her fears."

"But I can't let her continue to carry the guilt around."

"Maybe there's a way. What kind of windows were in Susan's room?"

That was an odd question. "What do you mean?"

"Were they short like these in here, or were they the tall, narrow ones some houses have?"

"Tall and narrow, why?"

"And do you remember how you found them? I mean if someone was going to climb out on a ledge I would think they would want to open the window just as far as it could go."

He was beginning to see what she was leading up to. "You're right, the window was opened all the way up. Penny could never have pushed it up so far."

"There you have it. You can tell her with complete honesty that Susan opened them up further after she left the room, that it wasn't her fault at all."

Eli gave her a hug. "Thank you."

The clock downstairs chimed midnight. In the distance a dog howled and was answered by another. Closer by, he heard the soft whicker of the horses, no doubt disturbed by the dogs. But all of that was mere backdrop to the beating of his and Sadie's hearts as he held that hug for a few seconds longer than absolutely necessary.

When he pulled away he saw the flush of awareness staining her cheeks, saw the longing in her eyes and he bent down to taste another of her oh-so-sweet kisses.

Sweeter than honey, special or otherwise, warmer than sunshine, gentler than a butterfly's touch—her kisses were like nothing he'd ever experienced. The fact that they were for him alone filled him with an overpowering joy. She was his—to protect and cherish and share the rest of his life with.

When they separated, he looked down into her bemused face and traced her lips with his finger. She was so beautiful, so absolutely kissable. "Someday, *Mrs. Reynolds,* in the very near future you will be sharing this room with me, I promise you, and we will be starting that family we discussed. But first we have a few matters to settle between us. And a little sister to help find peace."

Sadie gave her head a mental shake. His kisses were so wonderful. They made her feel like she was special, as if she were enveloped in a bubble of love and protection.

But he was right. Much as she wanted to explore this new side of their relationship, tonight they had to think about Penny.

He kept one arm around her and while she was glad of the contact, it did make it harder for her to concentrate.

"So what now?" he asked. "I want to just go marching over there and tell her all the things she needs to hear."

Sadie shook her head. "She was yawning widely when I left. I would guess she's sound asleep by now." Just the thought of it made Sadie yawn herself.

"You're right. It probably wouldn't serve any good purpose for me to wake her just to set her fears at rest. Perhaps I should wait until morning."

"Good idea." Sadie yawned again and felt her eyes drift close. With an effort she opened them wider. "But then you should talk to her first thing."

"Of course."

Was that a hint of amusement in his voice? If she wasn't so sleepy she'd call him on it.

When Sadie opened her eyes again, the black of night had turned to the hazy gray of pre-dawn. It took her another moment to realize she wasn't in her room. Turning her head, she met the amused gray-eyed stare of her husband. "Good morning."

Sadie sat up, not at all sure how to react. "Good morning." Taking quick stock she realized that both of them were still wearing the clothes they'd worn last night, though Eli had shed his coat and vest, and both had been laying crosswise on the bed, on top of the covers.

"You should have woken me up and sent me to my own room last night," she said, feeling slightly grumpy but not sure why.

"Ah, but you looked so comfortable I hadn't the heart to wake you."

"What if Penny had needed me for something?"

He waved a hand toward his door. "I left the door ajar so I could hear her if she stirred. There's been nary a sound."

She slid off the bed with as much dignity as she could muster.

He slid from the bed, as well. However his height allowed him to do it with much more grace than she'd been able to conjure up. Which was entirely unfair on a number of levels.

"Well then, thank you for your hospitality, but I think I'll return to my own room for my morning ablutions. I'll see you at breakfast."

"Of course." He made an exaggerated bow and then to her surprise followed her from the room.

"Where do you think you're going?"

"Why, to check in on Penny, of course. I'd like to talk to her before breakfast if she's awake." He grinned. "Where did you think I was going?"

Not bothering to answer his question, Sadie flounced

toward her room with a swish of her skirts. His warm chuckle followed her all the way to her door.

A moment later though, his exclamation pulled her back into the hall and rushing toward Penny's room. What was wrong? Had she had another nightmare?

She turned into Penny's room and at first didn't understand what she was seeing. Eli sat on his sister's bed, but Penny didn't seem to be there. Then she saw he was holding a piece of paper.

He looked up, holding out the paper, his expression stricken. "She's run away."

Chapter Nineteen

Sadie took the note from him and quickly scanned the lines, written in Penny's childish hand.

> Eli, it's my fault that Susan fell out of her window. Sadie can tell you about the terrible thing I did. I didn't mean for her to get hurt, honest. I'm sorry I didn't tell you before but I was afraid you wouldn't want me around any more. Please don't be mad at me.
>
> I know what I did was wrong and that I need to do something to make up for it. I don't know anything big enough, so I'm going to do like Annabel Adams and try to go around helping people and doing good things. I will miss you both and hope you will miss me a little bit, too.
>
> PS
> I hope you're not going to be angry with me, Sadie, but Skeeter wants to come with me so I'm going to let him.

Sadie's hands began to tremble and the letter fluttered to the floor. Penny was out there somewhere, trying to emulate Sadie's adventurous make-believe heroine. Sadie's knees buckled and she had to grab the bedpost to keep from falling. Eli had been right—she never should have written that story. She'd never be able to forgive herself if something happened to Penny before they could find her.

The only prayer she could form was *Dear God, keep her safe, keep her safe.* Over and over, the words tumbled through her mind.

Eli shot up, as if shaking off his momentarily paralysis. "She can't have gotten far. You let Sheriff Hammond know. I'll start looking."

"Of course. And she's got Skeeter with her, he'll watch over her." Then she had a sudden thought. *Please God, let me be wrong.* "Eli."

He paused in the doorway.

"Check the stable."

His expression whitened a bit more, but he gave a short nod and headed back to his room with long, impatient strides. She paused only long enough to jab a few pins in her hair, wash her face and put on more serviceable shoes. Yesterday's dress and less than tidy hair would have to do for now.

She headed out the back door and found Eli leading Cocoa out of the stable. He clinched his jaw and she saw a tic pulse at the corner of his mouth. "Buttermilk's missing." He mounted up and then looked down at her. "Tell Sheriff Hammond that I'm headed south and I'd appreciate it if he could go north."

Without waiting for her answer he set the horse in motion. Sadie dashed around the house and hit the sidewalk at a fast clip. It was still barely light out and not many folks were up and about. The few who were gave her curious looks but she didn't give them the opportunity to speak to her.

She reached the sheriff's office to find he was not yet in. What now? She had no idea where the man lived. But she knew who would know.

She set out immediately for the boardinghouse, a small part of her hoping that Penny had sought refuge there.

She burst in through the kitchen door without so much as a knock and almost sobbed with relief to find Cora Beth already busy stoking her stove.

"My goodness, Sadie, you gave me quite a start. What are you doing out this way so early?"

"Is Penny here?"

"Penny, why no—" Cora Beth seemed to finally take in Sadie's appearance and the import of her question. "Oh my goodness, is she missing? You sit yourself down here before you fall over, and tell me what happened."

"No time. Penny's run away and I need to let Sheriff Hammond know so he can help search for her. Only he wasn't at his office and I don't know where he lives. She's on horseback, Cora Beth, *horseback* and she's probably been out for hours so there's no telling how far she's gone. And it's all my fault. If anything happens to her—" Sadie felt her barely-held control start to unravel as a sob escaped.

Cora Beth took her arm and led her to the table. Then she handed her a cup of coffee. "Here now, you get this down while I go fetch Danny and send him for the sheriff. We'll find her, you'll see."

Sadie didn't know how long she sat there. She was

vaguely aware of Cora Beth sitting next to her, offering food and comfort, but she didn't emerge from her mind-fogging fear until Sheriff Hammond strode into the room. "Danny tells me little Penny has gone missing."

Sadie jumped up from her seat. "Yes. She ran away."

"You're sure she's not just hiding somewhere back at your place. Kids do that sometime when they're looking for attention."

If only that were the case. "No, sir. She left a note and her horse and dog are missing."

"Anything in the note or anything she say last night give you an idea of where she might be headed?"

"She just said she wants to be like Annabel Adams." Sadie's voice broke again but she managed to get herself back under control.

"Off looking for adventure, then." He rubbed his chin. "I take it Eli's already out looking for her."

"Yes. He left about thirty minutes ago. Said to tell you he was headed south and would appreciate it if you'd head north."

"I'll round up a few good men and we'll start checking all the roads and trails. I suggest you head home and stay there."

"But I want to help look for her."

"It's best if someone is at home in case she gets tired of adventuring and decides to come back on her own." He raised a hand to stall her protests. "And I'll pass the word to anyone that your house is our command post. All searchers are to check in with you from time to time to give you updates and see if she's been found."

Sadie nodded, still not happy with being on the sidelines but prepared to do her part.

The sheriff gave her a reassuring smile. "Don't worry, we'll find her."

After asking Cora Beth to get a telegram off to Griff, Sadie headed home. Not that she expected Penny to get that far, but somehow she felt better knowing her brother was aware of the situation. She also wanted him to call in favors from everyone he knew between here and there.

She turned in her front gate hoping against hope that Eli would have found her already or that Sheriff Hammond's prediction that she'd come home on her own would come true. But the only person she found when she arrived was Mrs. Dauber. She apprised the woman of the situation, then went up to her room to freshen up and change her clothes.

Then the excruciating wait began.

To keep herself busy, Sadie went to work setting up the command post Sheriff Hammond had requested. She had Mrs. Dauber prepare and keep at the ready plenty of coffee and food to feed any of the searchers who needed a quick break. She kept meticulous notes of every report that came in. Danny found her a detailed map Josie had made of the area and she used pins to mark the location of every road, trail, building or hidey-hole that had been checked. She took down the name of every person who had been talked to. And she kept the searchers updated as they came in and noted where each planned to go next.

Eli checked in about an hour after the search started. Sadie stepped right into his arms and he held her stiffly for a moment before his embrace momentarily softened. The stubble from his unshaven jaw scratched at her forehead, but she didn't care, she needed to give and take what comfort she could.

Neither said a word and after a few short seconds

he pulled away and reached for the cup of coffee Mrs. Dauber had at the ready. His jaw was clenched so tight Sadie didn't know how he managed to gulp it down. While he drank, he listened closely to the information she had gathered, then with barely a word, he set out again.

After he was gone, Sadie sat for a long time staring down at her map without really seeing it. She knew she shouldn't read anything into his stiffness, his silence. Naturally he was deeply worried about Penny. But she couldn't help but wonder if he blamed her for this as much as she blamed herself.

Then another pair of searchers stopped in and she was back into her role as information gatherer.

By the time she heard the train whistle shortly before noon, Sadie was beside herself. Penny still hadn't been found and she was going mad just sitting here waiting for the news to trickle in. She should be out there looking for her little princess.

When Griff and Ry came striding into her parlor Sadie felt a sob bubble from her throat and she threw herself into their arms. She quickly tamped down the urge to cry but her eyes were still moist when she pulled away. "Ry, it's so good to see you." She swiped a hand across her eyes. "I'm sorry I wasn't there to meet you but—"

"Hush, Sadie girl, I heard all about it." Her oldest brother offered her his handkerchief. "We were there when Griff got your telegram."

She looked past her brothers. "Where's Josie?"

Ry grinned. "She's at the boardinghouse getting showered with affection and questions by Viola."

Sadie put a hand to her mouth. "Oh! Ry, what was I thinking? That's where you should be, too. Viola will—"

"Time enough for that later. Right now it's another little girl who needs our help."

Griff put one of his arms around her shoulder. "Now, buck up and tell us what we can do."

With a nod, Sadie waved them over to her map.

By the time her brothers had determined where they would search, Josie was striding into the room, Viola in tow. As soon as Viola spotted Ry she ran across the room with her arms outstretched. "Daddy!"

Ry lifted her off the floor and twirled her around. "How's my special girl? I've missed you."

Sadie felt the tears prick the back of her eyelids again. What she wouldn't give to see Eli and Penny share such an embrace. *Heavenly Father, please given them that chance.*

Josie gave her a quick embrace, then stepped back. "What can I do to help?"

That was Josie, ready to dispense with the amenities and get right to the point as always.

"You can take over for me here. I'm going to help find Penny."

"Hold on a minute, Sadie girl—"

Sadie gave Griff and Ry both a hard look. "That's Penny we're looking for, and I'm as good at scenting a trail as either one of you. Y'all are going to have to hog-tie me to keep me from going out." She placed her hands on her hips. "And I promise even then you're going to have a fight on your hands."

Josie put an arm around her shoulder. "Ignore them, they're just being men. I'd do the same thing if it was Viola and there'd be no stopping me. Now, show me what you need me to do."

Griff and Ry headed out while Sadie quickly explained her system to Josie. While she was studying the map to pick out her own search area, though, she had an epiphany. Of course. Why hadn't she thought of this sooner?

"I'm going here," she said firmly. She placed her finger on the spot where she estimated the spot was that she and Penny had found yesterday, the special place that was just theirs.

Josie narrowed her eyes. "You know something." It was more statement than question.

"I think, I mean I don't know, maybe, but I may be wrong."

Josie made a shooing motion with her hands. "Then get on out of here. Go find your little girl."

Sadie was looking for the spot to turn off the main road when she heard a horse galloping up behind her. She turned in the saddle to find Eli bearing down on her and so she slowed her horse to a walk. Had Penny been found?

As soon as he got close enough for her to see his expression, she knew that wasn't the case.

Eli pulled alongside her and matched Cocoa's pace to Calliope's. "I checked in right after you left. Your sister-in-law says she thought you were on to something."

Sadie nodded. "I remembered the place where we went exploring yesterday and noticed no one had checked it out yet. It's kind of hard to find, but I thought maybe it was somewhere she'd try to go."

"Show me."

Sadie studied the tree line to their right. There were certain landmarks she had pointed out to Penny so they could find it again. "The trail cuts into those woods at an angle so you don't notice it unless you're looking for it. We only spotted it because Skeeter went chasing a rabbit that way."

Eli turned his horse from the road and moved closer to the trees.

"We're looking for a pair of pecans next to a cottonwood with a broken branch. The trail starts not too far from there."

Eli nodded, his eyes never leaving the tree line. A moment later he pointed. "There!"

Sadie moved up ahead of him and started counting oaks—it should be the third one. Even so she almost passed right by the trail. She pulled her horse up short and turned her toward the roofed opening. "You'll have to duck under these branches here," she told Eli. "But the trail opens up pretty quick once we get by this oak. And our spot's not very far in."

Eli let her lead, but he rode close behind her, so close Calliope could just about swish the flies from Cocoa's face with her tail. The trail was twisty and narrow so there was no question of riding side-by-side. They took turns calling Penny's name, then listening for a response.

Then she heard something that made her heart leap. She held up a hand to silence Eli. Then she heard it again. "That was Skeeter. We've found her."

Sadie nudged Calliope into a faster walk, continuing to call Penny's name. Why didn't the girl answer?

The trail widened just before they reached the clearing and Eli was immediately beside her. They entered the clearing side by side and saw Penny sitting under a tree with muddy tear tracks on her face and her arms around Skeeter. Buttermilk grazed nearby.

Eli vaulted from his horse almost before the mare had stopped.

Sadie, who was suddenly trembling so hard she wasn't sure her limbs could support her, dismounted more slowly. *Heavenly Father, thank You, thank You, thank you.*

By the time she reached them, Eli was on his knees with his arms around Penny and he was rocking her back and forth.

Penny clung to him as if she would never let him go.

Sadie let them have a minute, then knelt down beside them. "Mind if I share a part of that hug?" Her voice was as shaky as her hands, but she didn't care. Eli and Penny separated just enough to let her in, and all the pent up emotions of the day finally broke free in a flood of tears.

Chapter Twenty

Eli held tight to both of them, giving silent thanks to God that they had finally found Penny. He felt he'd aged ten years today. All sorts of horrors had been clawing in his mind since he'd first found her note. And threaded through all of it was a fierce, soul-wrenching regret that he'd never told Penny how very dear she was to him. He'd prayed all morning to have a chance to rectify that, and now that he'd been given that chance he wasn't about to let it pass him by.

As soon as Sadie's tears subsided, he broke off the hug and looked Penny in the eye. "Are you all right?"

"I hurt my foot and my arm is all scratched."

"Let's have a look at you."

Sadie scrambled up, pulling a handkerchief from the pocket of her skirt. "I'll wet this and be back quicker than a cat's sneeze."

That coaxed a small smile from Penny, which Eli suspected had been Sadie's intent. While they waited for her, Eli eased Penny's shoe off. "Where does it hurt?"

"Right here." She touched her arch. "I stepped on a pointy rock and it hurt something awful."

He examined it closely. The bottom of her foot appeared tender and bruised but the skin wasn't broken. He'd have Dr. Whitman take a look at it when they got back to town, just in case.

Sadie returned with her wet cloth and began to gently dab at the scratches. As far as Eli could see, they were superficial, as well.

Which meant it was time for him to have that talk with his sister. "You know, I've been very worried about you, Henny-Penny." The nickname, which he hadn't used since she was a toddler, slipped out as if he'd called her that all her life. "I would have been quite lost without you."

Penny's eyes widened. "You would?"

He raised a brow. "Of course I would. You're my sister and I love you." There, that hadn't been so hard to say, after all. In fact, it had felt rather good. He returned the squeeze Sadie gave his hand but didn't take his eyes from his sister. "I'm sorry if I made you so sad that you wanted to leave."

"Oh, no, it wasn't that at all." Penny bit her lip, then bravely squared her shoulders. "I did something terrible, Eli."

"Running away *was* terrible, and you must promise to never, ever do it again. But it all turned out okay, so we will give God thanks and put it behind us."

She shook her head. "That wasn't the terrible thing. I mean, yes, it was terrible and I'm very sorry, but I was talking about…"

He lifted her chin with his fisted hand. "About the night Susan died," he said gently.

She nodded, her eyes filling with tears.

"Sadie told me what you said."

"Don't hate me, Eli, please." Her voice rose to near-panic. "I didn't mean to do it. I would *never* hurt Susan."

He gave her a fierce hug. "Hush this nonsense. Of course you wouldn't hurt Susan. And I couldn't hate you, not ever. You're my sister, my Henny-Penny. Didn't I just say that I love you?"

She nodded her head against his shoulder.

Eli saw Sadie's tearful approval and it gave him the boost he needed to continue. "Besides, you have it all wrong."

"I do?" She pulled back, rubbing at her tears with her fist. "But I opened the window, Eli. I remember doing it."

He smiled tenderly, silently thanking Sadie for giving him the words he needed. "I went to her room that night, Penny. Her window was open, yes, but it was open all the way to the very tip-top."

Penny wrinkled her nose. "It was? But I can't reach that high."

He tapped her nose. "Exactly. Susan must have opened it wider herself. Which means it *wasn't your fault*."

He could almost see the moment she believed his words, could almost see the shadow of the burden she'd been carrying lift itself from her shoulders. She gave him another hug, then turned to Sadie.

"Did you hear what Eli said? It wasn't my fault?"

"Of course it wasn't, princess. Now, are you ready to come home? There's lots of people who are going to be very happy to see you."

Sadie came down the stairs to find most of the crowd of searchers and well-wishers had dispersed. But there were still a number of folks in her parlor keeping Eli company—Griff and Ry were there, as were Josie and Viola, Sheriff Hammond and Cora Beth.

"She's sleeping," Sadie announced. "Poor little thing is plumb tuckered out."

Sheriff Hammond stood. "Well, guess I'll be heading off to my place. I'm glad it all turned out okay."

Eli stood, as well. "Thank you, sheriff. We appreciate all you did to get the search parties organized."

The sheriff smiled. "Not much to it. Most folks around here will drop everything to help a neighbor in trouble, especially when there's a child involved." He smiled. "Besides, your missus did most of the organizing."

Cora Beth stood. "I'd best be getting on, as well. I left Uncle Grover in charge and I'm sure he's ready for me to relieve him by now."

Once Sadie had escorted the two of them to the door, she returned to her parlor. "Griff, Ry, I don't think you'll ever know how much it meant to me to look up and see my two big brothers striding through my door today."

"You know we'll be here for you, Sadie girl, any time you need us," Ry said. "All you gotta do is send word."

"We Lassiters take care of each other," Griff added. "All for one and one for all."

Sadie smiled at the reminder of their childhood battle cry. The she turned to Josie. "You, too. Thanks for all your help today."

Josie smiled. "Glad to help. But it seems to me you did most of the hard work." She turned to Ry. "I think these folks probably need some time to themselves. And I have a hankering to sleep in my own bed tonight."

"Yes ma'am." Ry put one arm around Josie, and held out his other to shake his brother's hand. "Good seeing you again, Griff. Maybe next time we'll have more time to visit."

Then he planted a kiss on Sadie's cheek, shook Eli's hand and lifted Viola. With a chorus of good-byes, they were gone.

Griff reached for his hat next.

"We have an extra bed if you need one tonight," Sadie offered.

"I already talked to Cora Beth about spending the night at the boardinghouse." He glanced Eli's way. "Like Josie said, you folks need some time to yourselves right now."

He gave Sadie a hug, then a peck on the cheek. "I'm glad everything worked out all right for you, Sadie girl."

Once they had the house to themselves, Sadie turned to Eli. She had to say this now, before her courage failed her.

"I'm sorry, Eli, I should have listened to you."

His lips curled up into a quizzical smile. "While those are edifying words to hear, you'll have to be a little more specific."

"It's my fault Penny ran away. My stories are what put all those notions about grand adventures in her head. She would have never gone off if I had listened to you and quit writing them."

"Sadie—"

She ignored his interruption, unable to stop now that she'd started. "I threw my new story in the stove this morning. I'll talk to Mr. Chalmers tomorrow and tell him that there will be no more stories from me. And I promise to stop filling her head with my nonsense. If anything had happened to her—" Sadie buried her face in her hands, unable to finish that sentence.

A second later she felt Eli gently tug her hands away. "Sadie, this is not your fault."

He was just being kind. She almost wished he would rail at her, would give her the chewing out she deserved. "I read her letter, remember. She ran away because she wanted to be like Annabel Adams. And I taught her how to ride a horse, and brought her to that place, so it's my fault she got so far, hid so well. I know you'll find it hard to forgive me, but I hope you'll try. From here on out, I'll try to be the perfect wife you'd hoped to find when you came here, to care for Penny just the way you want me to." She took a deep breath. "You two would have been better off if I hadn't—"

"Stop it."

His sharp command brought her up short.

"Don't you dare finish that sentence. I've been thanking God all day for bringing you into our lives."

Her breath caught in her throat. Thanking God?

His lips quirked up again, but there was no mirth in his expression. "That's right. I stopped on the side of the road and got down on my knees and prayed like I haven't prayed in years, like I never truly prayed before in my life. I not only begged God to help me find Penny, but I asked for forgiveness for being such a stubborn, mule-headed fool. For hurting you and Penny the way I have."

"But—"

He placed a finger on her lips. "You may have read Penny's letter but you obviously missed the most important part. She didn't leave because she wanted to be like Annabel Adams, she left because she was afraid I would be mad at her when I discovered her secret. I let my sister believe my love was contingent on her good behavior, let her believe she had a hand in her sister's death, all because I was too worried about fixing things, too worried about keeping everything under control, that I couldn't bother myself to spend time giving her what she needed most."

His self-recrimination tore at her. "You were just doing what you thought best."

"Best for appearances's sake you mean, not best for Penny." He stroked her cheek with the back of his hand. "No, if there is any blame to be cast here, it is all on me. What you brought her was the skill to survive out there, the protection of your loyal pet, and the knowledge that *someone* cared for her. It's why this day had a happy ending."

"Oh Eli, thank you for that. From here on out, I'll try to be the perfect wife you'd hoped to find when you came here, to keep your house in perfect order, to teach Penny to be a lady, to—"

Again he put a finger to her lips. "Sadie, all I really want is for you to be yourself. Because today I realized that, by God's grace, I ended up married to the absolute perfect wife for me."

Sadie was afraid to read too much into his words. After all, he'd had a long, highly charged day. Maybe he was just feeling euphoric. "Do you really mean that? Because you don't have to feel—"

"Mean it? I not only mean it, I'll shout it to the world if you want me to. I've felt this way for a long time but have just been too thickheaded to admit it, even to myself. I'm sorry I couldn't say it before, but I'll say it now. I love you, Sadie Elizabeth Lassiter Reynolds, just the way you are. I wouldn't change one tiny thing about you."

Sadie launched herself into his arms. "Oh Eli, I love you too, so very, very much."

Eli wrapped his arms around his perfect wife, savoring the just-right feel of her, the wildflowers and sunshine scent of her, the generous, joyous spirit of her. And he silently vowed to spend the rest of his life making certain she never had reason to question his love again.

* * * * *

WE HOPE YOU ENJOYED THIS BOOK!

Love Inspired ®

SUSPENSE

Uncover the truth in these thrilling stories of faith in the face of crime from Love Inspired Suspense. Discover six new books available every month, wherever books are sold!

SPECIAL EXCERPT FROM

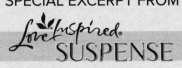

When a rookie K-9 cop becomes the target of a
dangerous stalker, can she stay one step ahead of this
killer with the help of her boss and his K-9 partner?

Read on for a sneak preview of
Courage Under Fire *by Sharon Dunn,*
the next exciting installment to the
True Blue K-9 Unit miniseries, available in
October 2019 from Love Inspired Suspense.

Rookie K-9 officer Lani Branson took in a deep breath as
she pedaled her bike along the trail in the Jamaica Bay
Wildlife Refuge. Water rushed and receded from the shore
just over the dunes. The high-rises of New York City,
made hazy from the dusky twilight, were visible across
the expanse of water.

She sped up even more.

Tonight was important. This training exercise was an
opportunity to prove herself to the other K-9 officers who
waited back at the visitors' center with the tracking dogs
for her to give the go-ahead. Playing the part of a child lost
in the refuge so the dogs could practice tracking her was
probably a less-than-desirable duty for the senior officers.

Reaching up to her shoulder, Lani got off her bike and
pressed the button on the radio. "I'm in place."

The smooth tenor voice of her supervisor, Chief Noah Jameson, came over the line. "Good—you made it out there in record time."

Up ahead she spotted an object shining in the setting sun. She jogged toward it. A bicycle, not hers, was propped against a tree.

A knot of tension formed at the back of her neck as she turned in a half circle, taking in the area around her. It was possible someone had left the bike behind. Vagrants could have wandered into the area.

She studied the bike a little closer. State-of-the-art and in good condition. Not the kind of bike someone just dumped.

A branch cracked. Her breath caught in her throat. Fear caused her heartbeat to drum in her ears.

"NYPD." She hadn't worn her gun for this exercise. Her eyes scanned all around her, searching for movement and color. "You need to show yourself."

Seconds ticked by. Her heart pounded.

Someone else was out here.

Don't miss
Courage Under Fire *by Sharon Dunn,*
available October 2019 wherever
Love Inspired® Suspense books and ebooks are sold.

www.LoveInspired.com

LISEXP0919

SPECIAL EXCERPT FROM

Love Inspired.

*Could a pretend Christmastime courtship
lead to a forever match?*

Read on for a sneak preview of
Her Amish Holiday Suitor, *part of Carrie Lighte's
Amish Country Courtships miniseries.*

Nick took his seat next to her and picked up the reins, but before moving onward, he said, "I don't understand it, Lucy. Why is my caring about you such an awful thing?" His voice was quivering and Lucy felt a pang of guilt. She knew she was overreacting. Rather, she was reacting to a heartache that had plagued her for years, not one Nick had caused that evening.

"I don't expect you to understand," she said, wiping her rough woolen mitten across her cheeks.

"But I want to. Can't you explain it to me?"

Nick's voice was so forlorn Lucy let her defenses drop. "I've always been treated like this, my entire life. *Lucy's too weak, too fragile, too small, she can't go outside or run around or have any fun because she'll get sick. She'll stop breathing. She'll wind up in the hospital.* My whole life, Nick. And then the one little taste of utter abandon I ever experienced—charging through the dark with a frosty wind whisking against my face, feeling totally invigorated and alive... You want to take that away from me, too."

She was crying so hard her words were barely intelligible, but Nick didn't interrupt or attempt to quiet her. When she finally settled down and could speak normally again, she sniffed and asked, "May I use your handkerchief, please?"

"Sorry, I don't have one," Nick said. "But here, you can use my scarf. I don't mind."

The offer to use Nick's scarf to dry her eyes and blow her nose was so ridiculous and sweet all at once it caused Lucy to chuckle. "*Neh*, that's okay," she said, removing her mittens to dab her eyes with her bare fingers.

"I really am sorry," he repeated.

Lucy was embarrassed. "That's all right. I've stopped blubbering. I don't need a handkerchief after all."

"*Neh*, I mean I'm sorry I treated you in a way that made you feel…the way you feel. I didn't mean to. I was concerned. I care about you and I wouldn't want anything to happen to you. I especially wouldn't want to play a role in hurting you."

Lucy was overwhelmed by his words. No man had ever said anything like that to her before, even in friendship. "It's not your fault," she said. "And I do appreciate that you care. But I'm not as fragile as you think I am."

"Fragile? You? I don't think you're fragile at all, even if you are prone to pneumonia." Nick scoffed. "I think you're one of the most resilient women I've ever known."

Lucy was overwhelmed again. If this kept up, she was going to fall hard for Nick Burkholder. Maybe she already had.

Don't miss
Her Amish Holiday Suitor *by Carrie Lighte,*
available October 2019 wherever
Love Inspired® books and ebooks are sold.

www.LoveInspired.com